About the author

Mark Durman is a former British Army officer who served on operations in several parts of the world. After taking early retirement from the military, he was Director for Europe, Middle East and Africa for a US international security company. He is a graduate of politics and economics and of the British Army staff college, Camberley and the NATO Defence College, Rome. He currently divides his time between Alicante, Spain and Paris.

VERIFICATION

Mark Durman

VERIFICATION

Vanguard Press

VANGUARD PAPERBACK

A CIP catalogue record for this title is
available from the British Library.

ISBN 978 1 784653 26 2

*Vanguard Press is an imprint of
Pegasus Elliot MacKenzie Publishers Ltd.*
www.pegasuspublishers.com

First Published in 2017

**Vanguard Press
Sheraton House Castle Park
Cambridge England**

Printed & Bound in Great Britain

To

Danièle, Anthony and William

Chapter One
December 1988

I pick up the phone on the third or fourth ring. It's the duty officer. "Colonel Peter Chambers? Gorbachev has just dropped a bombshell! He told the UN that the Soviets are going to withdraw six tank divisions, 50,000 troops and 5,000 tanks from Eastern Europe. Plus a lot more amazing stuff. In view of tomorrow's summit, the admiral wants you back in the office pronto."

I tell him, "OK, I'll be there".

I put down the phone and look across at my wife, Ann. Our two children have just gone to bed and we are in the middle of another of our "animated" discussions, this time about problems with our daughter, Chloe. Ann has obviously picked up on my saying "OK, I'll be there."

She says, "Peter, we must do something about Chloe. She's so withdrawn and moody. I really don't know how to communicate with her. And she always responds much better to you than to me. But you're not here half the time. And now you're off again!"

I know. Ann is right. Chloe is our daughter, I adore her but I realise it's not easy for Ann to deal with her at present. She's fourteen years old and just starting puberty. But it's more than that and we need to be very sensitive and patient with her.

I say to Ann, "You're right. I'll spend time with her, maybe we could all go skating at that rink at Sainte - Catherine this weekend. You know how she loves that and of course with Christian too." Christian is our ten-year-old son. I look at my watch. It's eight thirty. This discussion is going to have to wait. I've got to go. Ann gives one of her resigned shrugs as I prepare to leave. I've lived with this attitude since the Cyprus tragedy ten years ago. I give her a soft peck on her cheek, and get "that look" from her again. I pick up my jacket and head for my car.

To explain. Today is Wednesday 7 December 1988. I work in the Intelligence Division of the International Military Staff of HQ NATO in Brussels. Tomorrow is the annual winter summit of the sixteen heads of state of the NATO organisation. We've spent today preparing the briefing papers for these esteemed gentlemen (and lady!). The agenda and all the logistical admin and protocol arrangements are completed. The US President, the Canadian PM and the other heads of state are already either in the air en route for Brussels or about to travel here by train or car.

But here is the thing! Mikhail Sergeyevich Gorbachev, general secretary of the Communist Party of the Soviet Union, has today addressed the United Nations General Assembly in New York. From the few comments of our duty officer, I understand his speech has contained some highly unexpected announcements. At NATO HQ, we need to analyse these in detail and to do it right now as Gorbachev's speech could have a profound impact on the NATO meeting tomorrow and the international political decisions that could flow as a result of their deliberations.

It doesn't take me long to drive from our rented house in Woluwe, Brussels to NATO HQ in Evère - fifteen minutes at this time of the evening, thirty at most in the rush hour. I always enjoy the drive, as indeed I enjoy my job here - quite a change from previous operational tours. The commute gives me a short time on my own between the domestics at home and the issues at the office - a sort of transition or mind adjustment between the two.

I arrive at the NATO HQ entrance gates behind which is the large NATO symbol so often beloved by journalists to stand in front of when giving their press reports. Next to this is the NATO flag together with those of the sixteen member states. The pass sticker on my car and the ID that I show to the sentry on duty are enough for him to wave me through (pretty slack security in my opinion but there you go). I park on my allocated spot, C71, close to the side entrance of our division of the International Military Staff (IMS). Lights are on and I can see it's already busy in there. I hold my ID up to the electronic pass reader and I'm in.

We're slowly getting to grips with the new technology coming on stream. Gone are the old electronic typewriters and we've equipped the secretarial staff with word processors which clack away like a flock of woodpeckers. As a result, the speed of report production is now much quicker and simpler to amend and distribute. As the executive officer (XO) of our division, I've already attended a course run by Apple Coy and am beginning to get familiarised with the first computers that are coming on stream since the start of this year, 1988. All XOs will soon have them on their desks, first as an aide to office organisation and programming and there's talk of moving to an "on line" capability when this technology is proven by the so-called World Wide Web. This has yet to be reliably developed- we're hoping by 1990 or soon after. But that's all for the future.

As I walk into our divisional office block, the first thing I smell is fresh coffee. SuziB is already on the case. SuziB is a fellow Brit by origin but American by her marriage. She has been the personal assistant to the incumbent intelligence director for heaven knows how many years. Why the B in Suzi? No idea, but that's how she's known. Most of our directors, as the rest of us staff officers, only stay in post for two, or maximum three years. SuziB has mothered very many of us over the long period she has worked for NATO. She is large in both her personality and her waistline. Her age is uncertain and no-one feels inclined to ask. SuziB is a constant fixture, the division's continuity. She's a warm and caring lady but sometimes can be a little clumsy. We all love her as she makes us feel at home and that we work in a friendly and co-operative environment.

It's already about ten o'clock in the evening when I turn up and there's no reason why she needs to be here, but SuziB is SuziB. Before I even reach my office, she bustles up with papers in one hand and a steaming cup of coffee in the other.

"Heard you were on your way, Peter," she tells me, "I've got the main briefing papers together that you'll need to get to grips with. Dieter and Cheryl are already here getting stuck into the same material. They said they want to digest the speech, etc. then talk it all through with you and the admiral who told me he'll be here about midnight."

I thank her, take the papers and open my office door. SuziB follows and puts down the coffee on my desk, unfortunately spilling a drop right over the name Gorbachev. No problem, I can still read the text underneath. Discreet as ever, SuziB retires and not so quietly closes the door to let me get on with it. What a jewel she is! Without her, I suspect we might be more efficient but it would never be as cosy!

The papers SuziB has given me consist mainly of a complete English translation of Gorbachev's speech given today at the UN in New York with a few immediate reaction pieces from on the spot journalists. There are also copies of the briefing papers produced earlier for the incoming summit leaders with a hurried note from NATO's head of secretariat asking for our intelligence reaction to the speech and our advice as to what changes, if any, need to be made.

First I read the speech translation. What a speech! This is electric, world shattering stuff, turning the post-World War order upside down. Ever since the standoff between the western allies and the Soviet Union in 1945, the world has existed with a seemingly permanent split between West and East, between the so-called free world and communism, between NATO and the Warsaw Pact. Since Gorbachev became general secretary of the Communist Party of the Soviet Union in 1985, for the first time there has been the beginning of a dialogue between the two blocs. There have been face-to-face meetings. Our British Prime Minister has said: "I like Mr Gorbachev, we can do business together." The US president, a man who exudes both charisma and sound common sense has encouraged Gorbachev and this year Treaties have been signed limiting the proliferation of nuclear weapons and the deployment of intermediate range nuclear forces in Europe. All very encouraging after years of co-existence during our "cold war" period.

I read the speech again, all of it, not just the parts affecting the military. I'm really interested in the development of his argument. Gorbachev makes constant reference to a new world order, of co-operation, co-creation and co-development and how his earlier work on restructuring the Soviet Union, so fully described in his 1987 published book "Perestroika" is now moving from theoretical principles to implementation. He praises the contribution of the US president in continuing progress towards concluding a treaty on a fifty percent reduction in strategic offensive weapons, while retaining the ABM Treaty and developing a convention on the elimination of chemical weapons.

"So far so good," I say to myself. "All he has said is a logical development of his Glasnost (openness) and Perestroika (restructuring) reforms. Nothing unexpected there."

I now turn to the specifics of his proposals concerning military withdrawal. I note he says the Soviet Union has, by agreement with its Warsaw Pact allies, made the decision to withdraw six tank divisions within the next two years from Eastern Europe – East Germany, Czechoslovakia and Hungary and to disband them by 1991. Gorbachev goes on to say that assault landing formations with their associated armaments and combat equipment will also be withdrawn. In summary, the Soviet forces in Eastern European countries will be cut by 50,000 troops and 5,000 tanks. Gorbachev's announcement is lacking in specifics as to which formations and which countries but this is hardly surprising as this was a first bold statement to a non-military international audience. Details will surely follow later.

I open up my security safe and get out my copy of MC161 - our NATO agreed comprehensive assessment of the capabilities of Warsaw Pact armies and their order of battle. It has a NATO Secret classification. I then check how Gorbachev's announced figures might impact on the capabilities of Soviet forces known to be stationed in eastern Europe. My particular speciality is force levels in East Germany and the Group of Soviet Forces Germany (GSFG). So, I first concentrate on that Group of Forces. I look through the order of battle of GSFG - this comprises twenty Soviet divisions (including ten tank divisions), 7,000 tanks, 2,350 infantry fighting vehicles, 900 combat aircraft, 300 heavy/medium helicopters, a total of 370,000 troops. That's just in East Germany where there are also six East German divisions.

I make a less detailed check on the other East European countries. The Soviets have troops deployed in those countries but the main strike capability is with GSFG. I'll discuss the full order of battle with my colleagues Dieter and Cheryl later.

After an hour or so, I reach my own provisional assessment. Gorbachev's reasoning and troop withdrawal announcement are consistent with his change of direction for the Soviet Union in both internal and external policies. The withdrawal of the equipment and manpower that he has announced would reduce the Soviet capability for offensive action against the West but would still retain a formidable military force. Quoting Gorbachev here: "Our forces will be given a different structure from today's which will become unambiguously defensive."

I can see NO reason but to accept Gorby's speech as genuine. That's my view based on my personal experience and the facts that I now have available. But I am well aware that this a big wide world of interested parties. The US and all European and "free world" countries have a plethora of paid analysts, civil servants, sovietologists, political and economic experts. I expect many of these will be doing similar jobs to mine this evening because Gorbachev's speech today has the potential, if genuine, to change the face of strategic politics that has endured since the end of World War Two.

It's time to consult with my fellow analysts, Dieter Kuhn and Cheryl Walker in our small meeting room. I'm lucky to be working with such good guys. First Dieter. He's German and his background is in naval intelligence but he has spent some years working in Bonn on the Soviet affairs department via training and later instructing at the German Intelligence School at Bad Ems He's a tall slim man, with a rather long lugubrious face. This makes him look very serious and, in a way, he is. But he is very professional and thorough as is typical of his Germanic roots. He has developed a deep understanding of Russian politics. Since I've been in post, Dieter has taught me a great deal. I like working with him.

How to describe Cheryl? She's a US Air Force Colonel, always looking glamorous whether in her "slightly too tight" formal blue uniform displaying the silver eagle rank tabs of a full "bird" colonel or, as now, in roll neck sweater and jeans with her mass of jet black hair allowed to hang free. With her make-up and nails always immaculate and her curvaceous "all woman" figure, Cheryl is quite a personality. She has a strong character and is a persuasive speaker. She brings to our group, her background working in the Washington intelligence community at the Defence Intelligence Centre with attachments both with CIA Langley and the NSA Communications world. Apart from all this professional stuff, she's an attractive woman. She's not married and, as far as I know, she never has been. I like being with her, perhaps more than I should.

With my years in British intelligence, military school at Ashford and intelligence tours in Germany and elsewhere, we make a strong team.

Our meeting doesn't take long. We've all read and digested the great speech and are all agreed. Gorbachev has been consistently saying for some two to three years now that the standoff between East and West cannot continue to drag on. All the experts we have consulted between us, from US, UK, Germany, Canada and elsewhere, agree that he is genuine in this regard. He has developed evolving political policies leading to greater openness and freedom of expression. From a purely financial perspective, he knows the Soviet Union can no longer afford the vast drain on national expenditure of military research, development, provision and sustaining the Soviet military complex. In particular, he knows his country cannot continue to compete with the US development of the new versions of Pershing ballistic missiles and their deployment in Germany.

Our next job now is for each of us to contact our national governments to ensure we are all in step. We are about to close our meeting when our director, Admiral Ricardo Figo walks into the meeting room. He is Portuguese. He is a charming man who we all like and do our best to support. A problem with the sometimes incomprehensible protocol of NATO is that all the key appointments in the International Military Staff are political positions that have to be awarded to ensure there is an equitable balance between the member nations. Admiral Figo has a distinguished naval career but has virtually no intelligence experience, certainly concerning the Warsaw Pact Forces. Fortunately, he doesn't try to bluff and sensibly leans on the three of us to guide him on this subject.

I'm pleased that Cheryl seems willing to be our lead speaker.

"Welcome, Admiral," she says. "It's been quite an evening! Peter, Dieter and I have been through the speech and done our homework regarding analysis. To summarise, we're agreed that Gorbachev's words are consistent with all he has said and done of late and what he has so far delivered in terms of the missile treaties, etc. We have analysed the troop/equipment figures he has referred to and agree that, while limiting any aggressive potential, even with those reductions, the first line divisions would still retain a strong capability. His speech gives no details of which troops would be withdrawn or from which East European country but our feeling is that our leaders should give a welcome, though guarded, response at tomorrow's meeting - or is it now today?"

Cheryl looks at Dieter and me and asks us, "Are we all agreed?" We both concur.

Admiral Figo looks relieved that there seem to be no complications.

"Fine," he says. "And I'd like to thank you for responding so quickly to this issue. What do you recommend we need to do next?"

"Well," Cheryl continues, "we need to consult with our respective nations to check we are all in sync, then we can redo the position papers for our bosses' meeting as necessary. And we need to get on with this soonest as my guy is already airborne en route and the others are all probably also on their way here."

It all seems very straightforward. But it doesn't turn out that way.

Chapter Two

I ring through to the UK national office. This is located in another area of NATO headquarters where the sixteen nations each have their own national representatives. A sleepy sounding voice answers, identifying herself as the UK duty officer. I give my NATO ID number and explain I need to see the briefing notes given to our prime minister concerning the Gorbachev speech. This should be a routine procedure to ensure that what national experts are briefing their leaders prior to major international conferences is in sync with the NATO specialist staffs. I hold on the line while the briefing officer is found. This is Clive Thompson, a member of the PM's staff, who usually accompanies her on such occasions. I have met Clive a couple of times before. He's a short man with glasses who is always neat and alert. He is very bright and quick on his feet – he needs to be, working for such a formidable lady. He's just arrived in Brussels from London by air.

With his normal efficiency, Clive agrees to have the PM's briefing notes sent over to me by secure fax. I have to wait in line as the sole secure fax machine in our office is already sending through the US president's notes for

Cheryl's attention. Dieter has legged it round to the German delegation to collect his notes in person.

I start to read through the PM's briefing notes expecting a similar assessment to our own. I am completely wrong. The notes summarise the main points of the Gorbachev speech but reach a very different conclusion. The overarching tone of the assessment is one of great caution, suspicion, and even of mistrust. The advice to the PM is for her to be sceptical about the troop/tank withdrawal announcements, and take a "we'll believe it when we see it" line.

I'm shocked. This is unbelievable! I can see no justification for this hard attitude for all the reasons we have given to Admiral Figo. The UK national briefing seems to be completely out of step with our assessment within our NATO group.

Cheryl is sitting next to me and has been reading the US briefing notes as has Dieter, having returned from the German delegation.

Cheryl speaks first. "My God, my guys in Washington are advising extreme caution about the Gorby speech and are suggesting the Soviets are trying to dupe the West into reducing our defences. They are recommending we should be bringing in reinforcements in Europe. That doesn't fit at all with our view. What about your side?"

I reply: "Same here, total lack of confidence about the Soviet withdrawals." I turn to Dieter and ask him:

"What does the Federal Republic say?"

"Not at all the same as you Brits and Americans! Our German side supports exactly what we had assessed earlier – that Gorbachev is genuine and means what he says about the military withdrawals."

So, we have a total mismatch. Our NATO view is positive about the Gorby speech. This is in line with the assessment of the Federal Republic of West Germany (FRG) but is totally contrary to that of the US and UK! It's now about two o'clock in the morning and the leaders of our countries are to meet in a few hours' time. This has the potential of showing major disharmony between our western nations. Worse than that: it could destabilise West-East relations at the very time that so much positive progress has been made. Something has to be done – and fast!

Cheryl and I decide to go up to our respective national delegations to dig into this. What factors had made our national intelligence staffs so suspicious? What new intelligence do they have which has not been passed onto us in NATO?

I hotfoot it to the UK delegation and find Clive Thompson still at his desk. I tell him about the complete mismatch between our NATO assessment, with which the FRG agreed and the contrast with the US/UK line. I warn him that if we don't get our acts together, we will end up with the US president and our PM saying one thing and the FRG the opposite. That alone would cause a major rift within the Alliance but, more important, it could seriously undermine all the confidence building measures that had been built up between East and West during the past few years.

I ask Clive to press London for an explanation. He does his best but at this time of the morning, it's difficult to find anyone from the UK Joint Intelligence Committee (JIC) to discuss the issue. Plus, there's the problem of trying to establish secure communications. Eventually I find myself talking to a guy named Henshaw from the Defence Intelligence Staff (DIS) who was a note-taker at yesterday's JIC meeting convened to review the Gorbachev speech. I tell him of our NATO assessment, supported by the FRG.

I say to him, "After all the recent positive dialogue with the Soviets, why are the UK and US now so sceptical about Gorbachev's speech? What don't we know here in Brussels?"

Henshaw replies: "Even though this is a secure line, it's difficult to say much more about this. Only that our agencies have received some very delicate source information."

"About what?" I ask him.

"Sorry, but I'm not cleared to say more without higher level authorisation."

I'm starting to get pissed off but try to keep my cool.

"OK," I say, "but how long is that likely to take?"

Henshaw pauses then says, "Look, you must understand that all the key players who signed off on the briefing notes left for their homes hours ago. I could try to contact them individually to pass on your views but that's going to take time and in any case the assessment was made jointly by the JIC which, as you know, has reps from MI 5 and 6, GCHQ, the DIS and the Cabinet Office."

I can tell I'm wasting my time here. Before I could get to talk to anyone in authority, our PM would be reading her notes in preparation for the summit. In any case, the assessment was made jointly by the JIC who would be unlikely to change it just because of my objections. And who was this high-level secret source? The JIC probably wouldn't tell me. I can't blame Henshaw for being defensive. He is only doing his job. But I also have to do mine.

I hurry back to our NATO office nearly bumping into Cheryl at the entrance (not an unpleasant experience I must say). We compare notes and I learn that Cheryl has had a very similar experience. Apparently, the US intelligence coordinating committee had been split between those who had favoured the whole process of improved dialogue with the Soviets and the old guard of Sovietologists who still saw the "Soviet war machine" as continuing to pose a real threat to the West. The latter group have always been highly suspicious of Gorbachev's true intentions. Cheryl had been told of a new important source whose information swung the assessment against acceptance of Gorbachev`s withdrawal statement. This reservation had apparently been passed to the UK as part of our special intelligence sharing agreement.

I now realise that the UK have merely accepted the US assessment. We're stuck with it.

It's now about 0400 hours. I ask Cheryl what she thinks we should do about this mismatch

"Hell, Peter," she replies quickly, "Not our problem. I've given my people our assessment, told them it is shared by the FRG staffs. If the information from this goddam so-called high level source or sources is so persuasive, our people can get on with it. Fuck'em! I've done all I can for tonight, I'm tired and I'm going get my head down for a couple of hours. I suggest you do the same."

She heads out of the door with a look back at me that I could be forgiven for interpreting as "Why don't you come and settle down with me!" Good old Cheryl, she can swear like a trooper, knows her own mind and, in this case, is not prepared to rock the boat with her national intel staff. In many ways, I agree. Cheryl is very alluring in her "all woman" style. I tell myself to put any ideas about her out of my head. At least for now.

I check with Dieter. He is still convinced that Gorbachev's announcement is genuine. He tells me he has rechecked his German sources. Nothing has occurred for him to change his opinion. Intelligence from Bonn is still convinced that Gorbachev still holds the full reins of power in the Kremlin and that his speech is merely an evolution of his drive towards Perestroika and a rapprochement with the West. Dieter tells me he has a meeting with his FRG delegation at 0800 hours, meantime he's slipping home for a few hours rest while he has the chance.

Maybe I should do the same as Cheryl and Dieter and get some sleep. I check out of our meeting room and go back along the now deserted corridor to my own office. A coffee would be good but even SuziB has gone home. I sit behind my desk. There's still a few hours before the Heads of State are due to arrive and our hosting duties begin. I think about this total mismatch of interpretation of Gorbachev's speech. This cannot be right. Everything we know, everything we've researched, all the myriad of intelligence sources and agencies that feed into our department – all these say the same thing, that Gorbachev is genuine in his efforts to bring about fundamental change. Not just his words but also his actions to date, both within the Soviet Union and in all his dealings with Western leaders.

Cheryl is right in that we have both made representations to our respective national delegations and given them our assessments. What else could we do? It wouldn't be our responsibility if our nations reject the Gorbachev position and fail to grasp this unique opportunity to unravel the Cold War that has existed since the end of World War Two.

Somehow, I can't just leave it at that. For fuck's sake, I've been trained as an intelligence officer and have learnt and stood by the principles of the intelligence process all my career so far - centralised control, systematic exploitation of sources, timeliness, objectivity, etc. But there's one principle that stands out right now. It is that a professional intelligence operator must argue his case if the evidence is there to support him, no matter if it contradicts higher level decisions that have already been taken. I used to drum that principle into my students when I was lecturing at Ashford. The easy option now would be to shut up and get on with my job. I've reported our assessment to London. If they disregard it, it's not my problem. But I just can't do that. Am I a serious professional or not?

I decide to have another go at my national delegation. Again I walk through the cold empty corridors of our NATO headquarters building till I come to the UK Delegation section. The same duty officer is there and I tell her to call Clive Thompson. Like all sensible officials, Clive has also taken the chance for a snooze but, to his credit, he responds to my call and quickly adjusts.

"Look, Clive," I tell him. "This is serious. Unless there is compelling evidence to the contrary, involving top-level source intelligence that I'm not briefed about, I'm convinced we are about to make a major political blunder by giving our own PM false information. I think the Americans may also be making the same error. If, as a result, both the US president and our PM reject Gorbachev's statement, we could be thrown right back into a Cold War situation all over again. I need to have the chance to try to correct our PM's briefing in time for her to digest it before this morning's summit. You know how influential she is. What she says carries great weight with all the other nations. In my opinion, it would be a major political blunder for her to accept the present JIC assessment brief."

Clive hears me out. He doesn't have my background in intelligence but he is an astute civil servant. What he can do is get things moving quickly and arrange high level meetings if he judges the situation warrants it. He acknowledges I am seriously concerned about this issue. He makes a decision.

"OK, Peter, got your point. There's no time to go back to London now about this. I need you to come back here again and explain what you told me directly to Sir Geoffrey. He should be in by 0800 hours sharp. That suit you?

"Thanks, Clive," I tell him. "I'll be there."

Chapter Three

I wonder how to fill in the remaining time before my appointment. I could slip home, freshen up and get a change of clothes. But that might wake Ann and the children. In any case, I prefer to wear my army uniform for the meeting with Sir Geoffrey and it's already hanging up here in my office.

As always, when I have time on my hands, I find myself reliving that terrible day when our world, Ann's and mine, was turned upside down. It seems incredible that it's now nearly ten years ago. Ann and I will never be the same again.

It was in August 1978. An army friend of ours owned a beach house along the coast from Kyrenia, part of what's now the Turkish Republic of Northern Cyprus. Our friend lent it to us for a two-week holiday. I'd just finished a difficult unaccompanied tour in Northern Ireland and it was bliss for Ann and me to have a complete break with our three children Nicholas, then seven, Chloe who was four and little Christian, who was just a few months old.

The Kyrenia coastline is so beautiful and we were able to switch off completely. There was so much for all the family to do and enjoy and for Ann and me it was almost like a second honeymoon. We spent a carefree first week there enjoying being a family together. We were just into our second week when the tragedy occurred. I still remember it as if it were yesterday.

This is what happened. A few hundred metres from the beach house, the sea was edged by a lovely sandy bay. The previous year I had taught both Nicholas and Chloe to swim. They both loved it and spent hours during our first week there, constantly in and out of the water. That day, after we had had a lazy lunch at the house, Nicholas pestered me to go swimming again so I went with him and Chloe down to what we were now calling "our beach" as the whole time we were there we never saw another person. Ann stayed behind with baby Christian. Some distance from the coast was a small island which seemed to be uninhabited. We had all been intrigued by this and made up stories about what it would be like to explore it.

As soon as we got to the beach, Nicholas went straight in the sea with little Chloe following on behind her big brother. As usual, I called to Nicholas not to go out too far and for a time the two of them seemed fine. Then I noticed the wind was starting to pick up as is usual along the whole Mediterranean coastline in the early afternoon. The sea which had been completely calm, started to become choppy. I saw that my children were getting carried away by the tide and that Chloe was too far detached from her brother. I ran down the beach and threw myself into the sea, swimming as fast as I could towards them. By the time I reached them, I could tell little Chloe was struggling and frightened. I caught her in my arms then told her to hold on to my neck and shoulders so that my arms and legs were free to swim with her. We caught up with Nicholas who by now was also tiring and beginning to panic as the tide took us further out to sea. I'm quite a strong swimmer but I too began to tire as I fought against the tide to get back to dry land. As well as ensuring Chloe was holding on to me tightly, I was doing my best to keep Nicholas in front of me encouraging him to try to stay calm and keep swimming towards the beach. He was soon exhausted and I struggled to pull him along with one hand while using the other to keep going. At one point I really thought I was going to lose both my children but after what seemed like an eternity I eventually felt the sand under my feet and managed to get a firm footing and force my way back onto the beach. I had to pull Nicholas out of the water and when at last we were clear, he collapsed at my feet. Chloe had been clinging to my neck and shoulders and just continued to cling to me like a limpet as if in a coma as the three of us finally reached the safety of the beach.

I had almost to prise Chloe free and I laid her down on the sand next to Nicholas. She was taking short staccato breaths and shivering. At least she was alive. But my son – he lay at my feet and was completely still. He seemed to be unconscious. I knelt down beside him and tried to revive him using every means I knew. I massaged him, tried mouth to mouth, anything that might bring him back to me. "Come on, come on, come on!" I cajoled him. But nothing. No movement. He just lay still with no sign of life.

I don't know how long we were in the sea and I don't know how long I tried to resuscitate my son. It seemed an age but was probably no more than half an hour. When I found that I could do nothing more to revive Nicholas, I picked him up and put him over my shoulder. I then picked up Chloe and held her up against my chest supported by my left hand. Like this, I struggled back to our beach house as fast as I could. When I got there, I found Ann asleep in a recliner chair with little Christian by her side. I abruptly woke her, told her to look after Chloe and made for the old Renault car we had hired. We had no phone so all I could do was lay my son flat on the back seat of the car and drive as quickly as I could to Kyrenia to look for medical help.

When I got to the town, I had no idea where to go. It was mid-afternoon – siesta time in the Mediterranean. I drove round to the harbour and finally found a café still open. I parked outside and rushed in holding my son in my arms. I speak no Turkish but the word "doctor" is universal. The café staff immediately rushed to do what they could. I can only praise their kindness. They cleared a table and we gently laid Nicholas down. I continued to hold him, just praying that, somehow, he might yet revive. But it was no good. After some time, a Cypriot gentleman arrived and explained that he was a doctor. He examined Nicholas and told me what I already knew. My son was dead.

I tried as well as I could to cope with the aftermath. The police arrived and I had to make a full statement. Fortunately, the police inspector spoke passable English, learnt I suppose during the days when Cyprus was part British occupied. But this process took time as did finding a suitable medical facility where my son could be held for a post-mortem examination. I had to leave him there. I took one last look at him. He seemed so small, so vulnerable. My darling seven-year-old son.

Throughout this ordeal, I was overwhelmed by the feelings of guilt and responsibility. I am the father. I am responsible for protecting my children. But I had let them down. I should have reacted quicker or not allowed them in the sea without me being alongside them all the time. It was my fault and now my son was dead.

It was early evening before I got back to the beach house. When she heard the car, Ann rushed out and threw herself at me.

"Where is our son?" she screamed. But she already knew the answer.

I shake myself out of my memories and concentrate on the present. I go to the wash room, freshen up, then return to my office, put on my Colonel's uniform then wait for the time of my appointment with Sir Geoffrey.

I arrive at the UK delegation in good time for my appointment. Clive is there and tells me the foreign secretary is briefed about my concerns and is ready to see me. Clive opens the door to an inner office, announces my arrival and withdraws.

With his customary avuncular manner, Sir Geoffrey motions me to a chair and then sits down opposite. He is kind enough to remind me of our last meeting, when I had briefed him during the NATO exercise called Able Archer. I know he's got a busy day ahead so I get straight to the Gorbachev speech and stress how our assessment within NATO staffs varies radically from that given to him and the PM in London.

Sir Geoffrey hears me out, pauses reflectively for a while, then says:

"I think you'd better tell Margaret about this. Wait here for a moment."

He goes to a connecting door, taps, puts his head inside and I hear him talking quietly to the occupant of the other room. He then turns, beckons to me and says:

"Come and tell the prime minister about your concerns. She's ready to see you now."

I don't know what I had expected but surely not this. It is still early morning but the Prime Minister is sitting behind a desk here in Brussels looking fresh and impeccable - hair neatly groomed, navy blue suit with white edging, brooch over her left breast, pearl necklace, earrings – all in place as if ready to go right now straight into the summit.

I know I'm not here to discuss the weather so I launch into my party piece about the Gorbachev speech, trying to keep my words as succinct as possible. The PM hears me out then asks a few very sharp and pertinent questions about troop levels and what the main impact would be on military effectiveness of the withdrawal numbers Gorbachev had given. I have already rehearsed these points with my NATO colleagues so I'm able to give clear, short answers. She then asks me why I think London and Washington both have such a different assessment to mine. I reply that only they can answer that but as an intelligence officer who has specialised in Soviet political and military affairs for some years, I make assessments based on the evidence before me and now feel duty bound to ensure she is aware of our position following the Gorby speech.

The PM concludes our meeting by saying, "Thank you, Colonel, for your input today. I'll talk to Ronnie and Helmut and we'll get our act together before we formally meet with the other nations this morning."

That's it! I'm out of there. I leave the UK delegation and head back to my own office. I find I'm sweating. I really had no idea my little piece would escalate right up to this level but now it's done and I feel at least I've followed my conscience. Trouble is, due to the condensed time frame between yesterday's speech by Gorbachev in New York and today's summit here in

Brussels, there was not time enough to digest all the input from the mass of intelligence sources particularly in the US. I begin to have doubts. What if Washington and the London JIC are correct and I am wrong? I could have just dropped myself irredeemably in the shit.

Chapter Four

There's a set ritual that precedes every summit at NATO headquarters. It takes careful choreographing by our head of protocol. Each head of state/president/prime minister is afforded a personal welcome by our secretary general at the main entrance as their car draws up. He says a few words then passes the VIP on to his own national representative. The secretary general then returns to the entrance just in time to greet the next head of state. It all works to a tight time schedule and I'm always impressed by the smooth efficiency of the procedure.

I am at the entrance watching our arrivals this morning. President of the United States, Chancellor of the Federal Republic of Germany, President of France, Prime minister of the Netherlands, then I'm astonished to see our very own Prime minister stepping elegantly out of her car. How can this be as I was with her in this very building only a short time ago? I suppose she must have been escorted out again so that she could "re-arrive" to fit in with the NATO protocol. Amazing woman!

The summit meeting gets underway in closed session under the chairmanship of the NATO secretary general. It is open only to the heads of state with their accompanying minister(s), plus their close advisors. That includes Clive Thompson but not us military staff members. We are required to be on call if our expertise is called for. It rarely is and it isn't today. So, we hang around waiting until the great men (and woman!) have finished their deliberations.

They then have an interim break when the leaders pile out into the large atrium where coffee and light refreshments are available. Nominated NATO staffers do attend this session. This includes Cheryl, Dieter and myself. I find it fascinating to observe who talks to whom. I note there is a large group surrounding the burly and dominant figure of the German chancellor and in one corner the little socialist French prime minister is deep in conversation with the prime ministers of Holland and Belgium. Centre stage though is the tall impressive figure of the US president talking animatedly to our British PM. Their body language suggests they have a close relationship. Clive Thompson is included in this group. He spots me, comes over and says:

"I was watching out for you Peter. I wanted to let you know that the PM went for your line re: the Gorby speech. She wrapped it up pretty diplomatically by saying she was most encouraged by what he said at the UN and hopes this leads to further open discussions and cooperation. The US president backed her up and used the same term "trust but verify" he had been quoted as saying at an earlier meeting with Gorbachev. She told me she appreciated your intervention this morning and wants to have another word with you. You see she's chatting to the president right now. Let's just hover close by."

I follow Clive and we stand at the edge of this group. Sir Geoffrey is also there. When he sees me he beckons me over and steers me towards the PM. He says to her: "Prime Minister. Colonel Chambers is – "

"Thank you, Geoffrey," she interrupts him sharply. She introduces me to the president and says to him, "Ronnie, we need to straighten out this business of our intelligence contradictions in London and Washington. Why are our staffs at home being so timid and defensive about Gorby's speech? I'd like Colonel Chambers here to get straight over to London to meet with our people, review the intelligence and give me a revised assessment. Maybe he could then discuss all this face to face with your intel people. What do you think?"

This is a big moment in my life. Here are two world leaders discussing the issue that I had raised this morning. Wow! I am trying to keep cool but inwardly I'm wondering what the fucking hell is going on. I try to concentrate on the matter at hand. The president is speaking but I don't take in the precise words he is saying – only that he is agreeing with our PM and I'm getting my marching orders to get on with the job. I'm not sure at this point if I should be looking at my PM or the President of the world's greatest superpower. I try to get a grip. All I can think to say is:

"Yes, Prime Minister, I'll get onto it right away."

I feel my time has come to withdraw and Clive comes to my rescue and escorts me away from this illustrious little grouping. He says:

"Well, Peter, you certainly got our bosses thinking. My reading of their desires is that you hotfoot it to London sharpish and meet with our joint intel committee guys asap. Could you get there to meet with them tomorrow, Friday? I'll get our UK delegation to arrange flights, etc."

What else to say? I've just been given the most challenging and high-profile mission of my life! Of course, I must go.

I feel that my personal involvement in the NATO summit is now over. After the meeting, our protocol people allocate a number of separate rooms so that each head of state can give a press statement to their national journalists. This is scheduled to fit in with prime-time TV news in each country. I had hoped to listen in to our PM giving her version of events to the UK public. But now I realise I had better get organised for my new mission.

Once again, I walk back through the corridors of the NATO building to my office. My first duty is to check in with Admiral Figo to let him know what has developed. The ever helpful SuziB is on hand to escort me into his office. I'm expected in London tomorrow – after that I have no idea except I must pursue this issue. The admiral is as charming and supportive as ever. All he says is:

"Colonel, I congratulate you for having the moral courage to stand up and speak your mind. Of course, you must follow your national orders. Take whatever time is needed and let me know if I can help. Just call."

I'm just about to pack up my papers and file them away when Cheryl breezes into my office.

"Hey, Peter, you've really been stirring the shit! My people have just told me our president has ordered a complete intel review. I've been told I have to attend a meeting next Monday in Washington and your name was mentioned. Maybe we'll be making this a joint mission."

Maybe we will, I think. The idea is not at all disagreeable. I say to her:

"OK, Cheryl, at the moment I'm not sure where I'm going with this. I have to go to London tonight - after that, I'm not yet sure. Let's stay in touch, heh?"

I'm about to leave the office when my phone rings. It's Clive.

"Peter, we've got you booked on an 1830 hours Sabena flight this evening from Zaventem to London City, with a return tomorrow from City at 1600 local. The JIC is set up to meet you tomorrow in the Cabinet Office, Whitehall at 1000 hours. Can you make that and should we get you a hotel?"

Cor! - It's all happening, I'm thinking. I tell Clive:

"That's fine, I'll be there for the evening flight and the meeting tomorrow. Don't worry about accommodation. I'll call my club and stay there."

I clear my desk and head home. I notice it's still only 1600 hours but I'm bushed after having been up all night.

The Brussels traffic is heavy on the Ring on my way home and it's after 1630 hours when I pull up at my home. I'm still wearing my army uniform as I couldn't be bothered to change again in the office. I realise I've only got about half an hour to change and pack a bag before I'll need to leave for Zaventem airport. I notice Ann's car is not in our car port.

I open my front door and walk into the sitting room. No-one is at home. I suppose Ann is doing the school run. We're lucky that both Chloe and Christian are now at the same school - British School of Brussels at Tervuren. Chloe, who is now fourteen, is in secondary and Christian, who is ten, is still in primary. There's usually sports or clubs after school so they probably won't be back before I have to leave again. I change out of my uniform, take a quick shower, put on "smart casuals" for the flight. Then I pack a suit for tomorrow's meeting and a few overnight bits and pieces. Ready to go.

I write a short note for Ann, telling her I'm going to be away overnight in London and will call her from there. Then I ring through to my club, Special Forces in

Knightsbridge, and book myself in for one night. I still have a few minutes before I have to go. We have a three-bedroom house so we can give both of our children a room apiece except when we have guests to stay when they have to double up. I look first into Christian's room. It's always a bit of a mess but I suppose typical for a ten-year-old. He's an active boy and his room is festooned with sports kit and posters of sports stars - normal for a healthy ten-year-old. I see that on the shelf beside his bed he has books, well mostly comics, in all three languages - English, French and Flemish. This is down to Ann whose mother is Belgian and father is British. I admire the fact she has always ensured that our children got used to using more than one language from the start. Now Christian is in the French stream at school, he is becoming really bi- if not even tri-lingual. I also see he still keeps a couple of cuddly toys on his pillow. But he's only ten and is still a little boy at heart. Ann is highly protective of him. I can understand why. I suppose I am too. I love that boy.

Chloe's room is different. Always neat, almost spartan. I suppose I'm surprised that she doesn't go too much for the sort of "girly" things I would expect from a girl in her early teens. She's such a pretty girl but I do worry about her weight. Ann often accuses me of siding with Chloe if there's an issue between mother and daughter. She could be right. I adore my little girl. I would have loved to embrace my children before having to leave but it's not possible as it's now five o'clock and I have to head for the airport.

I leave my VW Golf in the short stay car park at Zaventem (HM government will be picking up the tab) and find my tickets are ready for me at the Sabena desk. I wait in line to board the plane and find I've got a window seat with two quite large gentlemen occupying centre and aisle. I feel cramped up but manage to manoeuvre my legs into some sort of space. I'm so tired that, despite the cramped legroom, I only just have time to get my seatbelt fastened before crashing out for most of the flight to London City.

I could get from London City airport to my club by tube but instead opt to take a taxi. I guess my "high level" mission entitles me to some privileges. I suppose I could also have opted for a smart hotel. But I like to take the chance to stay at my club whenever I'm in London. I often meet up with some army chum there and can relax and reminisce. The Special Forces Club was originally established just after the end of World War Two for members of the Special Operations Executive (SOE), particularly those brave souls who had worked with the resistance groups in German occupied France. However, the passing years have taken their toll and the numbers declined; so, some time ago, the committee decided to open up the club membership to members of the SAS, Intelligence Corps and Special Boat section of the Royal Marines. I joined back in the early '80s and have retained my membership ever since.

I check into the club, drop off my bag in my allocated room and head down to the bar. There are a few guys there but none that I know, so I down a quick beer and take a carafe of red wine through to the restaurant where I eat the set menu supper. Back in the bar again, there's no one I recognise so I decide to get an early night after a couple of phone calls. I use the pay phone in the hall to call up Philip Daniels. Philip is a Soviet studies expert I have known for some years. He is fluent in Russian and has spent long periods in Moscow and other parts of Russia. He heads up a research group based at Cambridge University. He knows more about what is really going on in Soviet politics than anyone else I know. I'm in luck. He's at his home. I say:

"Philip, hi. Peter Chambers here. Sorry to disturb you at home. Are you free to talk?"

"Sure, Peter, good to hear from you. What's up?"

I have to be careful with what I can say on an open line but I give Philip a general summary of my day's experience at NATO HQ and tell him I've got an urgent Whitehall meeting tomorrow. I ask him:

"I realise this is very short notice, Philip, but I would really like to get your views and advice. Any chance we could meet for lunch tomorrow? I was thinking we might meet at RUSI at, say, 1300 hours then find somewhere for a bite nearby?"

RUSI is the Royal United Services Institute. Both Philip and I are members and the Institute is based in Whitehall, right next to the Cabinet Office and Ministry of Defence main building.

I think Philip can detect I'm under some pressure here. He doesn't hesitate.

"Sure, Peter. See you there tomorrow," he replies. I'm in luck there.

Next I call home and Ann picks up straight away. I tell her I must have just missed her at home this afternoon but I had had to rush to catch the London flight. Ann sounds resigned and low key. There's no spark in her voice. I ask about our children and she gives me a matter of fact reply. I tell her I will be back tomorrow night and she reminds me I had promised that we would all go to the Vendome Cinema in Chaussée de Wavre to see the top film of the moment, "Saving Private Ryan". It's the last night before the programme changes. I say I'll be back in time. I tell her I love her and she responds. But I regret it's perfunctory – from both of us. Where has the warmth of love between us gone?

OK, I had managed to get some sort of sleep on the plane this evening but it was very shallow. I feel knackered and ready for bed. I go to my room, strip off, have a leak and brush my teeth.

I hope I can sleep.

Chapter Five

I'm so tired I expect to crash out as soon as I hit my bed. It doesn't happen. I turn on my left side and try to put my mind in neutral. That usually does the trick. Not tonight. After X minutes of sleeplessness, I turn on my right side and rearrange the pillow. Makes no difference. I get up, turn the light on, go to the sink and retrieve my wash bag. I hunt around in there hoping I might find a Zopoclone sleeping pill. I occasionally take one during stressful times. No luck, there's not one there.

My problem is that I can't stop thinking about the day's events. What the hell did I think I was doing by charging up to our UK delegation and making such a fuss about Gorby's goddamn speech? Cheryl felt the same about the speech but did the smart thing, registered her views then left it at that. I should have done the same. Now I've got myself stuck with a task which has escalated to the very top. I have no idea how this will work out. I can only stick with it and see where we go.

I still can't fucking well sleep! Maybe a pee might help. I get out of bed again then realise my little room in the club doesn't have an "en suite" bathroom. So, I grab a towel to cover my privates and stumble down the cold corridor to the shared loo in the hallway. It's a relief to clear my system. I'm amazed I had so much stored away in my bladder. Must have been the beer.

I get back into my bed hoping that at last I can sleep. Uh, uh – it doesn't happen. At least not yet. The Gorbachev business is not the only thing that's racing through my brain. I also keep thinking about my relationship with Ann. Are we ever going to get back to the times before the Cyprus tragedy when we might again be loving and content with each other? I am haunted by the look on her face that day ten years ago when I got back from Kyrenia without our son, Nicholas. I still remember her screams. The rest of that week was a nightmare as we struggled to find our way through it. I remember taking Ann, with little Chloe and our baby son Christian, back to Kyrenia. It took an age to complete all the paperwork that the Turkish Cypriots required us to do. I simply didn't know what was best. I suppose I thought that as Nicholas was now dead, perhaps we should bury him locally. But Ann wouldn't hear of it. She was adamant we must bring him back with us and insisted we take him to her parents' home in Somerset to be buried there. I didn't argue. She was probably right. But to do so involved a morass of bureaucracy first to get release documents from the Turkish Cypriot authorities, then to prepare little Nicholas's body for movement, no small job as the August temperatures in Cyprus were over thirty degrees. We had to negotiate our crossing via

Nicosia's Green Line border into the Greek Cypriot part of the island, then again persuade the British in the Sovereign Base Area at Akrotiri to permit the RAF to fly us with Nicholas's coffin back to the UK. It took the whole of a highly charged emotional week finally ending with a funeral service for our son at the local church at Ann's parents' home.

I've re-lived that experience in my mind so many times since, always haunted by my recurring feelings of guilt. At least Chloe was only four at the time and had no real understanding of what was going on and Christian was still a baby. Just looking into their rooms today reinforced how important my two children are to me. I must try never to let them down again.

Still no sleep! I turn over again. I think perhaps I need another pee, but then I realise that's ridiculous as it's only a few minutes since the last long flow. My mind keeps returning to depressing thoughts.

"The Cyprus tragedy" also marked a watershed in our sex lives, Ann and me. Before then, I suppose we were quite naïve. We just had sex together, whenever we had the urge, which was often. It just happened in a mutually loving way. We never questioned or analysed anything. We were a couple, a man and a woman in love with each other. What could be more natural? Was it every day, how many times a week? I have absolutely no idea. We just loved to have sex together, intertwined, loving each other's bodies in shared love making. We never used accessories, lotions, gels, sex toys – nothing like that. We were just two young healthy people together, just us two - and as a result we had our three (now only two) children.

It all changed after Cyprus. For a while, I suppose we just withdrew from each other, Ann with her conviction that I could/should have saved our son, me with the constant feeling of guilt and of letting my family down. Having sex together again seemed inappropriate and crude. But as the months wore on, nature reasserted itself - at least in me. I tried to woo Ann back through tenderness. In bed, I would touch her gently hoping she would respond. I hoped we could again renew the feelings we had shared before. It was not to be. Ann remained cold and frigid. It hasn't been a case of total abstinence. From time to time I have been a little more demonstrative and Ann has acquiesced to my sexual advances. And now after the ten long years since Cyprus, nothing much has changed. Yes, I have occasional sex with my wife but I always feel she is just putting up with it. She lies back and lets me do my thing. She doesn't participate in the process. She hardly ever, if at all, reaches an orgasm. It's almost as if she is, in her mind, in another place. She is merely allowing me to use her body. For me, this destroys the very essence of making love which I feel has to be mutually desirable to have any meaning. After I reach my climax, I no longer feel the joyful completeness of it. Rather, I feel unfulfilled and selfish.

Yet, more and more recently, I've felt myself aroused by other women and I have secret sexual fantasies about them. So far, I've done nothing about these feelings. Perhaps, as I'm now in my mid-forties, I'm starting a mid-life crisis.

My mind continues to wander off on this theme but I suppose sheer fatigue must have won out in the end as at last I sleep.

When I wake again, my watch tells me it's just on 0800 hours. The sole window in my little room in the club looks out onto Herbert Crescent which leads up to Harrods department store and the Knightsbridge Road. On this winter's day, it is only just getting light but already the London traffic is building up. I'm not a great fan of London, or of any big city really, but I do think this area is very gracious. Usually when I stay here I bring my trainers and grotty running kit and take advantage of the miles of interconnecting parks that link from Kensington Gardens and Hyde Park then via the underpass to Green Park, St James's Park and Buckingham Palace Gardens. Just the thought of the many times I've jogged round that route, lightens my depressed sleep-deprived mood of the night before. I usually find that the negative thoughts of the night never seem so bad in the light of the new day.

I trudge up the cold corridor, take a leak and more, then shower and put on the suit and tie I had brought for the meeting that Clive has set up for me this morning. I walk into the dining/breakfast room at the same time as a military chum called Doug Hammond. Doug's a big muscled guy whose suit seems to cling tightly around his broad shoulders. I haven't bumped into him since the early 1970s when we were on operations together in the Dhofar region of the Oman, both serving with Special Forces at the time. I was seconded from the Intelligence Corps and he, I remember, was from the Royal Engineers. We have much to discuss as we tuck into our "full English" bacon and eggs breakfast. This is one of the joys of this club. Usually there's someone you know and, by the nature of the membership, someone who probably shared some of the same experiences.

We chat over breakfast, pay our bills and leave for our respective meetings – Doug is going to HQ 23 SAS (TA) just off Sloane Square, while I have to adjust and prepare myself to meet these gallant souls of the UK Joint Intelligence Committee.

Clive told me our meeting is scheduled for 1000 hours in the Cabinet Office, Whitehall. I've never been to that building before but I do know the Ministry of Defence main building well, having once had an office there. So, I know the general geography. I'm wearing only a light coat but the English December morning seems quite mild and it's dry so far. I reckon it will take about forty minutes max to walk there and I've got the time. I've only got my overnight bag to carry so I decide to walk rather than take the tube or a cab. I enjoy the route as I stroll across Sloane Street into Belgravia, cutting across Eaton Square, up Victoria Street, past Westminster Abbey and into Whitehall. By the time I get there, my negative mood and dark mental clouds of the previous night have completely dispersed and now I feel in good spirits. I reach the Horse Guards in Whitehall with a spring in my step and in good time for the meeting. I remember all the work that Cheryl, Dieter and I put into our analysis yesterday and I feel confident of being able to hold my own with the JIC members this morning.

As I hadn't been in this building before, I find the entrance quite confusing due to the extensive renovation work that is going on. I show my military ID and Passport at the security grille and am told to wait to be escorted. By chance, my escort is a slim elegant young lady dressed in a smart dark suit. She introduces herself as Annabelle. Age? - Maybe late twenties. She has a slender body and a pert little derrière. I would not be truthful if I don't think it is a pleasure to walk up the stairs behind her. "Come off it, Peter," I say to himself. "Behave yourself!"

Annabelle leads me to a large door at the end of a wide corridor. She knocks then opens the door for me to go in, then she withdraws and closes it behind me. The room is organised with a large oval table surrounded by two or more rows of chairs. I'm surprised to see most of the chairs are already occupied and that the occupants' faces are turned towards me. I feel rather foolish standing in front of all these people while still in my coat and holding my overnight bag.

A young man appears and relieves me of my coat and bag while an elder gentleman stands and says:

"Ah, Colonel Chambers." He introduces himself as the chair of the Joint Intelligence Committee. He gives his name but as far as I'm concerned, he doesn't need to as I recognise him as a highly respected and very well-known Knight of the Realm and diplomat who I'd heard affectionately referred to as "Maggie's mandarin". He then introduces each of the main members sitting around the table, namely representatives of the Secret Intelligence Service (MI6), the Security Service (MI5,) GCHQ and a brigadier from the Ministry of Defence. I had been hoping Clive Thompson would be here but I can't see him. The chairman continues:

"As you see, our team is already gathered at the explicit instruction, I have to say, of our prime minister. On Wednesday, we learnt of Mr Gorbachev's fascinating speech to the UN and we later discussed its implications. As a result, we sent our considered assessment to the PM before she left for Brussels. Yesterday evening we were told the PM had not followed the line we had advised and, when she addressed the NATO summit, she changed that position following her talk with you. We understand the US president followed suit.

Furthermore, the PM has instructed us to talk with you – so here we all are!"

I take the seat the chairman offers me next to him at the head of the table. I suppose I had expected a hostile reaction from these people and indeed, there were one or two who are glaring back at me. But most seem just interested in the way this situation has developed, appear welcoming and appreciative that I have come direct from Brussels to meet and talk to them this morning. During my walk here from my club, I had been preparing a rough outline of what I might say at this meeting. I am well aware that everyone around the table is an expert in their particular speciality of the intelligence business. And these are the top representatives. Much of what I know about this subject has come directly or indirectly from their departments and I genuinely have much respect for the high-level work they do. I have these thoughts in my mind when I say:

"Mr Chairman, ladies and gentlemen. Firstly, I want to apologise for what probably seemed like an impertinent rejection by me of your assessment yesterday about the Gorbachev speech. I want to assure you that if routinely I have a different interpretation, I would surely represent it through the correct channels to your committee. I would certainly never try to go over your heads. It was merely due to the time scheduling that prohibited me from doing so yesterday."

I think to myself, "Right - stop there". I am quite pleased with that little act of eating humble pie. I turn to look at the chairman's reaction. He seems OK with what I have said, so I decide to push on:

"My intention had been to write a formal report of what transpired yesterday and submit it to your committee via our NATO UK delegation. But then I was told I was required to meet directly with you today so I delayed putting anything in writing. I'm now pleased to have the chance to meet and to discuss this issue in as much detail as you choose."

The chairman asks each of the lead representatives to make a short statement about how they interpreted the Gorbachev speech and its wider implications for Soviet policy and East–West relations. All except the MI6 rep spoke up. I was impressed by the response of each of these agency heads - well informed, articulate and succinct. I could take no issue with anything said around the table.

Back to the chairman. "Colonel Chambers. You've heard the views of our experts here, I'd now like to ask you for your views on what you've just heard and let's ferret out where our positions differ."

I'm impressed by the Chairman. I find him to be a clever and wily old bird. I've read about his diplomatic skills and think he's now setting me up. I feel I'm being tested and that this is a moment where I could succeed or fail.

"Thank you, Chairman. I shall try to be brief and to the point. In NATO headquarters, I work alongside two fellow colonels - one US and one German. We three all have the same rank grade and we all have years of experience as "Soviet watchers". Our added value is that our experiences come from different backgrounds: mine you know from a UK military background but I would add to that the additional knowledge I have gained through my work and studies with people such as Philip Daniels and his associates in the Soviet studies group, based in Cambridge. From Philip, I have learnt to set any political or military development into the context of Gorbachev's wider evolving strategic goals. In fact, I am having lunch with Philip after our meeting here. Our US colleague comes from a DIA, CIA NSA background and continues to keep close liaison with these agencies. Our German colleague similarly works continuously with his intel people but also has the added bonus of the great insight stemming from the German foreign ministry in Bonn. Remember that their minister, Hans Dietrich Genscher has until now in 1988, been foreign minister for fourteen continuous years. During this period, he has built up a formidable network of sources and contacts within the Soviet hierarchy. His office probably knows as much about what is going on in the Kremlin as they do themselves."

"So, by combining our experiences from UK, US and German inputs, we feel as qualified as any other body to judge what Gorbachev is up to and specifically to comment on his speech at the UN. Our conclusion was that the spirit and details of the speech were completely consistent and that our prime minister should give the speech a fulsome welcome. But of course, with some reservation. I can only say that the best way of summing up the situation is to re-quote the US President's phase which he said again yesterday, "Trust but verify"."

I realise I have been in full flow for some time and I had said I would be brief. But I haven't quite finished yet. As I had been speaking I had looked around the front row occupants at the table. I was pleased to see several heads nodding in agreement. But something still needed to be resolved. I continue:

"Mr Chairman, the crux of this issue today is for me to ask you why the assessment that your committee of the Gorbachev speech made was so negative. What factors persuaded you to advise our PM to be guarded and mistrustful in her response? I can only conclude that you have intelligence material within your committee here which has not been passed to us in NATO. This surely must be why there was such a wide difference in our assessments."

I stop speaking and there is a silence in the room. Everyone seems to be looking towards the chairman to respond. He pauses reflectively, then says to me:

"Colonel. Thank you for your presentation. You've hit the nail on the head. I think everyone here is in tune with your analysis. But, as perhaps you will have suspected, we did indeed receive some disturbing source material earlier this week which prompted our caution about the speech."

The chairman turns to the gentleman he had earlier introduced as from MI6. He says:

"John, I hand this one over to you."

I think his full name is John Evers. He's a man I would put in his early fifties. He is slim and has a tight, wiry build. He seems awkward and reluctant to say too much in front of this large gathering. I can't tell whether it's just because of his agency's natural tight security or that he's not convinced himself about his information. He says:

"We have been in close contact this week with our US colleagues at CIA. They have told us that the information received is from normally trusted and reliable sources. One source, for example, is close to a member of the politburo who is also in the secretariat of the communist party of the Soviet Union (CPSU). In essence, this is the situation; in the last few days, both the Soviets and the US have received very worrying information. From the Soviet side, reports picked up by both the GRU and KGB indicate that the West sees Gorbachev's détente initiatives as a sign of weakness and plan to exploit it by reinforcing conventional forces in West Germany. In reality, this is of course quite untrue. In turn, our US colleagues have had reports, again emanating from normally reliable sources that the Soviets are planning to exploit the transition period between outgoing and incoming presidents, together with a more relaxed security posture during the Christmas stand-down. No precise detail is available but could include troop reinforcements in East Germany or even threatening to re-blockade West Berlin. The US problem now, to be very frank, is that they are mystified by these reports. They are now trying to backtrack to those source origins to verify their authenticity."

Wow! In a worst-case scenario, if true, and if implemented, that would certainly undo all the initiatives for de-escalating the Cold War tensions and plunge things back to square one. Fucking hell, it could lead us back to the point of war.

I say to the Chairman: "Sir, now I realise why our assessments were so contradictory and why you felt you had to urge caution. But the big question is: are these reports really genuine? They seem so extreme and contradictory to everything that both the US and Gorbachev are trying to achieve."

"Precisely!" the Chairman replies. "It's imperative we get to the truth about this and I discussed it with the PM last evening. She urgently wants to know more from the US who provided us with the reports which, we have to say, lack detail. The PM also wants a fresh pair of eyes from an experienced professional to examine this development. She's read your CV file and liked your manner and expertise when you briefed her in Brussels. She told me to talk to you myself and, subject to my approval, to task you to go to the US soonest, discuss with their agencies and give us your conclusions. Having heard your presentation today, I'm pleased to support the PM's view. You've got yourself a job! You may need to follow this through yourself more deeply in Germany or elsewhere. You can count on the resources of our committee here to back you up as you require. Oh, and one word of warning. Do not make any mention of this matter to anyone who does not have the highest level of security clearance. What is your reaction, Peter?"

I look around the table and am pleasantly surprised to see that most seem to be supportive and cooperative. I'm not too sure about John Evers, the MI6 man. Perhaps I should talk to him separately. All I can think to say to the chairman is:

"Of course, and thank you for your confidence in me. I'll get onto it and report back as soon as I can."

The chairman makes some concluding remarks and I can see it's time for me to buzz off. I shake his hand and nod goodbye to the rest of the members and their staffs in the room. I collect my coat and overnight bag and I'm out of there. I notice Clive Thompson had come into the room at some point during our talks but he leaves again with me. To my great surprise, I see that the chairman has also left the meeting and slipped out behind me. He says:

"Look Peter - just a final word before you go. I didn't want to make too much of a big deal in there but I must emphasise that the PM is seriously concerned about the reports you heard from our MI6 people. If correct, this could have devastating consequences. We look to you to get us the facts so we can move forward with what we hope and pray will keep us on track with the peace process. We are putting a lot of trust in you. Don't let us down!"

The chairman then quietly returns to the conference room to continue or conclude his meeting of the committee. That is no longer my concern. Clive had discretely backed off while the Chairman was talking to me. Then, he comes back to my side and says:

"I've just got back from the PM's office and was told about your new mission and have now heard the chairman's confirmation. Things move fast, eh! Look, I've already jacked up a meeting for you at the Defence Intelligence Staff building in Washington for 1000 hours local on Monday morning. They said they will get all the relevant agencies to be represented there. I'm working on flight tickets, accommodation, etc. with the US embassy now. I'll contact you with details at your home in Brussels probably tomorrow. We'll also Fedex over to you credit cards, etc. for your expenses. That's about it. Have fun!"

Together, Clive and I make our way back to the entrance of the building. I hand in my pass at the security grille and walk out into the street. Clive and I briefly shake hands. He turns right, back towards Downing Street. I turn left, towards the Ministry of Defence main building.

I'm feeling numb and rather stunned. But I'm also excited. I've just been given the most important task of my life.

Chapter Six

I get to the RUSI building about half an hour before my scheduled rendezvous here with Philip Daniels. No matter. I always like to spend time here at the Royal United Services Institute. Founded way back in the 1830s by the Duke of Wellington, RUSI is a "think tank" for defence and security matters. I've been a member for some years now and whenever I am in London I try to drop in to listen to some of the excellent speakers, to use the library or just meet fellow members. The institute has a well-deserved reputation for forward thinking and free discussion. I have listened to several high-quality speakers here and have been impressed by their standards of accurate and objective analysis. One of those speakers was Philip Daniels and, since then, Philip has become a personal friend. Through him, I have also met several of his colleagues who are experts in various aspects of the Soviet Union and its Warsaw Pact allies such as politics, economics, military and technical research and development.

Philip is an academic, and not a security cleared member of the civil service or military. Because of this, I always need to separate out those areas we can discuss together and those, due to security caveats, that we cannot. I remind myself now that I must not mention my new mission to Philip or, come to that, to any other individual who does not have a security cleared "need to know". This is never a problem with Philip, firstly, because he understands and respects the sensitivities about classified information and secondly, because there is now so much information about the Soviet Union available through open source channels. Also, due to his fluent Russian language skills and the many contacts he has built up over the years, Philip has developed an almost unique knowledge of Soviet politics. I'm hoping today that he will give me an update on how he sees Gorbachev's philosophy of Perestroika developing and, from a Russian point of view, how stable his power base is within the Politburo.

I am in the middle of these thoughts when I spot Philip coming towards me. I recognise his tall lanky figure and mop of long blond hair. Although he must be in his mid to late forties, he looks much younger. We shake hands and I say:

"Hi, Philip, glad you could make it. Look, before you take your coat off, why don't we leg it up towards Trafalgar Square and get a beer in one of those pubs around there?"

Philip agrees and we stroll up Whitehall together exchanging pleasantries about our families. We reach the top of Whitehall and choose one of the many pubs nearby. They are always full at this time of day, and it's a scrum to elbow our way through to the bar. Eventually we get a waiter's attention. We order a couple of pints and some rather tired looking sandwiches and find our way through to a reasonably quiet corner. All that's left to sit on are two bar stools so we settle onto these and push our bags, my overnighter and Philip's attaché case, under the table next to us.

I get straight to the point, "Philip, about Gorbachev's speech to the UN on Wednesday. I'd really appreciate your take on that. What do you make of the speech? Why do you think he chose to make it at the UN? How secure is he as the Soviet supremo?"

Philip takes a swig of his beer while he assembles his thoughts. He then wipes the froth from his mouth and off he goes. As ever he is a compelling speaker. He summarises Gorbachev's rise to power culminating in his appointment as general secretary of the CPSU in March 1985. He talks through Gorby's political philosophy, the development through the stages of Glasnost or open discussion of political and social issues, to his launching of the programme of reconstruction (Perestroika), renewal (Obnovleniye) and acceleration (Uskoreniye). Philip refers to Gorby's main rivals in 1985 when he was appointed to the top job (mainly the dangerous Romanov) and how he has since consolidated his power base both within the Soviet Union and in relation to his ageing East European partners.

I am more than pleased to let Philip continue, interrupting him only to clarify a few points relevant to my understanding of Gorby's thought process leading up to his UN speech. After an hour or so, and another couple of beers, we are done. Philip summarises by saying he is convinced that Gorbachev is sincere and genuine in deciding to reduce force levels in Europe and that he has the power and authority to get the job done.

Philip's analysis makes me feel somewhat vindicated about the line I took at the NATO summit. Of course, his material is solely from open sources but I fully respect the depth of his knowledge of this subject.

I thank Philip profusely for giving me his time today and we prepare to leave. Most of the customers in this cosy pub have already thinned out and returned to their workplaces and, as we ourselves prepare to leave, I notice that a light drizzle has set in as London reverts to its normal dismal weather pattern. Philip gives me a last parting shot. He picks up his attaché case and extracts a document consisting of a number of A4 pages held together with string tags.

He hands it to me and says, "Look, Peter, I think this might be useful to you for your mission, whatever that is. This is the first proof of a book I'm editing. It's a compilation of some of my own articles and those of several of my compatriots from our Cambridge research group. It still needs a bit of refinement but we hope for publication sometime next spring. This is a spare copy so you're welcome to keep it. Oh, and one last word. Watch out for Erich Honecker. He's not a happy camper."

We shake hands, Philip walking off with his long loping strides back down Whitehall, while I turn in the opposite direction towards the Strand.

I realise it's time to get back to London City airport to catch my four o'clock return flight to Brussels. I can't remember how best to get there by tube so I walk through the drizzle to Charing Cross station and wait in line at the taxi rank there. I'm wondering what Philip meant by his remark about Honecker as I reach the front of the queue, climb into the taxi and out of the rain.

I reckon if I can check in at the airport by three o'clock, I should have plenty of time for the flight. My taxi driver does his stuff and deposits me outside the London City arrivals terminal at two fifty. I present my ticket and passport at the Sabena desk and I'm though to the departures lounge. I've promised Ann to take her, Chloe and Christian out this evening to the last showing of "Saving Private Ryan" at the Vandome. I know how important it is to her that we do things together as a family at the weekend and, for me, this evening has extra significance as I haven't yet told Ann that I have to get to Washington by Monday morning. I know the time this evening will be tight but my four o'clock flight should enable me to get back home in Brussels by six or six thirty latest even with the one hour time difference. The last performance starts at seven twenty so even with the fifteen- minute drive there and parking, we should make it on time.

I look up at the flight departures board and see my flight listed. "Sabena SN 0721 to Brussels - Flight Delayed: Fuck! I think, I hope it's not a long delay. I try to relax by making a start on Philip's draft book about Soviet affairs. But I can't concentrate. I look back up at the departures board. It still says: "Flight Delayed". I give it twenty minutes. No change. I get up and go to the loo, come back and look up yet again. Still no change. "Flight delayed". I decide to go to the reception desk but there's a long queue in front of me, probably mostly harassed Belgian businessmen trying, like me, to find out what's going on.

I'm still in the queue when I hear an announcement, "Sabena Flight SN 0721 has been delayed due to ????. (can't make out what she's saying). We apologise for the delay. Please wait for further information." That's all. I realise there's no point me continuing to wait to talk to the receptionist at the desk as she won't know any more.

I go back to my seat and wait. What else to do? Then I decide to try to use the public phone to call Ann. There are three phone booths. All are in use and behind the present users there are long lines of others waiting their turn to phone. I never do get to the front of the line.

After a frustrating hour or so of negative energy, at last I hear: "Will passengers for Flight SN 0721 to Brussels go immediately to gate number eighteen where your flight is ready for boarding." At last, I think, as I join the scrum of passengers who, like me, are both frustrated and relieved at the same time. As a positive, the boarding process is carried out smoothly and after the routine pre-flight safety info, etc. at last we are in the air.

I look at my watch and re-calibrate the time. We took off at five forty, the flight takes an hour, add another ten minutes to disembark, I have no hold luggage so, say, another ten to fifteen minutes to clear arrivals and retrieve my car, then another thirty minutes if I'm lucky to drive through Brussels Friday evening traffic. That adds up to one hour, fifty-five minutes. Add that to five forty-five and that makes – oh no! About eight o'clock! That's the earliest I could possible get home. Too late as the film begins at seven twenty!

I know I shouldn't get so wound up about this. It's counter-productive. And my God! There are so many far more important things going on in the world than just taking my family to the cinema – for fuck's sake! I tell myself to get a grip. It's been a pretty traumatic couple of days and I need to settle down and get things back in proportion. It's just that my family is so important to me and after the ten years since the Cyprus tragedy, still Ann and I have this distance between us. And Chloe and Christian were really looking forward to us all seeing the film together. Not turning up on time this evening, just makes things worse between us.

My time calculations prove to be over optimistic. All of the phases take longer – the plane doesn't get to its stand until seven o'clock local time, we seem to wait an age before we can disembark, there's no gantry so we have to get on a shuttle bus to the arrivals terminal, there's a queue to get out of the car park, then we grind to a halt several times on the Brussels ring. It's touching eight o'clock before I finally draw up in front of my house.

The house is in darkness when I enter. No sign of life so they obviously went on ahead without me. I find a note on the table. It reads: "Can't wait any longer, your supper's in the fridge." That's it, terse and to the point! I don't bother to investigate the fridge, just drop my overnight bag, lock the front door and go back to my car.

I drive straight to the Vendome cinema and struggle to find somewhere to park, eventually wedging in between two cars in a spot that's several streets way. I run from there to the cinema. It's just eight thirty. I go to the kiosk but it's already closed. I see that the film is showing in Salon One so I go there. There's an usherette at the door. I explain that my family is inside, and that I'm late due to my flight being delayed. I ask her if I can go in. I'd checked that it's a two- hour film and reckon there should still be an hour left. The usherette seems not to be impressed. She's says there's a capacity audience inside and there's no chance of a seat. I tell her I don't care and am quite willing to stand or sit in the aisle. I'll pay full price for the privilege. With a frown and pursed lips, the usherette is finally persuaded. I push a few Belgian francs in her hand and before she changes her mind, I slip through into the salon. It's pitch black in there except of course for the film, which is in the midst of a violent Normandy battle scene. I know the basic story of the film, ie. the four Ryan brothers are all called to war, three are killed and the action is about finding the fourth Ryan brother. My eyes slowly adjust to the dark and I search for my family. At last I see them, Ann in between our two children. All the seats are occupied around them. There's no way I can get to them, so I sit in the aisle for the rest of the film, hoping I don't get accused of causing a security or fire risk by blocking the exit.

When the film finishes, I notice there are two exits to the salon and I don't know which one my family will take. So I wait until the final lights come up and people start to leave. Sod's law, I see Ann leading the children out through the door on the opposite side from where I am so I push my way through to that side, rightly earning complaints from those around me. I say sorry, but I don't care, as I struggle to catch up with my family before they disperse as I've no idea where Ann has parked.

Then I see them up ahead and call out. Christian hears me, turns and shouts out, "Daddy, wow you made it. Mummy said you wouldn't but I knew you would!" He rushes up to me, throws himself into my arms and we hug each other. This one action makes it all worthwhile. We close in on Ann and Chloe. Chloe comes and gives me kiss. Ann does not. I come to her and kiss her on the cheek anyway.

"Well family," I say. "I have to blame Sabena airlines for making me miss half the film and there were no seats left when I eventually did get here. But that's now history. Who's for a Belgian waffle and ice cream?"

I know what their reply would be and we are quickly installed in one of the many ice cream parlours in the Chaussée du Wavre. Christian was thrilled by the film and we discuss it in some detail.

We stay there until after ten then Ann reminds us that both Chloe and Christian have school activities tomorrow and they need their sleep. We leave in our separate cars, both the children insisting they come with me in mine. I can tell Ann is not pleased. When we get home, it's the children's bedtime. When they've brushed their teeth and gone to their bedrooms, I go to say goodnight. Christian is still animated by his day and we agree I will come with him tomorrow morning to support his school rugby trial. I hug him goodnight. I go to Chloe's room. She's in her bed, quiet as usual. As I bend over, she reaches up and puts her arms around me.

She kisses me on the lips and whispers quietly in my ear, "Daddy, I love you so much!" That's all. I feel a surge of tender emotion towards my darling daughter as I switch out her light. It was worth a hundred times all the day's aggravation for this moment.

I come back into the living room to find Ann is already preparing for bed. I feel bad about not touching the supper she left me but it's too late now. I wonder whether I should tell her that I have go to the US for a Monday meeting but I don't have flight details from Clive yet so I decide to wait.

By the time I've switched off all the lights, checked the locks and had my ablutions, Ann is already in bed. I get in next to her and I can see her silhouette in the half light. She's still a beautiful woman. I reach over and stroke her shoulder but she does not respond. I know she's cross about my late arrival at the cinema and, I suspect, because our children preferred to ride back with me. She turns away from me on to her right side. I turn over to my left. There is a physical and emotional gap between us. Again we pass a loveless night.

Chapter Seven

It's been our custom on weekend mornings for our little family to sit down to breakfast together. As they've grown up, both Chloe and Christian have got more involved with school activities and with friends of their own age. But we still like to spend Saturday and/or Sunday mornings as a family. It's not of course possible during the periods when I'm away on operational duties but my staff job here at NATO HQ enables me to be at home at weekends most of the time.

This Saturday, Christian and I are first up. I give Christian a few Belgian francs and he's off to our favourite boulangerie that's round the corner to buy freshly made croissants and a couple of baguettes, or "tradis" as they are called locally. Meantime, I lay the table, beat up the eggs and get the coffee percolator on the go.

Christian comes back and we enjoy the joint experience of making the scrambled eggs. It's been a bit of a father/son activity since way back. Now that Christian is ten, he needs no instruction about this simple recipe, but we still like to keep it going. There's no great secret here – just four elements, beat up the eggs thoroughly, add just the right amount of fresh milk, a little salt and pepper, stir continuously and at the right temperature and gauge the "moment critique" when to take the pan off the stove.

Today the scrambled eggs look perfect, the bread has been lightly warmed, the coffee is percolating and ready for pouring. We can already hear movement from the girls but Christian likes to put his head round their bedroom doors and formally announce that "breakfast is served!"

Ann and Chloe appear, both in their dressing gowns, and we all sit around our dining room table. We attack the scrambled eggs first while they're still warm, then start on the croissants, bread and jam. Christian is always bright and talkative from first thing when he wakes up while Ann and Chloe take longer to get going in the morning. Already Christian is talking animatedly about his rugby trial at the British School of Brussels this morning. Ann and Chloe are listening and slowly adjusting to the day.

I look across at Ann, my wife, and yet again realise what a beautiful woman she is. She's wearing her dressing gown, has no make-up and has only lightly combed her long blonde hair. She is now in her early forties and a few lines are just beginning to form under her eyes. But her figure is still slender and firm and I always like to look at the elegant line of her neck and her angular shoulders. But, as always, there is the sadness in her eyes and the distance in her manner. If only she could talk openly about the "Cyprus tragedy", perhaps even now after the ten long years since that event, we might find closure and move on. Perhaps I'll try to raise the subject again tonight.

Christian begins to get impatient. He says, "Dad, do you think I should take the new pair of boots for the trial today - the ones you bought me as an early Christmas present? The other ones are getting worn out." I can tell Christian is getting nervous about the trial. It's the first time he's been picked. I tell him:

"No, stick with the old one's for today. I'll bring the others and keep them handy so you can change at half time if you want."

Reassured about his boots, Christian is still restless to get going. He asks the perfunctory permission to leave the table and then is up and quickly clearing his plates and taking them to soak in the kitchen sink next door. I say to Ann and Chloe:

"I think I'd better get going too or Christian will really start fretting. You know how keen he is about the rugby trial. I know you two want to do some shopping this morning. Why don't we all meet at the Woluwe Centre later?"

Chloe says, "Daddy, you know it's "Granny's chocolate buying day". We could go to Leonidas and choose them together."

That agreed, I get up and leave the girls to do the washing up. I go into Christian's room and check through his kit with him for the trial and I make sure I also bring along the new boots. We leave Ann and Chloe still at the table, go out to the car and drive the short distance to the British School of Brussels in its impressive grounds near the Museum of Central Africa at Tervuren.

Christian meets up with some of his school chums and they go off to the changing rooms together to get ready. The weather is still relatively mild for the Belgium winter and the morning is crisp and dry – good rugby conditions.

I stand around the touchline with some of the other parents and we chat about our sons. Although the school is called the British School, the pupils come from a wide variety of nationalities and backgrounds reflecting the cosmopolitan nature of Brussels. The city is host to the major institutions of the European Union and NATO but it's also the European hub for many international companies such as the proliferation of new electronics and computer companies. I feel lucky that we've managed to get both our children into this school. Chloe seems to be doing quite well, according to her teachers, though at fourteen she's just entering her puberty years and is quiet and not over communicative with either Ann or me. Christian on the other hand is an open and active boy.

I watch as the boys emerge from the changing pavilion under the supervision of one of the teachers. The aim of the trial is to select the first XV team to represent the school at the under thirteen level. I see that Christian has been put in the scrum half position. I'm watching my son with a father's pride! He seems much smaller than many of the other boys, but then he's only ten while some of the others are up to twelve years old. I try to remember how big I was at Christian's age. As far as I can recall I was a late developer. Now I'm 185 cms tall (or six foot one inch as our American friends prefer) and weigh about 80 kilos (or 176 pounds) but it wasn't until I was about fourteen or fifteen that my height started to shoot up. Ann is quite tall for a woman and I've always heard that boys grow taller than their mothers so it's likely that Christian will end up about my size when he's older.

The game is hard fought as the boys are all trying their best to impress and catch the teacher's eye hoping to be picked for the first team. They still make many basic mistakes, for example, too many forward passes, too often getting into off side positions, not binding properly in the scrum but all these errors will be reduced as they learn the intricacies of the game. The first half ends with the scores level at eight points each - one try (not converted) and one penalty apiece.

The boys change over on the pitch then go into a huddle to discuss team tactics. Other boys, not playing, come on with drinks and slices of orange to refresh the players.

The second half begins well but then starts to become ragged as the boys tire. At ten to twelve years old, the boys have not yet developed stamina or how to pace themselves for the full period of the game.

Christian's team seems the first to weaken and his opponents run in two easy tries. But although outgunned by a stronger team, I'm pleased to see that Christian never gives up. When his pack manages to heel the ball back, Christian is on to it quickly and either sends a well weighted pass back to his fly-half or makes a darting break himself then either chipping the ball forward or uniting back with his forwards to maintain the momentum of the game.

The teacher blows the final whistle and thirty tired boys first shake hands with their opponents as per the etiquette of the game of rugby, then make their way back to the changing pavilion. As they go, Christian turns and give me a wave. I give him a "thumbs" up sign, he smiles and re-joins his chums.

With the other parents, I wait for the boys to reappear. After a while, they start to emerge from the pavilion. Christian is there, looking fresh faced and with his hair still wet from the shower. He runs over to me. I would love to cuddle him but feel that might embarrass him at his age, Instead, I tell him, "Well played. I was pleased you stuck at it and gave it your all till the end of the game."

"Dad," Christian says ecstatically, "our teacher has just told me I've been picked for the first XV for our match next Saturday!"

I'm proud of my son. And he didn't need his new boots.

I take Christian home to drop off his kit and change then we go straight to the Woluwe shopping centre. It's not a large complex and we manage to find Ann and Chloe, not surprisingly coming out of one of the main ladies' dress shops in the centre. They are both carrying bags with the shops logo. Chloe says, "Hmm - no questions Daddy - we'll give you a fashion parade later. Now what about Granny's chocolates?"

We all go over to the Leonidas shop. This has now become our monthly routine. My father died several years ago and my poor mother is now a sick lady. She is in her early eighties and we've managed to get her installed in an old peoples' home in Somerset, near to Ann's parents. It's not ideal and I wish I could visit her more often but she's well looked after there and comfortable. But now it has become our ritual to send her a box of beautiful Belgian chocolates every month. Chloe takes the lead, selects the box size then we pick out a selection of chocolates. We know my mother really fancies marrons glacés so we always pick some of those but also vary the choice each time. The shop assistant indulges our deliberations as we make our final selections. She then ensures the packaging layers are in place, raps the box in protective foil, then in brown paper, even providing the string. All we have to do is write my mother's name and address, pay for the chocolates and the postage. The shop does the rest and usually they arrive with my mother in Somerset within a few days. Impressive Belgian retailing!

The sight of all those chocolates is making me feel hungry. I say, "Anyone feel like fish and chips?"

As expected, I get an enthusiastic nod from Christian and both Ann and Chloe also seem keen so we go to the café/restaurant in the middle of the shopping mall. It also has an outer deli section serving shell fish but we head inside and find a table for four. We sit down and I say with mock formality:

"I need to make an announcement. Ann, I can inform you that your son, and Chloe, your brother Christian, here is now a member of the under thirteen rugby first XV at the BSB!" I can see Christian is so proud when I made this announcement and he receives the congratulations from Ann and his sister. I love to see our family like this.

The fish here is always fresh and Belgium has a well-deserved reputation for the best "frites" in the world. It's self-service here and Chloe and Christian head for the counter. When we are alone, Ann changes our good mood. She looks accusingly at me and says:

"Peter, why didn't you tell me you are going to America tomorrow? When you were out, a guy called Clive something rang asking for you. When I told him you were out, he asked me to tell you that you're booked on a flight to London early tomorrow morning then to transfer to a BA flight to Washington. I've written the details down. He wants you to call him this evening to confirm the arrangements."

I think to myself, "Fuck it, she's right. I should have told her last night. There you go." I say, "Ann, I can see you're upset about this and I'm sorry I didn't tell you last night. I didn't know for sure when I would be going. I so want us to have a good family day together. Let's enjoy the rest of the day with our children. We can talk about this later."

Ann gives her usual resigned look which I suppose is because I've fucked up again.

"Come on," I say. "Let's join the fish and chips queue!"

After we've finished our meal, I ask our children what they want to do next. Christian answers straightaway.

"Daddy, you know that the Christmas market at the Grand-Place is on already - has been for a week according to my friends at school. Could we go there? And perhaps you should show us how to skate!"

I know Christian is teasing me. Both he and Chloe have learnt to skate well for some years now but I am hopeless! I never have been able to keep my balance. But so what? I know my children enjoy skating and can also have a good laugh at my expense. Christian and I had walked to the Woluwe centre from our house so now we all go in Ann's car. This works out well as it's smaller than mine and easier to park in the busy centre of Brussels. The Christmas market is a special event with stalls and Christmas decorations set up around the Grand-Place, the Bourse area, Place de la Monnaie and Place Saint-Catherine. We do the rounds of the stalls then go to the entry booth of the ice skating rink. We choose our skates and find a row of cubicles where we can change into the skates and leave our shoes there.

I let my family go ahead and watch from the side as they glide into the rhythm of the skating. Christian as ever skates with wild enthusiasm, competing with other children. I love to see him looking so animated and happy. Chloe too looks relaxed and at ease on the ice. She is more cautious than Christian but I can tell she too is enjoying the experience, in her own quiet way. Then there's Ann. She is a lovely graceful skater. She glides along with a seemingly effortless ease. Yet again I marvel at how beautiful she is. If only one day we could recapture our love!

"Come on, Daddy," Christian shouts out to me. "Let's have some action from you!"

I feel honour bound to take to the ice, but as always, I start to stumble and feel I'm losing my balance. Christian comes alongside and tells me to follow what he is doing. I try my best but I can feel my feet slipping away from me. I try to grab hold of my son to steady myself but it's no good, I know I've past the point of recovery and as gravity asserts itself, all I can do is brace myself for the fall. Here I am, an army colonel, spread-eagled out on my bum in the middle of the rink. My kids love it. Chloe has been watching and she comes over and helps Christian to get me back to my feet. They are both in hysterics.

"It's all right for you two experts!" I joke, "but what about your poor old dad's sore bum?" I try again but with the same result and give it up. Skating is definitely not for me! I decide to sit the rest of the session out.

When eventually my family have had enough of the skating and walking round the Christmas market, we head back home in Ann's car.

While Ann and Chloe prepare supper, I call Clive's home number. He picks up straightaway.

"Ah, Peter, thanks for calling back. I left the flight details with your wife earlier but it's good to get your confirmation. You'll be getting in to Washington tomorrow evening, which should allow time for you to rest up before your meeting with the intel guys on Monday. We've booked you into the Ritz Carlton Pentagon City, convenient because your meeting has been switched to the Pentagon. Don't know exactly why except the issue is becoming very political. There'll be a briefing pack delivered to you at the hotel. Oh, and Peter, just to let you know the PM has expressed a deep personal interest in this matter and needs to be kept fully briefed. I'm trying to set up a secure communications link for you to report back. Any questions?"

Wow! I have to make a mental leap from being a father on a family day out to representing my country in these high-level Anglo-American talks. All I can think to say to Clive is:

"OK, Clive. I've got the picture. I will need some cash I guess. Can you sort that for me? I'll be on the plane tomorrow and I'll keep you posted"

"Fine, Peter. Will do. Oh, and good luck – I know you won't let us down!"

During our supper, I tell our children I will be leaving in the morning to go to America for a few days. I say that I hope I won't be away for too long and I ask them to think of good ideas for what we could all do next weekend as well, of course, as supporting Christian's rugby!

When our children are in bed, I go to say goodnight. First I go to Chloe's room. She's in bed reading and I see it's a book about one of William Shakespeare's plays. Chloe tells me it's part of her English literature curriculum and we discuss the course for a while. I tell her I love her and kiss her goodnight. Then I go to see Christian. He is lying in his bed but still has his light on. When he hears me, he props himself up and turns to face me. I say softly, "Hi, Mr Rugby man, how are you doing."

"Hi yourself, Mr Skater!"

We joke a while then I tell him I was so proud of him today on the pitch and wish him good luck for next Saturday's match.

"You'll be there of course, Dad?"

I suppose I have been worrying about this. All I know is I have a top-level assignment in Washington starting on Monday. I sincerely hope we can quickly sort out what is concerning the US intelligence community, tidy up a report and get back to Brussels. But right now, I have no idea how things might work out. I tell my son, "Look, Christian, I hope to be back in time and I should be. But I can't promise because there are things I am involved with which I can't myself control. So, if by really bad luck I don't make it on Saturday, you can be sure it will have been beyond my control. Do you understand that?"

"Ye-es, I suppose, Daddy. But do try your best. Oh, and Daddy, why is Mummy always so sad?"

I'm rather stunned by my son's remark. Even he, at ten years old, has picked up on Ann's demeanour. All I can think to say is:

"Mummy just has some worries. She'll be fine. Make sure you look after her while I'm away. OK?"

I kiss my son goodnight. I go back to the sitting room where Ann is sitting on our settee watching the news on TV. I go and sit down beside her. I put my arm around her and try to draw her closer. She doesn't pull away but she doesn't move in towards me either.

"Look, Ann," I say to her, "We can't keep going on like this. Even Christian is concerned about you. We've got to find a way through this, you and I."

Ann doesn't reply. I can see tears in her eyes. She just pulls away and goes to our bedroom. The news is still on the TV. There a report of our PM being interviewed. I'm not sure about the details but it involved her September Bruges speech about our relationship with the European Community. She's looking fresh and composed as ever. I hope she still will be when I report back about the Gorbachev speech.

I turn off the TV and the lights in the sitting room, then go through to our bedroom. Ann is asleep or pretending to be. I get in next to her but know there will again be no physical contact between us.

Chapter Eight

I can't get off to sleep. I'm getting seriously worried about Ann. Right now, she is lying next to me. Is she asleep? I don't know. When I get back from this trip, if she continues to refuse to talk about our present negative relationship and her coldness towards me, what should I do? I suppose I'll need to go to our doctor, talk it through with him and ask for a referral to an appropriate specialist such as a psychologist. Perhaps for both of us. Then what if Ann refuses to see him/her? What then? Divorce? I hate the idea of that but I have to do something. We can't keep on like this.

Then I have another thought. A bad one. Before I was posted here to Brussels, I attended a six-month course at the NATO Defence College in Rome. I was allocated an apartment there and Ann joined me with our children during their school holidays. The rest of the time she stayed back in UK in the small house we had bought in Kent. At the end of my course, we had a mix up over dates and I arrived home a day earlier than expected. Ann was there. She was looking radiant. Her hair was beautifully styled and I noticed she was wearing a new dress. But she wasn't alone. A good-looking guy of about our age was also there. They seemed surprised to see me but the guy reacted quickly and introduced himself, I think, as Mike Hansen or something like that. He told me he had known Ann since they were at uni together and they had been good friends then. Shortly after he graduated, he got a job in Australia and had decided to emigrate there. He was back in the UK on a short business trip and had decided to look up Ann. He got her address from her parents in Somerset. He said he'd arrived just before me and had invited Ann for supper in a local restaurant in Hythe. Mike told me it was great I was back and could I join them at the restaurant for supper? Appearing to be gallant, I remember he said, that as I had just got back from Rome, perhaps it would be better if he dropped out and left the reservation for Ann and me.

I remember feeling pleased for Ann that she had met up again with an old pal. I told them to go ahead to the restaurant and have the chance to reminisce about their uni days and to enjoy themselves. That was about two years ago. I remember feeling relaxed about the guy. He had seemed open and honest. But now, well I'm not so sure. Could it be that he had been seeing her while I was in Rome? Perhaps he hadn't emigrated to Australia as he said and what he told me was all a con. Perhaps the guy had been fucking my wife while I was away!!!! I simply don't know and have no proof he was anything other than what he told me. But I have a doubt. Could it be that Ann's frigidness towards me is not solely about the

Cyprus tragedy? Perhaps she's still missing this Mike guy. I suppose I must have fallen asleep while my mind was still with those dark thoughts.

When I wake up it's seven thirty. My flight from Zaventem leaves at ten so I'd better get moving. Ann still seems to be asleep and, as it's Sunday, there's no need to wake the children. I don't know what I should pack as I have no clear idea about what our meeting might lead to or how long I might need to be away. I decide to travel in smart casual - i.e. jeans, leisure shirt and sweater, winter weight leather blouson. Then I pack a formal business suit, shirt, tie, change of undies and wash bag. At the last minute, I put in my sports kit, hoping I can get in a few runs or at least some gym sessions while I'm away.

I look in on Christian. He's still fast asleep so I leave him. Then to Chloe. As I lean over her, she turns towards me and puts arms around my neck. She pulls me towards her and whispers, "Daddy, I don't want you to go. I just want you to love me!" Then she turns back onto her pillow.

I am reflecting on Chloe's sweet and emotional reaction as I walk through to our sitting room with my bag, ready to leave. I am surprised to find Ann is there. She walks with me to the front door and we stand there together for a while not talking. Then Ann comes to me, puts her arms around me and lightly kisses me. She says quietly, "Peter, come back safely. We need you." Then she turns and heads back towards our bedroom.

My head is in a whirl as I get to my car, drive to Zaventem airport and park in the Long Stay. I feel totally mixed up.

Clive is as good as his word and I find my tickets for the short hop over to Heathrow, then the British Airways flight to Washington had been sent by Fedex for my collection at the BA desk. I clear through Departures and wait for my flight to Heathrow to be called. In the Fedex envelop I'm pleased to find the BA ticket is Club World Class but note that there's no return ticket. There's also an American Express card made out in my name. Clive has left a note giving me the PIN number and he's commented: "For you to use as you choose. We don't need receipts!" Wow, I think, things are looking up. I've never known that before! Seeing this expensive ticket and the limitless AMEX card makes me realise I must now get my mindset back to concentrating on the purpose of my mission to the US.

Today, our short flight across the channel is on time. I've brought the draft book that Philip Daniels gave me and now I start to get into its detail. I see that Philip has written the opening introduction and a couple of chapters himself but has included papers and analysis written by a range of experts on Soviet affairs, some British, some American and some of Russian origin. Philip has also included a list of very informative annexes. Of course, the work is all derived from open source material but I find most of the assessments given in the book are of extremely high quality and right up to date. Philip told me he hopes publication will be early next year, 1989. The chapters which I think are most relevant to my mission are entitled: 'Development of Defence Policy under Gorbachev, Perestroika and the Military' and 'Soviet Political and Defence policies: Current Developments'. I intend to read all these chapters thoroughly during my time travelling to Washington. I hope that, with the help of the details from Philip's book, combined with all our classified material in NATO that I'm fully conversant with, we should be able to reach a definitive and agreed assessment that I can feed back to the PM. Providing the Americans produce their top team at Monday's meeting, I can see no reason why we shouldn't get this business wrapped up in a day or so at most.

I follow the Transfers sign at Heathrow, check in at the British Airways desk and proceed through Departures for the flight to Washington. I've got nearly an hour to wait and I think about getting some breakfast at one of the fast food outlets. Then I realise that my Club World ticket should entitle me to a good spread on board so I decide to wait. Instead I continue studying the detail of Philip's book on Soviet affairs.

We're called forward for the flight about twenty minutes before it's due to take off. I present my ticket and am delighted to be ushered to the upper deck stairway of this Boeing 747. My allocated seat is wide and comfortable, one of two seats side by side – the second one being unoccupied. As the departure time approaches, I wonder if I shall have the two seats all to myself but the last passenger to board, just before the hatches are closed, is shown to the seat next to me.

The passenger makes a bit of an exaggerated show of pretending to check if she has the right seat, then she looks at me and gives one of her big wide smiles.

"Surprise, surprise, Peter!!" It's Cheryl, my American Air Force colonel workmate from NATO. I see she's wearing designer jeans that are ever so slightly too tight as is her roll neck sweater which emphases her ample breasts. I also notice that she is wearing her long black hair loose so that it falls down to her shoulders. In a phrase, she looks great! Just seeing her appear as if out of the blue and realising that we will be travelling next to each other for the eight-hour flight to Washington, is an immediate tonic and morale boost. I'm sure Philip Daniel will forgive me that I won't be reading his book anymore for the next few hours.

"Cheryl, this is great!" I enthuse, "What's going on?"

"Relax, Peter, remember I told you before you left the office on Friday that I had a call from our NATO US rep telling me I also have to attend the Monday conference in Washington? Well, I checked who was working your travel arrangements, talked to your chum Clive and fixed it that we'll be together. I saw you up ahead boarding and left it late to get on, just to surprise you. You don't mind, do you?"

I suppose I should hold back a little, play it cool, after all it's only a few hours since I left my house in a very emotional state as far as my relationship with Ann is concerned. But I find it difficult to contain my pleasure at the prospect of spending one to one time with Cheryl on this flight. I reply:

"Mind? Of course, not Cheryl. I can't think of a better travelling companion!"

I'm about to expand on this, probably too fulsomely, when we're told to fasten seat belts, given the security briefing and we're airborne. It feels almost as if a new chapter of my life is beginning. My spirits rise even more when the air stewardess comes to us to offer drinks. Cheryl and I both order champagne. What else?

We also study the lunch menu - lobster starter then a choice of grilled beef, medallions of fresh salmon, tortellini pasta or cold potted turkey. I go for the beef, Cheryl for the salmon. What we do agree on is the wine - we plump for a good red Pinot Noir Burgundy. Cheryl says:

"Do you know my father said that the last thing he wanted before he died was to drink a glass of fine Burgundy wine. And do you know what? He did exactly that!"

Cheryl is full of stories about her family, her friends and her life in the American Air Force. We find conversation easy between us. I ask her where she had been the previous day. She winks mischievously.

"Ah, Peter, that would be telling! You never know what this naughty lady next to you gets up to in her free time! No, seriously, I nipped over to Paris and spent yesterday with an old USAF friend who's vacationing there. But not before I made sure that you and I were booked on the same flight and with seats next to each other. I just managed to make the connecting flight from Orly this morning. And Peter, you can stop looking at me like that! I'm not going to tell you if my friend was male or female. It might make you jealous!"

Cheryl has this way of being part flirty all the time and I can't help but be flattered. Being with her makes me feel relaxed and good. We finish the main course of our meal and the bottle of red seems to have emptied itself. We order another with our dessert – fresh fruit for Cheryl, cheese platter for me. We decide to share the meal choices between us and give toasts to each other as our second bottle of wine goes the same way as the first. The stewardess clears away our trays. Cheryl says, "Peter, I saw you looking at her tits as she leaned over you to take your tray. I know she's pretty but you shouldn't make it so obvious or it'll be me who's the jealous one. Oh, and you shouldn't call her an "air hostess" or "stewardess" any more. That's supposed to be politically incorrect. They're all now "flight attendants" both male and female. Remember, it's now 1988 and we're into an age of sexual equality."

"I'll try to remember," I tell her, "And as for her being pretty, I think you were just kidding. You know how I looked at you when you turned up on the plane, particularly when you reached up to stow your bag in the overhead locker!"

"That's better, Peter," she teased. "I like it when you talk dirty to me!"

Cheryl really is irrepressible.

I find the meal and our demolition job on the wine is beginning to have its effect on both of us. Cheryl moves towards me and links her arm through mine.

"What about we find a good film to fall asleep to?" she slurs.

We check through the film offerings and are pleased that BA are right up to date. We can watch "Rainman" starring Dustin Hoffmann and Tom Cruise or the just released "Stormy Monday".

"Oh, I like the sound of "Stormy Monday". It's got that hunk Sean Bean in it. Let's watch that!"

So, we settle down, snuggling up close and, with our heads touching, we watch the film from one screen. At least we start to watch it but neither of us can stay awake. I remember drifting off in a rather drunken haze, thinking life is wonderful. I suppose I should think that it is somehow being disloyal to my family to be so close to another woman but my mind at this time doesn't want to go there.

Chapter Nine

We both sleep for a time lulled by the steady drone of the Boeing 747's powerful engines and the after effects of the wine. I'm the first to wake up. Cheryl's head is still resting on my shoulder. I gently ease her back into her seat so that I can extract myself. My first over-riding priority is to have a pee! That done, I ask the air hostess, or rather, the flight attendant, as I suppose I must now call her, for some cold water. She brings a large bottle and two glasses.

Cheryl slowly opens her eyes, adjusts to her situation and sees the water. We both drink down two full glasses. We don't talk much. I suppose we both realise we overdid it with the wine. But what the heck! No harm done.

We enjoy an easy conversation for the rest of the flight and land at Dulles International airport, Washington DC on schedule, 2100 hours UK time which, with the five hours' time difference, makes it four o'clock in the afternoon in Washington. We wait to collect Cheryl's bag, I just have my walk on wheely, and when we pass into the arrivals terminal, we spot a uniformed guy holding a sign – "Colonel Walker and party". Cheryl is the Colonel Walker in question, I suppose I'm "the party"!

The US military protocol organisation is highly efficient if perhaps rather over the top for us Brits. Everything is taken care of. Cheryl and I are whisked away in a large military staff car and driven the twenty odd miles from the airport at Chantilly, Virginia to the Washington downtown area where our hotel is located. At the Ritz Carlton, Pentagon City hotel, our bags are taken from us and deposited in our pre-allocated rooms. We are asked to be in the lobby for 1900 hours when we will be taken to a reception that has been arranged for us.

The evening passes pleasantly enough. Our hosts are a selected group of US intel people, a mix of military and civilian, male and female. I notice Cheryl has created a complete makeover. She has swept her long raven hair back from her face into what I believe is called a chignon knot. She is wearing a low-cut dress, long earrings and her red lipstick emphasis her wide sensuous mouth. She looks fresh and ready to go. That's Cheryl!

We are taken to a nearby restaurant, first for a cocktail in the outer lobby then for supper in the main dining area of the restaurant. Cheryl and I are placed at different ends of the table. My two companions sitting either side of me are both civilians. They introduce themselves as Ed Morgan from the CIA and Jo Suter who is a senior exec with the National Security agency. We talk about our backgrounds and Ed and Jo press me about the workings of the NATO summit and how it is to have all the main Western leaders together. We specifically don't talk about the detail of tomorrow's meeting at the Pentagon but they tell me they will both be attending. I get the firm impression that the Americans are taking the Gorbachev speech and the politics around it very seriously indeed. I know I'm going to be pressed to hold my own and need to be well prepared.

We work our way through a full menu and when I think I can get away without offending our hospitable hosts, I take my leave. I think to take a taxi back to the hotel but my hosts insist I take a government car. Back in my room, I turn in early. I feel I'm going to need all my wits about me tomorrow.

I wake early and am pleased I had packed my training kit. I pull it on and head down to the gym. As I expected, it's well stocked with all the usual range of training appliances. I spend some time warming up, then use several of the arm and thigh strengtheners. I end up with a thirty minutes session on the running machine, starting with slow jogging than speeding up to a full striding session before back again to jogging speed to cool down. I go back to my room, take a shower, and dress in the only suit I have brought with me. I meet up with Cheryl at breakfast and notice she's decided to wear her formal US Air Force full colonel's uniform.

Perhaps I should have brought my service dress uniform. Too late now!

A military staff car collects us at nine o'clock sharp and deposits us at one of the several Pentagon entrances. Our escort is there to meet us. He checks IDs and in my case passport, gives us passes to wear around our necks and leads us along a labyrinth of corridors to a conference room. It seems Cheryl and I are the last to arrive as the room is already full. I am offered a seat next to the chairman's while Cheryl is shown to the back of the room.

I feel this is rather déjà vu after my meeting last Friday in Whitehall. But there is a very different set up and atmosphere here. There are about twelve people around the table with probably twice that number sitting behind. About half are in some form of uniform. There are name cards in front of all those sitting around the table. I see the abbreviations CIA, FBI, NSA and DIS but others are unknown to me. Behind the CIA and NSA labels I recognise the two guys Ed Morgan and Jo Suter who had sat next to me at the restaurant last evening. As far as I can tell, I am the only non-American in the room which feels rather intimidating. I would have appreciated some support from my own people, perhaps from our embassy here. But what the heck, here we are. I shall soon find out what it is that's so concerning the US intel community.

Behind the sign "Chairman" sits a silver-haired gentleman, probably in his mid-sixties. He opens the meeting, "Colonel Chambers, we appreciate you coming all this way to meet with us today. Your defence ministry has sent us your CV and we understand and respect your background. Let's get to it. During this meeting today, we may need to share with you some of our national sensitive intel material which we consider needs to be reserved with a US eyes only caveat. Are you prepared to sign an agreement as part of our Special Access Program?"

I haven't expected this and have had no indication or dialogue about it with the UK authorities. I know this meeting has our PM's personal blessing but no more. I reply, "Sir, you know my security clearance levels for UK/ CANUKUS and NATO classifications. I have no authority from the UK authorities to whom I owe my primary responsibility and allegiance for any further access. I will sign your agreement if you so wish but with my own caveat that I reserve the right to brief my own people as I feel necessary."

The chairman pauses and looks around the room. In the end, it is the guy representing the FBI who nods agreement. A staffer produces the agreement document. I read it through and sign. This formality over, the chairman continues, "Last week, before the NATO summit, we expressed reservations about Chairman Gorbachev's UN speech in our briefing to our president. Following a discussion that he had with your prime minister, he did not stick to our recommended line. We understand she had been persuaded to change her own briefing following her discussions with you, Colonel. Am I correct?"

"Sir, I did make representations to her and she did change her response at the summit. So yes, I suppose you could say I did persuade her."

"What was your rationale, Colonel?" I feel I'm being squeezed here and I don't appreciate it. It seems like I'm being tested. But OK I'll go with it and see what happens. I reply.

"Due to my knowledge of Soviet and other Warsaw Pact force levels and deployments, I considered that the reduction numbers Mr Gorbachev announced were consistent both with a move from an offensive military posture to a defensive one and also in line with the political and strategic relaxations he has already brought about and is moving further towards in the future. I would add that my German colleagues fully supported my assessment. All I did was represent this view to our prime minister. Detailed discussions and co-ordination with our people in London was not possible due to the short time between the speech and the Brussels summit." I might have added that Cheryl also agreed but I don't want to drag her into the discussion as I have no idea where it's leading.

The chairman now turns to a guy in an Army uniform which I notice has the two silver stars of a Major-General on the lapel – that's two jumps up from my own rank. He asks me, "Could you give a brief summary of the group of Soviet forces facing West

Germany and any noted recent changes in their deployment?"

"Fuck it," I think, "this is getting to be an inquisition. But OK, you asked for it. I can go with this." So I run through the main order of battle of the three Tank Armies and two Motorised Rifle Armies that are lined up facing our NATO forces in West Germany. I am most conversant with the details of Three Shock Army so I itemise each of the Divisions - 25th, 12th, 10th 47th Tank and 207 Motor Rifle Divisions and break down each of these formations to regimental and battalion size with their present barrack locations. I end by saying, "And to answer the last part of your question, General, no, as at last Friday when I was last in my office in Brussels, we have detected no recent deployment changes."

The general isn't finished yet.

"Would you give us an outline, Colonel, of your understanding of Soviet planning for a military invasion into West Germany?"

"Great question, General," I reply. I'm really getting into my stride here. In my reply, I start by referring to Marshal Ogarkov who revolutionised the Soviet Operational Art during the early 1980s. I continue, "Ogarkov has initiated the all arms doctrine of the Rapid Strike Complex whereby command and control could be maintained throughout the simultaneous prosecution of fluid, fast moving operations on multiple fronts. His work has formed the framework of the General Staff plans which the Soviet troops have trained for regularly in both Army and Front level exercises in the Letzlinger Heide and other training areas of East Germany. And of course Marshal Ogarkov, who in 1984 was dismissed as Chief of the Soviet General Staff, still retains his post on the Central Committee and today is the operational commander of Soviet forces in the Western Theatre of Strategic Military Action. So really we could say he was merely moved sideways rather than demoted."

I decide to stop there. I'm itching to develop the principles by which the Soviet planners estimated that in an attack against the West they could achieve a major breakthrough over the Rhine within ninety-six hours using conventional forces. But I think I've already said more than enough on this subject. The senior CIA and NSA reps both have questions. These mainly relate to Soviet strategic assets and political issues. After my initial hesitancy, I confess I am beginning to enjoy this. The questions are the sort of subject material we deal with on a daily basis in NATO HQ. I also bless Philip Daniels for his excellent book I've just been reading. That's kept me right up to date from a political viewpoint. From my side, I'm trying to understand what is the purpose of all this. What do they want from me?

After what must have been a good half-hour's grilling, I turn to the chairman and say, "Sir, I hope you accept I do know this subject, so may I now ask in return. What is it that is concerning your intel staffs here?"

He replies, "My turn to say great question, Colonel. But one more for you first, if I may, your CV shows you passed an exam at German linguist level six years ago. Are you still fluent in the language?"

I'm thinking - what a strange question following on from all our discussions about the Soviets.

I don't really know why, but I give a straight answer and say, "Yes, Chairman, I took that exam prior to starting a tour in Bielefeld, West Germany and used the language quite extensively during that period. Since then I've had less chance to practise but try to converse with some of our German nationals in NATO HQ in their language whenever possible. To summarise: yes, I can understand and converse in German but absolutely not to a level which is really fluent. I know I still make many grammatical errors in that demanding language."

"Thank you for your frankness, Colonel." The chairman turns to address the others in the room. He says, "Right, it's now time to reduce our numbers here. He indicates to certain individuals, mainly those occupying the front row seats around the table, saying, "I need you, General Allen, to stay together with Messrs Morgan and Suter here and the two main staffers from the offices of each of the outgoing and incoming presidents." He sees Cheryl, who had taken a seat at the back of the room, and says to her, "Ah yes, Colonel Walker, we need you to stay. I'll explain later."

Those indicated move into seats closer to the chairman while the remainder file out of the room. I notice each leaves a slip of paper on a tray next to the chairman's seat. I wait, wondering what the fucking hell is going on. The chairman steadily works his way through the slips of paper taking his time to review what was written on each.

Eventually, he puts the papers down, turns to me and, speaking in a quieter more informal voice, says, "It's now time to come clean with you, I want to apologise for putting you through such a grilling. It was for a good reason. I will be frank. We need the expertise of someone who has a fundamental up-to-date knowledge of what indicators would trigger a genuine increase in Soviet military preparedness to launch a surprise attack against the West. We are impressed by your CV but needed to know more about you. I pressed you for answers about various Soviet military and political issues. I had asked several of the others you saw in the room today to witness our conversation and advise me on their opinion of your personal suitability for a task which is of critical importance to our two countries. I have just reviewed their responses. They all tallied and I can now confirm that we need your assistance."

Quite a speech! I don't know how to react. I certainly was not expecting this. But I simply don't understand why these top-level US officials are so concerned, with their panoply of intel sources to advise them. Before I reply, the chairman continues, "What I'm now going to say is very sensitive to our nation. That's why I asked you to sign that agreement earlier and why I've reduced our numbers here to only those who vitally "need to know". Colonel Chambers, I'll be very frank and explain that we in the US intelligence community are faced with a number of conflicting elements."

"One: The composition of our intel professionals. There is a major split between those who have been "Soviet watchers" for many years and still see the Soviets and their Warsaw Pact allies as a continuing major threat to the West. They either don't trust Gorbachev or feel he does not have the power base in the Politburo to do what he says. Then there are the others who are convinced he is genuine and are pushing our president to move quickly and exploit this unique opportunity for major reductions in both nuclear and conventional forces. The Gorbachev UN speech has brought the two differing sides into almost open conflict, each giving their own version of advice to the president's office. We are finding this lack of coordination unprofessional and frankly embarrassing for our nation."

"Two: This is also highly sensitive. Last Wednesday, one of our CIA operatives in East Germany was murdered. He had been shot in the head. His body was found near the headquarters of the Group of Soviet Forces Germany (GSFG) in Zossen-Wùnsdorf. We don't know the circumstances. We have another operative who is working with a very highly placed East German employee who is an agent of ours. Communicating with him has become very difficult recently and we know they are both under close surveillance either by the Soviets or the East German Stasi secret police. He has sent us reports indicating that there has been a striking recent increase in encrypted communications between Berlin and Moscow and we believe there may be some reinforcement of Soviet forces in Poland and East Germany (GDR). Again, we don't know enough about this. Is it the Russians or the East Germans who are being so aggressive at the very time that Gorbachev is proposing close détente and troop reductions? We simply don't know."

"Three: Our counter Intel people have just arrested an American serviceman who has been spying for the Soviets for some years, seven to be precise. His name is Hall. He is a warrant officer in US Army Signal Intelligence and is an electronic surveillance expert who has had highly classified assignments in Germany. He is still being interrogated by our CI people but so far, he has revealed that for years he has passed to the Soviet, details of our most top secret political and military information. This is causing much nervousness here in Washington while we try to determine exactly what has been passed to the Soviets, how they might make use of it and what countermeasures we can take."

"Four: As you know, we are "between presidents". Our nation elected our new president last month,

November 1988, who will not be inaugurated until January. In this interim period, there's something of a vacuum in policy making as the outgoing president's personal staff prepare to leave and the incoming incumbent brings in his own people. These new people will take time to get fully up to speed. This leaves us with a lack of a consistent and coordinated reaction to the events of last week. Your UK JIC Chairman tells me he has informed you of the disturbing reports of an increased threat that supposedly emanated from previously reliable sources. Unusual communications protocols have been used to transmit these reports and we are simply baffled by them. Our NSA guys are backtracking to check the veracity of these reports but, at this time, we cannot reach any positive conclusions. There are even rumours which we believe are extreme but which we cannot readily disclaim. One is that the Soviets are playing a highly efficient disinformation game and that they are aware of our current weakness and may try to spring a surprise attack stemming either through the Fulda gap or astride the Magdeburg - Braunschweig Autobahn, another is that it is the East Germans who are stirring the pot and intend to make a land grab to reclaim West Berlin, perhaps as we relax during the Christmas period. These possibilities may seem far-fetched but we have to examine them until they can be disproved."

I'm listening to the chairman's comments in a stunned silence. Except for the briefing I was given at the JIC last Friday, I had no previous idea of most of this. Now I realise why the issue has escalated to such a level. But I'm still asking myself what all this has got to do with me. I soon find out as the Chairman looks sternly across at me and continues, "Colonel Chambers, we urgently need to clarify the situation and believe you have the expertise and balance to assist us. We want you to lead in assessing three things: first, has there been any evidence of Soviet or East Germany military reinforcement of combat troops in the GDR? Second, who is behind the heightened tensions in East Berlin, leading for example to the murder of our operative – the Russians or the East Germans? Third, how should we respond to those in our nation who feel we must react now by increasing our own alert measures?"

He pauses then continues, "We have contacted your PM's office about this and they are prepared to back us in assigning you. They offer any further assistance that may be required. We have also been in touch with Admiral Figo from your NATO office. He has temporally released you and Colonel Walker from your present duties. From our side, we will provide you with total support. In particular, Messrs Morgan and Sutter, who you met last evening, have been tasked to assist you."

The chairman then turns to Cheryl who has been listening throughout and tells her, "Colonel Walker, I asked for you to attend today as your experience with all three of our main intel agencies (DIA, CIA and NSA) plus your present NATO assignment, qualifies you to assist in this mission. You are to act as liaison to Colonel Chambers with particular reference to establishing communications between him and our agencies. Your Admiral Figo has also been informed that you are required for special US duties. That's it, any questions from either of you?"

I now realise at last what this is all about, why I had been called over here to Washington and what they want of me now. Incredible, and all because I was crazy enough to insist on challenging our PM's briefing three days ago. What have I got myself into? I see the chairman is waiting for me to respond. So what the fuck, let's go for it. And having Cheryl along as well can't be bad.

I turn to the chairman and say, "Very clear, Chairman. Of course, I'll do my best!"

The chairman gets to his feet, comes over and shakes my hand. I realise I have just been given one hell of a responsibility. We agree I will now spend time with Ed Morgan and Jo Suter to work out how to set about this daunting task and what assistance I can expect from them. I need Cheryl to help here also.

The chairman then concludes, "Colonel, you have the mission, now get to it! I've cleared my agenda to meet back with you at five this afternoon. I then need to hear your action plan. Clear?"

"Yes, Chairman," I reply, "Quite clear!" That's what I say but my head is still spinning and I'm trying to think what the fucking hell I'll need to do to fulfil this mission!

Chapter Ten

I now understand why I had been seated next to Ed and Jo last evening. It was all part of the chairman's plan to find out if I am the guy to go forward and find out what is really going on. What seemed so clear and straightforward a few days ago – a world heading towards a better, safer place with a rapprochement between East and West, now, with all the issues the Chairman has outlined, no longer seems that simple. We need to rework the whole issue.

A separate room in the Pentagon has been set aside for our group. Initially, it's just Ed, Jo, Cheryl and me. It looks like I'm going to be working very closely with these guys. Ed is the CIA man. I'd say he's in his late thirties/early forties. He's about my height and is slim and rangy in build. He's got a full head of hair, dark but not black like Cheryl's. He looks very fit and, with his CIA background, I know he's been well trained in self-protection. A good guy to have watching your back on operational assignments.

Jo, the guy from the National Security Agency (NSA) is very different in stature from Ed. He's short and round with thick pebble glasses. From the conversation that I had with him at the supper last evening, I got the impression he's a very clever guy in his speciality of government communications. I've learnt that NSA is responsible to the US government for the global monitoring of data for foreign intelligence and counterintelligence purposes, and for the protection of US government communications. This is an area of expertise that I absolutely do not have, so I can foresee that Jo could be a very useful member of our team.

Then there's Cheryl. She had remained firmly in the background during the meeting - unlike her usual extrovert character. I can see why the chairman has chosen her to work with us. Not only does her background span all the intelligence disciplines but she also has the personality to make things happen. Added to which, personally, just having Cheryl as part of my team, gives me a warm feeling of confidence, or of something – it's just good for her to be here!

We're just starting to scope out our new mission, when the two-star general who had been sitting next to the chairman during the meeting, arrives to join us. He's a man of medium height and build but seems to exude a natural confidence.

He comes over to me, shakes my hand and says, "Colonel Chambers, the chairman didn't choose to introduce me by name at the meeting so I'd like to put that straight. I'm Dwight Harris. At present, I'm working directly for the chairman of the Joint Chiefs of Staff here at the Pentagon and it was he who told me to set up the meeting this morning. I have previously served with the Defence Intelligence Staff so you could say I am acting in both capacities today. Firstly I apologise for grilling you so heavily about Soviet deployments, etc. but you will now understand that we had to be sure we were entrusting this mission to the right guy, particularly as you, Colonel, are not an American!"

General Harris paused and made a point of shaking the hands of Ed, Jo and Cheryl. I wasn't sure what he intended but he soon clarified this by addressing all four of us.

"Look, I need to make this totally clear. The Joint Chiefs are seriously disturbed by the rumours of possible offensive action either by the Soviets alone or by the East Germans with Soviet complicity during this transition period between our presidents which of course coincides with the normal Christmas stand-down. As a result, there's a strong lobby for the US to upgrade our threat alert status but we are aware that this could precipitate retaliatory measures by the Soviets and their allies. As a consequence, such actions could return us back to the Cold War stand-off situation. No one wants that after all our outgoing president's work at détente with Mr Gorbachev and the de-escalation of strategic nuclear missiles through the recent Treaties that have been signed. Our chiefs of staff are concerned by our lack of firm intelligence and that's why they have sanctioned your mission. They've told me to provide all the support you need. Colonel, feel free to call me at any time for additional resources. I will act as your link to our chiefs and the president's office and I am also patched in to your British Ministry of Defence and your PM's Cabinet Office in London. Is there anything you need from us at this early stage?"

Frankly, I haven't yet got a clue. I need to talk with my gallant new team here to clarify precisely our mission, to study the potential courses open to us, then to work out a plan of action. I look at my watch and see it's now 1130 hours and the chairman told me he would be here at 1700 hours to hear our plan. So, we've got to get a grip and get on with it.

I say to General Harris, "General, could you arrange for some refreshments to be brought to this room so we can work the issue continuously through till the chairman comes for our briefing. It seems a long time since breakfast! Also, I'd like you also to come to that meeting. By then, we should have had a first shot at what additional resources and support we will need."

I confess I had wrapped up my reply in somewhat clipped language, but it seemed to work and the general replies, "Fine. Refreshments will be fixed and I'll see you at five." With that, he leaves.

I turn to my little team and say, "Well I guess we're going to get to know each other very well as we move forward together on this task. I also know that I will have to rely massively on each of you. My first thought is to make sure we're all agreed on the detail of the task."

The chairman had posed three questions. There was a whiteboard and marker pens in the room, so I write on the board:

Mission

To determine:

One: Has there been any recent evidence of either Soviet, East German or Czech military reinforcement of combat troops in the GDR or Czechoslovakia?

Two: Who is behind the heightened tensions in East Berlin – the Russians or the East Germans?

Three: How should we respond to those in our (i.e. the US) nation who feel we must react now by increasing our own alert measures?

Ed, Jo and Cheryl have been watching intently as I wrote the above. All three nod their agreement that this is an accurate interpretation of the mission.

Ed is the first to comment, "I reckon we can cope OK with questions one and two by tapping into our existing resources. But I'm not at all happy about mission three. That's entirely a political matter. I guess all we can do is present our findings about missions one and two. If our conclusions are that there's no evidence of Soviet reinforcement and we can find a benign explanation about Berlin, then that is the best argument not to increase our US alert measures. But if we conclude either there has been reinforcement and/or the tensions in East Berlin could pose a threat to Western interests, we can merely report that. But then it will be up to the politicians to decide what action to take, not us."

This is the first time I've heard Ed's logic. I like what I hear. So, do both Jo and Cheryl as both nod their heads in agreement.

Under the mission statement, I make my first tentative attempt to list what indicators we should be concentrating on: I write:

Indicators

. Ground, air, sea deployments: out of routine, exercise areas, increased troop movements.

. NSA/GCHQ: Changes, intensity of comms patterns: eg between Berlin and Moscow

. Increased activity in Berlin: Soviets and East Germans

. Debrief of WO Hall and other arrested spies: What info had they been tasked to provide?

. Signs of power struggle in Politburo eg Ligachev, Zaikov.

I know this is only a first stab at it and there will be changes and increases to this list as our work proceeds, but at least it's a starting point and we can make our first assessment of what additional resources we will need to ask General Harris to provide. We are just discussing this indicators list when there's a knock at the door and a young lady appears wheeling a large trolley of refreshments – platters of meats and salads together with cold drinks. General Harris has kept his word.

During the next few hours, we agree an outline plan of action and prepare a list of our requirements to present to the chairman and General Harris. In summary, we agree that Ed, Cheryl and I will go soonest to West Berlin. I will initially link in with the US and UK intel people there and use their resources to carry out a comprehensive check of all Soviet, East German and Czech troop deployments stretching back to and beyond the Polish border. Ed will try to contact his undercover operators in East Berlin and check on the background to the recent murder of the CIA agent and other unexplained activities there. Cheryl will base herself at the American Mission in the US zone in West Berlin. Her role will be to coordinate communications with Ed and me in Berlin, and with Jo and the Pentagon in the US. Jo is to remain in NSA HQ in Maryland, focusing on Soviet and East German military and political communications and then feed any relevant details through to Cheryl.

At precisely 1700 hours the chairman and General Harris are back. They turn to me so I take on the role of spokesman for our group. Firstly, I point to the whiteboard and ask the Chairman to agree the wording of our mission to prevent any future misunderstanding. He does. Likewise, he agrees our preliminary indicators list.

I say to the chairman, "Sir, so far this is an exclusive American/British show. I do have good intel contacts particularly in Germany with their extensive sources in

Moscow and with the French, who, like the US and Brit missions, also run an efficient organisation in West Berlin. Can we include either of these nations in this project?"

The chairman is quick to reply: "Definitely NOT at this stage. Our counter intel boys have major concerns about KGB/Stasi penetration of West German government bodies and we can't risk compromising this operation. Regarding the French, I'll review this and keep you informed."

OK, that's clear. I then go through our outline plan and tell the chairman we need for Ed, Cheryl and me to get to West Berlin soonest. General Harris says he will fix the flights, etc. Cheryl also presents our list of requirements. This includes flight/travel, clearances from US and British authorities, additional communications, secretarial support, etc. It's a long list. General Harris scans through it, purses his lips then nods and tells us OK. Our flights and admin will be set up and we will get the details later today.

The chairman and General Harris shake us all by the hand and wish us good luck. We're in business!

We've all had a heavy session so I suggest we go back to our hotel and have a beer or whatever. Ed and Jo excuse themselves saying they would like to get back to their homes to sort out their domestics ready for our assignment to commence tomorrow. Cheryl and I share a car back to our hotel.

We decide to have a wash and brush up and then meet back in the hotel restaurant for supper. Before leaving my room that morning, I had put all my clothes in the hotel laundry bag less the suit I wore for the meeting. I am delighted to see it's all been returned, fresh and clean. I try to call Ann in Brussels but no answer. With the five-hour time difference, I reckon she's probably on her way to pick up our children from school. I'll try to call her again later. I also find I'm short of cash and probably won't be able to rely on my free gratis AMEX card for everything. So, on my way back down to the hotel lobby I use an ATM to stock up on US dollars.

Chapter Eleven

I get to the hotel restaurant to find Cheryl is already there. She's left her Colonel's uniform behind and is wearing tight designer jeans and a shiny red satin top. She favours red and she always looks good in it. We'd had a good buffet spread at lunchtime and neither of us want to repeat our overindulgence of the wine like yesterday so we both order Caesar salads and a glass of red Californian. I also take a small beer on the side while I'm waiting. Our conversation is light and we purposely keep off the subject of our new mission. We're getting towards the end of our light meal when a smart young lady officer whose uniform has captain's insignia, comes directly over to our table.

She says, "Colonels Chambers and Walker? Good evening. I'm Captain Terri Berger, an aide to General Harris. Our office is responsible for your travel arrangements. I apologise for interrupting your meal but I need to inform you that we have booked both of you and Mr Ed Morgan on a flight leaving Andrews at 1000 hours local tomorrow. I've arranged for a car to pick you up from here at nine. Mr Morgan has separate transport from his home. Is that OK for you?"

I think "full marks for US military efficiency". I look across to Cheryl and she nods her acceptance.

I say to the captain, "That's fine Captain Berger, we'll be ready. There's something else I need your office to do, tonight or first thing tomorrow. Please inform, classified of course, General Officer Commanding, the British Sector in Berlin of my arrival in Berlin, hopefully tomorrow, and ask for an appointment to see him as soon as practical. Ask his staff to check with the UK PM's cabinet office about the priority of our mission. Also, please inform him that I shall need to meet with the head of our BRIXMIS organisation there. Can do?"

"Yes, sir, I'll pass your requirement to General Harris. He will confirm back to you."

The captain then leaves to attend to her duties. She looks a smart and competent operator. I didn't explain the reason for my request which, frankly, was pretty cheeky of me to start giving orders to an officer way senior to me. But why shouldn't I milk it – I've never had the chance before. The reality is that the GOC British Sector in Berlin had been one of my instructors when I had attended the British Army Staff College way back in 1975. We had not always got on well. I found him to be somewhat old fashioned in his military thinking. He thought I was a rebel and he was probably right. The main point now is that I must have freedom of action when I'm there and I will need our senior brass to be briefed to give our team the maximum assistance from the start. I also plan to give Clive a call to get the wheels turning in London.

I must have been frowning while having these thoughts because Cheryl looks across at me and says, "Come on, Peter, lighten up. We've got our marching orders for tomorrow and there's nothing more for us to do until then. Look, I know a neat little club near here, they play great music, disco style. How about it?"

Bless Cheryl, a bit of light relief is exactly what we need after such a heavy day! I'm not a formal dancer but I confess I do love to muck about on the dance floor and I reckon Cheryl is just the tonic I need this evening.

We take a cab to the club and Cheryl leads the way down to a basement where there's a bar, soft lighting and music. It seems to be a Donna Summer tribute evening, fine for me, I love her music. When Cheryl and I arrive, the DJ is working through her "I feel love" album. Then we're into "A hot summer's night".

Cheryl and I don't hang about, we're both right into the rhythm from the start. My efforts at dancing are totally unstructured. Pretty pathetic really but I don't give a damn – this type of music just gets me going as I pick up the tempo. Cheryl takes my mood and we're away – moving, swaying, improvising, anything goes just to keep to the beat of Donna's music. The DJ changes to what must be Donna's newest releases this year, 1988. He tells me they're called "Thank God it's Friday" and "Bad Girls". Both are fun pieces. I'll try to buy them when I'm back in Brussels.

After an hour or so and uninhibited fun, we decide to call it a night and take a cab back to the hotel. During the ride, Cheryl links my arm. She doesn't let go when we walk through into the lobby and we continue to the elevator and ride up to her floor. We walk along to her room and she extracts her room pass key. She then lifts up her arms and encircles them behind my head. She gently pulls me down and kisses me on the lips.

She says softly, "Peter, would you like to come in?"

I hesitate. Cheryl is a fabulous woman and I love her company. But I'm a married man and have never strayed since I've been with Ann. And there's another thing. We are going to be working very closely together on this mission and I don't think we should blur our lines by having an affair - as tempting as it is. Then, when we get back to Brussels, we have interconnecting offices. Work and pleasure don't usually mix.

I'm into these thoughts when Cheryl intervenes. She's a perceptive woman. She gently pushes me away and turns towards her door.

She says, "You don't have to spell it out, Peter. I understand. Let's say goodnight here. Thank you for a great day."

She opens her door and closes it behind her.

I go back down to my own room on the floor below. I lie on my bed fully clothed. I reflect on the events of this long day. I've just been given the most challenging mission of my career and just now I've turned down Cheryl's seductive invitation. She's a very attractive woman. I'm now into my mid-forties and my sex life is limited to the occasional session with my frigid wife. I love Ann and I love my children but I'm still a normal healthy man. I feel frustrated.

I check my watch and see it's only eleven thirty. I'm not yet ready to sleep so I decide to go down to the hotel bar and have a nightcap. When I get there, I find the bar is quiet with just a couple of groups having their own conversations. I sit on a stool at the bar and order a whiskey on the rocks. I must have been deep in my thoughts because it's some while before I notice a young woman has taken the bar stool next to me. I turn to look at her. I would judge she's in her mid to late twenties. She's wearing a close-fitting silver dress with small beads embedded into it. Her dress is low cut, revealing the full curvature of her shapely breasts. I wonder why she has no coat on this winter's evening but reckon she probably left it in the lobby cloakroom. She has long blonde hair which frames her oval face. Although she is seated on the stool, I notice she has a perfect, slim, hour-glass figure. She is stunningly beautiful. But I realise she is a hooker, a gorgeous up-market hooker, but a hooker just the same. She lets me carry out my appraisal of her.

Then she says, "Care to buy me a drink?"

I suppose I should shut it down right now but I don't.

I reply, "I'm drinking whiskey. Will that suit you?"

She says "fine" and I tell the bartender to bring her a whiskey. We sit side by side. There's no small talk between us. I finish my drink.

Then I can't resist to say, "I'm in Room 604. Why don't you come and join me when you've finished your drink?"

I sign the chit for the drinks and go back up to my room. My mind starts to question what the fucking hell I'm doing but I block it out and push my thoughts away. Then there's a light tap on the door. I open it and there she is. She comes into the room and we stand facing each other, still not talking. I notice she has a zip at the back of her dress. I pull it down gently and it lowers right down to the cheeks of her bottom. She steps out of her dress and slips off her high heel shoes. And there she is – standing naked in front of me. I know I absolutely must have her. My mind refuses to consider any thoughts of guilt or responsibility. Not right now.

I don't know how I get undressed, except that it is very quickly. I don't know how the covers get onto the floor and we are lying on the bed sheet, and I don't know how she slips a condom on me. All I do know is that I must have this gorgeous sexy woman. It's like a primeval lust. And urgently, as by now I'm fully aroused. I need her in a basic, natural, uncomplicated, raw way. I know she's ready for me and I feel the joy of coupling with her. I feel assertive and strong as I push and thrust into her delicious body. I feel I'm in a different world. Nothing else exists.

At long last I can contain myself no longer and I feel the rush of emotion as I reach my full climax. After a time, I ease out of her and lie back with my head on the pillow, my mind and my breathing slowly returning to normal. She lies next to me and again we don't speak. There's no need for words. Then she gets up, goes to the bathroom and I hear her washing herself. She has put on the light in the bathroom and I see her beautiful body in silhouette as she comes back to me. She cleans me with a flannel then gently rubs me with a towel. Already I am feeling aroused again.

She whispers quietly, "Do you want me to go or stay?"

I answer in one word, "Stay!"

Now we take it more slowly. I caress her body. Her skin is flawless. I gently massage her back, her bottom, her breasts. She in turn kneads my chest and runs her hand down to my loins. I am now erect and stiff again and, gently this time, I enter her again. We move together in harmony, sometimes me on top, sometime her and sometimes I come into her from behind. Nothing seems wrong. Nothing is off limits. My mind is in a different place. I feel I could lift her up and carry her to a world where no-one else exits. After what seems a lifetime, a blissful lifetime, I climax again and lie back with a feeling of utter exhausted satisfaction.

When we have rested, we go together to the bathroom, wash each other under the shower and then towel each other down. When I come out of the bathroom, she is already pulling on her dress, slipping into her high heel shoes and freshening her make up. I go to retrieve my wallet and give her some of the dollars I had got from the ATM earlier this evening. To my surprise, she doesn't bother to count them but puts the money into her purse.

We go to the door. I lean over to her and lightly kiss her on her cheek. I open the door and she is gone.

I call down to reception for a wake-up call for 0700 hours and fall asleep immediately with a feeling of total fulfilment.

Chapter Twelve

I wake up feeling totally refreshed. I had asked for an 0700 hours alarm but it's still only 0630. I ring down to reception to tell them to cancel the wake-up call. I feel the need for exercise so I throw on my jogging kit and hit the gym.

After warming up, then pushing a few weights, I concentrate on the treadmill running machine. I start off slowly but soon build it up to a medium to fast jogging pace. I find I think best when I'm jogging. Needless to say, my thoughts about last evening come flooding back. First there was Cheryl's invitation which I had declined. It had been tempting as she's a lovely woman. I know I had played it straight and when I had got back to my own room after that incident I was feeling almost virtuous. Then I had ruined the whole fucking moral thing. Of course, I should on principle never have gone back down to the bar and found myself with that hooker. Or at least I should have walked away when I realised what was on offer. I feel like I've been a total shit, disloyal to my wife and absolutely not acting like someone who has just been entrusted with a major international mission. What the fucking hell did I think

I was doing? But then I start to wonder if I'm not now making it all worse by pretending to be shocked by my own behaviour. Am I not adding hypocrisy to my list of failings? Then I ask myself two questions. One: What harm did it do to anyone as no one else is likely to find out? Answer - none. Question two. Did I enjoy having sex with the hooker last night? Answer - absolutely yes! I don't know what to make of all this self-analysis. So what? What happened, happened!

I find myself sweating profusely and realise that I've been on the treadmill twice as long as I had intended and running at a speed I'm struggling to maintain. All because I had been carried away by this self-critique stuff. I turn the control to a reduced speed and begin the cooling down procedure. I decide to put the whole business of my night of passion with the hooker out of my mind at least for now.

I go back up to my room, shower, dress into my casual set of clothes and pack the rest of my stuff into my bag. I go down to the breakfast salon, hoping to meet up with Cheryl and I'm pleased to find her sitting there alone. She's changed back into her colonel's uniform and looks refreshed and ready to go. We greet each other and pick up our light easy conversation. I make no mention of last night's parting. Neither does she. I feel we can put that little incident behind us. We discuss today's travel and Cheryl tells me she's been informed we are taking the regular shuttle from Andrews Air Force Base, Washington to Ramstein Air Base, near Stuttgart, West

Germany then we'll transfer to another aircraft which will take us through the Air Corridor to land at Tempelhof airport in West Berlin.

We have some time after breakfast before our 0900 hours pick up so I go back to my room to make some phone calls. I reckon it's about 1430 hours in Brussels and 1330 hours in UK. I ring my house number but get no reply. We don't have an answerphone so I can't leave a message. In a way I'm relieved that Ann is not there as I'm still feeling rather mixed up about her and, fuck it, truth be told, I'm still feeling guilty about last night's hooker.

I then ring Clive Thompson's number in London. I'm in luck there as he picks up straight away.

He says, "Ah, Peter, glad you called. I had a good chat with General Harris last evening on our secure link and he filled me in on your meetings and confirmed mission. We put that before the PM and she's right behind you. I've also got your travel itinerary to Berlin. Looks like you'll be getting there about 0330 hours local time tomorrow morning. Just to set your mind at rest, the General Officer Commanding, British Sector will be putting you up at his residence during your time in Berlin. He didn't sound too keen at first but he quickly acquiesced when I told him your mission has the PM's personal blessing. Should be someone there to meet you on your arrival at Tempelhof."

I thank Clive and sign off. Wow! We're really getting the VIP treatment. Everything seems so far to be going to plan and I hope it stays that way. I'm wondering what we're going to find out when we start digging in earnest into the what the Russians and/or the East Germans are up to. I'm wondering what's going on in East Berlin. I hope our contacts will unravel the background to the CIA agent's murder but I'm feeling uneasy about Philip Daniel's warning about Honecker.

I link up again with Cheryl in the hotel lobby and we're met by the same Captain Berger, the smart young lady officer who had informed us about the flights last evening. She tells us she is our escort to Andrews. We arrive in good time and I'm surprised to find General Harris is there in person to meet us. He's with Ed Morgan, the CIA guy who's arrived by separate transport. The general escorts us through the departure procedures at Andrews and takes us into a private room within the departures hall.

He says to me, "Everything is arranged for your reception in Berlin and I'd like to get your initial thoughts about your action plan on your arrival there so that we can get things in place while you're airborne. I also need to brief you on some overnight developments."

"First, concerning East Berlin. I've just been discussing this with Ed. We told you that last week one of our CIA operatives had been murdered and his body was found near the Soviet GSFG headquarters. Our government has protested to the Soviets but they claim they know nothing about it. We don't know whether to accept the Soviet's story and we're doing our best to sort this out. Meanwhile the CIA sent another operative to re-contact our local sources there. Our people had secure radio comms with him until yesterday when he twice failed to respond to the contact protocol. We fear he has been arrested by the Stasi, the East German secret police. If so, he will surely be interrogated. If they break him, as they will eventually, what he could tell would irrevocably damage our source network there."

I don't know how to react to General Harris's report. These events concerning the loss of the CIA guys is clearly perturbing but I can't see how they connect to our main mission of checking out the reliability of Gorbachev's intended arms and troop reductions.

General Harris continues, "There's more. There have been further reports overnight from the source our chairman briefed you about yesterday. The most disturbing is a rumour that there is a conspiracy being planned within the Politburo of the Communist Party of the Soviet Union to oust Gorbachev. Details, like the previous reports, are vague and lack detail. However, the names of L.N. Zaikov and E.K. Ligachev have been mentioned as the possible instigators. Both hold important and influential positions as full members of the Politburo and are also members of the Secretariat. We are doing all we can to check the facts through other sources to confirm or reject the veracity of these reports."

The General is not finished, "These reports are causing a feeling of unease among our senior military and political personal here in Washington. Last evening there was a hot debate about whether or not we, the US, should now be raising our security alert status as a response to these reports. Conversely, we do realise that, to do so would send a clear signal to the Soviets and they in turn would feel they must react. That could start off a dangerous chain reaction. Look, Peter, it is now more urgent than ever that we sort this. Your mission is of the utmost importance to us all."

I listen intently to what the general is saying. I know that when we get to Berlin, we're going to have to hit the ground running. My mind is beginning to go into overdrive. I realise we need to have our intelligence guys set up an urgent meeting, while Cheryl and I are in flight, so that we can get immediately on with the job as soon as we arrive in Berlin. I'm well aware that General Harris outranks me but, from his demeanour, he seems to be waiting for instructions from me, a mere colonel!! I realise I need to be diplomatic here. Harris is a very bright man and I feel he will be influential in the success or failure of our mission.

I turn to him and say, "General, I believe we should arrive in Berlin at about 0330 hours local. I'd appreciate it if you could arrange the following: firstly, set up a meeting soonest of key source intelligence staffs to include G2 military personnel from both your USAREUR command in West Germany and from our

British staffs. We also need Ed Morgan to be there and British MI6 to be represented. I suggest the best location for the meeting would be at the offices of the British sector Berlin Brigade Headquarters but I leave that for your staff to decide. At whichever location is chosen, secure communications need to be set up to both US and British agencies such as NSA, coordinated by Jo Suter and GCHQ. The numbers involved should be as few as possible commensurate with coverage by all sources - human, electronic, air, etc. plus senior analysts."

"Got it, I'll get my guys onto it pronto. Anything else."

"Yes, there is. I need to see a consolidated report of all the tour operations within the past week by BRIMIS, MMLF and USMLM."

General Harris interrupts me. "Sorry, Colonel, I don't follow those abbreviations"

"Forgive me. I need to explain. These are the three accredited missions to the Soviet authorities - British, French and US which, under the 1946 Robertson - Malinin agreement, are permitted to tour widely throughout all of East Germany, except those areas designated by the Soviets as permanent or temporary restricted areas. Their tour reports are a primary source of establishing troop deployment details and any recent changes to equipment or units."

"OK, I now understand. But you mentioned the French there. Remember our chairman said the mission should be restricted to US and British personnel only."

"I know he did, General, but I have worked with the French military intel people. They're professional, discreet and can add value to our work in Berlin this week. We need the best assets available and I need the French teams to be involved. I will take full responsibility. I'd like that meeting to be held immediately following on from the first. Oh, and for the head of BRIXMIS to also attend the G Intel meeting."

"So be it. We'll get onto it."

I hope that I hadn't come across as too arrogant but we have to be organising this stuff now otherwise we'll lose the best part of a day sitting on a plane. The general doesn't seem phased by my string of demands, a mark of his intelligence and character. He then says:

"Look, your plane departure time has already been delayed by our conversation. Too bad, this is of vital importance. I'm clear about your immediate requirements and will smooth out the necessary diplomatic angles. One final thing before you leave, Colonel. You've met Captain Berger already. I'd like her to join your team and fly over to Berlin with you. She's a very bright and talented officer and, as her mother tongue is German, I think she could be a useful asset to you. I also want her to act as my liaison officer to link between us and keep me informed of your progress."

I am more than pleased to agree. Clearly Captain Berger had previously been told about her new attachment as she had come ready with her travel bag. I can see the flight staff hovering nervously as we are already behind schedule. General Harris shakes our hands and Cheryl, Ed Morgan, Captain Terri Berger and I leave to board our flight en route for West Berlin.

We are the last group to board and after the routine safety briefing we get airborne. This is the first time I've been on a plane of this type which I'm told is a Boeing C-17A Globemaster and is used regularly to transport US personnel and equipment between the States and West Germany. It is owned by the US Air Force. We have been allocated seats in the front row which I gather are normally reserved for senior officers and officials.

I've hardly had the chance to talk to Cheryl since we left the hotel together this morning. I take a seat between her and Captain Berger and I tell Cheryl that I see her role as providing the vital link between our operation in Berlin and the rest of the intelligence community in the US, the UK and, depending on our progress, perhaps also linking through to Admiral Figo and the rest of our team in NATO headquarters in Brussels. In practice, this means that Cheryl is now working for me, at least during this mission and, as we are of equal rank, I'm concerned how she's going to react. I need not have worried. All she does is give me a mock salute and she says:

"Always wondered what it's like to be under a Brit. Guess I'm now going to find out – even if it's only in an office!"

Good old Cheryl. She can find a smutty answer to everything.

I spend some time talking to Ed Morgan, who has got an empty seat next to him in the row behind. He is naturally most concerned about his missing colleague in East Berlin. We agree his first task will be to oversee the investigation into the disappearance and, if he so judges, to get himself infiltrated into East Germany and make contact with the local network. We agree he will need secure communications to report back to our headquarters in the West. From our conversation, I can tell he's a very perceptive and intelligent guy and I'm encouraged that he will be a great asset to our team. He says he is worried that he is not a fluent German speaker and this limitation could restrict what he could achieve in East Berlin. I think our mother tongue German speaker, Captain Berger, could well be useful to Ed. But that's for the future.

We have a long flight ahead of us. I feel there's nothing more I can do now until we eventually get to Berlin. It's important to conserve our energies till then. I settle down in my comfortable airplane seat and set it back to maximum. I am sitting, or rather reclining, between these two American military officers. On my left is US Air force Colonel Cheryl Walker - she's sensibly decided to relax and I can tell she's already asleep. She's undone the buttons of her uniform jacket and I notice her large breasts rise and fall with her breathing. Her head is turned away from me, to her left, revealing the soft outline of the side of her face which is in repose in her sleep. She looks as attractive sleeping as she does when she's awake. I wonder how I could possibly have resisted her invitation last night.

Our new recruit, US Army Captain Terri Berger is on my right. Her age? I would guess late twenties. Like Cheryl, she is also wearing her uniform. And also like Cheryl, she is sleeping. Until now I had only seen her wearing her formal military cap with her hair neatly tucked under it. She had been always very straight and correct in her manner when she had addressed Cheryl and me - her senior officers. Now, she is still all buttoned up but has removed her army cap and her shoes. In sleep, her hair has come slightly untied and a lock has found its way down the side of her face. She has curled her knees up and turned onto her right side. From my seat angle, I can see the outline of her shoulders, her back and her hips. I can't help myself thinking that under her formal uniform is a very attractive young woman. Shorter and slimmer than Cheryl but also very feminine in her own style.

I like my seat here between these two American lady officers and feel a vague stirring of desire. Then I scold myself for even countenancing such thoughts. For fuck's sake, Peter Chambers, I tell myself. You are sitting next to two intelligent and professional military officers. Keep your mind on the job. Easy to say, but nature is nature. My thoughts are roaming between being a simple male of the species and acting my part as a military officer, charged with a major mission. Then I realise that the time in Brussels must be close to my children's bedtime. Metaphorically I kiss Chloe and

Christian. I wonder what they're thinking. I also wonder about Ann, my beautiful but disturbed wife. With this jumble of thoughts, I slowly drift off into sleep mode.

Chapter Thirteen

Our flight en route to West Berlin is routine. It is already dark when our large transport aircraft lands in Ramstein. I only know it's Ramstein because we are told it is. To me it's just another large expanse of tarmac in the middle of somewhere. Our party is the first to leave and we notice all the rest of the military passengers gathering up their belongings ready to leave the aircraft and be guided to their ongoing transport to their new units in West Germany.

Our little group is given a VIP reception and we are taken to a well-furnished room in the terminal building to wait for our ongoing flight through to West Berlin. Bless the Stars and Stripes – they even provide a courtesy drinks bar. I am about to play the host role and dish out the drinks but I am pre-empted by a military steward who solicitously comes to each of us with notepad in hand. Ed and Captain Berger order Coke but bless Cheryl as always, she goes for a large gin and tonic, so I do the same, thinking maybe we can get in a second round before our onward flight. I'm learning that US Air Force transports are very efficient and feed us well but are always dry of any alcohol in flight - boring!

General Harris said we would be an hour in transit at Ramstein but the system seems to have geared up a notch because almost as I am downing the end of my G & T, we are called for the onward flight. We troop back onto a smaller aircraft, type to me unknown. Again, the other passengers have already been embarked when we climb on board. This time, I just about remain conscious for the safety announcements before the gin effect helps me off to sleep. I don't even have time to have naughty thoughts about Cheryl.

I crash out and am oblivious of any announcements but I understand we had to stick to a rigid flight programme through the air corridor from West Germany into Tempelhof airport in the US Zone of West Berlin. The change of the aircraft's engine noise must have woken me up. As we land and slow to a stop, I see the sign "Tempelhof". I bring my mind and thoughts into focus. We are now in Berlin - our mission starts here.

We are reminded of the local time here in Berlin - 0345 hours. Our group - Ed Morgan, Cheryl, Captain Berger and me, are again first to leave the aircraft. The immediate thing to hit me, almost literally, is the temperature - it's very cold! I see deep snow has been cleared from the main runways but is still piled up around the airport. I remind myself it's mid- December, we had it lucky in Brussels until now but here in Berlin the temperature has plummeted. We get to the bottom of the aircraft steps and are met by one US and one

British military officer, both with captain's rank insignia. The American salutes smartly and introduces himself as Captain Garathy, US Air Force.

He says, "Welcome to the US Sector here in Berlin. My unit is USAF 7350th, Air Base Group. I am instructed to ensure your safe arrival and to inform you that arrangements have been made for you to be accommodated for your mission at the residence of the General Officer Commanding, British Sector. The general has also cleared the operations room for your meetings this morning at the Olympic Stadium barracks complex in the British Sector. I also want to introduce you to Captain Thomas, British Army who will escort you."

The British captain then salutes and takes over. He explains that he is the aide de camp to the British general and is here to escort us to our accommodation. We make our way in some haste to get out of the cold and wait in a transit area for our bags to be offloaded. I'm glad that at least I had brought a winter anorak with me but the rest of my clothes are pretty flimsy and will need to be upgraded.

Once our bags arrive, Captain Thomas leads us through to two staff cars that are lined up outside Tempelhof airport. Cheryl and I get in the first car while Ed and Terri Berger take the car behind. At this time of night there is little traffic but the evidence of recent snow clearance lines the quiet streets. It's a short drive from the US to the British Sector. Captain Thomas gives us a running commentary en route. In fact, I have been here before during my tour with First British Corps in Bielefeld and probably know rather more about this beleaguered but fascinating city than he does, but I don't want to steal his thunder. For Cheryl, it's her first time here so that's fair enough.

We arrive at the general's residence and, with their usual slick efficiency, the military house staff escort us to our rooms. I'm relieved mine has good working radiators. Before leaving, Captain Thomas informs us that the meeting I had asked for has been set up for 0800 hours. Before that, the general would like to meet us all and suggests we convene for breakfast in the downstairs dining room at 0700 hours. I realise that is in only a couple of hours' time but, what the heck, we've just had our full ration of sleep en route from Washington.

I lie on the comfortable bed the general's staff have provided and think about how we are going to proceed in carrying out our mission. Thanks to General Harris in the States and, I suspect, this British general here in Berlin, together with Clive Thompson in London, we will be able to get moving quickly this morning. I had requested all the main US and UK intel agencies and staff to be represented at the 0800 hours meeting. From my past experience of working with these guys, I think we will have a thorough coverage of the warnings and indicators we will need to be examining to analyse whether or not the Soviets are increasing their military readiness. I also know that Ed Morgan will get stuck into solving the mystery of his compatriot's murder in East Berlin.

One weakness in our information requirements could be our lack of inside information within the Soviet Politburo itself. Here I would like to consult both Dieter, back in our Brussels NATO HQ and my academic colleague Philip Daniels. But that's going to be difficult. The US Chairman expressly vetoed me from consulting German nationals for security reasons. This could be justified but I just don't know. What I do know though is that Dieter, through his political contacts, would be very well placed to find out if there is any serious present opposition to Gorbachev in the Kremlin. Likewise, with Philip but in his case, being an academic and not a government employee, he has no UK security clearance. But I'm still determined to consult them and so I draft a note to each which can be sent to them this morning. I choose my words with care so as not to alert either of the true nature of my questions.

I've also asked for the head of BRIXMIS or his rep to be at the meeting. BRIXMIS is an abbreviation of the formal title: The British Commanders'-in-Chief Mission to the Soviet Forces in Germany. I know from reading their "tour reports" that they provide excellent ground sighting information. I tell myself I need to know more about their mission and its role.

I reckon that about covers how I see the rest of today developing so that we can get into the detail of answering the US Chairman's questions.

There's nothing more I can do right now and my mind turns to thinking about my children back in Brussels. I just hope I can get back by Saturday to support Christian's game of rugby. It's already Wednesday and there's still much to do here. I remind myself I must try to phone home today at least to let my family know I'm still around. My darling daughter Chloe is more of a worry to Ann and me than Christian. She's becoming very introvert and it's almost as if she's hiding something from us. The other worry we have with Chloe is that she is terrified of water. A few years ago, we took a holiday in the South of France. It was a big mistake. Chloe became agitated and distressed by the sight of the sea and absolutely refused to swim. Of course, her attitude brought the memories of the Cyprus tragedy flooding back. Although Chloe had been only four years old when her brother Nicholas died, the event must have left a deep mental scar. I hope we can find a way to help her about her fears. Chloe's problems and my relationship with Ann must be priorities when I get back to Brussels.

I realise it's 0630 hours and I need to get ready for our breakfast with the general. For the second time this trip I wish I'd brought a uniform with me. My casuals have already seen a few days wear so I decide to put on my suit as the only option.

My experiences of British officers with the rank of "General" have been decidedly mixed during my career so far. Some are real "soldiers' soldiers" who have been involved in operational situations around the world and have led their soldiers fearlessly and by example. Regrettably, there are others who have risen up through the officer ranks without apparently getting their hands dirty - except perhaps from their horses in the stables! Most of these are guards or cavalry officers who have followed their fathers into their regiments and who's monthly Mess bar bills are higher than most soldiers earn in a year. I hope that our breakfast hosting general is in the former category. But as I understand he's from an old cavalry regiment, I fear the worst.

Ed, Cheryl, Terri and I all arrive at the dining room at the about the same time but the general and his wife are ahead of us waiting at the door to greet us. The general is a tall man in his fifties, dressed in military olive green trousers, a "wooly pully" sweater, with the Major General's rank insignia on his shoulder tabs. I recognise his regimental colours on the stable belt he's wearing around his still slim waist. I introduce our team and the general ushers us to the table. He sits Cheryl next to him while I have the pleasure of sitting next to his wife, who tells me her name is Susanne. She's a tall good-looking woman, who despite the early hour, is well groomed and fresh looking. Our conversation is light and easy.

The general reveals himself to be utterly charming. He is most solicitous to our two lady officers, asking about their careers in the US forces and commiserating with them about their long tiring journey from the States. He recognises Terri's slight German accent and speaks to her for a while in the German language. As far as I'm able to tell, he is far more fluent in that language than I am. We don't discuss any detail of our mission here but the general is insistent that he and his staff are determined to give us every assistance possible.

In summary, we are treated to an excellent English style breakfast and hosted wonderfully by the general and his charming wife. Their gracious manner teaches me a sharp lesson: that I must not stereotype people before I've met them!

After our breakfast, the general accompanies us to the administrative area of the Olympic Stadium. He asks to have a short personal chat before we start our main meeting in the conference room there.

Inside his office, he says, "I've been in close touch with London since I heard about your work and we're also linked in to our military headquarters in Rheindahlen, West Germany. Rest assured we'll give you and your team every support. What is troubling me though is that London has told us there may been an increasing threat from the Russians to our situation here in West Berlin. In your view, Colonel, should we be increasing our threat level or cancelling leave for those who were planning to be out of Berlin during the Christmas period?"

I reply, "General, I can only give you my opinion as of course any decision to change the alert status would be made by those way above my pay grade. I hope to have a clearer understanding after our meeting here this morning. My view is that any increase in alert measures would be immediately picked up by the Soviets and they would be likely to follow suit. That could result in a totally unnecessary escalation. We'll do our best to resolve this issue as soon as possible and I will personally keep you informed."

After our meeting with the general, Ed Morgan says he has to go to meet with his CIA people in the US sector. He tells me he expects to be going himself into the Eastern sector of Berlin later today to tie up with their agents over there and dig into the murder of their one operator and the disappearance of the second. We know that communication between us will be difficult.

Our meeting room in the Olympic Stadium barracks complex is full when we arrive at 0800 hours. We first all introduce ourselves and state our areas of expertise or specialisation. There is a mix of mainly US and British uniforms but I also recognise Lieutenant Colonel André Bouchard, the head of the French equivalent to our BRIXMIS. I am also heartened to notice a few familiar faces who I've worked with before. There is a smattering of civilians so I don't feel too out of place in my suit.

I thank everyone for their attendance, stress the strict "need to know" security caveat, give an outline of the conflicting reactions to Gorbachev's speech and tell them of the high political necessity to determine whether or not the West should accept the speech as sincere and genuine. I say that, in order to make such a determination, we need to examine, in as much intricate detail as we can, any intelligence which might indicate reinforcement into or towards the forward area by GSFG or their allies.

The intelligence staff have already rigged up a large map which covers much of one wall of the room. It comprises joined up 1:50,000 scale maps covering the whole of East Germany. Onto this are superimposed symbols of the intelligence assessment of the locations of all known units of the Group of Soviet Forces Germany (GSFG) and of the East Germany Army (NVA) down to at least battalion level and, in some cases, individual unit level. Where applicable, designated wartime deployment areas are shown, which in many cases, are several kilometres from their peacetime locations. It has today's date marked on it.

Next to this map, is a duplicate, dated one month earlier. There are only minor variations between the two maps indicating that no major changes have occurred during that period.

We use these maps as templates for our discussions. We also discuss recent activity in such training areas as: Letzlinger Heide, Altengrabow, Juterbog, Wittstock and Lieberose. There has been considerable activity in these areas but nothing that our analysts describe as out of routine. The only new equipments, sighted from a BRIXMIS report of two weeks ago, was a unit of SS-23 short-range ballistic missiles. While of considerable intelligence interest, this is not considered to pose a major significant change in the overall military posture of GSFG.

Our findings at this meeting merely confirm what our intelligence community had already assessed. But we have to be absolutely sure about this in light of the conflicting reports in the US. We agree on what indicators need to be checked if a change of posture were to occur. Our list includes: major moves from barracks to wartime deployment areas, new sightings of equipment that could be used for offensive operations such as: short/medium range ballistic missiles, air assault troops, engineer amphibious bridging, move westwards of heavy artillery and associated radars, chemical warfare units, changes in the pattern of communications particularly at Front or Theatre level. We also need to ensure we verify that no new equipment is being brought by sea into Rostock or by air into any of the airfields in East Germany. I'll also get Cheryl to send a tasking to Jo Suter, back at the NSA, to monitor the latest

Soviet satellites, Kosmos 1220 and 1574 to check their orbits for any recent variations.

These discussions take us about two hours. I close the meeting by summarizing the above and arranging to meet up again this evening. Meantime, I ask all present to use their assets to recheck once again the accuracy of all our assessments.

I leave the meeting feeling we have covered all the angles and I feel confident that our original assessments were correct. I'm hoping Ed will be able to sort out the US agent problems in Berlin and get his fellow CIA operator freed from the Stasi. I'm feeling buoyant. Who knows, perhaps we can get this whole business wrapped up quickly, write up our reports and get back to Brussels.

I was pleased the Head of BRIXMIS had attended the meeting in person and I'm walking with him to his Ops room in the London Block, when the general's aide rushes up to me looking flustered.

He says, "Colonel, I'm glad I've found you. We've just received this morning's UK papers. The general says that you should see them straightaway."

He hands me several papers. I scan the headlines of one of our most sensationalist tabloids. It reads, "RETURN TO THE COLD WAR? US MILITARY BRASS DEBUNK GORBACHEV AS A FRAUD!" It goes on to quote unnamed sources as saying that senior officers in the Pentagon have evidence that the UN speech was just a bluff to encourage the West to begin a disarmament programme." The article continues in a strident tone, encouraging NATO to upgrade its vigilance levels. Other papers take a similar though less virulent line.

Fucking hell, I think. That's exactly what we DON'T need. The Soviets will surely pick up on these reports and we'll be right into the "tit for tat" situation we've been trying so hard to achieve.

I am just trying to digest this new turn of events when I'm called to the phone in the BRIXMIS office. It's Ed Morgan.

He says, "Peter? Look, we're in trouble. I can't talk on this open phone line but I'm sending you a message via the secure link to the BRIXMIS office. Can you stand by there?"

"Got it, Ed. I'll be there."

I don't have long to wait. The secure fax springs into life and I read the message from Ed.

It reads, "Our last CIA operator in East Berlin has just managed to make his way back to us. He's been shot and is in a serious condition. He reported that at least three of our remaining agents have been arrested today. The East German Secret Police must have broken our communication codes. It's vital I go in myself to see what I can salvage. We're now speculating that it could be the East Germans who are behind all these recent false reports. I need to try to get the proof. Can you assist? I'm coming over to your London Block asap."

I fax him back, "I'll be waiting for you."

So much for my idea of wrapping this up quickly today!

Chapter Fourteen

We are waiting for Ed in the BRIXMIS operations room in the Olympic Stadium complex. I use the time to ask the chief, a British brigadier, to explain the background of his organisation. I have the feeling we are going to need the assistance of his team and I need to know what his capabilities to help us might be.

I'm learning that the brigadier is a great enthusiast of his organisation, and with much justification. It doesn't take much to get him going.

"Pleased to oblige," he begins. "We are very proud of our unique mission. First some history. BRIXMIS was created in 1946 under the terms of what is known as "the Robertson–Malinin agreement" to exchange military missions: for the British, American and French to be based in the Berlin area and for a reciprocal Soviet mission to be based in Bunde, West Germany. The role of these missions was described as being: "to maintain liaison between the staff of the two Commanders-in-Chief and their military governments in the zones". For reasons that seem to have got lost in time, our British mission is as large as both the US and French combined. We Brits have thirty-one accredited personnel, the

French have eighteen and the Americans only fourteen. However, we work closely with our American and French colleagues and we coordinate our tours with each other. I mention our unique situation. One major example is that it's the Soviets who provide and maintain our splendid Mission House in Potsdam in East Germany. We permanently occupy the house and regularly entertain there. But we are well aware that all its rooms are almost certainly bugged so we don't talk about our work while we're there. That's why we run our operational planning, administration and logistics in the Olympic Stadium complex here in West Berlin."

The brigadier is really getting into his stride. He continues, "The liaison role allows BRIXMIS and the other missions to tour widely throughout East Germany limited only by certain areas designated by the Soviets. These are known as Permanently Restricted Areas (PRAs) and on occasions by Temporary Restricted Areas (TRAs). This relative freedom of movement throughout East Germany enables the missions to collect intelligence about Warsaw Pact forces, in particular those of the Soviets and East Germans. As you can imagine, in the forty-two years that we've been operating here, we've built up a substantial knowledge of force composition, deployments, movements and indications of increases in force levels and of new weapon systems being brought into East Germany."

I interrupt him to remark that there seem to be a lot of abbreviations involved.

He agrees and continues, "You're right, Peter, and I'm afraid I need to use a few more here, so that we're clear on our definitions. Our point of contact with the Soviets is through the Soviet External Relations Bureau or SERB for short. In its turn SERB is answerable to the commander in chief of the Group of Soviet Forces Germany or GSFG. Incidentally, while on abbreviations, we all refer to East Germany as the DDR which, as you well know, Peter, stands for Deutsche Demokratische Republik. Then there's the DDR Ministry of State Security, known as Stasi, the dreaded Stasi I might add!! And then the local police are called VOPO, meaning Volkspolizei."

I ask the brigadier what tour vehicles are used. He explains, "Under our agreement with the Soviets, our vehicles must be clearly marked and identifiable. We answer only to the Soviets in East Germany and specifically we do not recognise the DDR government. So, on the occasions we are challenged by the VOPO or Stasi, we refuse to deal with them but insist they call the closest SERB representative to handle the incident. As you will appreciate, we need vehicles which give us a mix of good road and cross country mobility, durability and reasonable comfort to support our three-man crews during their time away from our base in Potsdam. These tours can last for up to six or seven days. In the early years, we experimented with various vehicle types. For example, we initially thought the Range Rover would suit us well. In some ways it did, but our tour people found it a clumsy vehicle to take on an extended tour, not as manoeuvrable as its prestige would suggest and decidedly cold and draughty in winter. For some years now we use two vehicle types: the Mercedes Geländewagen which has of course four-wheel drive but also a front mounted winch for extraction if it gets bogged down when driving off road, and a spare 90 litre fuel tank giving the vehicle a range of some 500 kilometres per day. Our aim is for the crews to be completely self-sufficient while they're on tour. The Geländewagen has proved to be a sturdy, tough and reliable vehicle. It does of course have speed limitations so, depending on the tour parameters, we also use the Opel Senator. Again, we've made many modifications to the standard Senator model to suit our tour purposes. Oh, and I need to mention that, for good historic reasons, crews are not armed and they do not have radios or other means of communicating back to the Potsdam Mission House."

The brigadier concludes, "I hope that gives you a good feel of our activities, Peter. Routinely we have four or five vehicles out on tour at any one time. One has just returned. In fact, I've asked Major Tim Arnold, the tour leader, to stand by to brief us together about his tour findings. He's been touring the northern part of the DDR."

Major Arnold is still wearing his somewhat dishevelled olive green army uniform with his major's crown insignia under a large Canadian style Parka. He is unshaven and will clearly be heading for the showers after his debrief. Like his boss, he is an articulate and enthusiastic speaker.

He explains to us, "During our tour, we managed to sneak in between the Wittstock PRA and those at Retzow and Parchim. Of course, we had fitted chains due to the snow. This area is occupied by elements of Second Guards tank army of the GSFG. Our sightings of Soviet equipment and personnel for the first few days were routine and all are itemised in detail in my tour report but I would highlight that yesterday and last night we noted elements of two of the divisional headquarters, the ninth and thirty-second, deploying from their normal peacetime barracks into what we have identified as their wartime locations. Our team also noted the presence of self-propelled air defence systems, ZSU–X or 2S6. We've got some good photography of these weapons which we're getting to our analyst guys right now."

I ask him and the brigadier, "Wartime locations - in mid-winter? What do you make of that?"

The Brigadier replies, "Well, no conclusions yet of course, we'll have to look at it in the overall context of other deployments and reactions throughout GSFG. But it certainly is interesting and we'll check with the rest of our teams and other sources to see if this type of activity is reflected elsewhere in GSFG. It could be just a test alert exercise within Second Guards Tank Army. And the ZSU systems - well, that's normally part of their defensive posture rather than anything offensive that might concern us."

We are interrupted by a call for the brigadier from the duty officer at his mission house in Potsdam. He reports that the leader of another tour is en route via the Glienicker Bridge to the Olympic Stadium. Indeed, it's not long before the team leader, an army captain, walks into the Ops room and reports to the brigadier.

"I'm afraid our Senator is in a bit of a mess, brigadier. We had only just left this morning intending to head west to skirt round the Rathenow PRA then on to the southern edge of the Letzlinger Heide. We were barely clear of the Potsdam outskirts, when we were pursued by two Lada cars. We thought they were Russian at first but they had DDR plates and we identified the grey uniforms of Stasi guys rather than VOPO. Their cars were fast and must have had up-tuned engines. They flashed their headlights at us indicating that we should stop but we decided to try to out run them in the Senator. This led to a pretty hairy chase on the compacted snow-covered roads around the Ragosen area. We were aiming to shake them off while avoiding accidents to other civilian traffic. We thought we had got away clean but as we turned a corner we found the single-track road we were on was blocked by another Stasi vehicle. They must have been in radio contact. Sergeant Josh Clifford, our driver, slammed on the breaks but there was not enough road left to stop on the icy surface. So, we smashed right into him. I'm pleased to report there were no serious injuries to either our crew members or the Stasi. After we were forced to stop, the two other Stasi cars that had been giving chase turned up and we found we were completely hemmed in."

"We followed procedure and refused to deal with the Stasi, insisting they call the nearest Soviet SERB officer. Meanwhile we locked ourselves inside the car and apart from bursting for a pee, we were all OK. It took a couple of hours until our old SERB friend Colonel Anatoly Orlov arrived from Zossen. We explained to him that we had been ambushed by the Stasi and improperly detained. Orlov took his time to write up a report but eventually he ordered the Stasi to clear our way and we limped our car back first to the Mission House where we carried out minor repairs and then back to our workshop here. I'm afraid our mechanics will have quite a repair job on their hands. That about covers it, Brigadier. I'll of course submit a full report."

I can tell the brigadier is puzzled by this incident and I ask him if this type of harassment was a regular occurrence. He replies, "Not like this. Our crews are often chased but mostly by the Soviets themselves to try to impede our surveillance activities. But it's very rare indeed to have such a determined ambush by the Stasi. It does seem to fit in with a pattern of Stasi behaviour we've been noticing in the last day or so, particularly in the East Berlin area. Their activities have been more overtly aggressive. We've also noticed that their relations with the Soviets seems to have deteriorated. There's a general feeling of unease there which could have something to do with their reaction to the Gorbachev speech last week."

We are still discussing the implications of this incident when Ed Morgan arrives. I introduce him to the brigadier. I can tell Ed is quite distressed.

He explains, "Further to the fax I sent you earlier, Peter, our organisation in East Berlin has been seriously disrupted. Our main guy has been shot. He's made it back to our zone via Check Point Charlie, heaven knows how, but he'll be out of action for some time. I need to get over there asap. We've managed to get a message through to one of our main local agent groups who have urged me to meet them at a rendezvous point in East Berlin this evening."

I share Ed's concern about the decimation of his network as I had hoped this could be used to resolve whether it is the Stasi who are involved with the recent negative reports about Gorbachev's policy of détente towards the West. Now that the press is stirring it up, relations between East and West will only deteriorate further and we need to act fast. From my side, all our intelligence sources are tasked to detect any deployment change. The recent BRIXMIS tour report is disturbing. But there's nothing further I can do here.

I need to do all I can to support Ed and I feel that could include going with him to East Berlin if that will help - but I really don't know how it might. We agree I will come over to the US zone where hopefully the wounded operator will be fit enough to be debriefed by Ed. We'll then make a plan of action. We agree a meeting point in the US zone for 1800 hours this evening.

I now have two priorities. First, to try to get warm. I must get out of my flimsy suit and find some more practical clothes especially now that I could be in freezing East Berlin this evening with no idea what may develop there or for how long. Fortunately, help is right at hand here in the BRIXMIS offices. I'm directed to the quartermaster's department and find an obliging storeman who issues me with a set of cold weather kit from Parka to woollen sweater, shirt, trousers and boots - even a pair of woollen underwear! I'm now set up.

Second priority is to try to contact Ann. It's now been four days since I left Brussels. I use the phone in the HQ registry and my home number rings. Again, no answer. So, I try my Brussels office and am delighted to hear SuziB's warm and welcoming voice.

"Hi, Colonel" she purrs, "We're all missing you here. Are you having fun?"

"Well, Suzi, I suppose you could call it that! Look, could you do a couple of things for me. I can't get through to my wife Ann. Could you call her up later and let her know I'm fine and I'll call her when I can but I'm tied up with work so I don't know when I can call next time or when I'll be back."

"Will do of course, Peter. Where are you now?"

I suppose I should be careful what I say on this open line phone but I'm worried that Ann will think I'm just being evasive. I say to SuziB:

"Well I'm in Berlin - the west side at present but who knows? I'll try to contact you or Ann, direct if I can reach her, as soon as I know when I'm likely to be back. Look after yourself SuziB and send my best to Admiral Figo."

"I will and you be careful over there!"

It was good to talk to SuziB. I probably shouldn't have hinted to her that I might be going to East Berlin but I know she'll be discreet and will say the right things to Ann.

I feel we're beginning to make some progress. Our intelligence teams are on full alert and will report anything relevant. Cheryl will be the point of contact while I go with Ed to see what we can uncover there.

While I'm in the HQ building, I'm told there's an open line fax message for me. It's from Philip Daniels replying to the query I sent him this morning.

It reads, "There's a report in both the Soviet Army Daily Krasnaya Zvezda (Red Star) and Pravda today that NATO forces are to be reinforced in West Germany including a new US missile system. It rants on about the West's duplicity. No sources are quoted. Thought you should know this following our discussions last week. Good luck. Philip."

So now the Press are getting hyped up from both the West and the East. And again, no sources are quoted. It seems as if some agency, somewhere, is intentionally trying to stir up trouble. I hope that we'll find the answer in East Berlin.

Chapter Fifteen

I'm trying to get used to the idea that I might accompany Ed to East Berlin but I have serious reservations about what help I could provide. As a soldier, I have no direct training in this type of political undercover stuff. That's the job of our civilian intelligence services. I think back to the meeting in London when the MI6 guy, John Evers I think his name is, was talking about a direct exchange between Washington and Moscow to try to prevent any escalation of tension. That's surely the best approach? But since then, I've heard nothing more about these supposed talks and they were not mentioned at all when Cheryl and I were in Washington. So, as far as I've been told, the East–West direct exchange hasn't happened. So I guess it's up to us here to get on with it.

There's still some time before my RV with Ed in the US zone. I'm well aware that last week I had cut through the established chain of command about the Gorbachev speech by my direct intervention which landed me in front of our prime minister. I don't want to be accused of that again if I rush off to East Berlin without informing my superiors.

I manage to get the use of an office in the secured area of the main UK Berlin Brigade HQ and I wham off a report to the chairman of the JIC in London. I report that, as at today, Wednesday 14 December 1988, our analysis is that there has been no indication either of GSFG troop reinforcements in the DDR or of preparation for offensive action. The only noted change of deployment has been by elements of two divisional headquarters taking up defensive positions in their war locations. I report that all US/UK intelligence sources and agencies have been tasked to report any further changes. I also refer to the heightened level of suspicion and rumour which has been exacerbated by both the Western and Soviet press. I tell the chairman of the serious disruption to CIA covert operations in East Berlin and that the CIA rep in our team suspects that the reports from unquoted sources of escalation of troop readiness may have emanated from the Stasi. He has no proof of this and is planning to be inserted into the Eastern sector later today to re-establish his network there. I say that I may accompany him and ask him to inform the MI6 organisation.

When I'm content with my report, I take it on myself to classify it TOP SECRET and get it sent to the JIC chairman in London by secure fax with copies to the chairman of the US meeting in the Pentagon and the general here in Berlin. When that's done, I feel quite chuffed with myself that, at least this time, I've acted through the correct channels.

I wonder what the hell I should be taking with me on the East Berlin expedition – that's if I do go. Ed's gone back to his US sector for now and I don't know who else to ask for advice. In the end, I settle for acquiring a good supply of both Deutschmarks and DDR marks and just hope for the best. Pathetic but, fuck it, there you go. At least, thanks to the quartermaster, I've got good warm clothing.

I've still got some time in hand so I hitch a lift back to the general's residence. I pack my casual clothes and suit into my wheely bag and leave a little "thank you" note to Suzanne, the general's wife. Very proper!

It's already been dark for some time when I meet up again with Ed as agreed in the US zone headquarters at 1800 hours. Ed takes me through to the medical facility and into a private room where he introduces me to his colleague, the CIA operative who has just made his enforced return from East Berlin. He is propped up in bed, is heavily bandaged up and has a saline drip next to his bed. Ed introduces him as Bill Harman. Bill seems to be in pain but is conscious and is keen to talk.

He says, "Good to know you, Peter." He looks around at all the medical equipment surrounding him then he continues, "Don't be put off by all this hospital stuff. I got shot but I'm already on the mend. They're doing a great job fixing me up. I wish I could get back over there but I guess I'll have to give it some time to heal. Ed has given me the background and I've got the OK from the States to talk to you about our ops in the DDR. And I need to do so because the situation over there is critical. We are into a phase we call "soft ops" that is to say we are supporting groups who are strongly opposed to the Honeker regime, his Socialist Unity Party, or SED for short, and its enforcers, the Stasi. We are providing them with funds and items they cannot acquire locally such as communication equipment. We've also been providing copies of Gorbachev's latest book "Perestroika" with a German translation. We find it good psyops to be passing them Russian rather than US material. They have cells throughout the DDR, in East Berlin of course but also in Leipzig, Rostock, Halle, Magdeburg and other towns. They are well organised and include some top brains including senior university people, doctors and former civil servants. They have to operate in the tightest security as the Stasi and their informers are everywhere."

Ed and I have taken up positions either side of the bed. Bill is showing a lot of guts but we can see he's weak and that a nurse is hovering outside the door.

Bill continues, "Last week, everything hotted up following Gorbachev's speech at the UN. The SED party got prior notice of what he was due to say and did their best to block it out from the DDR. In Berlin, there was a major effort to get programmes covering the speech on West German TV put off the air. Of course, they were only partly successful. From our part, we circulated

German translations of the speech as widely as possible. Since the speech, the SED party and the Stasi seem to have gone into overdrive. They are far more ruthless than ever. You must realise, Peter, that for the first time in the forty odd years that they have been in power in the DDR, they are feeling really threatened. Until now, they have always had the Soviets behind them to ensure they remain in power. Now they can see that support beginning to ebb away. In his speech, Gorbachev not merely announced the military force reductions but he also stressed that each Eastern European country is free to choose its own path. In other words, there will be no more Soviet crack downs against insurrections such as have occurred in the past in Hungary, Czechoslovakia and Poland."

This was fascinating background but we can tell that Bill is weakening so Ed prompts him by asking, "Bill, you said there's a meeting this evening we need to attend. What are the details?"

"Yeah, you're right. The meeting is to be at a small Kneipe. It is near the centre in the district of Prenzlauer Berg. The address is: Meisenweg 13. Here, I kept a street map out when I knew you were coming this evening."

Bill struggles to turn on his side and pulls out a map from his bedside cabinet. The map is worn but useable. It is already folded to expose the area of the address. Bill straightens up and calls Ed to come closer.

He continues, "Look here, Ed, this is the street. As you see it's just on the edge of the Prenzlauer Berg district. Memorise the address but don't write it down or mark it on the map. The guys are due to meet there at 2030 hours tonight so you'll have to get a move on! Approach the pub very carefully and park some distance away. Remember, there are informers everywhere."

Ed asks, "How do we identify each other?"

"Don't worry. They will identify you."

At that point, a doctor and nurse come purposefully into the room. We can see poor Bill is exhausted and already has lapsed back into semi-consciousness. We'll get no more from him today.

Ed and I leave Bill's room and sit down on a seat in the hospital corridor.

I say to him, "If you're going to make that meeting, you'll really have to get your skids on. But look, Ed, I have to tell you of course I will support you but I'm not at all sure I need to accompany you on this trip. I can't see what I can achieve by being over in East Berlin with you. Perhaps it just adds to the risk ---"

I haven't finished making my point when Ed interrupts me: "Listen, Peter, I need you in on this. To be frank, although I've been with the CIA some years now and have had the so-called training: the truth is this will be the first operational mission of this type I've been called upon to do. Another thing is that my German language ability is quite modest. I've read your CV and your operational record. I really do need you there!"

OK, I think, that settles it. Let's get on with it.

Ed then says, "I've been talking with our US planners here and we're all set. We've got a car with West German plates, fuelled up and ready to go. I'm advised that, at this short notice, we'll have to take the direct route into East Berlin, that is to say via Checkpoint Charlie/Friedrichstrasse. It's the only crossing open to us non-German nationals without a full visa and we don't have time to get those. Apparently, we can just turn up at the checkpoint, exchange twenty-five Deutschmarks into DDR currency at the exorbitant exchange rate of 1:1 and buy a temporary visa. We of course show our passports rather than any military ID, you a UK one, me a US. And no weapons. If we're asked we'll just have to say we're on a business trip. There's no time for anything more elaborate. That's it. We then cross our fingers and hope for the best!"

It all seems very amateurish to me especially from such a professional organisation as the CIA. But I realise, if we are to make the meeting over there on time, there's no option but the most direct.

We go to the car pool and find the transport section is ready for us with a small Opel Corsa. Ed checks the paperwork, up to date tax and insurance, signs and gets in the driver's seat. I climb in next to him. I have nothing on me except my passport, a wad of money, oh and a good set of warm clothing!

It takes only a few minutes from the US facility to the approach to the check point. We recognise it straight away by the bright overhead lighting. There is a single line for traffic in each direction. Ahead of us there is a steady build-up of vehicles - mostly private cars like ours but also a bus and a couple of commercial trucks. We edge forward and pass opposite the US checkpoint covering traffic entering into the West. I notice this is a simple metal building protected only by a few sandbags. The traffic on that side is lighter and moving faster than on our side.

I leave Ed to stick in the traffic lane, get out and go to the booth where temporary visas are issued. There is a rather bored looking woman behind the counter grille. I do the mandatory exchange of marks from west to east - total fifty to cover twenty-five each for Ed and me, and indeed I get only fifty east marks back. I then hand over both of our passports and ask for visas for us both. I give her fifty marks. The woman gives me a cursory glance, makes out the visas, stamps them and passes them and the passports back through the grille. She should give me ten marks change. She does not. I move away from the counter to make room for the next traveller.

I re-join Ed's Opel car and we continue to edge forward to the DDR side. Here I can see guard towers and, as we approach, we have to negotiate around concrete barriers. The car in front is stopped and the two occupants are ordered to pull into a small lay-by and get out. We wait our turn. A guard comes to Ed's side and indicates to him to wind down his window. Ed complies and offers up our passports and visas. We wait again. The guard looks at the passports and matches them with the visas. He comes up close to Ed's window and shines a touch inside the car and at our faces. He then hands back the passports and visas and waves us on. Ed engages first gear and steadily pulls away in our little Opel. We hear no shouting for us to stop and are not immediately followed or impeded.

We are through. We are now in East Berlin.

I'm immediately struck by the total contrast between East and West Berlin. The obvious difference is about lighting and colour. Here in the east, traffic lights are few and far between and only official buildings, it seems, are lit up. There are virtually no advertising boards. Traffic is light and mostly consists of the little utility two stroke Trabants turned out by the East Germans. The snow has also been cleared from the main roads but is still piled up along the side of the pavements. We don't have far to go as, from the map Bill Harman gave us, we know we first have to cross the River Spree. We safely negotiate that then up ahead we manage to identify Alexanderplatz. We are watching out for any following vehicle. I'm not an expert in detecting a vehicle tail but as far as I can tell we are clear as Ed drives at a steady fifty kilometres an hour. From the directions of the map we make our way through Kollwitzkiez and Winsviettal districts into Prenzlauer Berg. We had studied the map closely before we left and have identified that

Meisenweg is a small road close to the junction of Wicherstrasse and Pappelallee. We are there. We check the time. It's 2015 hours.

We turn into Pappelallee. The map tells us that Meisenweg is the third road off to the left. We ease past this but can see no street sign. We carry on past another three streets before turning off into a road similar to Meisenweg. It's a quiet cul de sac. We drive to the end, turn around and come back toward Pappelallee. Ed parks the car and turns off the lights.

Then Ed says quietly: "Well, here we are! Meisenweg is just around the corner. We don't know the name of the Kneipe but we do know it's number 13. So, if the numbering system works the same as in the West, number thirteen should be about the seventh on the left from the junction with Pappelallee. Let's give it a few minutes to see if we've been followed then get to it."

We turn back into Pappelallee and walk up to the junction with Wicherstrasse, do a little loop and make our way back again towards Meisenweg. We are only too well aware of the strict informer network that the Stasi have organised to keep watch on its own people. We've learnt that the *inoffizielle Mitarbeiter* informal reporters represent something like two to three per cent of the DDR population and that every block of apartments has its dedicated informers in place. Despite this, we see no-one and decide to chance going to the rendezvous.

Ed is correct and we find number thirteen just along on the left.

Bill Harman had described the place as a Kneipe, which according to the German I've learnt means a small pub. And I suppose it is, though there is no pub-like sign on the outside. Just a normal house door. We take the chance to go for it but we can't see a bell or knocker. Ed uses his knuckles and knocks lightly on the door.

Chapter Sixteen

We wait apprehensively for a few minutes then the door is opened by a young guy. He is quite short but burly and thickset. Inside, it is dimly lit and we can just make out other people standing at a small bar area. All of them are looking towards us. The young man stands barring the entrance. He says; "*Wer sind Sie und was wollen Sie?* – who are you and what do you want?" I answer because Ed has told me he's not too confident speaking German. I reply: "*Wir sind Freunde von Herrn Harman. Er gab uns diese Adresse und sagte, dass wir uns hier treffen* – we are friends of Mr Harman. He gave us this address and told us to meet with us here. *Mein Name ist Peter Chambers und das ist Herrn Ed Morgan.*"

We watch as a woman detaches herself from the others and comes up to the door. She says to the young man, "*Es ist OK, Klaus, ich kann damit umgehen,*" then switching to good English, she continues: "Mr Harman said he would try to get someone here. Come on in out of the cold."

The young man, who we now know as Klaus, steps aside and Ed and I go on into the small room. There are three men there besides Klaus and the woman. She continues in English, addressing us both sharply:

"Tell us what you know and why you are here." I leave it to Ed to reply. He says:

"Bill Harman was shot today, somewhere here in East Germany. He made it back to the US zone and is conscious but hospitalised. He told us about your meeting and urged us to come in his place. So here we are!"

The woman listens intently to Ed, then she says: "Thank you. I needed to check that you are who you say. Indeed, Bill gave me your name Mr Morgan. I was with Bill when he was shot. I'm so relieved he got back OK and has survived."

We take off our Parkas and move into the centre of the room. The woman indicates that we and the other three men present should all sit down. Young Klaus remains by the door. The woman remains the spokesperson.

She says, "We all only use first names here, so we will call you Ed and Peter. My name is Heidi. I work at Stasi headquarters but don't be alarmed! It's not quite what it seems. Before we can discuss why we are all here today, I think it would be helpful to you if we all tell you a little about ourselves. You will then understand better why we meet in this way and how we can best cooperate together. Oh, and don't worry, all of us speak passable English, except Klaus, so perhaps it would be best if we stick to the English language."

Heidi is a petite woman who I would guess is in her mid to late thirties. She's not beautiful in the classical sense but I am immediately struck by her presence. She seems to have an inner strength despite her frail and slight physique. Her face is highlighted by her pronounced cheekbones and her crystal clear blue eyes.

She continues, "I want to introduce you to my colleagues here - Adel, Bernd and Frederik and to ask them to explain their respective backgrounds. Would you start first, Adel?"

Adel seems to be older than the other two, perhaps in his sixties. He wears round rimmed spectacles and has a long rather sad face.

He explains, "I am a professor in Mathematics and Computer Science at the technical university of Leuna-Merseburg in Halle. Like my colleagues here, I joined the communist party in my youth as a counter to the horrors carried out by the Nazi party. I have always conformed to the requirements of our SED party without having any real enthusiasm for politics and in my early days as a mathematician I was always given encouragement to pursue my own line of research. However, over the past years I have become totally disillusioned with the dominance of the Stasi movement who more and more seek to control our academic work. Today we are living in a police state. I want to see an end to this oppression and that is why I'm working with our group here. But more of this later"

Bernd now takes up the story. He is perhaps around fifty, slim and fit looking.

He says, "I am a medical doctor - initially as a general practitioner having graduated from Humbolt University here in Berlin. In 1970, I was recruited to join the Research Institute for Physical Education and Sports or FKS as we call it. This Institute specialises in high performance sports research. Initially I was inspired to be working as a sports physician to monitor and work towards the improvement of our young sports men and women. However, the sport became more and more politicised as the Sports Medical Services organisation controlled the policy of all our work. Every activity in High Performance sports is kept strictly secret and we are cautioned that we have to treat all our work with total confidentiality. Although not my direct domain, I learnt that selected athletes are being given what is termed "supportive measures" but this is in reality the use of universally banned drugs which the authorities go to great lengths to cover up so that athletes can deceive any drug tests. I am repelled by this and other repressive aspects of our political system here in the DDR. That's why I belong to this group."

I find these two stories fascinating. Here are two eminent specialists in their respective fields. Both highly educated men but both disillusioned by the communist DDR state. I notice that while Bernd was speaking, young Klaus had opened the door and slipped outside. I was about to ask Heidi about this when he returns and gives Heidi a thumbs-up sign. She acknowledges it with a nod of her head.

The third man in the group, Frederik, is about my own age. He is tall, fit looking and with an unmistakable military air about him.

He now takes his cue and introduces himself to Ed and me by saying, "Gentlemen, I am a Major in the Feliz Dzerzhinsky Guards Regiment, which is under command of the Stasi organisation. I suppose you could call our Regiment, the armed wing of Stasi. It sounds a strange name to the uninitiated so to enlighten you the name is from the founder of Cheka, the Bolshevik Secret Police. Of course, today I am wearing civilian clothes but on duty I wear an East German airborne forces uniform as I belong to the commando branch of our regiment. We have our base in the main Stasi headquarters complex in Normannenstrasse, Lichtenberg and our main mission is the protection of senior personnel and the overall security of the Stasi organisation. Our Regiment, while part of the regular East German Army or NVA, comes under the direct orders of the Stasi. My background is that of a regular infantry soldier but I was later drafted into our Guards Regiment. Since I've been working in Normannenstrasse, my men and I are frequently required to assist in the transport and handling of prisoners in the Hohenschönhausen prison in the Mitte district. There I have witnessed scenes of torture and mistreatment that I never thought possible could be carried out by my fellow countrymen. For long I've wanted to find some organ of protest that would have a chance of succeeding in the overthrow of this group of thugs. I think our group here has the potential to do so. That's why I'm here today."

This was a powerful statement. I'm seriously impressed by the quality of these people. I just hope that Ed and I can assist them in their cause.

Up to this point, we have all been very serious and earnest and with every good reason. All of us were taking great risks to be here today. The statements of Adel, Bert and Frederic would be considered as highly treasonable if overheard by the Stasi. Heidi has been following the conversation intently, her face wrapped in close concentration. Then suddenly she smiles and the room seems to light up with the warmth of that smile.

She says, "Gentlemen, let's try to ease our mood a little. After all, we have two distinguished guests who we haven't yet welcomed in appropriate style." She gestures to Ed and me and continues. "In the hope you might be joining us this evening, I put a bottle of our best East German Sekt in a bucket of ice. Let's have a drink together before the ice melts in reality as I hope it is also beginning to do metaphorically! But only one glass each I fear because we all need to stay alert and sharp tonight."

We do the rounds of toasting each other. Then it's Heidi's turn to tell Ed and I where she fits in.

"First and foremost," she begins "I must stress our vital need for security. We have chosen this meeting place today with care. We have checked the neighbourhood and there are no known *"inoffizielle Mitarbeiter"* in this part of Meisenweg, but we can never be sure as informers are everywhere. Ed and Peter, I need to explain that Klaus here is acting as our look out. After you had arrived, he went out to check the whole area for any sign that your approach here had been observed. When he returned, he gave me the all clear sign. But let's not be complacent. We have a reserve plan in case your arrival was spotted and reported to the Stasi. If we were to be raided, the door at the back of this room opens onto a small passageway which leads to the Pappelallee. Frederik's car is parked there ready for a quick getaway. Meanwhile Klaus will keep watch."

I am impressed by this small but dynamic woman. The other three men are high calibre operators but despite this, they all seemed to defer to Heidi and look upon her as their natural leader.

She continues, addressing her remarks to Ed and me, "I need to tell you where I fit in. Like Frederik, I work in the Stasi headquarters block in Normannenstrasse. I am a secretary in the Department for the Main Administration for Reconnaissance. We call this the *Hauptverwaltung Aufklärung* or HVA, Stasi's foreign intelligence section. Our department is now very large consisting of thirteen sections directing espionage or counterintelligence operations. Perhaps you know that for many years our Chief was Markus Wolf who, during his time with us, achieved great success in penetrating the political circles of West Germany. He is a very intelligent and impressive man. However, he retired two years ago, in 1986, and his successor, Werner Grossman, is an entirely different character. More about this later."

Heidi pauses and realises she hasn't finished her glass of Sekt. She picks up the glass, holds it up high in a mock salute and throws the remaining liquid down her throat. She then gives another of her fabulous smiles.

She then continues, speaking directly to Ed and me, "Bill Harman was involved with supporting our work in organising groups such as ours here consisting of East Germans who could provide leadership in the event of an uprising against the ruling SED party and their Stasi enforcers. We have been quite successful in these efforts and now have cells set up in most cities and townships in our country. We still have much yet to do but we are content to move slowly to ensure that we have the right people in place and always with the top priority of protecting our security. In a country with an estimated 500,000 Stasi informers, you can imagine we have to move very carefully indeed!"

Heidi glances again towards Klaus at the door. He gives her an all clear nod.

She continues, "Bill has been helping us with the production and distribution of leaflets and we have found a means of printing these securely and of good quality. Recently, much of the content has been extracts from Gorbachev's recent book, Perestroika, particularly Part Two under the heading "New Thinking and the World" where he outlines how the Soviet Union and the US are moving together to a new relationship of détente and disarmament. These articles are very well received by our supporters but of course, are seen with great dismay by the SED party. Then last week, Mr Gorbachev made his historic speech at the UN. This has already had a major impact. It has infuriated the SED even more and caused a sense of unease and restlessness amongst our citizens."

Heidi pauses and I notice Klaus has again gone out. Heidi continues:

"I now turn to how we might turn this situation to our advantage. My section in the HVA is called Division X. I should add that during Markus Wolf's time here, although we were technically controlled by Erich Mielke, the chief of Stasi, HVA had acquired a de facto independence of operations. In Division X, much of our work has historically been directed against West Germany but since Gorbachev's rise to power in the Soviet Union, the division has shifted its emphasis. The SED realises that the DDR is becoming highly vulnerable as it can only retain its power base with the support of the Soviets. So, it is currently involved in inserting rumours and reports of increasing military preparedness. Under the management of our Department Head, Colonel Konrad Krause, it is simulating Soviet intelligence sources and feeding these into the US intelligence community and similarly simulating US reports and feeding these into the Kremlin. The aim of course is to reignite suspicion between East and West and thus retain the DDR's position as a loyal defender of Soviet led communism. As Mielke said in a recent speech to his staff. "Remember Comrades, the most important thing you have is power. Hang on to this at all costs. Without it you are nothing"

I am immediately stimulated by Heidi's remarks. Speaking from a position of knowledge due to her job in the HVA, she is substantiating what we had been suspecting - that these increasing threat reports had all been initiated by the Stasi.

I interrupt Heidi and say, "Heidi, what you've just said totally confirms our suspicions. But I must tell you that your Colonel Krause has already been quite successful in casting doubt on the genuineness of Gorbachev. There are some indications that the Soviets are reacting to the reports which in turn are being countered by increased vigilance alerts in the West. And just before we left West Berlin earlier today, we found that the press, both West and East, have jumped on the bandwagon and are stirring things up further. Before these reports gain more political currency, and more "tit for tat" reaction and response, it's vital we expose them for what they are - a cynical attempt to re-establish the cold war between East and West.

I notice that the others in this dark little room are nodding in full agreement.

Heidi says, "Exactly, Peter! We now need to work out how we can expose Colonel Krause and produce definitive proof to both sides that the reports are initiated by Stasi. The first—"

Heidi is interrupted by the sound of shooting nearby. The door is suddenly flung open and Klaus stumbles into the room. Blood is already oozing through his parka and we can see he has been shot in the shoulder and chest. Before he collapses, he manages to tell us:

"Es ist die Stasi! Sie haben das amerikanische Auto gefunden. Sie haben die Gegend abgesucht. Als sie mich sahen stoppten sie mich, ich fing an zu laufen und sie fingen an zu schiessen. - They found the American's car, are searching the area and shot me."

Our meeting is over. Bernd, the doctor, is immediately on his feet and attending to Klaus. He undoes his parka and pulls up his sweater and shirt. The rest of us grab our coats and prepare to make for the back door as Heidi has explained. But we can't leave Klaus. We wait while Bernd does a quick examination.

His face is grave as he tells us, "He's alive - just. He needs proper attention soonest. If we leave him to the Stasi, they'll either shoot him or patch him up and then interrogate him. We'll have to take him with us."

Heidi has the presence of mind to lock the front door and turn out the lights. Then she leads the way out through the back door into a narrow alleyway. Bernd and Frederik carry Klaus between them. We make our way along this alley and reach Frederik's parked Trabant car. Behind us we can hear shouting from the Meisenweg road as the Stasi carry out house to house searches.

Bernd and Frederik carefully lay Klaus on the back seat and Frederik then goes around to the driver's seat. Adel takes the front passenger seat and Bernd stays in the back with Klaus. It's a small car and only capable of squeezing in one more passenger in the back. Behind us, we hear the sound of the door to the room we had been in being broken down.

Heidi says to Ed, "Ed, you get in the car. It's important you get word back to your Americans in the West. I'll stay with Peter here"

She then shouts out to Frederik and the others. "We'll meet tomorrow at the location you all know, now get going!!"

The little Trabant two stroke fires up and, takes off belching out a stream of smelly fuel. It's already turned into Pappelallee and heading up towards the Wicherstrasse junction before the Stasi react.

Heidi breaths a sign of relief.

She says, "Frederik's a great driver and he knows this area like the back of his hand. I'm confident he'll lose those goons. And we're lucky that Bernd is there to attend to Klaus – let's hope he'll be OK."

Of course, I share her hope about Klaus but I have to wonder what the hell we're going to do now with the Stasi guys closing in. We've no weapons and if we try to make a run for it, I haven't got a clue where we should go.

Heidi seems calm and I admire her composure.

"Come with me, Peter," she says as she leads me back along the alley, past the back door of our meeting room. We can hear sounds of movement inside. The Stasi are obviously already there. At the other end of the alley, Heidi stops next to a small motor scooter.

"Welcome to my little Zündapp Bella. She'll get us safely away. Hop on behind me, Peter, and hold on tight!"

Heidi gets up front and kick starts the engine of the Zündapp. It fires up straight away. I do as Heidi says, climb up behind her and off we go. Heidi doesn't hang about but any vehicle on the quiet East Berlin roads at this time of night must surely attract attention. We are soon off the main roads and onto smaller cobbled streets, covered in compacted snow. Heidi drives at speed and find I have to cling onto her as we speed around a series of sharp bends. I again give thanks to the BRIXMIS quartermaster for issuing me with warm clothing. I certainly need it now on this open scooter in Berlin's freezing winter temperatures.

I have no idea where Heidi is going and no clear plan of what our next action will be. At present. I'm totally dependent on this diminutive, fascinating woman. I don't know why but I feel good about it.

Chapter Seventeen

Heidi's little Zündapp rattles along over the compacted snow covered cobbled streets. I've never been here before of course and I don't have the faintest idea where we are or where we are going. I usually have a good sense of direction which has been developed during my army training but now it's dark, cold and overcast and I don't even know if we're heading east, west, north or south. I know we passed through an area of what looked like recently constructed drab housing estates lined up in almost regimental orderliness, all made of some sort of concrete slab. They are depressingly similar in size and height. I think this could be the Hellersdorf area from the description I've read and the distance I reckon we've travelled since we left Meisenweg.

I decide to stop even trying to work out where we might be - it's an impossible challenge. Instead, I concentrate on holding on to Heidi and trying to keep as much of my head down out of the rushing cold wind. Conversation is not possible and in case, not relevant. What are we going to discuss anyway? How fucking cold it is? We know that already. Politics? I don't think so. I decide to grit my teeth and try my best to enjoy the ride.

Heidi confidently works her way through a maze of small roads somehow managing to keep the Zündapp upright on the snow compacted surface. Eventually she brings the motor scooter to a stop outside yet another square apartment block. No car or motorbike seems to have followed us. Even in the dark, I can see the building is a grey colour as its silhouette stands out against the white, cloud covered sky. There is a small open area in front of the building which is surrounded by a line of trees all now bare of leaves. There are signs that the front area is used for children to play as there's a plastic slide in one corner and a miniature football goalpost in another. Near the communal entrance, is a line of metal bars designed as a stand for bicycles and, in Heidi's case, motor scooters. I descend stiffly from the scooter and wrap my hands up under my armpits to try to restore some warmth into them. Each time I breathe I emit a cloud of icy mist. I've been wearing decent gloves but these were not up to the task of coping with roaring along in the open on a freezing Berlin winter's night.

Heidi seems as relaxed as if she's just had a spin on a fine summer's day. She turns to me and gives me another of her magical smiles.

"Journey's end for now, Peter," she says "We are in the borough of Pankow and we're going to have to hole up here for a while. My own apartment is in Lichtenberg but I'm afraid that's out of bounds for us tonight. An old couple, Herr and Frau Neubert, live here. They were close friends of my grandparents and they're my own dear friends now. I sometimes come to visit them to see if they're OK. On occasions, I even stay the night. They don't speak English so I'm afraid we'll be stuck with German for our conversation but don't worry it probably won't be for long. You'll see what I mean when you meet them."

"But if I'm spotted here, won't it compromise them?"

"No, it'll be fine. I'll tell you more later. Come on, let's get out of the cold. I've brought some things for them. Can you give me a hand?"

There are two saddle bags attached to the side of the scooter, in fact I had had to curl my legs awkwardly around them during our trip here. Inside each are full bags which Heidi now pulls out. We carry these between us up the several flights of dark concrete stairs. Leading off each corridor are doors with each apartment number written in exactly the same type-case. Heidi stops in front of one and knocks on the door. Nothing happens for a time so she knocks again. Eventually we hear the shuffle of someone's feet coming to the door. It opens slowly to reveal an old lady. She is neatly dressed in a skirt with a floral blouse covered by a thick sweater. She has grey hair, cut short and neatly combed. When she sees Heidi, her wrinkled face lights up.

"Heidi, how lovely to see you!" she exclaims in German. "Do come in. Gerhardt and I were just talking about you."

Frau Neubert ushers us into her living room. It is small and sparsely furnished with two armchairs placed either side of a brown tiled coal heater. There is a square table with four chairs around it. The floor is covered in a brown coloured linoleum. As a concession to individuality, there is a small floral rug in the centre of the room and flower pots on the table and window ledge. Despite the cold of winter, the flowers are still in bloom - a tribute to Frau Neubert's careful attention. Sitting in one of the chairs is an old gentleman, presumably Herr Neubert. He does not get up and I notice a walking stick placed beside his chair. He is hunched into his chair and I can tell he's a sick man. Both Herr and Frau Neubert look as if they are in their eighties. Heidi goes over to Herr Neubert's chair, kisses him on the cheek and gives him a hug. She says:

"Herr and Frau Neubert, we were in the area attending a meeting and I couldn't resist calling to see you. This is my friend Herr Peter. We have brought you a few things which we hope you might like."

Heidi opens the bags and produces a roll of fresh sausage and a variety of fruit and vegetables. She says:

"I know how hard it is to get fresh produce here in the winter. I'm lucky with my job that I can use our concessionary so I'm only too pleased to pass some on to you."

Frau Neubert seems delighted with her gifts. She busies herself taking down glasses from a sideboard next to the table. She says:

"You must stay and drink a little Sekt with us while you're here." Then looking at me, she says, "Perhaps you could help me Herr Peter. The bottle is in the fridge just there in our kitchenette. Unfortunately, neither my husband or I are as mobile as we used to be."

I'm only too pleased to have something useful to do. The kitchenette is just off the living room. It contains a wash basin, a small cooking stove and an old fridge. I can tell these kind people live very simply but, despite their age and lack of mobility, the house is kept immaculately clean. I find the fridge and notice it's nearly bare shelves. Heidi has chosen her present to them very well. I take out the bottle of Sekt and observe that it is produced from the Gewürztraminer grape: despite their modest lifestyle they have good taste! When I get back to the main room, Frau Neubert has already lined up four glasses on the table.

I bring the bottle through to the sitting room, remove the top wrapper and ease out the cork. Frau Neubert gives a little squeal of delight as the cork pops and I pour four equal measures into the glasses. I get the impression that this is a ceremony that they cannot afford to enjoy very often. Heidi takes one of the glasses and brings it over to Herr Neubert. She kneels down next to him and carefully hands him the glass. He takes it with a trembling hand and Heidi stays next to him to ensure he doesn't spill any of the liquid. I take a second glass over to her next to Herr Neubert and she stays close to him. I give the third glass to Frau Neubert and pick up the last myself. In our allotted positions, Heidi and Herr Neubert close together next to the stove, Frau Neubert and me in the middle of the little sitting room, we raise our glasses and together say "*Prost*" in unison and take a sip of the Sekt. Already I am warming to this old couple. I imagine they have experienced much hardship in their lives. Herr Neubert is clearly a very sick gentleman. He doesn't speak at all, is clearly very immobile but he is alert and I can tell he is understanding everything yet somehow is incapable of responding.

Perhaps encouraged by the Sekt, our conversation is light and easy. At some point, Frau Neubert has produced plates and cutlery and we eat a light meal consisting of some of Heidi's sausage and tomatoes with a few cold boiled potatoes from Frau Neubert's sparse fridge. I want to know more about the lives of this couple and, when I feel the time is acceptable, I ask Frau Neubert about their past. She takes her time to answer and I say:

"Frau Neubert, I hope I've not offended you by my question."

She sighs and replies. "No, not at all. I'm flattered that you, a stranger to us, should ask such a question. I'm just wondering where to begin."

Again, she seems to be collecting her thoughts, then she says: "To answer your question, Herr Peter, I have to take you back to the beginning of our lives. My husband was born in 1908 and now in 1988, he has just turned eighty years old. I was born two years later. We used to live near Leipzig and that is where we met, fell in love and married. You could say we had the good fortune to have been too young to have suffered much directly from the first world war but we grew up during a period of great difficulty as our country struggled to regenerate during the 1920s after the end of that war. We suffered greatly from the period of mass inflation and the devaluation of the Mark. There was much political infighting and Hitler's National Socialist Worker's Party seemed to us to offer stability to our country that no other political group could match. Remember that at that time we were young and idealistic. In 1925, my husband decided to sign up as a party member and I actively supported him. Adolf Hitler seemed to have the potential to be the saviour of our disjointed country."

Frau Neubert pauses and I wonder where her story is going. Heidi and I say nothing and wait for her to take her time. At last she continues, "We got married in 1932, just after my husband qualified as an architect and for a few years our lives went well. We had hoped to start a family but I did not get pregnant in those early years of our marriage. Then, in the late thirties, there was a major recruitment drive to join the armed forces. My husband was patriotic and felt it his duty to volunteer. In fact, due to his training, it is possible he could have escaped any compulsory draft, at least for a time. We'll never know."

Again, she pauses. Heidi has all this time remained at Herr Neubert's side. She now puts her arm around him. I think we know that there is great sadness in the story to come. Frau Neubert takes a deep breath and continues, "My husband was very fit at that time and was assigned to the infantry. He has always had a very true eye and controlled emotions and, due I suppose to these characteristics, he was selected to be trained as a specialist sniper. After his training, he was assigned to the Sixth Army which was formed in October 1939 at the declaration of the new war. It was commanded by General Walther von Reichenau. In 1940, my husband was involved in the invasion of the West and spent most his time in the fighting originally in Belgium. He was directly involved in the attacks on Liège and Namur and later with the Sixth Army's successful sweep into France. When France capitulated, we then thought the war would end and my husband came home on leave hoping he would be discharged and could resume his career. But it was not to be."

I could tell the story was now getting difficult for this dear lady. I said to her gently, "Frau Neubert, please don't distress yourself."

I was going to say more but she cuts me off, "No, no, it's good to talk. I really want you and Heidi to understand how it was. After a very short leave, my husband was told he had to return to duty and his regiment, still part of Sixth Army, took part in the invasion of the Soviet Union in June 1941. That September, they were at the gates of Leningrad, succeeded in taking Smolensk, and had a major victory at Kharkov. My husband's morale and that of his compatriots was again high as they prepared for Operation Blau, the summer offensive of 1942. Earlier that year, General Reichenau was killed in a plane crash and his post as commander of Sixth Army was taken by General Paulus. That summer it all went so very wrong as the German Wehrmacht and the Soviet Army fought themselves to destruction at Stalingrad. My husband's role as a sniper was vital as the battle degenerated to fighting street by street and even house by house. He was involved in the heart of the battle throughout from August 1942 until the Sixth Army was forced to surrender in February 1943. Miraculously, my husband survived the battle, unlike the nearly 150,000 German soldiers and their allies who perished there."

There was more to tell and Heidi and I knew that Frau Neubert wanted to finish the story, "My husband was one of some 90,000 to be held captive by the Soviets after the surrender at Stalingrad. At home, it was some long weeks before we were informed about the tragedy and very much longer than that before we knew what had become of our men. At the end of the war, Germany was in total ruins. Our home near Leipzig had been destroyed by air raids and I, like many German women, were forced to live in miserable circumstances. But of course, my husband and his colleagues had it much worse. The Soviets treated them appallingly and many died in captivity, weakened by disease, starvation and lack of medical care. They were dispersed around the Soviet Union and employed as forced labour in the Soviet wartime economy and post war reconstruction. After the creation of the pro-Soviet DDR state, our men were gradually released in groups, sometimes in hundreds, sometimes just a dozen or so at a time. Each time I clamoured for news of my husband but was unable to get any information. Then one day in the summer of 1950, a train arrived in Berlin carrying a party of fifty ex-Prisoners of War. The DDR authorities produced a list of the men and I saw my husband's name was included. I rushed to take the first possible train to Berlin and to the camp where they had taken them. There, after a heart-breaking separation of nine long years, I re-found my husband. He was so thin, weak and sick, but he was alive and I had got my man back."

Frau Neubert is shaking with emotion as she relives her tragic memories. She stops talking and starts to shake. She takes out her handkerchief and sobs quietly. I can't resist but to put my arms around her and hold her to me. She leans into my chest. I notice that Heidi is also comforting Herr Neubert. She is kneeling down next to him with her arm round him and her hand gently stroking his face. He has been listening intently to his wife, his head down, in his own space. We stay like this for a few moments, just quietly absorbing Frau Neubert's story. I would like to know more. What support did they get from the DDR authorities? What medical treatment was available? How did they come to be living here in this part of East Berlin? But now is not the time to ask these questions.

After a while, Heidi gently disengages from Herr Neubert, gets back up to her feet and walks over to the bags we had brought in when we arrived. She smiles in that unique way of hers. She says, "I intentionally left one little present till later. I think now is the time!" She takes out from her bag a small wrapped parcel and goes over to give it to Frau Neubert, "It's just a little something for you and Herr Neubert. For later perhaps?"

I'm learning to love the way Heidi seems to have the knack of gauging when to lighten a mood. There's no need for her or me to make a big expression of sympathy about their life story. Our unspoken gestures are enough. They know we understand what they have had to endure. We don't need to put it into words.

Frau Neubert responds to the mood change. She turns to Heidi and says, "You naughty girl, what is this?" She makes a big deal of taking the parcel from

Heidi and of fussing to untie the string and uncover the contents. Inside are two large blocks of gourmet Swiss chocolate. Frau Neubert exclaims, "Heidi, you know that's my absolute number one favourite. I haven't tasted that since before the war!" She comes across to Heidi and hugs her. Our sad, sombre mood has been lifted, thanks to Heidi.

Frau Neubert wants to insist that we all share some of the chocolate but Heidi is firm and says she and Herr Neubert must enjoy it by themselves together later. I resist asking any more questions about their lives. Enough is enough for one session. Heidi and Frau Neubert tell me about how they know each other through Heidi's grandparents who were close friends for many years. I gather that Heidi's grandparents are now dead but again, I don't want to ask more questions which might lead back to sad stories.

I can tell that Herr and Frau Neubert are tiring. It's been a long evening for them. Come to think of it, it's been a long day for me too. I'm not at all sure where we go from here – that is as far as Heidi and I are concerned. My watch tells me it's past midnight and I've no idea where we are to sleep tonight. I'm not unhappy when Frau Neubert says, "Herr Peter, how good of you to come to see us this evening. When Heidi comes over to visit us, she often stays the night. We have a little bedroom next door to ours. You're most welcome to sleep there but I'm afraid there's no heating so it's rather cold." She looks at us both in a way I find difficult to interpret and says, "You know, you really are a lovely looking couple, I thought that when you arrived, now I'm sure of it. Please excuse us but I must now take my dear husband off to bed."

That is it. She goes over and helps Herr Neubert to his feet and supports him as they slowly make their way to their room.

I look across at Heidi. I'm not sure what to say. As I'm learning to expect, she helps me out and says, "Come on, Englishman, time for bed!"

Chapter Eighteen

We stay discreetly in the living room area for a while longer as we can hear Herr and Frau Neubert preparing for bed and using the bathroom. We try to make ourselves useful and tidy up the glasses and plates we had used earlier. That is all we can find to do as Frau Neubert keeps their apartment spick and span. Heidi then rummages around in the bags she had brought with us. First, she pulls out a well-used but readable street map of East Berlin. She points with the tip of her finger to what the map refers to as small park area and says that is where she has arranged to meet the others in the group tomorrow at six o'clock. She warns me not to mark anything on the map. Then Heidi goes back to her bag and manages to produce a tube of toothpaste, a single toothbrush and a small hand towel. She tells me we'll have to share and hopes neither of us has too many germs!

We go and inspect our bed for the night. It's not big by Western European standards - bigger than a single but smaller than most doubles. It has a top sheet and a single eiderdown. There is no fire or other means of heating.

When the sounds from the Neubert's bedtime preparations have ended, I say to Heidi: "Why don't you go ahead and use the bathroom. I'll get our parkas and put them on the bed for extra warmth."

While I wait for Heidi to attend to her ablutions, I sit down in Herr Neubert's chair by the dying coals on the stove. I can't help but think I've somehow got myself into a surreal situation. This morning I was enjoying a traditional English breakfast with the general and his wife in the British Berlin zone. Now, here I am in this little apartment somewhere in East Berlin having earlier this evening been close to capture by the Stasi, freezing my goolies off on a motor scooter, listening to Frau Neubert's harrowing life story and now being about to lie down for the night next to a German lady who I know fuck all about. I'm not even sure that Heidi is her real name. And apart from her telling me we are now somewhere in the Pankow district and giving me the little map, that's about the limit of my knowledge.

As I'm pontificating about my lot, Heidi comes back out of the bathroom and whispers brightly, "Bathroom's free - don't forget to brush your teeth!" She makes it sound like we've been a domestic couple for some long time.

I complete my ablutions and make my way through to the cold little bedroom. I don't know if it has a separate light. If so Heidi hasn't put it on. But there's a small table lamp in the sitting room so I leave the connecting door open so we can vaguely see inside the bedroom and hope we might get some benefit from the dying embers of the fire.

Heidi is already in bed. I strip off as far as my "Long John" thermal undies and slip into bed next to her. She also is just in her underwear. We both lie on our backs facing the ceiling. I am on the left side, Heidi is on the right. Symbolically, it's like I'm the West, Heidi is the East. For a while we lie there with our hands down by our sides, our bodies not quite touching. The width of the bed only just allows this to be possible. And not for long. Heidi turns on her left side towards me. She says, "Peter, it's cold. I need you to warm me up." I put my right arm under her shoulders as she turns and I pull her towards me. She moves with my arm and cuddles up onto my chest. I gently rub my hand up and down her back and feel the slender shape of her body now snuggling up to me. Her face is close to mine and I lightly kiss her already feeling a growing tenderness towards her. I like the feeling. We stay like that for a while, neither of us yet ready to sleep.

Heidi says quietly, "Peter, we know almost nothing about each other. You arrived at our meeting this evening and identified yourself just as Peter Chambers but I didn't even give your surname to Herr and Frau Neubert. I know you're British and I think you told us you are in the military. But that's it. I want you to tell me about yourself. But we must talk very quietly so as not to disturb the Neuberts."

"You have just said what I was thinking about you Heidi," I whisper back. "Yes, it's good to talk for a while. But, ladies first, as we Brits say. Tell me about yourself. I think I have the right to know who I'm lying next to in this bed."

"OK, Peter. Here goes. Where to start? Well... I was born not far from here on the outskirts of Pankow in 1950, in fact my 38th birthday was last month. You see, I've even told you my age which I believe English ladies are very shy about. I was brought up as a single child because my mother was pregnant by a Soviet soldier who disappeared somewhere before I was born. I know nothing about him. My mother was not strong and when I was about five, she got cancer and died. So I was brought up by my grandparents, who were best friends with the Neuberts. That's how far back our friendship goes."

Heidi turns in a little closer to me and puts her right leg between mine. She's still wearing her underclothes but I can feel the full outline of her body as she leans in towards me. She continues, "My family situation was very poor and from the start at school in Pankow there was always a strong political element. We had lectures referring regularly about the principle of overturning the social classes. Indeed, children of working or peasant classes received preference in admission to higher education. I was a beneficiary of this system. After classes at school, we were encouraged to stay behind in the "*Schulhort*" where teachers supervised our homework and encouraged us towards more advanced study. I also joined a "Young Pioneer group" until I was about fourteen when I moved on to belong to a free German Youth organisation. So, as a young teenager, you could say that I was a proper little swot and a good communist."

She gives a little giggle at this last remark. We turn slightly to my right to adjust our position. I put my left hand over onto her back and keep her warm by rubbing her between her shoulder blades and the base of her spine. She continues, "I was always good at languages. My English is OK, no??"

"I think you're fishing for compliments," I tell her, "but seriously, you're pretty good!"

"And you're good at German too," she counters. Then she continues, "But it was the Russian language that really fascinated me - perhaps it was something to do with my unknown father. I don't know. Anyway, I passed my final college exams with good grades and was thrilled to be offered a place at Moscow State University. So I spent three years there graduating with a degree at interpreter level. When I came back here to Berlin, I think it was in 1975, I was offered work with the Stasi starting as a secretary and building up to work for the *Hauptverwaltung Aufklärung* or HVA department. I was lucky to have Markus Wolf as a patron. He often used me as an interpreter when he was dealing with the Russians although he also spoke the language well enough. Markus retired two years ago but I'm still working at the same place."

I ask her. "OK, Heidi, you say you were a good communist so why are you now so against the regime here?"

"I'm not so much against communism, indeed I think Herr Gorbachev is a wonderful man. What I've come to loathe is the total blind repression of the SED ruling party. It is run by old men who are living in the past. It's only due to the Stasi that they can hang on in power. While I was working for Marcus Wolf, I was exposed to the culture of the West. Marcus is a brilliant man and while he was head of our department I could turn a blind eye to many of the excesses of my employers. Since he's left, I realise more and more how the Party uses force and intimidation to retain its grip on power. Every day I see examples of the violence the Stasi uses to enforce its power over our people. I've now come to hate that and will do all I can to help in its overthrow."

I could feel Heidi getting emotional during this last outburst which she was finding difficult to express while still talking in whispers. I hold her tightly and we lie still for a while wrapped in each other's arms. She's an enigmatic person. Sometimes passionate and serious yet at other times light, funny and frivolous. I wonder about her personal life and ask her, "Heidi, are you married or do you have a regular partner?"

She takes her time to reply, then she says, "Married? No never. Regular partner? Not really but I did have a friend who I thought I was in love with. I met him here in Berlin after I got back from Moscow. He was Russian. His name was Yuri Krivosheev, a captain in 6 Guards Motor Rifle Division. That's part of 20 Guards Army which is based here in East Berlin. We knew each other for about three years and I think we were both seriously considering making it a permanent relationship. Yuri was ambitious and had the good pedigree of attending the Frunze Military Academy. He was also parachute trained and when the Soviets got seriously involved in fighting the Mujahideen in Afghanistan, Yuri got himself transferred to the 103rd Guards Airborne Division based near Kabul. We used to write to each other often and Yuri used to write about the search and destroy operations he was involved with using Mil Mi-24 helicopter gunships in support. Suddenly his letters stopped and it was some weeks later that I found out that he had been killed when insurgents shot down the plane he was in as it was about to take off at Kandahar airport. That was four years ago, in 1984. There's been no one serious since then."

Again, we lie still and quiet for a while. It's time to change position. My right arm is getting numb so I gently pull her over and she instinctively turns to lie on top of me. I fold my hands behind her, one resting on each of the cheeks of her bottom. I am amazed at how frank and forthcoming she has been in answering all my questions so directly. Already I feel I'm getting to know this woman. I like the experience and already the sharp shiver of the cold as we got into bed has been replaced by a warm glow as our two bodies are entwined together. It's a joy to have her so close. She is lying on top of my crotch and I can feel myself beginning to become aroused. I'm tempted just to go with my nature but decide to resist my natural impulse. I pull her up higher against my body so that my groin is now clear of hers. As I move her, I can feel the full outline of her body pressed against my chest and stomach.

"So, Mr Englishman," she whispers, "I've bared my soul to you. Now it's your turn. Are you married?"

Her question jolts me back to the real world and I recognise that this is a sobering question from her just as I was beginning to lose myself in the joy of holding her beguiling body and having thoughts of surrendering to my male instinct. I compose my thoughts. By nature, I'm a private man particularly as far as my personal life is concerned. But I've just been listening to Heidi's whispering earnest voice and I feel I must return the compliment and be just as open to her as she has been to me.

I tell her, "Yes, I am married and have been for nearly twenty years. I have two children, Chloe who is fourteen and Christian who is ten. I love my children dearly."

"I understand, Peter. But you say you love your children dearly. But what about your wife? Don't you love her so much?"

It's amazing how perceptive Heidi is. In the one phase I used she picked up on the nuance that I was implying that there is a problem with my wife. My first reserved impulse is to gloss over her question with some sort of glib reply. But I know that's not right. Not here. Not now. I suppose I feel it's like a sort of release valve. I've held back on my emotions for so long, With Heidi, I feel I need to let it go. So, I tell her about my wife Ann, how much we were in love, about our early life together. Then I tell her about the Cyprus tragedy ten years ago, something I have not told any other person for many years now. I tell Heidi all the details, and of my feelings of guilt as a father and husband who has let his family down and of the consequence of how it has affected the rest of my relationship with Ann, my wife.

Heidi hears me out. She slowly moves off my chest and turns on her left side next to me. With her right hand, she reaches over and gently strokes my face, then runs her hand slowly down to my chest and kneads my chest and stomach. I know she can sense the grief I still have about losing my darling son Nicholas. Then we lie still and silent.

We all live in our own worlds and have to react to what presents itself before us. I have lived with my guilt about the Cyprus thing all these years. It's serious and has had a major impact on my life with Ann. Then I think about what Heidi and I have listened to earlier when Frau Neubert related the incredibly moving and heart churning story of the life she and her husband had to bear all those years after Herr Neubert was taken prisoner at Stalingrad. It gives a perspective I could hardly have imagined before and seems to make my worries pale into insignificance.

Heidi asks me about my career so I run through some of the military postings I have had – in Africa, Borneo, Aden, the Oman, Hong Kong and of course in West Germany. This is not the time for detail about these jobs which is a blessing because, although we are being very honest with each other, my inbuilt reserve about revealing classified information forbids me from saying anything about my work in Germany. Also, Northern Ireland, where most soldiers of my generation have spent several years. Ireland is such a complex mixture of politics, religion, tribal alliances and outright thuggery that it's best to leave that subject well alone. As I'm talking about my postings, I'm well aware that this alluring woman next to me is a trained communist who is working for the Stasi, so I think to myself, "Attention Peter Chambers – be very careful what you say." So I stick to generalisations and Heidi doesn't try to probe.

All she says is, "Peter, what you tell me highlights what incredibly diverse backgrounds we come from, you and I. So much has been due to the political forces that has shaped our world since the end of the last World War. There could have been so many different outcomes but here we are with Europe still split in half between East and West. Probably what I have told you about my background is alien to you and the culture you were brought up in. From my viewpoint, what you've told me about your travels around your "free" world is so difficult for us East Germans to grasp. Again, I think about what we discussed in our group this evening and hope that Mr Gorbachev will be the catalyst for change we all want."

As I'm now getting used to, Heidi decides to change the mood completely. She raises her right hand and gives me a mock slap on my chest. She says, "Now, Peter Chambers. I have an important announcement to make!"

I wonder what's coming next. She continues to whisper in a conspiratorial way, "I must tell you that I am bursting for a pee. So, you'll have to make space for me while I get up and brave the cold. I implore you to keep the bed warm for when I get back!"

She doesn't hang about. Soon I hear her scurrying quickly back to the bed. She jumps back in and plants her icy feet directly on top of mine. I massage her feet and body and start to feel the warmth flowing back into her. But that is not all I feel. She is still wearing the top part of her underwear but has removed the bottom part. I continue to stroke and massage her and feel the movement of her receptive body as she responds to my touch. Her invitation is clear,

I'm instantly aroused by the delicious feel of her nakedness. I'm so tempted to let go. This seems such a natural progression of our situation, lying so close together in the little bed. Yet, I hold back. I'm learning that Heidi is a very special person. Maybe we will never be together again - at least not like this. But maybe we will. My body craves to have sex with her now but I force myself to resist. Somehow, I feel it's too soon.

"Heidi," I whisper to her, "We've had a magical night that I'll never forget. Let's just keep it at that."

She stiffens and I worry that I've upset her. But then she reaches over and puts her right arm across me and replies, "Yes, I know you're right, Peter. But be prepared. I intend to proposition you again some day soon. And maybe we can find a warmer bed!"

Without another word, she turns back onto her right side. I caress her back and shoulders until soon I hear her breathing deepen as she falls asleep. Then so do I.

When eventually I wake up, Heidi is no longer next to me. I reach out across the bed but she is not there. I find my watch that I had left on the floor next to the bed. It's seven-fifteen. I get up and stumble out into the living room. I see that the bags we had brought in last evening are gone.

All I can find is a note which says: "Peter, thank you for a wonderful night! I have to go to work. See you tonight, you know where and when. Love Heidi." That's all.

Chapter Nineteen

I suppose I should have expected this. Heidi is a working girl and has to show up every-day to prevent any suspicion about her loyalty to the wretched Stasi regime. But this leaves me with a lot of problems. Heidi left me a map which is useful but it doesn't go down to street level. I sit down under the table lamp in the sitting room and try to orientate myself. I know I'm somewhere in Pankow but from the map it seems this is a borough which covers a large area. Tracing my hand down over the map, at last I find Lichtenberg, this also seems to be both a town and a district. But if I can get there, I should be able to locate the rendezvous for this evening's meeting with Heidi and her colleagues from last evening plus Ed, that is if they managed to escape the clutches of the Stasi.

I can see it's still dark outside but my instinct is to get moving straightaway. There is no sound from Herr and Frau Neubert so I presume they're still sleeping. I was incredibly impressed both by how charming Frau Neubert is and by the harrowing story of their lives. The last thing I want to do is to implicate them in any way by being found here by the authorities. I slip round to the bathroom and use the loo, then dress back into my BRIXMIS issued kit. I bless the warmth it provided me yesterday and that they also gave me a good pair of stout walking boots.

I write a short note to Frau Neubert. I say I was so honoured to meet her and Herr Neubert and wished them well. I try to phrase it in my best German and to use a Germanic type of script. I don't even sign it to prevent, I hope, any chance that it could incriminate them in some way.

I let myself out of their apartment and make my way down the grey staircase to the exit of the apartment block. The cold hits my face and I see my breath. I pull up the BRIXMIS issued scarf around my head. I have a pang of sadness when I notice that Heidi's Zündapp has gone from the bike rack at the entrance to the block.

It's just on eight o'clock, still fully dark and a light powdery snow is falling. I decide I mustn't hang around. I need to get well clear of the Neubert's apartment area. The problem is, I've absolutely no idea which way to go. I need to occupy about ten hours in this city doing something - heaven only knows what. I realise I am totally untrained for this kind of work. I need to try to fit in and look natural as if I know what I'm doing and where I'm going. Not easy when I haven't got a fucking clue!

I'm in a small street which doesn't seem to have a name. I can't see one anyway. The last snowfall has mostly been cleared but piled up on the sides of the road and frozen over again. I find I'm walking on a surface of hard impacted snow. I walk up the road and soon find myself at a junction with a larger street running at right angles. I notice it has a tramline running down the middle of the roadway. Should I turn left or right? I have no idea. For some reason, I decide to turn right and set off I know not where! On this road, there is a steady stream of traffic, mostly the two stroke Trabants, farting along noisily. Then I'm also passed by a few of the bigger Wartburgs, also with their two stroke engines but slightly smarter and less obnoxious than the Trabbies. There are also a few vans and trucks.

I notice that most of the traffic is passing me rather than coming towards me. I wonder if this could mean that most of the occupants are on their way to work, either to businesses in Pankow or to reach the U and S-Bahn transport systems. I latch on to this idea and decide to keep going in this direction, reasoning that it could take me to the centre of town. From there, I'd have options and it should also be easier to lose myself in the middle of a busy town. I notice a tram coming towards me and I peer through the gloom at the sign on the front as it passes. I can't quite make it out but I think it reads "Heinersdorf". That doesn't mean anything to me so I keep plodding along. Some short time later, I hear the clanking of another tram, this one behind me going in my direction. As it approaches I turn to look at the sign on the front. I think it reads "Pankow Centrum". I reckon I'm heading in the right direction.

Slowly it's getting lighter at the start of another cold drab day in East Berlin. The snow has stopped but it's just as cold. I trudge on in the same direction and soon pass a tram station with a queue forming up waiting for the next tram. It's tempting to line up behind them. I've got plenty of Ost marks in my pocket but I don't know the system of how to buy a ticket. I'd only draw attention to myself if I ask someone or try to pay the driver when, for all I know, that's not the system. So, I press on again.

I come to another large intersection and notice the tram tracks veer off onto another road on the right. I take this road following the tracks. At the junction there's a signpost. It reads, "Pankow Centrum 3kms". So now I know for sure that I'm on the right track. I think it would be a relief to get out of the cold and take the tram but I've got all day and I decide it's better to play safe by walking.

Gradually I find myself passing more buildings. There's more traffic and I feel I must be approaching the town centre. So far, most of the buildings have been of the grey square slab variety, the majority I suppose having been erected during the past forty years of communist rule but as I reach the town centre, I pass some more substantial elegant older buildings. One in particular stands out. It has a sign in front it saying it is the Gymnasium Pankow. I now feel I'm reaching my first destination. Another tram passes me and turns into a station terminus of sorts and I see all the occupants getting off. We are now in a big square and I see up ahead the terminal building of what is clearly the Pankow's main rail station.

It's taken me just over an hour to walk here. Despite the exercise, I'm cold and I'm also hungry. Next to the station I see a building which appears to be a mix of a café and waiting room for the station. I decide to chance it, get out of the cold for a while and see if I can get something to eat and drink while I work out what to do next. It's quite crowded inside and smells of stale food and sweat. I join a queue that has formed up at the bar. I watch what the customers ahead of me are ordering and notice the favourite seems to be soup and black coffee. That suits me fine. I listen hard to the precise words used to order and to pay and when my turn comes I mumble the same as the guy who was in front of me.

I take my purchases and a plastic spoon on a small tray and en route to a table, I see a box containing leaflets with the routes of the Bahn network. I take one and then pick my way carefully through the crowds to a seat which has just been vacated. First I try the soup which somewhat to my surprise is hot and very pleasant. It's bearably warm in here and I'm beginning to relax while I study the rail network. I see Pankow is shown as having three stations, there's Vinestrasse, Pankow central, which I suppose is where we are now and, just to confuse me, I see the third is called Pankow - Heinersdorf. So now I realise that had I turned left instead of right at the road when I first hit the tramlines, I would have got to a rail station anyway. And it looks to be much closer than Pankow central – I could have saved myself the long trek all this way – too late now!

I see that Pankow central is on an S-Bahn network and with a change of trains after some five stops, I can get to Lichtenberg. From there, I should be able to find the meeting rendezvous. It also occurs to me that riding on the metro would give me a good means of using up the day while keeping moving and also out of the cold. I'm feeling better already. My next concern though is to try to work out how tickets are bought for the train. I think I'll have to watch very carefully what others do then try to copy them.

I'm still refining my route planning when I'm brought back into the present by a guy who has now found a seat next to me. He's a skinny fellow, with round pebble glasses. He's wearing mittens and holding out an unlit cigarette towards me. He asks, "*Hast Du Feuer*?" I try to remain nonchalant and I tell him, "No, I don't smoke, sorry." This doesn't put him off and he seems intent on starting up a conversation. I try to give noncommittal answers to his continuing questions but he doesn't stop. He then asks me what I thought of the football last night. I don't have a clue what he's on about but from his remarks I gather the DDR played some international match which hadn't gone well. I tell him I didn't watch the game but I realise I'm on a loser here. I can speak quite good German but I was taught at the language school in Mühlheim/Ruhr and I'm struggling to follow this guy's thick Berlin accent. He detects I'm not German and asks me where I'm from. This is bad. In fact, it's exactly the situation I was hoping to avoid. So much for my aim of remaining anonymous throughout the day! I know there's no future in trying to bluff this guy with a pseudo cover story. It simply won't work. I decide I've got to get out of here. I pretend to check my watch and indicate I'm late for my train.

I get up, bid him a quick, *"Auf Wiedersehen"* and leave the café. I go straight to the entrance to the platform and look around to see how I should pay. I can't see a conventional ticket office or hatch as per most of the metro systems I'm used to in the West. I glance round and think I see my chatty table neighbour has also left the café and is up behind me. I decide to abort trying to buy a ticket and get behind the short queue waiting to get onto the platform. There is barrier but it has an opening in it where passengers are filing through. I don't see any official checking tickets so I go through amidst the flow of the other passengers as a train pulls up at the platform. I get aboard, the doors close and we're away. As we pull out of the station, I can see my nosey neighbour watching. I have to assume he'll go directly to inform the Stasi.

It occurs to me that I didn't check the direction of travel of this S-Bahn train. We could as easily be heading North back towards the Heinersdorf station instead of south towards the centre of Berlin. If the former, I would be right back near where I had started out and I could find a Stasi reception committee waiting for me there.

The S-Bahn slows as we enter a station. To my relief, I see the name Schönhauser Allee on the station board. At least we are indeed heading south towards the city. The doors open, some people get off, even more get on. I check for officialdom, police or military uniforms. I see none but I realise Stasi probably operate in plain clothes anyway so I'm none the wiser. I decide to sit quietly and try to let a few stations get between me and Pankow. I'm confident we're now heading in towards the centre of East Berlin and I hope there's more chance I can lose myself among the Berlin city crowds. The doors close and we're off again.

I check my network chart. I see I could have got off this train at the last station and taken a U-Bahn line down to Alexander Platz. I've never been there but from what I've read and heard, it's one of the main squares in East Berlin and the most cosmopolitan. I think I could well hole up there until my meeting this evening.

The train stops again, this time at Prenzlauer Allee, confirming the network plan is accurate. I stay put and we're off again. The seating is arranged with all passengers facing in towards the centre. There's an old gentleman sitting on my right who was there when I got on at Pankow Central. He is engrossed in his newspaper and seems well settled for a long ride. On my left, the occupant has already changed. A young teenage boy had been there when I got on at Pankow. He left at Schönhauser Allee and his place is now taken by a large woman who smells of smoke and garlic. She is clutching a bag of something on her lap – perhaps it's full of garlic hence the smell! Neither seem the slightest bit interested in me or, to my relief, to engage me in conversation. Opposite are a mix of passengers who seem to be going about their routine business.

I think I'm in the clear for now. But if I'm right in thinking the guy who gave me the third degree at Pankow is a Stasi informer, he would have phoned in and reported me straightaway and that I was on the S-Bahn heading south. I've no idea how quick the Stasi network is to react or how high a priority I would be. But based on the recent shooting of the two CIA guys and the reports from Heidi and her colleagues of Stasi extreme nervousness particularly following the Gorbachev speech, it seems likely the authorities will want to know all about a guy who speaks German with a foreign accent and acted as I did at Pankow. I decide I need to change trains soon. I see from the network plan that in four more stops we will reach Frankfurter Allee and that there I can change to an S-Bahn line and take that to backtrack through to Alexander Platz.

I tick off the next three stops – Ernst-Thälmann-Park, Leninalle and Storkower Strasse, all activity there seems routine. We slow to a stop again and I'm ready to move as we pull into Frankfurter Allee station. I wait for a few people to get off before me then, trying to act casually, I get up and leave the carriage. The doors close behind me and the train pulls away. I see the signs for the U-Bahn lines and make my way there. This time I check carefully my intended direction of travel. One way, the end of the line is shown as Tierpark. The other is shown to end at Thälmannplatz and it routes through Alexander Platz. I decide to take that line.

I join the queues for the S-Bahn, direction Thälmannplatz, and a train quickly arrives. I'm impressed by the speed and efficiency of the system. The carriage I'm in is crowded and I, with several others, have to stand. I like that – less chance of conversation! I tick off the five next stops and prepare to get off at the following one, which I'm relieved is indeed Alexander Platz. I join a jostling crowd who are also getting off at this station.

With the crowd around me, I emerge out of the S-Bahn station and arrive almost directly in to a vast pedestrian zone. Looming up ahead is the enormous Ferneshturm TV tower. Around the square are a collection of shops, centred by a large department store called "*Centrum Warenhaus*". This seems to be the closest the DRR can come up with to a Shopping Mall in the West but it lacks colour, style and originality. I walk around the giant square wondering how best to spend my time as I'm again back into the cold bleak Berlin winter chill. I see a group of people gathered in one area and go over to see what's there. It seems to be some sort of meeting place centred on a large monument. On it, there's a sign which reads, "*Brunnen der Völkerfreundshaft* – fountain of Friendship amongst Peoples". I continue my wanderings and come across a building called "Press Café" on the side of which is a giant mural displaying a Marxist view of the Press.

I'm still in the open and the chill factor is again setting in. I look for somewhere to get out of the cold and chance upon a museum. I don't really care what it's displaying provided there's some heating inside. I find this place is called the Hanf Museum and it traces the origins of the agriculture, manufacturing and use of hemp. Entrance is free. As I go from stand to stand I find it genuinely interesting, a useful filler of my day and a chance to get out of the biting cold.

After an hour of learning all there is to know about hemp, I decide I'd better leave the Museum or I would be causing suspicion there. Already I can see that one of the curator staff is showing an interest in my tour. I don't trust another café and being subjected to a grilling like in Pankow. So I guess it's back to Bahn riding to fill in my time and keep warm. I pass by a bookshop en route back to the metro station and spend a while looking for a book that I can use as a prop while I'm travelling on the Bahn. I pick a turgid tomb about Marxism, hoping no-one in the Bahn will want to quiz me about it.

I consult my network plan again and see that there's a straight run on an S-Bahn line connecting Alexander Platz to my evening destination of Lichtenberg. But that will take only a few minutes. I plan to get there at about five o'clock to give myself an hour to find the rendezvous. I don't want to be hanging around there too long and arouse suspicion. It's now only two o'clock, meaning I still have some three hours to use up. I also reckon that I'm probably being over cautious. I do believe the guy at Pankow was a Stasi informer and would have reported me in. But if the Stasi had decided to follow up and arrest me for questioning, surely they would have intercepted the S-Bahn I was on earlier. And nothing happened. Anyway, I can't think what the informer could have told them about me that would have been of much long-term interest to the Stasi.

I go back to the Bahn station and immediately see a ticket office. There must have been one like that at Pankow but in my haste, I didn't spot it. I queue and buy my ticket routinely and move through to the platforms. I decide to take the S-Bahn line heading towards Lichtenberg but to change at Ostkreuz and head off towards Adlershof. Why? Why not? It will fill in some time. I'm feeling more relaxed now. I understand how the S and U-Bahn systems work, I've had no further interest shown in me, I've not had anyone making conversation and at last I'm tolerably warm.

I'm jolted out of my complacency when the train stops at Baumschulenweg soon after I've changed at

Ostkreuz. I see there are armed men on the platform. They are wearing the grey uniforms which could be from the East German National Army, NVA or from the Stasi military arm that Frederik had described last evening. I have no idea, only that they are serious and that our train is to be searched. I can see train police getting into a carriage further up from mine. They are escorted by a couple of armed guys in these grey uniforms. I remain in my seat and try to keep composed. There's nothing else to do but wait. The carriages of our S-Bahn train have remained shut and the train police open each in turn to enable the search to be made. My seat is adjacent to a door but this remains firmly closed.

The search team moves to the next carriage up from mine and I can see the station police use a spanner like tool to open the door from the outside. I see them enter the carriage with the armed escort but I can't see what they're doing as they are out of my line of vision. They are taking their time to inspect each carriage and seemingly doing a very thorough job. I have nothing incriminating on me, only the Bahn network plan and the small-scale map of East Berlin. And I have my British passport and the entry visa that Ed and I obtained when we came over to the East yesterday. I hope maybe they'll be satisfied that I'm just an ordinary tourist.

I see the search team, which is all male, leaving the previous carriage and locking the door closed behind them. They do not seem to have made any arrests. I tell myself to keep calm. Perhaps this is just a routine spot check that the authorities carry out from time to time. I see them coming up to our carriage. The station police chief takes out the spanner tool and inserts it into the outer lock. He turns it and our carriage door slides open. One soldier guards the door entrance while the other escorts the station police. They begin at the top end of the carriage. Each passenger is required to stand up, produce their identity document and state their business. Our carriage is half full. The search team is very methodical and they slowly work their way down to the middle of the carriage where I am sitting. I watch the procedure. Each passenger duly complies and produces his or her documentation. The police pick the odd individual and carry out a body search. No woman is searched.

Now it is my turn. I show my British passport and the visa document and when asked, I say I am here as a tourist. I say I've always wondered how life is in the DDR and this is an opportunity to find out. The chief police officer does not look convinced. He tells me to put my hands behind my back. I glance down and see he is holding a document. To my horror, I recognise the photo on the document. It's a copy of **my** passport photo. I also see one of the guards is holding a pair of handcuffs and is preparing to fit them on me.

I have no choice. I turn around, grab hold of the chief guard by his shoulders and propel him directly at his soldier escort. I push him as hard as I can so that both are rammed against the side of the carriage and into the path of the guard at the entrance. The heavy jolt causes the entrance guard to drop his weapon. Now I'm on the move. I leap out of the open carriage door and make for the station exit. I can see the remaining soldiers on the platform beginning to react but I'm already on them. By now I've built up a good momentum and I charge into the two guards at the station exit at full speed and slip between them. By the time they can turn and fire, I'm already away. I run at full pace up a road leading from the station, then I see a smaller road leading to an apartment block. I slow to walking pace and listen. There's no one following.

I'm clear for now but I know this is temporary. For reasons I don't understand, the Stasi have my details and it seems I'm a prime target. I know the name of this station but I don't have a clue about the area. I only know that it won't be long before the Stasi organise themselves and come to hunt me down.

Chapter Twenty

It won't take them long to get a serious hunt going. I'll be an easy target out here in the open. It's still just light but already the winter gloom is closing in. I have no knowledge of the area and no support out here. Anyone who sees me and hears about the search is likely to contact the Stasi. I desperately need to find some cover – somewhere to hide up until I can make sense of why the Stasi seem to have targeted me so specifically.

I force myself to keep walking at a normal pace, trying to keep roughly parallel to the line of the S-Bahn track. I find I'm in an area of mixed housing and industrial buildings. Up ahead I see a row of large storehouses. One has a sign saying *"Möbelgeschäft"* – furniture store. As I get level to it, I see a large furniture truck pulling out from an open door of the store. The driver pulls forward so that his long vehicle is well clear of the door. I see my chance there and slip in through the vehicle door into the dark interior. Moments later the driver appears on foot, slams the door shut and I hear him turning the lock. I wait inside quietly until I hear the sound of the driver engaging gear and driving off.

It's pitch black in here and I can't see a thing. I wait for my eyes to grow accustomed to the dark and gradually I can see the outline of the interior of the store and that it is full of rows of mattresses and bedding. I wryly tell myself I could sleep in great comfort here! And at least I've bought myself some time, hoping that the Stasi won't think to look for me here – just yet.

I search around for a light and find a switch near the door which has just been closed. I grab a thick duvet from a pile on one of the rows of racking and push it in between one of the mattresses near the top of the rows. I go back and turn out the light then return again to the racking. I stumble to feel my way to where I have lodged the duvet and slide under it, hidden by the mattresses. The duvet acts as a buffer to prevent me from being suffocated under the weight of the mattresses. I tell myself it'll make a good temporary hiding place and at least I will be warm while I try to work out what to do.

There's the sudden sound of cars and sirens near by the storehouse I'm hiding in. Then I hear voices with someone shouting out orders. It sounds like the Stasi have got their act together and a serious search is under way. They know I'm on foot and that I couldn't have outside help, so they must have decided to make a detailed search of this local area. I know my only chance now is to wait it out. I don't think they'll search through all these storehouses.

But I'm wrong. I hear orders being shouted out and the sound of an industrial door being slid open. It sounds like it's coming from the adjacent store to the one I'm in. I can hear several voices and I visualise a team of searchers going methodically through the storehouse.

After some minutes, I can hear someone call out, *"Alles klar. Er ist nicht hier."*

Now the team of searchers moves to the storehouse where I'm hiding. I hear the sound of a bunch of keys being examined and then one being inserted into the lock of the main vehicle door. The Stasi must have commandeered all the keys from the storehouse proprietor. The door opens. I have squeezed myself deep down between two mattresses high up on the racking. It's the best I can do and I can only hope it's not conspicuous. The search team is thorough. I hear their footsteps as they take their time to walk slowly down the rows of racking checking the contents of each rack. One of the searchers comes close to where I'm hiding. I can hear his breathing and the flashing light from his torch as he moves it from side to side. He stops right next to where I'm hiding and I hold my breath hoping that an end of the duvet isn't showing. Then I hear a voice from somewhere further down the storehouse saying. *"Kommen Sie Wolfgang, wir müssen in Bewegung bleiben"*. Slowly the searcher next to me starts moving again and I hear his footsteps carrying on down the row of racking. Then I hear the team of searchers returning to the entrance door. One calls out, *"Alles klar!"* the door is slid shut and I hear the key turned in the lock. I allow myself to let out a long sigh of relief. At least I'm still clear.

I check my watch and see it's now just after half past three. I need to be in Lichtenberg by five or soon after in order to locate the rendezvous point by six. But I'm stuck here and if I try to make a move, I'm bound to be spotted easily. Even if I do evade their search, I don't know the way and I reckon I'm a good ten kilometres from Lichtenberg. There's no way I could make it on foot in time. I consider alternatives, perhaps a bus or tram. I didn't notice a tramline on the road by the Bahn station but that doesn't mean there isn't one nearby. It would be logical that there's either a tram or bus as well as the Bahn leading into the city centre but I have no way of knowing for sure.

My best bet would seem to be to take a chance on the Bahn again. If I can get back to the Ostkreuz station, my network plan shows me I can change there back onto the line coming from Alexander Platz that I was on earlier. From there, Lichtenberg station is only couple of stops further down that line.

I stay hidden in my mattress cover for some minutes. The voices of the searches get fainter as they continue looking through the rest of the store complex. Then I hear the sound of the slamming of vehicle doors, engines revving and the vehicles driving off. I stay where I am for another fifteen minutes or so. Silence.

I can't afford to wait here much longer if I'm to have any hope of getting to Lichtenberg on time. My next decision is whether I can chance going back to the Baumschulenweg station where the Bahn police check had been made. That station is only a short distance from here. Problem there is that my somewhat dramatic escape would have been witnessed by station staff and they could well identify me if I go back there.

Alternatively, I could back track to the previous station on the line and see if I can pick up the Bahn there to get to Ostkeuz. My network plan tells me the station is called Plänterwald. The staff there wouldn't have seen me as we had passed through that station earlier. I have to make a decision and get going. I decide to plump for the Plänterwald option.

It's tough extracting myself from the warmth of my mattress nest. I could have holed up here for the night. But I know I don't have that luxury, there's no choice. I get down from the racking and go over to the entrance to the storehouse. Although the vehicle door is locked from the outside, I had earlier noticed that there's a personnel door next to it which has a spring lock that can be opened from the inside. I pull back the lock and step back out into the cold bleak winter's night. It's now completely dark. I wait and listen. There's no sign that the searchers are still in the area. The vehicles that had brought them have gone. In hindsight, I wonder why there's not a perimeter fence around these storehouses – there almost certainly would be in the West. Perhaps the "ossies" are more honest over here. It was my good fortune.

I set off along the snow lined road back in the direction of central Berlin, trying to keep to roads that don't have too much traffic and which, as far as I can tell, run roughly parallel to the line of the Bahn. My muscles seem to have stiffened up during my enforced rest among the mattresses and I struggle to get back into a walking rhythm. Then there's my feet. I am delighted with the boots I got from the BRIXMIS quartermaster. They're warm and fit me well. But I've been wearing them continuously all day and they're not yet worn into the shape of my feet. I can feel the start of a blister forming on my right heel and my left big toe keeps on stubbing into the top of the boot. But these are the least of my worries as I seem to be getting further away from the main route leading to the next station.

I don't know how long I'm walking and the sameness of the piled-up snow makes it difficult to know my direction. The road I'm now on is quiet and I seem to be the only pedestrian. I keep my head well down and my scarf pulled round my head and hope I don't attract the attention of the few cars that are passing. I hope my posture would be taken as natural for anyone walking out here in the cold.

At last I come to a road junction and to my relief see an S-Bahn sign with an arrow pointing down a road leading off to my right. It doesn't give any details of place or distance. I don't care. I know I'm heading in the right direction so I follow this road. Now, there are more pedestrians about and most are heading in the same direction. I follow on and soon I see the station up ahead.

It has a big S-Bahn sign and words "Plänterwald". I've reached my destination.

The station is busy. A train coming from central Berlin is just pulling up at the platform and I watch as a mass of commuters get out and head for the exit. I take the chance of this exodus to slip into the station hoping that the next train heading back towards Ostkreuz will arrive soon. I look around at the group of travellers waiting for the same train so I line up with them. As far as I can tell, there are no police or obvious Stasi personnel around.

Then it all changes. I hear a vehicle pulling up outside the station, then a group of uniformed and armed men push their way into the station and head directly for the platform. They seem to be looking for one particular passenger. Instinctively I know that passenger is me. I think to myself, "Here we go again!"

There's no future in lining up with the other passengers and trying to pass myself off as the innocent tourist. It didn't work the last time and I know it won't this time either. So yet again I have to make a run for it. I ease out of the queue and try to blend in with some of the passengers from the previous train who are on their way out of the station. I get to the station exit and pass through. I begin to think I'm clear when I hear a shout behind me, *"Das ist er, das ist der Mann,"* I break into a run and try to put distance between me and my pursuers. But this time, their reaction is much quicker than at the Baumschulenweg station. I can hear at least two or three guys giving chase. I gear up into a sprint and head for an area where I can see a development of large apartment blocks. My lungs are struggling to cope with my laboured breathing in the freezing air. I'm still in good shape and pride myself on my fitness level. But I not winning this footrace and I fear I'm being chased by men who are younger and fitter than me. I might be able to wear them down over a long distance but I don't have that luxury right now as I hear them steadily closing down the space between us.

I'm now in among the apartment blocks and as I turn a sharp corner I'm momentarily out of their view. I pick at random a doorway entrance to one of the apartment blocks and slip inside the dark entrance lobby. There's no real place there to hide but it's dark and similar to the other apartment buildings. I crouch down trying to conceal myself as well as I can behind a rubbish bin at the foot of the stairwell. I try to slow my rasping breath. I watch as my pursuers turn the corner and come into my view. I see they are young, maybe all in their twenties but I can't really tell in the dark. They realise I am no longer running on ahead of them so they pull up and stop close to my unsatisfactory hiding place. They seem determined and professional. Also, I can see they are all armed with pistols.

The pursuers have a quick debate among themselves, then one of them, presumably their leader, decides that I must still be in this area. They are correct!! He directs the other two to start checking the other blocks while he searches the building that I'm in. If I stay where I am, he'll be bound to see me. I'll have no chance. I get to my feet and as stealthily as I can I climb up the steps in the stairwell. I know he will soon follow. He has a gun, I don't.

The stairwell is dark and I see no sign of a light switch. I continue up the stairwell steps. On the first landing, there are doors to individual apartments. All these doors are closed. I can see the flashing light of my pursuer as he starts to climb up behind me. I carry on again up the stairs to the next landing. Up ahead, I see a lady with a child's pushchair. She has just opened the door to her apartment and has turned to bring in her child's pushchair. I see this as my only chance available. I reach the door, push the child's chair into the room, step inside myself and hastily close and door behind me.

"Was machen Sie da?" she exclaims. Her child is crying. She is a little girl of about three or four years old. It's no wonder she's frightened. The mother looks to be in her late twenties but I can't see her features as both mother and daughter are still well wrapped up in their protective winter clothes. I desperately want to avoid the mother from screaming out so I reckon it's best if I tell her the truth, or at least to explain why I'm here."

"Ich bitte Sie, mir zu verzeihen. Ich werde von der Stasi verfolgt. Sie sind draussen. Sorry to disturb you. I'm running from the Stasi. They are just outside."

This is a critical moment. The woman looks scared, then angry, then if, as I hope, I'm reading her expression correctly, she softens. Then she asks:

"What have you done? Are you a criminal? Did you kill someone?"

"No, I've killed no one. But I've upset the authorities and the Stasi want to capture me and take me for questioning. All I ask is that I can stay here until they go away. Then I will leave you and your daughter in peace."

My explanation seems to satisfy the woman - for now. She bends down and undoes the retaining strapping on the child's pushchair. She then picks up the little girl, holds her to her chest, pulls down her fur bonnet and strokes her hair. She says soothingly to her daughter,

"It's OK, my darling, the man won't hurt us." She then lowers her to the floor and proceeds to undo the child's thick topcoat. The child sits on the floor and mother and daughter together pull off her fur boots. I take this gesture as a sign of confidence that she's not going to rush off to report me to the Stasi.

Emerging from all her winter top-wear is a pretty little girl. She has now stopped crying. I look around the apartment. It's small, which seems to be standard for East Berlin but well-kept and clean. The woman then proceeds to unwrap herself from her heavy outer clothing and I can now see she is a slim attractive woman. She has good features and her blonde hair is plaited and tied up around her head. I can tell she is still nervous but trying to adjust and be sociable.

"My name is Inge Schultz," she says, "and this is my daughter Beatrice. She's four years old."

I reply in a formal tone, "I am Peter. I'm pleased to meet you Frau Schultz but I would have wished it would have been in more fortunate circumstances." I then lean down and shake little Beatrice's hand and tell her, "And I'm pleased to meet you too, Beatrice. I hope we will be friends." The little girl looks up at me with her clear blue eyes. She just smiles and nods. That's enough for me.

Inge Schultz continues, "You speak German, Herr Peter but you don't have a German accent. Where are you from?"

"I'm British and unfortunately have a visa problem. That's why the Stasi are after me." Not fully the truth but it'll have to do.

"Yes, they can be swines and they never give up. My husband will be home soon and I know he will understand your situation. Meanwhile why don't you take off your coat? We manage to keep ourselves quite warm in here."

Inge is turning out to be very sympathetic but I can't afford to trust her. So, I stay close to the door just in case. I'm pleased to see her curtains are fully drawn and the telephone is on a small table close to the window. I decide to take off my scarf and open out my coat but I keep it on as I can't relax. I've no idea what's happening to the Stasi hunt and I may need to move quickly again.

Meanwhile, Inge busies herself around the apartment. I hear the sound of a kettle boiling and she soon appears with a cup of coffee and a plate of sausage and potatoes. I accept her kind gesture with much pleasure as I realise this is the first food I've had since the soup at Pankow this morning.

I jump at the sound of a key being turned in the front door behind me and I brace myself. A man enters. Like everyone here, he's wrapped up in winter clothing. As we come face to face, I can see the predictable hostility in his face but Inge intervenes immediately.

"It OK, Hermann, this gentleman has asked for shelter for a while. He's a British man and is being chased by the Stasi. I told him he could stay."

Her husband reacts with commendable nerve. He looks me up and down, then at his wife and daughter. He then relaxes and shakes my hand.

"Hermann Schultz," he says, introducing himself. "I've just walked through a gauntlet of them myself as I was coming home just now. I wondered what poor blighter they were after. They gave me the third degree and I had to show my ID and proof that I live here before they let me through."

I realise these are good people. I even have thoughts that I might persuade Herr Schultz to drive me to Lichtenberg.

Then the situation changes again. We hear the sound of more vehicles arriving outside the apartment block.

Then a voice using a loudspeaker cuts through the winter air.

"Attention. Attention. There is a dangerous man hiding in this apartment block. All residents are to open their doors while we conduct a search for this man. Anyone caught sheltering or helping him will be arrested. The search will begin immediately."

I looked across at Herr Schultz, his wife and his little daughter and I realise this is the end of the road for me. They are good people. Even if they were to try to assist me, I could not accept that. This is my problem. No one else's. There is no way I can escape and there's no way I can rendezvous with Heidi in Lichtenberg this evening. There are no rabbits to be pulled out of the hat.

I quickly shake the hands of both Herr and Frau Schultz, button up my coat and wrap my scarf round my head. I go out of the door and walk back down the stairs. As I'm descending the last flight, the flashlight from a powerful torch shines on me. I raise my hands and advance slowly towards the light. Two uniformed men come out of the gloom and roughly pull me to the entrance of the apartment block. Then my hands are forced behind my back and a pair of cufflinks are attached. This is it. I am now a prisoner of the Stasi.

Chapter Twenty-One

Suddenly I am surrounded by a squad of soldiers. I don't know what force they're from, whether the DDR national NVA army or the uniformed Stasi. I suspect the latter. I am unarmed, handcuffed and defenceless. That doesn't stop one of them from coming up to me and punching me hard in the stomach. I think he wants to hit me again but his superior warns him off. I still don't understand why I have been singled out as such a major target. Since the skinny guy back in Pankow early this morning, the authorities seem to have devoted major resources to hunt me down. Well, now they have succeeded.

No one speaks to me, but I can sense the soldiers' satisfaction that they have successfully achieved their mission of my capture. I also realise that they had plenty of opportunities to have shot at me but no one has fired. I don't know why they didn't fire. Perhaps I am going to find out.

A vehicle is driven up near to where we are standing. It looks like a conventional food or vegetable delivery van. The back is opened up and I am force marched up towards it. I am pushed up inside and find that the interior has been reconfigured to consist of a number of small cells. My guards roughly push me into one of these cells and slam the inner door shut. I can't stand up straight and there is nothing to sit on. I am totally cramped up. There are no windows and all I can see is blackness.

The vehicle starts up, grinds a gear into place and we move off. I remain wedged into this small space, unable to move into a reasonable position. The roof above me seems to be pressing down on my head, the space around me is too small for me either to turn or to slouch down into a sitting position. I am stuck. I am unable to straighten up, to turn or to move.

The vehicle grinds along sometimes in a relatively smooth rhythm as the driver holds his top gear, at other times we lurch around as he double de-clutches through his gears, jerks and stop/starts I assume through city traffic. I have no idea where we might be going and I lose all sense of time.

I try to fight off my growing sense of claustrophobia. I feel like I'm in a coffin and can't break free. I try to control myself but feel I'm beginning to lose it. I remember the only other time in my life before when I had experienced claustrophobia like this. It was during Special Forces army training. As part of our tests, we had to go into a small road culvert pushing our packs and rifle in front of us. The culvert had water flowing through it and as we pushed forward, our equipment and our bodies formed a dam which built up around us.

The water level rose up to the point where there was only a small gap of air left below the top of the culvert. I remember then having to get a grip of mind over body and to keep crawling slowly on. Then eventually, we reached the end of the culvert and emerged out into the open. Somehow I had passed that test then. Now I must try to get into the same mind-set.

Easy to think, more difficult to do. I am feeling on the point of utter desperation when the vehicle finally grounds to a halt. I hear shouting and then the sound of gates opening, we move forward a short distance and then we stop again. Another gate, another move forward and finally another stop. By then I am in some sort of mental limbo.

I hear shouting and the back of the van is opened. Someone gets in, moves up to my cell and opens the door. I am pulled out, bundled into some building and manhandled along a dark corridor. My body has been so constricted during the time of the drive here that I struggle to get back the use of my limbs. I am roughly pushed into a cell. My handcuffs are taken off me and the door is slammed shut behind me. I try to get my bearings but have no control over my thoughts. The only thing I do register is that I am now a prisoner of the Stasi. Beyond that, I cannot begin to think rationally.

I look around my cell and realise I am the only inhabitant. It is clean but smells of heavy disinfectant. It consists of a small cot bed, a lino floor, washbasin and tap, a small mirror and a chemical toilet. On the floor is a low stool. The ceiling is high and in one corner I see a window but this is fitted with opaque glass block. The overall colour scheme in the cell is brown - brown lino floor, brown painted walls, just about brown everything.

When I had first been arrested at the apartment block back in Plänterwald, I had been body searched for a weapon. They found none. Later, when I was pushed into this cell, the handcuffs had been removed. Now I'm surprised to find that I still have my passport, visa and both West and Ost marks. I also still have all my winter clothes so, although there doesn't seem to be any heating in the cell, at least I feel reasonably warm. I go through a series of stretching exercises trying to get the circulation back into my body.

I can only have been in the cell for about ten minutes when the door opens again and two guards come in. They put the handcuffs back on and frog march me out of the cell and along the dark gloomy corridor. I notice there is a bright red overhead light flashing. Occasionally we pass by other prisoners but each of these has been made by their guards to stop and face towards the walls of the corridor. They cannot see my face and I cannot see theirs.

After shuffling along the corridors for some time, the guards bring me to a stop outside another door. They knock and a voice from inside tells them to enter. I am pushed into the room and forced to sit on a small stool, low to the ground. My handcuffs are removed and the two guards take position just behind me and to either side. In front of me is a desk and behind that sits a man dressed in the uniform of a Stasi officer. He is clean shaven and looks as if he's just come out of the shower. I can smell the aroma of strong aftershave. I think his rank insignia is that of a colonel but I expect he's going to tell me. He is writing some sort of report and we wait for him to finish. No one speaks.

After a wait of perhaps fifteen minutes, the Stasi officer caps his ink fountain pen and ceremoniously places it on a stand on the side of his desk. All very theatrical, I'm thinking. I suppose I should be impressed.

He doesn't yet speak to me but he tells the guards. "*Ihre Papiere*!" The guards rough body search me again and produce all I have – my passport, the temporary visa, the East Berlin map (happily with no markings on it), the U and S-Bahn network plan and my West and East mark notes. A guard takes my precious belongings plus my watch over to the officer then resumes his position behind my back. The officer looks at my papers as if with distaste. I notice that his desk is positioned significantly higher than the stool I'm required to sit on – all I suppose designed to give the interrogator (who I presume he is) a sense of superiority. Again, there's a long silence before the officer at last deigns to speak directly to me.

"*Ich bin Oberst Albert Weber. Und Sie sind…?*" He makes a show of referring to my passport. "*Sie sind Herr*

Peter Chambers, ein britischer Staatsbürger. Ist das richtig?' You are Mr Peter Chambers, a British subject - correct?"

I nod my head. I am determined to make this Colonel Weber make the pace. I hope at last to discover why it is I am such a high priority for the Stasi.

The Colonel continues, *"Ich habe Ihnen eine Frage gestellt. Ich brauche eine vernüftige Antwort. Ein Kopfnicken ist nicht ausreichend.* I asked you a question. You are Mr Peter Chambers, a British subject - correct? I need you to say it in words. I do not recognise a nod of your head."

I try again and this time say, *"Ja, Oberst Weber. Ich bin Peter Chambers, ein britischer Staatsbürger.*

"That's better. And I see you can speak our German language well. However, this is a good chance for me to practice my English so we will carry on in that language."

Strange, I'm thinking, I would have thought we would continue in German to keep me at a disadvantage. Perhaps he's just conceited and wants to show off, especially in front of the guards. That's fine by me.

"Mr Chambers, why did you come to the DDR yesterday?"

I stick to the story I gave earlier, "I was visiting West Berlin and had some free time. I had always wanted to see a little of the east of the city, so I came over yesterday. It was just to do some sightseeing"

"What is the nature of your business in West Germany?"

"I was doing some work in the British zone?

"What kind of work?"

I can tell that in the few short questions, I'm already pushed to give a convincing answer. I have no cover story which might be credible. I know it and clearly Colonel Weber also knows it.

He waits for me to answer and he can see I'm struggling to think of something plausible. I can tell he's enjoying seeing my struggle. Then he says:

"Let's stop playing games. Right now! I know full well that you're not **Mr** Peter Chambers but **Colonel** Peter Chambers. And that your dear travel colleague **Mr** Edward Morgan is an operative of the American CIA."

I have no idea how he knows my and Ed's background, but I do know there's no point in trying to bluff this guy. I've just got to see where this goes.

Colonel Weber continues, "So, to start again. Colonel Chambers, why are you in East Berlin?" I know I must stick to one story alone. I know Colonel Weber won't believe me and will continue to push and probe.

I answer as before, "I just wanted to do some sightseeing here."

"Oh yes! And what sights have you seen?"

As chance would have it, I can answer this question honestly. I tell him about my visit to Alexander Platz and all that I had visited there. But that doesn't satisfy him.

"Yes, that was for a part of this morning. What about the rest of your time. For example, who were you with last evening and where were you last night?"

Now we're getting to it. Clearly, the Stasi have some knowledge of our meeting in Meisenweg last evening and needs names and details of our contacts. I know he will not give up with these questions until he gets his answers. Any fictional story I might invent will be checked and found to be false. It's time for me to say no more in order to avoid being tripped up and unintentionally slipping out some vital information. In the military, our training is, if taken prisoner of war, to give regimental number, name, date of birth and nothing more. Here of course I'm not a prisoner of war in the conventional sense and there's no Geneva Convention to protect me. But I guess anything else I say could incriminate me more, so best to shut up and see what happens.

He asks again, "Who were you with last evening and where were you last night?"

I try to appear angry, "Colonel, I am getting bored with your questions. You have told me I am a colonel in the British Army. Yes, I'm willing to confirm that. As far as I know our countries are not at war with each other. So I resent your questions and demand that you stop. We are of equal rank, you and I Colonel Weber. So let's have some equal respect!"

I'm not expecting that getting on my high horse is going to work but it was worth a try. As I thought – no dice.

"To have merited equal respect, Colonel Chambers, you should have complied with protocol and informed the agreed channels of your wish to cross to East Germany and requested a meeting with me or one of my colleagues. You did not do that. Instead you and Mr Morgan chose to slip in using a tourist visa and did not report to our authorities on your arrival."

I think to myself, he's right - so back to the drawing board!

"I ask you again, Colonel Chambers. Who were you with last evening and where were you last night?"

I don't answer. He asks again. I don't answer. He goes on with the same questions continuously for a considerable time. All this time, I am sitting on the small stool. It's short and to keep my balance I have to keep my legs raised up above my shoulders. To see my interrogator, I have to look sharply upwards. Apart from putting my interrogator and me in a constant configuration of superiority and inferiority, the position is extremely tiring and painful. My interrogator knows all this only too well and is using this advantage to wear me down. I try to put my mind into neutral and to keep my silence no matter how repetitive the questions are.

After some long time, even Colonel Weber appeared to become bored. Suddenly he changes tack. "I will tell you a little more about yourself, Colonel Chambers. I can tell you that you work in the Intelligence Division of the International Military Staff of Headquarters NATO, based in Evère, Brussels. Am I right?"

This startles me, as he knows it would. How the fucking hell does he know that? He hasn't finished.

"You might also like to know that we at Stasi HQ receive a copy of your NATO "secret" document MC161 before it is even distributed to your NATO national authorities. As you very well know, MC161 is issued by your office. It is the annual NATO agreed assessment of the Warsaw Pact Order of Battle, formations, deployments, capabilities - the lot! Indeed, we are impressed by its quality. We of course immediately send a copy to our allies in Moscow. From it, we can interpret accurately the capabilities of your intelligence services and determine how best to exploit your weaknesses."

This has stunned me as he knew it would. What he has said about the document we call MC161 is indeed classified NATO SECRET and handled within the strict rules laid down by the NATO security authorities. Clearly, there has been a major security breach occurring in our department. If ever I get out of here, I need to sort this out. I feel the interrogator is taunting me now as he continues:

"Surprised, heh? But my dear Colonel, that is just the start. And it's how we knew you and Mr Morgan were coming over to be with us here in East Berlin yesterday evening. We know the CIA have their little friends here. One of Mr Morgan's CIA chums got shot yesterday and hence your and Morgan's trip. We know you were due to meet his contacts. During the evening, we traced Ed

Morgan's Opel Corsa car and knew the meeting must have been nearby. Am I right so far?"

This is shattering that he knows so much. It also explains how the Stasi had found out about last night's meeting place. But their efforts to trace and capture me also means that they do not yet know the identity of Heidi and her group. That must be why my capture was so important to them. And hence all his questions now. He's not finished:

"You see Colonel Chambers, we East Germans have no particular grievance with you British. But we do need to be informed about the activities of our own citizens. If you tell me who you were with last evening and where you slept the night, I feel confident we can find a way to let you go and get back to your lovely wife Ann and your two delightful children Chloe and Christian."

Again, he's throwing in his knowledge of my personal life which is disorientating as he must have known it would be. I wonder what else he knows and is holding back until later. I only know I must resist answering his key questions. I realise these guys are highly professional at extracting information and it will be impossible to hold out for ever. But I remain determined to do all I can to keep from this guy for as long as I can, details of who I met last evening and what we discussed. I hope Heidi and her colleagues will find out I've been captured and will be interrogated. I hope my resistance to answer Weber's questions will buy them enough time to disperse and reorganise.

We have now been at this interrogation for what seems like hours. I can only guess as they also took my watch. And it hasn't finished yet.

The interrogator continues with the same questions. I say nothing. The position I have to sit in becomes excruciatingly painful but each time I try to move, a guard pushes me back down.

The questions go on and on. I try again to put my mind in neutral, hoping there must eventually come a time when even the interrogator will have had enough. At last I feel his questions are beginning to lose their bite and he is tiring. He says:

"Colonel, we will break for now but I want you to understand that you will eventually answer all my questions. We've just started. The guards will take you back now and we'll meet again soon. I urge you to reflect on all that we have so far discussed. I've not asked you for any of your national secrets. We know most of them already! By telling us who you met last night will not compromise British or Western allied secrets, so your conscience will be clear. I'll see you again soon. He pauses then says:

"Oh, and Colonel Chambers, one thing while you're our guest here in our establishment. We do not use names, only numbers. Yours is: NM 061. Remember it well because from now on that is how you will be known."

With that last remark, he reverts to German and orders me to be returned to my cell.

Chapter Twenty-Two

Again, I go through this flashing red light business as I am being manhandled back to my cell. When I pass others in the dingy corridor they have all turned in towards the walls. I suppose it's because the Stasi authorities here want to ensure that no one knows anyone else.

I get back to my cell. My guards remove my handcuffs but also this time they take away my parka, boots and sweater. My interrogator has told me I'm no longer an individual, just a number. I'm NM061. My watch has already been taken from me so I've no idea of the time. By my rough calculation, I reckon it's still the middle of the night, perhaps about four a.m. but that's just a guess.

My morale is fucking awful. I failed to make the Lichtenberg rendezvous and so I've lost contact with Heidi and her team. Even if I was free, I've no way of contacting them now – no address or phone number. I wonder if Ed and the others got clear last evening. I have no way of knowing. So, to summarise. My great incursion into East Berlin has achieved absolutely fuck all. In hindsight, I would have been far better off staying in the West and probably trying to mobilise the experience and skills of BRIXMIS and/or the US and French missions to follow up on the provocative reports which are causing such concern in London and Washington. I'm now also totally out of contact with Cheryl and our team back in West Berlin. There's no way they can know where I am and no way for me to contact them. So much for my mission, tasked directly by our PM. Let's face it, I tell myself, I'm really in the shit.

I feel shattered after chasing around East Berlin all day and ending up facing hours of Colonel Weber's third degree. I can achieve nothing by worrying so I decide to crash out on the cot they've provided in the cell and see what tomorrow will bring, or is it already today? I lie down on the cot and pull the thin blanket over me. As I'm on the brink of sleep, there's a loud knocking on my door and the overhead light is switched on to full power. The door opens and two guards appear. One stands to block the door, the other comes over and in rough German says:

"You are not allowed to sleep like that! You can only lie flat on your back and keep your hands outside the cover. If you don't comply, the cot will be out of bounds. Do you understand NM061?"

Fucking hell, I think, what has my life come to. But OK, just do it. I'm so tired I don't care anymore. So, as instructed, I turn around so that I'm lying flat on my back and I place my arms outside the blanket. The guard seems satisfied and I'm thinking at last they'll leave me alone and I can sleep.

But I can't sleep. Probably my mind is too active or I'm overtired or it's this fucking stupid arms outside crap. Or perhaps a mixture of all these. I suddenly realise it's already Saturday, or is it? The day I'd promised Christian I'd do my best to be there to support his rugby match. The first time he's been picked for the team and now for sure I'm going to let him down. And I've not had a decent conversation with Ann since I left for Washington last Sunday. I hope SuziB managed to call her and straighten things out. Suddenly the penny drops. SuziB, our warm and cuddly SuziB! How did the Stasi get hold of our sensitive and classified NATO document MC161? It's produced and printed under tight security but who always has access to it – SuziB of course! How did Colonel Weber know all about my family? Now I remember that I asked SuziB to call Ann and tell her I was in Berlin and hinted I might be going to the East of the city. That could be the only way the Stasi knew I was going across with Ed and that I would be meeting CIA contacts. That was why it was so important to them that I was found. It all begins to fit together. SuziB knew I was hurriedly called to London and must have had a good idea of my mission for the PM and the endorsement from Washington. I now realise she must have called her contacts and told them to track me down. It's the only thing that makes sense. When I think about it, what do any of us in our division in NATO really know about SuziB? She's been there for years and is always makes herself available and indispensable. I suppose we just all came to accept her as part of the history and legacy of the branch. We accepted she had a husband somewhere, thought to be American but I never met him and I wonder how many others in the division ever did? I've read about the Stasi "Romeo" campaign whereby personable young Stasi men are trained to target and pursue eligible single females working in sensitive Western government jobs. They would then have an affair with them and once their target has fallen in love they would turn them and recruit them to pass classified information to their Stasi lover. Now I realise that is surely the case with SuziB. And what a stupid name. How naïve we have all been!

And there's another thing. Why did Weber tell me about MC161 and that he knew all about my family? No interrogator would normally give away such detail because it could compromise the source. It's not professional and yet I found Colonel Weber to be a very determined and switched on guy. I can only think of one reason why he chose to tell me about MC 161. It's because he knows I am to be killed! But surely not until they have extracted from me the names of Heidi and her team. Apart from refusing to name them out of my loyalty to them, I now realise that my very life depends on it. I've no idea what further interrogation techniques I can expect only that I must somehow find a way of resisting Weber. Once he succeeds in cracking me, I'm history!

I think I must have eventually dropped off and got some sleep. I am awoken by the noise of someone bashing on the cell door. A tray is pushed through a trap at the bottom of it. On it is a bowl of thin soup and a piece of stale bread. I feel hungry enough to finish the lot. Shortly after, there is banging again on the cell door and I am ordered to return the tray. I can tell I'm under regular surveillance through the spy hole in the door. Despite this, I manage to have a shit in the appliance provided. When I decide to go back to the bed, I am shouted at and told it is out of bounds during the day and I am to sit on the stool. I do so wondering what the rationale is. I can only deduce that it is policy to weaken us prisoners through sleep deprivation. That seems to fit as when I close my eyes, even though I remain on the stool, there is banging on the cell door ensuring that I keep awake.

I don't know how long I am kept sitting on this fucking little stool but suddenly the cell door opens and two guards enter the room. I think they are the same two as last night but they all seem to be alike - expressionless, carrying out their orders in robotic fashion. I wonder if they have home lives, wives, children, watch football, do normal human activities. I don't think I'll ever know.

Again, the flashing red lights in the corridor, again the other prisoners we pass are all turned to face the wall. Then, once again I find myself facing Colonel Weber. This time he makes no formal introduction. I have no name as he addresses me solely as NM061. Then it's the same as last time:

"Who were you with last evening and where were you last night?"

"Who were you with last evening and where were you last night?"

"Who were you with last evening and where were you last night?"

The same questions, over and over again. I say nothing in reply. I sit there and listen to the questions as he repeats them endlessly. I don't know how long this goes on for. I try to put my mind in some sort of faraway neutral place where I can park it in storage so that I no longer have to listen to the questioning.

After a long time of enduring this, Weber tries another approach. He says, "You had the chance to think about the offer I made you last night NM061, but I see you have stupidly decided to decline. Very well, we'll see how you like to have a bath. You are to take off all your clothes.

This is a new procedure and I must have shown some confusion because the guards are soon on me and strip off all my clothing. It is left in a bundled heap on the floor. When I am fully naked the guards turn me about and march me to a small cubicle and push me inside. There is barely room to stand. The door is locked behind me. I wonder what is going to happen, then I hear the sound of water and feel it flowing over my feet. It is freezing cold. I hear a tap continuing to run and the water level keeps on rising up, to my waist, then my stomach. It keeps on rising. I think I'm going to be forcibly drowned but when the water level reaches my neck, I hear the tap turned off. I am now stranded in icy water and can keep my head above its level only by standing upright. There is no light and no sound other than the water as it swirls around me.

I start to panic as I slightly lose my footing. My head drops and I swallow a mouthful of water. I straighten up and find my head is again above the level of the water. I realise that provided I'm standing straight up or on tip toes I can keep my mouth clear of the water. This means I have to keep standing in this position. If I start to slip or bend my knees, I can drown.

I realise this is a form of torture to weaken my resolve. I suspect there are cameras on me to watch my reaction. Probably if I were to call out and say I 'm willing to answer their questions, I would be brought back into the interrogation room. I have no idea how long they will keep me in this hellhole but if they were to let me drown in here, they would not get the information they seek. This stiffens my resolve to do my best to stick this out as long as both my mind and my body can stand it.

I try to focus on other parts of my life. Of course, my family comes into my mind first. I love my children and I think about each of them and how they are both growing up. I vow to do all I can to support them, Christian as a fit young boy, always enthusiastic and keen to learn. Then my beautiful daughter Chloe, unsure of herself at present. She just needs to find her way. I think about Ann and how I must renew my efforts to bring back love into our lives. Or maybe even to decide we should split. I just don't know. Then there's Heidi. I confess she had a tremendous impact on me in the short time we were together. I only hope I will see her again.

I think about my life in the army, of the different countries I've been to, in the Cameroons and the Congo when on secondment to the Nigerian Army, to Borneo involved in fighting alongside the Gurkha soldiers, in Aden during our disastrous British withdrawal, in the Oman with our own special forces, in Northern Ireland where a lasting political solution still eludes us. Then in Germany, where we prepare for a war we hope will never happen. This mental meander brings me back to the mission I am supposed to be involved in right now. I swear to myself I can't let it end like this. I have no idea if I will ever be able to leave this place but at least I will try with all my mental strength to ride it out here as long as I can. I'm determined not to give in to Weber's interrogation.

My body is weakening in the icy water I'm immersed in. I feel the need to bend and stretch my legs but I know I can't do that without swallowing more water. I try again to think of other things way outside this watery world. It doesn't seem to work anymore. My mind is dragged back to the present reality of my situation here. I feel I'm weakening. If I were to call out to Weber and say I'll give him names, perhaps I might get some warmth and peace.

Then I hear the sound of running water. The level begins to drop and I hear the gurgling of a tap as the water drains away. Now it's down to my chest, then my waist and finally my body is free again. I'm shivering uncontrollably in the cold dank cubicle. Then the door is opened. Strong hands grab hold of my arms and return me back to the interrogation room. I'm ordered to put my clothes back on. I do this still dripping wet as no towel is provided.

When I'm dressed, I'm told to sit back down on the small stool. Colonel Weber is still behind his desk. He starts all over again:

"Who were you with last evening and where were you last night?"

"Who were you with last evening and where were you last night?"

"Who were you with last evening and where were you last night?"

I say nothing. This same ritual continues for some time. Then the colonel says, "Enough for now. But you will tell me in the end NM061.They always do." As I am led back to my cell, I feel I've won a small victory.

The time is starting to drift by and I feel my existence here is now becoming something of a routine. There's only artificial light so I can't tell whether it's day or night. It's only the routine that changes. During the days, we have to sit on our wretched stools, at night we lie on our cots with our hands outside the thin blanket. I say "our" but I have no idea who "our" or "we" are as I have no contact with any other prisoner. I see shapes when I'm taken to the interrogation room but never a face or a name. This is a soulless, cruel place – dark, drab, utterly depressing. Judging by the distance driven when I was arrested, I suspect we are still somewhere in East Berlin, but I have no confirmation. My only contact remains Colonel Weber, my interrogator but he only asks the same question like a metronome. I have no reading material. I'm cold again and cannot see any future. There seems to be a direct policy to deprive me of sleep. It's working. I'm so tired all the time and feeling weak and sick. I'm losing track of time as it's now days since I've been here. I suppose I should have started making marks on the wall to count each day like those resourceful prisoners I've read about but I don't. So far, I've resisted answering Weber's perpetual repetitive questions but I don't know how much longer I can stand it. I've had the water treatment again and managed to hang on still but each time I can feel myself getting weaker and it's more difficult to keep standing upright in the freezing water.

Then suddenly there's a change. During one of the tedious day sessions in my cell, the door opens and two guards come in. They say nothing but come over and snap cufflinks on my wrists. They then take an arm each and lead me out into the corridor. This time we turn left not the usual right to the interrogation room. We keep straight on until I see natural light ahead, the first since my incarceration here.

They lead me towards the same type of van that brought me here and I'm pushed up inside. Like before I get shoved into one of the tiny cell type structures that have been built in to the back of the van and I'm locked in. There is no window. The van drives forward and I hear a gate being opened. Forward again and I hear one gate being closed behind us and another opening in front. Then the van moves forward again.

Like the journey before, the space is very restricted and I cannot turn my body or bend. By the number of stops and starts I think we are still in the city. After a while, the van stops and we go through the same ritual of gates being opened and closed. The van stops again and I hear the driver and passengers getting out. I suppose I'm being moved from one prison to another but I have no idea why.

The guards who pushed me into the van now reappear, unlock the inside cell and lead me out of the van. My cufflinks are taken off. I see I'm in some sort of inner courtyard of what looks like a military barracks. The guard produces a document and presents it to a smartly uniformed officer. He looks at the document then looks at me. He signs the document and passes it back to the guard. The driver and the guards then get back into the van and it drives up to a barrier bar. A sentry then raises the bar and the van is driven away.

I'm feeling dazed from the cramped ride and I try to adjust to this new situation. Something is very different. I recognise the officer's uniform and his smart ushanka fur hat. I look around at the other soldiers. These are not Germans. I am totally confused as I realise that I am now in a Russian barracks surrounded by Russian soldiers.

I've no idea why I've been transferred to Russian custody. I'm expecting to be taken to one of the cells in this military barracks where perhaps I will be interrogated again. The officer comes up to me and to my amazement shakes my hand. Beside him is another soldier who says in English, "You are Colonel Chambers. I am Sergeant Gordievsky and my captain here is called Kaganovich. We believe you don't speak Russian so I have been detailed to interpret for you."

He continues, "The captain wants you to understand that, at the request of the Commander of the Soviet Forces in Germany, the DDR authorities have agreed to transfer you from their custody to ours. We know you have been held for some days in Hohenschönhausen prison and that you are likely to have been subject to interrogation there. Is that correct Colonel?"

"Yes, quite correct," I reply. What else to say?

"Exactly, we anticipate you will be exhausted after your ordeal there. Captain Kaganovich sympathises with you about the ordeal you must have faced. He offers you accommodation in our officers' Kaserne and has a medical orderly standing by to attend to you. So, if you would be kind enough to come this way, Colonel, we will show you to your quarters."

I'm in a complete daze. What the fuck is going on? I stare hard at the faces of this officer and the sergeant and both seem sincere and caring. I haven't eaten properly for days and I've had precious little sleep. I'm filthy and unshaven. Yet here I am being treated with the utmost courtesy. After my confinement in the prison, I can't walk properly so I stumble after the officer and sergeant. They invite me to sit in the front of a smart clean Lada staff car that is parked alongside. I'm still bewildered when we pull up at a building which Sargent Gordievsky tells me is the officers' Kaserne. We get out of the car and I'm escorted along a clean polished corridor to a room at the end. Inside are two individuals dressed in medical uniforms. I am introduced to them as the duty doctor and a nurse from the local Russian hospital. The sergeant then says,

"Sir, we will withdraw now and leave you with the doctor. As you see, there is a bed made up for you here and we anticipate you will need to rest. We hope to see you later." With that they leave.

Neither the doctor nor his nurse speak English but they have some German so we can get along. The doctor asks me to undress and then gives me a full examination. He tells me I'm OK but weakened by malnutrition and lack of sleep. He gives the nurse some pills for me to take and then leaves. The nurse tells me she has already run a bath of hot water and suggests I take it now. I don't argue as I step into a bath full of soapy hot water. I can't believe how my fortunes have changed. While I luxuriate in the bath, the nurse turns up with a brush and shaving foam which she spreads liberally on my face. I lay back in the bath while she expertly shaves off the heavy growth of stubble that has accumulated over the past days in prison. I get out and dry myself on a soft clean towel. Then I put on a gown that has also been provided. The nurse then brings a glass of water and suggests I take the pills the doctor has left. I suppose I should be suspicious but I don't care. I take the pills and go over to the bed. I notice my parka and winter clothes are hanging up there, my boots are lined up on the floor and on the bedside table I see my passport and watch. I can't think about anything else. I climb between the clean sheets and this time I immediately fall into a deep sleep.

Chapter Twenty-Three

I wake up slowly after a long dreamless sleep. I'm warm, clean and lying between crisp clean sheets. I open my eyes and look into that beautiful smile. It's Heidi. She's sitting on a chair that she's pulled right up next to my bed. She leans over to me and kisses me lightly on my forehead. I can't resist but to reach up to her and pull her down close to me so that we can kiss fully on the lips.

"I missed you, Peter," she says, "I thought I'd lost you, but now you're back!"

I pull myself up so that I can see her properly. She has that elfin look that attracted me when I first saw her. Short dark hair cut almost in a boyish way. An oval face with even white teeth which she shows often with that beautiful radiant smile of hers. She's wearing a woollen roll neck sweater and a plaited skirt. She's in her socks and I can see her heavy winter boots on the floor where she's kicked them off. Her eyes are shining and again she gives me that smile. As I come out of my deep sleep, I try to come to terms with the total change in my life – from the horrendous depravity of my prison existence to waking up feeling clean and refreshed and looking at this gorgeous woman.

"I guess we have a lot to talk about, Heidi" I tell her. "I don't even know what day it is."

"OK, Peter, let's start there." She looks down at her watch then tells me, "It's six o'clock on Wednesday 21 December 1988. There, is that precise enough for you?"

"Wednesday? That means I was in that place for – what? Five days? I had lost all track of time in there."

"I can imagine. There are some terrible horror stories coming out of there. We were shocked when eventually we found out the Stasi had got you and taken you there."

"When you say "we". Are all your team I met last week OK? And what about Ed?"

"All fine – now! But they've got some stories to tell from when we had to make our enforced departure from the meeting that evening. I'll tell you all about it. But Peter, how do you feel? Captain Kaganovich told me the dreadful state you were in this morning when the Stasi guys handed you over."

"Well that's another thing. What the hell am I doing in this Soviet camp? I don't understand anything."

"I know, there's so much to explain. Look, Peter, if you're up to it, I'd like us to move away from here this evening. Do you think you're fit enough? I talked to the doctor who examined you this morning and he told me he found you to be basically sound but obviously weakened by your ordeal in the prison."

"Well lying here after a good sleep and looking at you, Heidi, I feel terrific. Let me get up and see if everything is working OK." I get out of the bed and find

I'm still wearing the light gown the nurse had found for me. I walk around the room. I feel stiff from all the ridiculous postures I had been made to adopt in the prison – otherwise, well – OK. I notice my winter clothes are neatly folded near the bed. Amazing, I find they have all been washed and dried while I was sleeping. There too are my passport and watch but, hardly surprising, no money or credit card. I am seriously impressed with my Soviet hosts.

I tell Heidi, "Yes, everything seems to be in basic working order. Give me a few minutes to have a pee and get dressed into these clean clothes, *grace à* our hosts, and I'll be good to go."

"While you do that, I'll go and organise some transport for us." She turns and comes up close again, "Oh, and Peter, it's so wonderful to have you back!"

It doesn't take long before we're ready to go. As we step outside the officers' Kaserne, which is fully centrally heated, we are hit again by the cold of the Berlin winter. There are signs of a recent snowfall but I had been completely unaware of that while I was languishing in the prison I now know is called Hohenschönhausen. The snow has been cleared away from the main roads in the barracks and is piled up on either side. The cleared areas are icy and we walk with care to the car that Heidi has organised for us. As we approach, a driver jumps out and opens the back door for Heidi and me to get in. He salutes smartly. He is accompanied by the captain I had met when I was brought here early this morning. Heidi reminds me his name is Captain Kaganovich. He also salutes and gets back into the front passenger seat. As we set off, he explains, through Heidi's translation, that we are only going a short distance, still in Berlin Mitte, to one of the apartment blocks occupied by Russian officers, mostly from the 6th Guards Motor Rifle Division, 20 Guards Army which is based in the city. He lives there with his wife and two children. As we drive, Heidi does not offer any individual comments but acts only as an interpreter for the captain as he gives us a short running commentary. I'm thinking how strange this is as Cheryl and I were treated in such a similar style by a young British captain when we had been driven from Tempelhof to the British zone. That was only last week but it seems much longer. The main difference today is the state and style of these drab buildings compared to those in the West. Up ahead, I notice a large area that is blocked off by a barrier bar and armed sentry. Behind it I can see a large rectangular building. Captain Kaganovich sees me looking at it and says, "You probably don't recognise that place from this side, Colonel. That was your home for the past few days. That is Hohenschönhausen prison!"

I'm pleased we're not stopping near there. The place sends shivers down my spine. Indeed, our driver takes us to a smarter area of the city. We have to clear a sentry post there, then we arrive at another group of apartment blocks. These are the usual square shape but the whole place looks neat and tidy and well maintained.

Through Heidi, Captain Kaganovich explains, "This is where most of our married officers live and if you'll excuse me, I'll leave you as my married quarter is just over there. I'll bid you good evening, Colonel" With that he gets out of the car, salutes and walks away.

"This is very interesting, Heidi," I say to her, "but what's next?"

"Well, Peter, I have a little surprise for you. Be patient, We're nearly there." She gives the driver an instruction and we set off again. But only a short way, to another apartment block in the same area. The driver stops again. He gets out of the car, comes around to my side, opens the door and salutes. Heidi and I get out and the driver climbs back in and drives off. Heidi and I are left standing in the road beside a pile of cleared snow.

"Come with me, Peter," she says. She has an air of mystery and I wonder what she is up to. I follow on behind her as she enters the nearest apartment block and we climb up two flights of stairs. We walk along a corridor and stop at a door to one of the apartments. Heidi takes a key from her pocket and turns it in the lock. It opens and Heidi leads the way into a nicely furnished room.

"Here we are," she explains. "This is my surprise. It belongs to a Russian army friend and his wife. They are away on leave and have told me I can use it whenever I want. It's ours for the night, Peter, just you and me!"

She turns and gives another of those smiles of hers. Then she says, "Peter, as we were saying back in the Kaserne, we have so much we need to talk about. I thought this is an ideal place. For one thing, we are in the middle of the Russian owned married quarters which are secure and regularly patrolled. The Stasi would not dare to set up listening devices here. Another reason is that I want to have one evening in my life when I don't have to share you with any other living soul. Is that clear enough for you, Mr Englishman?"

What else to say but, "Perfectly clear, ma'am!"

We take off our winter coats and leave our boots near the door so as not to tread in snow. The apartment is heated and pleasantly warm. Heidi goes over to the sideboard and takes out two glasses. Then she goes though into a small kitchen and reappears holding a bottle of vodka. She pours the drink and brings the glasses over.

"Let's have a drink to celebrate your release, Peter. We are in a Russian apartment so I think it appropriate for us to do it with vodka. "Good health - *Khorossheye zdorov'ye"* – (That's what it sounded like to my non-russian speaking ear).

"Now I want you to sit down here at the table, Peter. You must be very hungry so I'm going to take care of that."

I sit down and sip my vodka while Heidi bustles off back into the kitchen. Soon she reappears with a bowl and two plates. I look mystified and she explains that our starter is caviar that she got from the Russian commissariat. She serves it with the freshest bread I've had since the general's breakfast back in West Berlin. Heidi is a very resourceful woman! We eat some portions of the delicious caviar and wash it down with another glass of vodka. After praising the caviar, I say, "Heidi, I'm still completely at a loss to know how it was the Russians got me out the prison today. How was that possible?"

She takes a while to reply, then says, "It's a long story, Peter, and I'll tell you everything. But let me just get our next course started and then we can talk." With that she goes back to the kitchen. I can hear her busying about preparing things. But soon she's back again.

"Right, first things first, everything is on the slow burner in the kitchen so we can leave it for a while. OK, here's the story. When you didn't turn up at our rendezvous on Friday we feared the worst but at that time we didn't know what had happened to you. All the others you met at Meisenweg were there including Ed Morgan. It was important we carried on, so we had our meeting as planned and made a lot of progress. Of that, more later. We were naturally very worried about you. You remember Frederik, the Stasi military officer? Yes? Well he made enquiries among his colleagues and the next morning found out that you had been caught and taken to Hohenschönhausen. This was terrible news. You will understand, Peter, we were of course worried about you personally but also if they broke you and forced you to tell them about our group, this would have ruined so much of what we are trying to achieve."

"I understand, Heidi, you don't need to spell it out. And that was exactly what the interrogator there was trying to extract from me. But don't worry now. He got nothing from me. But if I had been there much longer, I just don't know. Their psychological methods are very powerful and I think in the end it becomes impossible not to tell them what they want."

"We all understood that and realised we needed to act quickly."

"But what did you do to persuade the Soviet's to intervene. I'm British and on "the other side"."

"I'm coming to that, Peter. Remember I studied in Moscow, had a Russian boyfriend from the 6th Motor Rifle Division and I work regularly with the Soviets as an interpreter. So I have good contacts and relations with the Soviet hierarchy here. Anyway, I decided I had to act quickly and to go to the top, or at least to the highest-ranking officer I knew. That is Colonel Anatoly Orlov, who is head of the Soviet External Relations Branch, or SERB as it is known. I have worked on interpreter duties with him for some years. His office is at Zossen-Wünsdorf about one and a half hours drive from here. I asked Captain Kaganovich to drive me. Anyway, I got to see Colonel Orlov. I had to be quite open with him. I told him that I knew the West is concerned that the DDR is putting out rumours and false reports with the aim of implying that Gorbachev is not genuine in his moves towards a détente with the West and specifically that he is lying about the force reductions he made in his speech to the UN. In order to investigate these reports, the West had sent you over here. But the Stasi had intervened and arrested you. I tried to convince the colonel that if the false reports are indeed the work of the DDR, then this would be to completely undermine Gorbachev's work. It was therefore in the Soviet's interests that you, the British officer, should be handed over to the Soviet authorities immediately. I don't know if Colonel Orlov was convinced but he heard me out and told me he would investigate. I heard nothing more until this morning when I was told you were to be handed over to the Soviets. And that's what happened. Tomorrow, you are to report to Colonel Orlov yourself. We have an appointment at his office at eight o'clock. I am to be your interpreter."

I had listened intently to Heidi's story. What an enterprising person she is! All I can think to say is, "And here I am, thanks to you. You are an absolute star!"

"I don't know about being a star, Peter. But I am a determined woman. Particularly where you are concerned. But that's enough for now. Our next course should be ready"

She gets up and goes back into the kitchen then shortly she reappears with a tray containing a pie with vegetables and a side sauce. Apologetically she says, "I had to improvise at short notice today, Peter, so you'll have to put up with this. Someday, I'd love to cook for you properly."

She has no need to apologise. What is more she produces a bottle of good French Burgundy which she says she also got from the Soviet commissariat. I tell her, "Your pie is delicious, Heidi, just what I need. We didn't exactly eat "haute cuisine" in Hohenschönhausen!"

We eat for a while in silence. I'm still absorbing Heidi's story about how my release came about. In fact, I look forward to the meeting with Orlov tomorrow. I've heard and read a lot about Zossen-Wünsdorf and never thought it would be possible to go there while we in the West were still facing off with the Soviets.

We finish our meal with some fruit that Heidi had chopped up and covered with a ball of ice cream that she's spirited away in her friend's fridge. We take our time and enjoy the rest of the Burgundy.

Feeling replete and relaxed, I offer to do the washing up but Heidi won't hear of it, insisting that's not the work of a Colonel. Cor, I think, it's certainly not like that in the West! I ask Heidi about last Friday's meeting – the one I missed.

She replies, "It went really well in that now we've got solid information about the work of Colonel Krause in the X Division of the HVA, to remind you that's the *Hauptverwaltung Aufklärung* or overseas spy service. He's still very actively churning out this stuff. Our team feel it's time for us to act if we are to prevent it causing a serious rift in East-West relations. Now I've broached the subject with Colonel Orlov of the SERB, I'm hoping we can enlist the Soviets active support in sorting out this guy. Our group are all keen to be involved but none of us are from the military except Frederik and he has to play it very carefully with his Stasi bosses. That's why we hope you can lead us on this, perhaps with the direct help of the Soviets."

"That would really be something – the idea of a joint British/Soviet operation against the DDR! I can't see that happening. But you're right and we'll see how it goes with Orlov tomorrow. I know he deals regularly with our BRIXMIS people who say he's a flexible and pragmatic guy, so who knows? How is it left with your group? When do you plan to meet with them again?"

"That's already fixed. While you were sleeping, I got word to them that we will meet up again after you've met with Orlov. I'll give them a time and RV when we know how you get on."

"A question for you, Heidi. We need seriously to think about physically kidnapping Colonel Kraus and with him hard evidence of the false reports he's sending out. That's the only sure way of proving categorically to the authorities, both East and West, what the Stasi are up to. If I think the response from the Soviets tomorrow is positive, I'll float the idea to them. If we do consider kidnapping him, how best do we get him over to the west?"

"We discussed that at our Friday meeting, Peter. There are several possibilities. The DDR authorities are very nervous at present and have increased their security at the main checkpoints so we'll have to plan that very carefully. I've got some ideas we can talk through depending on your meeting tomorrow."

Heidi gets up and starts to clear the dishes. She says: "I know you had a good sleep today, Peter, but you've just come out of a major ordeal in the Hohenschönhausen. Why don't you just relax while I clear up these few things? I'll be right back. Remember we've got an early start tomorrow. Oh, and Peter, just so that you know, the compound that we're in now is the property of 6 Motor Rifle Division of the Soviet army. It has a perimeter fence around it and is permanently patrolled. That's why the Soviets were relaxed about you staying here. So, I suppose you could say you're my prisoner tonight! You'd better behave yourself!" With that remark, she winks and gives another of those smiles as she waltzes off into the kitchen with the dishes.

There's a two-seater settee in the room and I sit down there while I hear Heidi running the tap in the kitchen as she clears up from our supper. I reflect on what an amazing day it's been. If it hadn't been for Heidi's initiative in going to the Soviets I would still be in that fucking prison now. And I don't know how much longer I could have held out. There's still a lot to sort out. I need to contact Cheryl and update her and of course I need to ring home. But that will have to wait until tomorrow. Meantime, here I am, refreshed, well fed and warm. And I've got a beguiling young woman for company. Can't be bad!

It's not long before Heidi has finished her housework and comes back in to the room. She sits down next to me, rests her head on my shoulder and cuddles in. We stay there quiet for a time. Then Heidi says, "Peter, I think tomorrow is going to be a big day for us both and some major decisions may have to be made. But, my darling Colonel Peter Chambers, that's for tomorrow. Right now, I've got you all to myself. My friends who have this apartment tell me the bed is very comfortable. I think we should go and check it out. Do you agree?"

"I agree," I tell her. And so we do.

Chapter Twenty-Four

Heidi told me last night that she has booked the Soviet staff car to pick us up at 0615 hours and she had set her alarm for 0530 before we went to bed.

I am awake before the alarm bell rings and I think Heidi is also but we don't talk. It's not necessary now after the night we have just shared together. We get up and fall into a smooth domestic routine of using the shower and bathroom, in my case shaving, and preparing to leave. We even have time for a cup of coffee and a yogurt. Heidi does a quick clean around, strips the bed and leaves a "thank you" note for the wife of the officer who normally lives here. We dress in our winter clothes and put our boots on in the corridor so as not to leave a mess in the apartment. All very polite and civilised.

We walk down the stairwell and find the Soviet staff car waiting outside the apartment block, engine running to keep it warm inside. The driver sees us and immediately jumps out of the car, comes around to the back door, salutes and opens the door for us to get in. I'm impressed, although I realise that our car and itinerary today have been arranged by the Soviet General Staff so we are getting the VIP treatment.

I understand that Zossen-Wünsdorf is some fifty kilometres due south of Berlin. I have not been there before and would like to get some idea of the countryside but of course it is still completely dark and will be for the duration of our journey.

We don't talk much in the car as we drive through roads now cleared of the snow which is piled up on either side. Although our driver is Russian and in theory would be most unlikely to speak any English, I am well aware that the Soviet intelligence services, GRU and/or KGB, could well be involved today and be using one of their operators to pose as our driver. In any case, at this time of the morning, neither of us feels like making bright conversation. I sit back and reflect on the marvellous night I've just spent with Heidi. Unlike the other night, which we spent together in Herr and Frau Neubert's cold little flat, this time we were not constrained by having to wear our winter undies and to speak only in whispers. We lay together and slowly explored each other's bodies. Gradually we came to the point of sex but we didn't rush anything. It was deep and strong and sensitive and full of caring and, well yes, even of love. We didn't use the word "love" but lying there together, we both felt we were with the person we had been searching for all our lives. It was sincere and at a level I have never known before.

I bring my mind back to today and what we might expect from the meeting at 0800 hours with Colonel Orlov. I'm full of admiration for Heidi that she had managed to get to see this officer and that it had resulted in my release. It is also useful that he is head of the SERB and knows the work and personalities of our BRIXMIS members and those of the US and French Missions. I hope to be able to build on that. What I don't know is the present state of relations between the Soviets, particularly those operating in East Berlin, and the German DDR authorities. This could be critical if I try to enlist Soviet help to take on X Division of the Stasi HVA. All I know for sure is that the Soviets had sufficient influence to get me released from the Hohenschönhausen prison yesterday.

Our driver keeps up a steady pace and as the first signs of daylight are appearing, we drive into a large built up area. As far as I can see, all the signs here are in the Russian Cyrillic script. Heidi explains that we are now entering the complex of Zossen-Wünsdorf. She says that they are in fact two separate places, several kilometres apart but merge into one vast area of Soviet military life.

"Some call this area Little Moscow," she explains. "I've heard that altogether there are some 75,000 Soviet men, women and children living here. The area is well served with facilities such as schools, hospitals, supermarkets and even local businesses. I also understand there is a daily train running between here and Moscow."

We now turn into a military barracks area and a smart sentry flags our car down. Our driver stops the car, gets out and goes over to the guard post and reports. After a few moments the driver reappears, accompanied by two other Soviet soldiers. I can see an officer's insignia on the shoulder board of one of them as they approach our car. He looks at Heidi and me and tells the driver to open all the doors and the rear boot. The second soldier searches in and around the car while the officer comes to us and speaks to Heidi in Russian. She translates that the officer has been told to expect us but he needs to ensure our car has not been tampered with before allowing it into this headquarters block. He also inspects my British passport and Heidi's German identification papers. He then instructs our driver to proceed and tells him exactly where he has to park. I now realise I am in the Headquarters of the Group of Soviet Forces in Germany. Quite an experience for a British NATO colonel!

We park as directed. There must have been a phone call from the guardroom because as soon as we pull into the allotted parking space, another officer appears. He opens the rear door, salutes and invites Heidi and me to get out. He introduces himself and says, in good English, that he will escort us to our meeting with Colonel Orlov. I glance at my watch and note it is 0755 – perfect timing!

We walk along a well-polished corridor and then are shown into an outer office. We see two female secretaries who hardly look up from their typewriters as we enter the room. Our escort asks us to wait and he goes to the door. It has a sign in Cyrillic script, which I can't read, but I assume says "Colonel Orlov". The escort knocks and almost directly, the colonel appears. He is quite short and stout with a large wide open face with crease lines suggesting he likes to laugh a lot. He has the strong chunky frame of a wrestler. He is wearing full uniform, less hat, and I see his left breast is adorned with medal ribbons. I glance at my watch and note it is 0800 hours precisely.

Orlov advances towards me with his arm outstretched and shakes my hand with a decidedly firm grip. He says effusively in passable English:

"At last we meet, my dear Colonel Chambers. We have been so concerned about your welfare since we learnt about your incarceration. I'm pleased to see you are looking good."

I don't know quite what I was expecting from Orlov but this is certainly a promising start. I reply, "And I'm feeling good too, Colonel, thanks to your intervention yesterday and for the care and hospitality that you arranged."

He looks towards Heidi and says, "We both have to thank the Fräulein here for taking the initiative to come and see me and explain about your situation." He then says directly to Heidi, "Fräulein, in appreciation of your efforts, we have arranged a separate tour for you while you are with us today. My aide here will escort you and explain to you the history of this extraordinary complex we Russians have been proud to occupy for some forty years now. I hope you will find the tour interesting and informative."

This is a surprise. Clearly, Orlov has decided to distance Heidi from our conversation. I glance across at her and give her a questioning look. She returns my stare and gives a little nod of acceptance. The colonel's aide makes a gesture to her that she should follow him back out of the room and, somewhat meekly, she follows on behind him.

Orlov then beckons me into his inner office. It's a large room containing a desk, strewn with papers but also has two comfortable armchairs facing each other. Orlov indicates that I should take one of the armchairs and he sits down on the other. He clearly has an informal chat in mind. He says, "I think it good, Colonel, that we take a little time to get to know one another. Firstly, I'm delighted you are now recovered from your ordeal at the hands of the Stasi and…" he gives me a conspiratorial wink, "that you spent a comfortable and fulfilling night!"

He doesn't follow up on that remark and I don't react to it. I think he's just letting me know he's well informed about my relationship with Heidi.

He continues, "Perhaps you know that my job here is head of what we call our External Relations branch. You English speakers call it SERB. Actually, my normal office is located outside our main headquarters complex here so that I can be more easily accessible to your British and other Western missions. Are you familiar with this protocol, Colonel?"

It's interesting to hear the story from the Soviet side - also a useful way of getting our relationship off to a good start as I know I'm likely to need this guy's good offices if we're going to get the support we need from the Soviets. So, I reply, "Yes, I'm aware of the Robertson/Malinin agreement and some of what has developed since with our BRIXMIS and the US and French missions. All I've heard is that their liaison with your office is very good."

"Indeed it is, though sometimes we do get into local difficulties which we have to resolve. For example, a few days ago, one of your American mission tours, flagrantly disobeyed the rules of the PRA system - that's the Permanently Restricted areas. They were apprehended several kilometres inside the Letzlinger Heide training facility and were caught by our boys openly filming one of our equipments. There was nearly a punch up involved which could have escalated to a serious confrontation. I had to intervene and have since withdrawn the accreditation passes of the whole of that three-man team."

I can tell that Orlov likes to talk and reminisce. Also, that he likes to practice speaking in English. OK, I'm thinking, let him, that's fine by me. He continues, "Look, we keep calling each other Colonel. We are officers with the same rank. So why don't we use our first names just between ourselves. I'm Anatoly and you, I believe, are Peter. Correct?"

"That's right. Anatoly and Peter it is."

"You know, Peter, I must confess to you that I get on very well with you British and I am a frequent visitor to your splendid BRIXMIS lakeside villa in Potsdam. I enjoy the film nights and other excuses for us to party together. I like your British sense of humour though I confess I do not always understand it! I've also been to observe your queen's birthday parade which you hold at the Olympic Stadium in your British zone. The next invitation I've had from your Brigadier Head of BRIXMIS is for your annual Christmas party at your Potsdam House in a couple of days' time. Maybe you will join us? Although we communists are not Christians, we like the way you celebrate and we're always up for a social get together."

I have no idea where this conversation is going. It's not yet nine o'clock and I feel Anatoly is already in the mood to break out the vodka! But I can't deny he is a very engaging individual and I find it easy to go along with his light mood.

"You know, Peter, I'm very impressed with the standard of training of your BRIXMIS people. They all play the part of just being on liaison duties yet we all know that in reality they're using these tours to try to get as much intelligence as they can. We know it and they know we know it! It's all something of a game, but there are rules and your guys seem to know just how far they can push the boundaries. I would one day like to visit your training school in England. I believe it's in Ashford now but one of your guys tells me you're going to be moving out soon to make way for the building of your new high-speed railway. I heard the training school is going to be moving to Bedfordshire. I think it's called Chicksands. Is that correct?"

Woo steady!, I'm thinking to myself. This guy is a smooth operator. What he's asked me to confirm is in fact correct, but I'm sure he's just pumping me for information to see how far I'll go. I think it's time to move things along.

"Now, Anatoly, I think you and I both know that it's not my job to get into that area. I'm sure you would feel the same if I were to ask you about details of your sensitive training facilities. I think we have other matters to discuss today."

Orlov smiles ruefully, "You're right of course. Point taken. Forgive me, Peter, sometimes I do get a little carried away, especially when I get the chance to talk to someone such as you."

I have to admire him. He knew he had been caught out there but he glosses over it with disarming ease. He certainly has charm but I know I'll need to keep up my guard – and keep off the vodka! I'm keen to get on with trying to enlist the Soviet's support for tackling the Stasi disinformation people, so I get to the point and ask him, "We in the West were all impressed by Mr Gorbachev's speech to the UN last week. How has it been received here by the East Germans?"

"Well of course, we Soviets had prior warning of what our general secretary was going to announce so it came as no surprise. But it was very different for the East Germans. My reading of the mood here, particularly by the ruling SED party and their henchmen, the Stasi, is one of great anxiety. We notice there is a feeling of nervousness and unease. To be straight with you Peter, the SED is only kept in power, apart from the Stasi of course, by the historic ties they have with my country and the feeling we are here to support them. Our General Secretary's new policies of Glasnost and Perestroika, culminating in his speech last week, has left the SED ruling party feeling very exposed. Incidentally, the reason I sent your German lady friend away is so that we could discuss this more freely."

I don't of course tell him that Heidi, due to her job, her drive and her contacts, will be an essential part of any operation against the Stasi that I hope we may be able to carry out. This is not the time to get into that detail.

Instead I say, "I think you know the reason I came over to East Berlin, a Mission which would have ended in disaster had it not been for your intervention at the

Hohenschönhausen prison yesterday. In fact, your support there, reinforces my view that we are on the same side concerning our mutual desire to get to the source of this disinformation that can cause further tensions between us at the very time when Mr Gorbachev and the leaders of the Western countries are working so well together towards a genuine détente."

"Yes Peter," Orlov confirms, "We are indeed. I think I should now give you a little more background concerning our actions yesterday. When the German Fräulein came to see me, I in fact had previously been informed about your arrest. As I'm sure you understand, we Soviets like to keep ourselves well informed. We in the military use our formidable GRU intelligence organisation. They had informed us last week that you and a CIA operator named Mr Ed Morgan had gone through the Checkpoint Charlie crossing point in an Opel Corsa car. We were intrigued and decided to follow up on this information. Our people lost your track for a time until we found out about your arrest and captivity. So, when the Fräulein came to see me, I was already aware of the basics. We dug deeper. Our sources produced details of your full CV. We were intrigued enough to obtain your release and to ask you to come here today for further discussion about your mission here. I have to tell you Peter that your case quickly escalated right to the very top. The reason I asked for our meeting to be so early is because I have been instructed for you to be available to meet our commander in chief."

Orlov pauses for effect. I don't know where this is going only that I now seem to be a pawn in a game that has got way beyond anything I was expecting. Orlov is about to continue when his phone rings. He excuses himself and answers, speaking only in Russian which I do not understand. By his body language I can tell he is receiving instructions from someone superior to him in rank as he's almost standing to attention while holding his phone. The call ends and Orlov turns back towards me and says:

"That was the commander in chief's office. The marshal is in his office and has told his staff he wishes to speak to you directly. Our appointment is in fifteen minutes."

I ask Orlov, "When you say marshal, who are you referring to?"

"I'm referring of course to Marshal of the Soviet Union Nikolai Ogarkov, the commander of our Western Theatre of operations including our Group of Soviet Forces in Germany!"

This is a major and dramatic development. During my military training, I have studied the writings and policies of Ogarkov and consider him to be one of most brilliant military minds of the post-World War two era. He has revolutionised the Soviet military science and his book "History teaches Vigilance" which was published just three years ago in 1985, is now required reading for any serious student of modern warfare. The book stresses the very important demands that advanced technology is having on the Soviet military. I understand that Western experts were confused when in 1984, Marshal Ogarkov was dropped from his former post as chief of the general staff of the USSR. Many saw it as a demotion due to political rivalries that were current at the time. However, his appointment here as commander of the Western Group of Forces, of which the Group of Soviet Forces Germany would spearhead any attack against the West, is now believed to have been a more rewarding appointment for Ogarkov, enabling him to develop and refine the policies he had been promoting in his lectures and writings.

Now I am told I am to meet the great man himself. I must say I feel both nervous and excited. I know it is critical to have the support of Marshal Ogarkov and that he is the absolute key to whether my mission will succeed or fail.

Chapter Twenty-Five

Colonel Orlov insists we leave immediately for the main GSFG building which houses the command element of the Headquarters. I can tell that Orlov is nervous as I suspect he has rarely come directly face to face with the great man. We could walk there, but the weather is still as uncompromising as ever so Orlov lays on a staff car to whisk us over to the HQ block.

Inside the HQ building, I sense an atmosphere of orderliness and calm efficiency. I suspect only the very brightest personnel are selected to work at this level. This is the hub of the command and control of the Group of Soviet Forces Germany which I'm told today directly controls some 370,000 men 7,000 tanks and an Air Army. I suspect this headquarters also commands the remaining European Groups of Forces that make up the Western Theatre of Operations (WTO). All are under Marshal Ogarkov's command. Just to be able to communicate securely with all the army group and divisional commanders, must require a major signals capability: yet there is no apparent sign of complicated wiring or cables. All must be hard wired and discreetly fed into a major communications node nearby.

Colonel Orlov and I are escorted along an immaculately polished floor and taken directly to the marshal's office. Before I have the time to fully organise my thoughts, we are shown into his office. This is large but relatively sparsely decorated. I suppose I was expecting there to be large photos of Lenin and other former Soviet dignitaries and grandiose Hammer and Sickle insignia but this is not the case. There is one photo of Ogarkov himself with General Secretary Gorbachev and another of him in combat uniform surrounded by a group of his soldiers. I see no caption under either photo. Ogarkov is alone in the office when we enter except for a smart young female officer who I understand is to be our interpreter. I would have thought that Orlov could have coped very adequately but clearly Ogarkov prefers to have his own.

In my earlier studies of the man, I remember he was born in 1917, so he must now in 1988, be in his early seventies. But he is well preserved. He comes around from behind his desk and shakes the hands of Orlov and myself. It's a moment I shall always savour! He then returns to his desk but indicates we should take seats drawn up close to the other side of the desk.

The marshal speaks in Russian, but the young lady officer is translating immediately into excellent English. It's so slick it's almost instantaneous. "Colonel Chambers. You will understand I am a very direct person and like to come straight to the point but I think you British may find my manner blunt. I was made aware of your situation by Colonel Orlov here and our intelligence staff produced your CV. They inform me that your mission in East Germany is to get proof of the origin of all the false reports being fed into both the US and British Intelligence services and equally into those on our Soviet side. Is that correct?"

Wow, no messing about here! And I see no merit in trying to say anything other than the truth. I reply, "That is correct, sir, we in the West are seriously concerned that there is a disinformation campaign being launched with the sole aim of driving a wedge between the good relations that have been developing over the past year or so between the East and the West, more precisely between the countries of your Warsaw Pact and our sixteen nation NATO organisation. We in the West have been greatly heartened by the evolving thawing of relations between our two blocs, by the close personal contacts between our leaders and the ensuing missile treaties that have been signed. So much of this new détente has been due to the personal drive of your general secretary. We hope none of this will be put at risk"

"And how do you intend to achieve your mission?"

I'm into this now and there's no point in trying to bluff this great man. He's too sharp and has the full range of his intelligence services at his command. So, I continue, "Sir, all the evidence we have unearthed to date indicates that the source of this disinformation comes from within a division of the Stasi HQ in East

Berlin. The Americans and we British do have some useful contacts within the Stasi organisation. We hope to exploit these to get the hard proof we need. Once we have that, we can expose this fraud and pass the proof to both our Western leaders and yourselves."

Ogarkov hears me out, then says, "When you say "a division of the Stasi HQ" do you mean," and here he glances down at a note before continuing, "Division X of the *Hauptverwaltung Aufklärung,* the Stasi's main administration for foreign intelligence?"

I can tell he is very well briefed. All I reply is, "Exactly so, sir."

"And how do you intend to proceed in obtaining the hard proof you seek?"

I am wriggling here as I can see any independent plan I might propose will seem very thin. Better to try to enlist Soviet cooperation and resources, so I say, "Sir, as you know I failed in my initial effort and was arrested by the Stasi. Thanks to your intervention, I am here now. May I ask, sir, if you share our opinion that it is in our mutual interest to reveal to our governments that these reports are in no way stemming from our countries so that we can dismiss them as fraudulent and return to the position of détente that both sides desire?"

I waited while the marshal reflected for a moment then said, "Yes, Colonel, we are on the same side concerning this issue and have the same objective. These Stasi initiated reports have become a major irritant and must be exposed. There are those in my country who would like to believe that the West is still an aggressor. They are mainly from the old school of thinking but they still wield some power and influence in the Kremlin. Our general secretary and I need to treat very seriously the issue of exposing these lies. The recent highlighting in both your Western press and our own is also contributing to fan the flames of mistrust. Additionally, you also need to understand that we Soviets at present are in a very sensitive and volatile relationship with our allies here in the DDR. In summary, I will support you in your mission but this will have to be limited and deniable. Is that acceptable to you, Colonel?"

I am delighted by the marshal's remarks. I couldn't have asked for more. I say at once, "Certainly, sir, totally acceptable and I appreciate the sensitivities involved."

I am expecting that, the decision of limited support to my mission having been made, that would be that and Orlov and I would be dismissed with the details left to a subordinate to organise. But the marshal seems to be in no hurry to turn to other matters. Instead he is a reflective mood.

He says, "Mikhail Gorbachev and I go back a long way and we have found common cause, I as a soldier and Mikhail as a politician. We both knew fundamental changes needed to be made. In my view, we were throwing too much money at the wrong things. We were still thinking in terms of the last great war and failing to realise the value of new technology on the battlefield. I initiated major rethinking for much of our battlefield tactics, to be more mobile, nimble, and have a more flexible application of all arms combat. Secondly, I recognised that our soldiers were mainly poorly trained and we needed to invest more time and inventiveness in our training programmes. Thirdly, I came to realise the total folly of basing our war plans on first strike nuclear options. Fourthly, I realised that we Soviets were falling further and further behind the Americans in terms of new weapon technology particularly in surface to surface missiles. We were slowly being priced out of the market. I used to discuss all these issues regularly with Mikhail. I am of course older that he is but in many ways we are kindred spirits.

"We were both very much affected by the Chernobyl disaster two years ago in April 1986. To contain this, involved the displacement of some 500,000 people at a cost of 18 billion roubles and we are still paying social benefits to seven million people across three countries. This incident brought us to a total rethink about the use of nuclear weapons in modern warfare. To me, the primary purpose of holding nuclear weapons is to deter the use nuclear weapons against us! Can you image the effect of the use of such weapons in a built up industrial area of Central or Western Europe!"

It is fascinating to hear the marshal expressing these thoughts especially to a Brit like me. I am more than content for him to continue, which he does, "Colonel, with your background, you will be aware that we held a meeting of Warsaw Pact Chiefs in Budapest last year.

Mikhail and I were keen to use this summit to show our intent to scale down the unwieldy size of our forces. In our final communiqué we called for, and I quote, "the reduction of armed forces to a level where neither side, while making sure of its own defences, would have the means for a surprise attack on the other side or for mounting offensive operations in general." So, you see, both the political and military objectives are in line and Secretary Gorbachev's speech last week to the UN was completely consistent with the Budapest Communique and many other speeches that Mikhail has made. That is why it is particularly galling to have these false rumours now being spread around."

It seems he has still not finished. After a pause, he continues, "There's another thing I'm going to tell you, Colonel, which is very sensitive but which I feel you should know. You are to treat this with full discretion. Our friends in the SED party here in the DDR have drawn up a plan to use their own East German forces, backed by Stasi, to invade the Western Sectors of Berlin. They only intend to activate this plan if their situation gets desperate particularly if they feel we Soviets are deserting them. Such an action would totally upset the present balance of power. The political situation in the DDR is deteriorating and we believe they are using the disinformation tactic to try to undermine our US/Soviet relations and shore up their own position with us Soviets. We are also concerned that this transition period between outgoing and incoming US presidents, when decision making is stagnant, together with the usual Christmas stand-down, is a very sensitive period.

"I've given you this background so that you fully understand our reading of the situation here and it's why I'm backing your project, Colonel. I've instructed a commander of one of our Special Forces units to provide the backup we assess you will require. I'll leave it to you and him to work out the details. I wish you success. Colonel Orlov here will also assist as you require and he will report back to keep me informed. Good luck!"

With that he shakes our hands, Colonel Orlov salutes and we leave the presence of one of the most brilliant men I am ever likely to meet.

Orlov and I return to his own office. I had noticed that the marshal's conversation had been almost exclusively directed at me and Orlov had hardly been brought into the conversation. I don't push it with him but it just seemed so out of character as Orlov was a naturally talkative and ebullient individual. I put it down to his understandable reticence in the presence of such an outstanding commander.

Orlov is quickly back to form and clearly wants to be involved in my mission. He is soon on the phone and when he ends the call, he tells me, "That was Major Nikonov. The marshal has already given him orders to support your mission. I propose we now go over to his unit to meet him and his guys. You can then judge how best to use his support but with the limitations the marshal has stipulated. You know, Peter, this will be the first time I've ever felt I'm going to be on the same side as a Brit."

We get back in Orlov's staff car and drive around part of this vast HQ complex, eventually finding the Special Forces accommodation in a remote corner of the compound. Major Nikonov is there to meet us. He makes us welcome and gives a short brief of his role and capabilities. He tells us his unit is a formation of *spetsialnogo naznacheniya,* which is abbreviated to Spetsnaz. He is a young very fit looking guy. I like him straightaway and find him and his unit have distinct similarities to our own SAS and the American "Seal" special force units. He asks me how he can support my mission.

This is first time I've really put my mind to the detail of precisely how we can achieve the mission I've been given by the UK and US governments. Up until this point it had always seemed more of an aspiration rather than a practical operation. Now at last I realise that everything is different as I have the backing and resources of the Soviets. It's time to get serious.

I will need to talk again to Heidi when she's returned to us from her "educational tour" and we need to get together with her colleagues and Ed soonest. Then we must complete our detailed plan and get on with carrying it out. Time is not on our side. Marshal Ogarkov made that very clear this morning. I give Major Nikonov a brief outline of the mission I had discussed with Marshal Ogarkov and ask what resources he would have available. His reply is simple. If Ogarkov has authorised the mission, the resources will be unlimited. I tell him to have his guys available for an operation in Berlin this evening and for him personally to be ready to attend a planning meeting sometime later today, details of time and place to follow.

I know it's going to be important that, apart from the Soviet Special Forces, at least some of our own group, will need to be armed. Now is the opportunity to get this sorted. I ask Major Nikonov to show me his armoury and I'm staggered by the range and variety of weapons he has here. He tells me I can choose what I want and he'll get me the matching ammo.

I'm surprised to see the arms store includes some of the American Armalite Combat rifles AR-18s which fire the 5.56mm x 45mm calibre round. I like this weapon. It's light, robust and very deadly at short to medium range. It has a twenty-round detachable box magazine and a cyclic rate of 750 rounds per minute. I used this Armalite throughout my tour in the Oman in the mid-seventies. Provided I kept it well cleaned and lightly oiled, it never let me down and it saved my life on several occasions. Trouble is that it's of US manufacture, although Sterling Armaments in UK is also manufacturing this weapon under licence. I'm very tempted to book some of these sub machine guns from

Major Nikonov but I'm concerned about their distinctive signature origin.

I decide instead to go for the trusted omni-available gas-operated 7.62mm Kalashnikov with its 30-round detachable box magazine. This is the most deniable weapon. It's robust and simple to operate though I've always been surprised that it has a no hold-open device on the bolt to indicate an empty magazine or any method of holding the bolt open. Nonetheless I decide that this should be our sub machine gun and I ask Major Nikonov to set aside ten of the East German MpiKM version. This has a plastic stock and pistol grip, but a wooden fore-end with appropriate loaded 7.62mm magazines. If any of these were to be lost during our operation, their source of supply would be difficult to prove.

We'll also need some handguns and I see the arms store here is well stocked with these. My eyes light up when I see an array of Browning GP 35s. This gun fires a 9mm parabellum with a thirteen round detachable box magazine. Manufactured in Belgium, it has become the standard side arm for military officers in many NATO countries including my own. But again, it would be conspicuous if discovered so instead I plump for the East German manufactured version of the 9mm Makarov. It's a light and reliable handgun and its limited eight-round detachable box magazine is compensated for by the small size and lightweight of the magazines.

While I've got the opportunity here, I search through Major Nikonov stores and set aside a couple of pairs of handcuffs, some flares, ropes, bullet proof vests, knives and holdalls. Then my eyes light upon a shelf containing small lightweight battlefield radios and ask how these operate. I find they are very similar in technology to the tactical radios we use in the British army. I add some of these to our list of requirements. Major Nikonov notes all that I have selected and says they will all be available and serviceable when required.

It's time to get going and I'm now determined to get this job done, today if at all possible. I need to establish the ground rules between me and Colonel Orlov as we have the same rank. I say to him frankly:

"Look Anatoly, your marshal has given me the support I need to achieve the mission and stressed the urgency. We've now got the special force group with us so I plan to get the job done asap. I need it to be clear between you and me, Anatoly. I value your participation but I will take the lead here. Do you have any problem with that?"

Orlov comes straight back with, "Not at all, Peter. You are the boss here. Tell me what I am to do."

That settled, I tell him to get Heidi back from her "tour" because I need her to arrange the meeting to be held soonest back in Berlin.

"Incidentally, Anatoly," I tell him. "You keep calling her "Fràulein", her name is Heidi. Please use it!"

By the time we get back to the compound exit point, Heidi is there. When she sees me, she gives me one of those special smiles of hers. It's great to see her again! I tell her we now have all the support we need to get going and that she should reconvene her group, plus Ed, to meet in East Berlin this afternoon. She says she needs to use a phone and we go over to the guard post. Colonel Orlov gives instructions to the Guard Commander and Heidi is taken to the guard communications room.

Some minutes later, she emerges and announces, "All fixed for four o'clock!" I have no idea how she communicates with her group and its best I don't ask. We decide to get Major Nikonov to come with us now and join our meeting. A few minutes later, he arrives and reports that he has instructed his troops to be ready to move to Berlin on his orders.

We have the same driver who brought us to Zossen-Wünsdorf this morning. His passengers have increased by two - Colonel Orlov and Major Nikonov. We also have the backing of the commander of the Soviet forces in Germany. One other element has changed. The temperature has gone up and the snow has turned to rain.

Chapter Twenty-Six

A lot has happened since I was last in this car. Apart from the increase in passengers and the shitty weather, I feel I'm returning to Berlin with a clearer perspective. Since this whole business post Gorbachev's speech, I made the one positive move to challenge the preconceived wisdom of many of my superiors, found myself exposed to a political level way above my previous experience and, when I'm being really honest with myself, I've been living in a sort dream world and swept along by events. My nature, my experience and my training has been as a soldier – carrying out the tasks I have been given, and trying to balance the sometimes-conflicting roles of being a soldier and being a husband and father of my children. Now, due to Gorbachev's speech, the whole focus of my life has changed. I'm not a politician or political civil servant, I'm not a spy trained to operate alone in an alien environment. I'm a soldier. That's my motivation and my training. Now is the time to get down to basics and sort this fucking business out!

As we drive through the outskirts of Berlin, Heidi acts as navigator and directs the driver through the mass of Trabants and Wartburgs towards the Lichtenberg district of the city. She tells the driver to pull up in a small street and that we should all disembark. She then tells the driver that he should park up here and wait for instructions. She says to the rest of us, "Our meeting place is next to a bakery at number thirty-seven Heilstrasse, in the next road on our left. The bakery is open till late so it's perfectly natural for clients to be in and out of there all day without attracting Stasi informer attention. We should split up individually and make our way there. When you reach the bakery, you will see a door just to the right of the shop. It's not locked. Go in there and up the stairs. Our meeting room is at the top."

The bakery is easy to find, not least due to the appetising smell of fresh bread as we individually make our way there. I note the door to the right of the shop, as Heidi has described. As I climb the stairs I think I missed a trick and should have routed via the bakery shop and stocked up. It's been a long time since our yogurt breakfast. Then I realise that the Stasi have stolen all my money!

I need not have worried though as, when I go into the room that has been reserved for the meeting, I see a table has been set up with a buffet of an assortment of sausages, breads and savouries. Good planning Heidi!

I'm delighted to see that Ed Morgan is here and we greet each other like long lost friends. He knows about my incarceration and sympathises and we have a quick catch up session before we start our meeting with the rest. His eyes pop open wide when I tell him about my meeting with Ogarkov.

Also, here are the three guys I had met in the aborted Meisenweg meeting, Adel, the computer science professor, Bernd, the doctor and Frederik, the Stasi major. I introduce this group to Colonel Orlov and Major Nikonov and am sensitive that the two Soviet officers are apprehensive about Frederik's presence. I realise we're all going to have to get used to trusting each other in this group – and quickly. There's also a woman here who I've not seen before. Heidi introduces her as Ruth and that she'll explain later why she's been invited.

We help ourselves from the buffet and then take seats around a table that has been set up in the middle of the room. I notice that Klaus, the guy who was shot in Meisenweg, is back on guard duty by the door. He seems to have recovered from his injuries, thanks I suspect to Bernd's quick and efficient actions that night.

When we are seated, I see that everyone seems to have turned towards me to get things going. I feel my time has now come. I speak in German and ask Heidi to translate to Major Nikonov as necessary. I start by saying, "Welcome everyone. Although many of us here don't know each other well right now, I'm confident that by the end of this day, all that will change. I want to thank Heidi for organising our meeting today. Everyone here has special expertise and I'm confident that when we put all our various skills together in a co-ordinated way, we will be able to achieve our goal. You all know the background. The Stasi have been disseminating disinformation to both the Soviets and the West with the aim of undermining the détente between our two political blocks. This is proving to be far too effective in destabilising relations, particularly now that it's being fanned up by the world's media. Both the Western nations and the Soviets want this stopped before it gets out of hand. That's our job."

I look around the table waiting for Heidi to translate that to Nikonov. The rest seemed to have understood my somewhat rusty German and I see nods of agreement.

I continue, "I see two main elements to the task. The first is to infiltrate into Stasi headquarters in Normannenstrasse. We are confident we know the source of the disinformation – that it is being initiated by Colonel Konrad Krause from within X Division of the *Hauptverwaltung Aufklärung* or HVA. We need to isolate his office, confront this officer and obtain written proof of his work. If practical, I intend that we will either kidnap or coerce him to come back with us to the Western zone. I realise this is no small undertaking but I'm confident that, between us, we will succeed. I shall shortly ask you, Frederik, to give your assessment of how we can best achieve this while evading the considerable security obstacles we will need to overcome.

"Secondly, with our proof of the dissemination reports – including, I hope, Krause himself, we will need to cross over to West Berlin so that we can present evidence to the authorities there and in turn transmit them back to Marshal Ogarkov and the Soviet political authorities."

I had intentionally spoken in clipped formal terms because I need our group to be thinking the task through and asking themselves how they can best contribute to achieving it. I turn again to Frederik and say, "We need to lean heavily on your knowledge and expertise in order to infiltrate into the headquarters and reach Krause's office. What is your assessment?"

Frederik begins by explaining his background to those who have not met him before, that he is a major in the Feliz Dzerzhinsky Guards Regiment and has detailed knowledge of the layout and security of the Stasi headquarter buildings. He explains, "Krause now operates from a separate building from the main seven storey block. During his time in charge of the Department, Marcus Wolf gained a large degree of independence from Erich Mielke, the Head of Stasi. Wolf established his own operating ground rules. Since he retired two years ago in 1986, his successor as head of the East German foreign intelligence service, Werner Grossmann , has continued this independent line and has set up a small separate complex where Krause works, supported by a small team with their own communications."

I ask him, "To be successful, Frederik, we will need to get into the main Stasi compound then infiltrate to this HVA complex and isolate Krause's office. I understand from Heidi he normally works there in the evenings but we'll need to check that out. I foresee that I will need to be there myself with perhaps five or six others from our group here. Incidentally, Major Nikonov here will be providing us with weapons. How do you see us getting there undetected?"

I realise this could be a major issue but am relieved when Frederik replies, "There is of course tight security but we will have some advantages. The first is that to the best of my knowledge no one has ever tried to break into the Normannenstrasse complex before - no one has the slightest desire!! So we will have the benefit of surprise. The second is that all the guards know me and are used to me doing my security rounds there often during the evenings or at night. Provided there are just a few of us involved and any weapons, etc. are concealed, I'm confident I can get you to the compound undetected."

I like Frederik's positive thinking. I then ask him, "Once we're at Krause's office, how practical will it be to isolate it so that we can really get at this guy uninterrupted?"

"Well, as I said, the complex there is detached from the main buildings. We'll just have to ensure we keep watch from outside while you're in there and alert you if any of the guards decide to patrol that complex. It won't be without some risk but I think that can be minimised."

I ask him, "Do you think it would reduce the chances of the guards checking on that complex if, during the time we're there, there were to be a major incident nearby, say in the Normannenstrasse area which might distract the guards from doing their normal internal patrolling?"

Frederik looked puzzled and said, "I don't quite follow."

"What I have in mind is for Major Nikonov to create an incident outside but close to the Stasi HQ. I'm thinking about staging a traffic accident or starting a fire - something like that which would lead to the emergency services being called - fire, ambulances, etc. and therefore distracting attention from our operation at Krause's office." I turn to Nikonov and say to him: "That's within the terms that Marshal Ogarkov stipulated. Could you initiate some decoy to assist us?"

After Heide's translation, Nikiniv's reply is immediate, "Certainly, Colonel. We'd enjoy that!!"

I can see that also Frederik is in agreement. It's good to see we're making progress and satisfying that I'm getting positive co-operation from both German and Soviet input.

"OK." I continue, "That will be the basis of our infiltration plan. It's critical that we know for sure if and when Krause will be in his office this evening. Who can help there?"

Heidi answered right away, "As you know I often liaise with Krause's office and have a close friend who works there. I'll ask her to let me know when Krause comes in. There are many innocent reasons why I should do so and she won't be suspicious."

I say to Heidi, "Good, you do that." Then I say, "We need to keep our infiltration team as small as practical, but that indeed includes most of us here. I propose it should consist of Frederik, myself and Ed plus the following: Heidi as interpreter as my own German is not fluent enough, Adel for his technical expertise concerning signal transmissions etcetera, Bernd whose medical skills could be very useful, and Klaus as our watch man. That's seven people altogether. We can discuss what weapons and other supplies we take later. Are we agreed?"

I waited while the group digested my proposal. Then to my relief, all agreed.

I concluded. "Fine, that's how it will be. I intend that we go this evening if Krause turns up. There's no reason to delay."

The next big issue we need to tackle will be how the hell we get back to the Western zone if/when we succeed in phase one of our operation, particularly if we have to lug a reluctant Krause with us. But I think we need a break first to digest what we've just agreed before moving on. Everyone seems relieved when I suggest we have another attack at the remaining food on the buffet.

While we're having our break, I take time to look around our group to check on their reaction to what we've agreed so far. I realise I'm asking a hell of lot of some of these people who have no previous experience of this type of operation. But I'm encouraged by what I see. Everyone seems well motivated and I'm not aware of any dissension or any resentment that I have now taken charge.

When we reconvene I tell them that, on the assumption that the phase one of our operations is successful, we've now got to work out how we get over to the West. I ask them for ideas. I suppose it's natural that it's Heidi who is the first to speak. She turns to the German woman called Ruth and says, "I asked Ruth here to attend because I think we've found a novel means of crossing. Ruth, would you explain?"

Ruth is a lady, aged between forty and fifty, who is clearly nervous but also determined. I feel that by being here with us today, she has made a big decision in her life. She says, "I work in the Palast der Republik which, as you will know, houses our parliament. Herr Honecker and many of his top SED members have their offices there. I am a secretary in Herr Honecker's office. The Palast is also used for a variety of cultural events. In fact, there is a concert there this evening given by the Leipzig symphony orchestra which will be attended by many thousands of our citizens. However, the reason Heidi asked me to come to this meeting is to inform you about a construction that Herr Honecker has had built which has been kept top secret even from most of his own aides. There is a hidden passage clad in reinforced concrete that runs from inside the Palast under a main road to a building which has direct access to the River Spree. Herr Honecker has instructed that the passage, which is about fifty metres long, should always be kept in a readiness state and a boat with outboard motor fitted is to be moored at the river access point. The passage, which is kept permanently guarded, is intended for the use of Honecker and his closest aides in the event of a calamity overcoming our republic."

I don't think anyone, except Heidi, was expecting to hear anything like this revelation. We all knew that the job of exfiltrating back to the West would be a major undertaking, made more demanding by the heightened state of unrest due to the present rise in tension. This Honecker tunnel would seem to be our solution.

I ask Ruth, "Do you know exactly where the entrance is and about the guarding arrangements?"

"Yes, it's just next to his office in the Palast. I know because I had to make some of the administrative arrangements when the work was being carried out. As far as guarding is concerned, there are three or four men always on duty even right through the night. And you should know that there is also an alarm system fitted which the guards can use to call reinforcements if needed. But I can say, as with the other gentleman's earlier remarks about the Normannenstrasse complex, there has never been a security incident there and the guards are usually very relaxed."

I feel very excited about this and I notice the others do also. We agree that we will use this as our "escape" route, thanks to the work of the leader of the DDR! We decide that we should be able to get into the Palast this evening easily enough, taking advantage of the crowds attending the concert. Having made her stand to support Heidi's opposition group and brief us about the tunnel, Ruth now seems more relaxed and says she is willing to lead us to Honecker's office and show us the location of the tunnel.

There are still several administrative details we need to cover. The first part of our operation will be in Normannenstrasse, then we will need to move, possibly carting a reluctant Krause with us, from there to the Palast which I'm informed is located between Schlossplatz and the Lustgarten area known as Marx-Engels Platz. We estimate the distance between the two locations is about eight kilometres. I ask Nikonov if, as a back-up, he can provide our transportation. He confirms that he can.

We then get into logistics and I ask Nikonov, with Heidi translating, when we can get the supplies of weapons and the other stores I had asked to be provided. Expecting some delay, I am pleasantly surprised when he tells me that before we left Zossen, he had already ordered his troops to drive down to Berlin. He tells me they are now in the barracks of sixth Guards Motorised Division located close by here and can supply all the equipment to us directly on our command.

I also discuss with Nikonov our diversion plans to cover our entry into the Stasi compound and our later exit. This will involve the use of at least one BRDM armoured personnel carrier. He tells me, no problem, he can get them from Sixth Division. We also agree how we can communicate using the short-range radios I had earmarked in his stores in Zossen and the code words we will use. I am getting to appreciate the efficiency of Soviet Spetsnaz Special Forces. Who knows, one day we might find that they and our own SAS lads might be allies fighting alongside each other. What a formidable combination that would be!

From Frederik, I ask for the use of two VIP cars from his regimental pool. He replies that he often has to escort dignitaries into the compound and staff cars are always available. He can book two just by making a quick call to his unit. I also ask him to provide two uniform jackets from his regiment. I plan we will use these cars to enter the compound. On our exit, we will have the flexibility to choose between using these same cars or the transport provided by Nikonov, depending on the situation.

I guess that's as far as we can take our planning for now. I'm confident we have agreed upon an infiltration means that should get us safely there thanks to Frederik's extensive knowledge. Much will depend on him and we can only hope that, as a German national and Stasi trained officer, he will remain true to his conviction to support our objective. For the rest of our mission, I feel our plan is sound, but as always in operations we will need to have some luck on our side and to be ready to adjust and be flexible to face any unexpected contingency.

I am preparing to wrap up the meeting when the phone rings. Heidi jumps up to take the call. It does not last long. Heidi puts down the phone and tells us, "That was my colleague from the HVA. She tells us that Krause has just arrived in his office. He's told his radio operator to be on hand to transmit the reports he's planning to send out later tonight.

Now we know the operation is on for this evening. Frederik tells us that the usual time for the night shift to report is 2000 hours when several thousand employees arrive. I decide we will make our own entry at that time.

Next I turn to Colonel Orlov and say to him, "Anatoly, your role is to make contact with the brigadier of BRIXMIS and meet him as soon as possible - at the Mission House in Potsdam or wherever is best for you. Brief him on our operation and tell him it's on for tonight. Ask the brigadier to brief his general and also Colonel Cheryl Walker, US Air Force. Ask the colonel to arrange a reception group to be stationed on the edge of the River Spree opposite the Palast, from say 2300 hours tonight but they may have a long wait. They are to watch out for a flare and/or sighting of a boat crossing from the Eastern side. That, if the gods are smiling, will be us."

I have a few further words for our group. I say, "Thank you for your co-operation and for the enthusiasm you are showing. Between us, I believe we'll succeed in this mission which is of the highest importance to the leaders of both West and East. We mustn't let them down. One final point which I address to all our German nationals here this evening. Once we commit to this operation, there can be no turning back. That means that once we are over the River Spree and safely in West Berlin, it is very unlikely that you will be allowed back without being arrested. Having said that, I want to know if any of you feel that is too high a price for you to pay."

I look around the room - at Heidi, at Adel, at Bernd, at Frederik, at Klaus, even at Ruth who may get more involved than we intend - all of our East German national colleagues. But none of them move. All have decided to stay with us and go through with the operation.

I now tell Nikonov to get us our weapons and other supplies and I task Frederik to get the cars. Once we have these, we'll be on our way.

Chapter Twenty-Seven

It's difficult to believe. What the fucking hell am I doing? Whenever and wherever I've been on military operations before, I've always been with other well-trained soldiers - guys I've been with before or at the least I know they've been through the same training regime and they know how to react under the sort of pressure I suspect we're going to experience this evening.

But this is different with our disparate group. One exception is Ed who has been through the vigorous demands of the CIA training establishment. Then there's Frederik who has been trained within the tight East German army norms but can I trust his loyalty to our cause one hundred per cent when it's really put to the test? And what do I know about the rest of these people? Even Heidi, the enchanting Heidi. I know more about her body than what's going on in her mind! But here we are now, it's too late for doubts. If we are to work as a close-knit team we can't run it by committee! I know that I have to take charge here, be firm, but clear and fair. That's the only way we can succeed in our mission.

After our earlier conversation, Orlov leaves to make contact with our BRIXMIS people as we discussed. We have a brief handshake and tell each other we hope to meet up again soon.

Then Nikonov and Frederik go off to organise our logistics. Frederik is soon back. He has brought the two uniform jackets which I issue out, one to Klaus and one to Bernd. They are to be our staff car drivers! Frederik tells me the two VIP vehicles have been fuelled up and are on standby awaiting his call.

Nikonov then reappears with a large haversack on each shoulder. He opens them out onto the table. We first deal with the weapons I have ordered. All are there, each with the matching magazines filled with ammo. I decide that Ed, Burnt, Klaus and I will have Kalashnikovs and so will Frederik as I reckon it might draw too much attention if he were to get one from his own armoury. Adel will have a Makarov pistol as he has never handled a sub machine gun before. Likewise Heidi. Poor Ruth shied away from the sight of the firearms and decided she would take her chances being unarmed. She's probably right.

I give one of the haversacks to Klaus to carry. He's the youngest and fittest of our group and seems keen to be involved and to prove he's fully recovered from his wound. In this bag, we load the rope, handcuffs, knives and the flares I had ordered. Nikonov had also brought along a flash light so we decide to take that with us as well.

Next, we deal with the short-range radios. I've not handled a Soviet model before. Nikonov gives us a short demonstration and we find they are remarkably easy to use. I issue out one to each of us and we carry out a short test. They all work well. But I need more than this as I'll require to be in contact with Nikonov separately as his group will be operating from outside the Stasi perimeter in compliance with Marshal Ogarkov's orders. We also have to deal with the language issue between us and I can't rely that Heidi will always be on hand to interpret for us. We solve this problem in true military style as Nikonov tells me he has learnt the NATO standard phonetic alphabet as part of his Spetsnaz training – ALPHA, BRAVO, CHARLIE, DELTA, ECHO, GOLF, FOXTROT, LIMA and so on down to ZULU. He can only spell the words in Cyrillic but that's of no importance. We'll only be saying the words not writing them down! So we agree, he and I, on a set of procedures for him to implement when I transmit to him a fixed alphabet word, for example, when I need him to execute the diversion outside the Stasi compound, I will tell him over the radio. "ALPHA!" and he will know what to do and confirm by reply "ALPHA confirm". We run through several permutations and practise how we will communicate them. Then we reserve a separate channel on the radio to be used exclusively between us for these executive instructions.

We go through our plan several times. Nikonov's diversion will occur on my radio call which will be at about 1945 hours. Our group will approach the main entrance guards ten minutes later at the time of maximum activity when the day shift leaves and the night shift arrives. We will use the two VIP cars that Frederik has supplied. The first car will be driven by Klaus, wearing his uniform jacket with the front passenger seat occupied by Frederik, wearing his full guards regiment uniform. He will be our spokesman if challenged. Ed and I will be in the rear, keeping quiet.

The second car will be driven by Bernd, our doctor posing as chauffeur wearing the second uniform jacket. Heidi will be in the front passenger seat. She will have her Stasi pass to show if challenged. Adel will be the backseat passenger. Ruth will not be involved but will make her own way back to the Palast and be ready to meet us there later. We will contact her by radio when we are about to arrive at the Palast and she will tell us which entrance to take.

I run through the entry plan several times and our subsequent move to the compound where Krause works. Everyone says they understand precisely what we are going to do and what part each will play. I've taken this initial stage of our infiltration in a slow and pedantic fashion but, in my mind, I make no apology for that as I'm dealing with a disparate mixed national group, most of whom have never been involved in anything like what we are now about to undertake. I think it's also important that they get used to, and accept, that I am in complete charge of this operation. So far, I've had no problems from anyone about that.

We clean our meeting room and Nikonov takes away the stores we decide to leave behind. At 1915 hours, we are all dressed and ready to go, wearing the bullet proof vests and with our Kalashnikovs hidden under our parkas. We leave the bakery and follow Frederik to the two cars he had arranged to be parked in a nearby street.

I don't want to be tied down by a precise time for our infiltration as I first want to gauge how the personnel shift change procedure goes at the main entrance gate to the large perimeter of the Stasi headquarters compound. So we park up where we can observe the process from a distance. By 1940 hours, the build-up of employees seems to be beginning in earnest. I've been told there are some 5,000 persons employed overall in the compound so, if there are three shifts, there could be a combined number of arrivers and leavers of over one thousand people passing through the entrance during the change-over period. Time for our diversion. I switch to the dedicated radio channel between Nikonov and me, press "send" and say to him clearly, "ALPHA". I get an immediate, "ALPHA confirmed" and we wait.

But not for long. We watch as a Soviet BRDM-2 Armoured Patrol Vehicle turns around the corner into Normannenstrasse and ploughs straight into the side of an incoming tram. The tram screeches to a halt, is knocked off its tracks and is pushed partway onto the tracks running in the opposite direction. There's an initial silence then pandemonium breaks out as frightened passengers start to disembark from the shattered tram. We see several of the passengers have been wounded and are being assisted by others. As they disembark, we see groups of the survivors huddled together in the cold. Tram traffic in both directions has been paralysed.

Soon, we hear the sound of sirens. Clearly the local police and emergency services have been alerted and are hurrying to the scene of the "accident".

"Great stuff, Major Nikonov!" I say to myself, "just what we needed!" Then I lean towards Frederik as our lead driver and tell him, "It time to start the show, Frederik, let's go!"

Frederik engages gear and we move towards the vehicle check point at the main Stasi compound entrance. We line up behind two other official cars. I notice the time is just past 2000 hours. Over to our right, we can see the flashing lights as Police and Ambulance vehicles home in on the scene of the crash. Everyone's attention seems to de directed over there.

Our staff car slowly moves forward in the line. Now we are at the check point. Our guard approaches the window that Frederik has just lowered. Before the guard can speak, Frederik calls out to him, "What the hell is going over there?"

"There's been a bad accident, sir, we've heard there are several casualties but we haven't been given any further information."

"Right, soldier," Frederik says authoritatively. "You stay at your post here. I'll need to get over to the VIP parking and go to assist there myself. We have a doctor in the car behind so we'll need to get on with it. You're doing a good job, soldier."

The guard salutes and raises the barrier. Frederik drives through with Klaus bringing the second car close up behind. The guard doesn't check for IDs. Frederik leads us to the VIP carpark and brings the car to stop. Klaus follows and parks next to Frederik. We all get out. We have successfully negotiated our first obstacle. We are now inside the Stasi compound.

Following the procedure, we had rehearsed in the meeting room, Frederik takes the lead, I go second and Ed comes last acting as our rear guard. Under Frederik's expert guidance we make our way round the right-hand side of the large seven storey building that we see outlined in the night sky ahead of us. We follow first along a built-up road way, then Frederik veers off and leads us between a number of smaller buildings. Having passed several of these, he approaches another of a similar square shape, then stops and points to one particular building.

He whispers to me, "That's the one. That's where Krause has his office."

I know this is a critical time. We need to take control of Krause's office quickly and with minimum noise. We must neutralise any chance of those inside getting to a phone or panic button to raise an alarm. But first we need to be sure we know who is inside and what guard and/or other security they have there.

I tell Frederik and Heidi to go ahead and carry out a quick recce of this compound while the rest of us wait outside. If challenged, those two have legitimate reasons to be here. The rest of us do not!

It's not long before they return. Frederik whispers his report, "The compound has two stories but the top one is unlit and seems deserted. On the ground floor, there is a guard sitting behind a desk. He's reading something, comic I think, and doesn't seem at all alert. Behind him, there's a shut door leading I presume to Krause's domain. There's no way of knowing how many are inside."

I know we have to act quickly as we are all exposed out here and a random security patrol could spot us. I make a quick plan and call our team to come close. In a low voice, I tell them. "We need to act now. I will lead with Klaus right behind me. The rest of you follow on. When I enter the building, I intend immediately to immobilise the outer guard. I plan to threaten him and disarm him. If he resists, I'll have to shoot him but only with single shot to keep noise to a minimum. Then Klaus, you guard him while I lead the rest into Colonel Krause's office area. We will confront all the staff there and do not under any circumstances allow anyone to reach a phone or press an alarm. Is that clear?"

They all nod their understanding.

There's no merit in hanging around so I start off immediately. I open the door of the complex and walk brusquely up to the guard. As he glances up from his comic, I point my Kalashnikov at him and tell him, "Put your hands up and turn around and face the wall." He's a large bovine young man who has been completely taken by surprise. I suspect nothing like this has ever happened here before. At first, he looks at me and my aimed Kalashnikov in bewilderment but then I say, "I shan't tell you again. Now DO it!"

At last his brain engages, he drops his comic, raises his hands and turns around. I say to Klaus. "Now over to you. Check him for weapons and keep his hands where you can see them. I'll be back again soon."

Now it's time to gate-crash Colonel Krause's domain. I'm sure he won't be alone in there but we have no way of knowing who else will be on duty with him. I would say there will be at least a couple of assistants and some communications people but how many and where they will be positioned in the office, we have no prior means of establishing. There's only one way to find out.

I say quietly to my team, "OK, we're going in. Spread out behind me and keep your weapons at the ready. I hope we can do this without bloodshed but if anyone in there tries to get to a phone or alarm button, we'll have to be ruthless. Understood?"

More nodding from the team. I decide it's time to go. Leaving Klaus behind on guard duty, I lead the way. There's an outer door leading to a short passage one side of which has toilets and on the other side is a small kitchenette. At the end of the corridor I see another door which is closed. I move up to the door, stop and listen. I can hear the hum of a radio transmitter of some sort, the scraping of chairs as people move about. That's all. From the sounds, I try to build up a mental picture of the inside layout. But there's not enough to go on. Then I clearly hear a male voice. I can't pick out the words but the tone sounds authoritative. I'm guessing we've found Colonel Krause!

I glance behind and see everyone, less Klaus, is right up behind me. They all have their weapons at the ready and are tensely waiting for me to move. So, I do. I turn the handle of the door, push it open and we move swiftly into the office. I see eight individuals, more than I had thought. I move to the centre of the room and shout out in German.

"Drop what is in your hands. Right now. DO IT!" I see looks of startled shock on their faces. But they all comply with my order.

Then I say, "Right, put your hands up so that I can see them, slowly walk away from where you now are and move towards me." My intention is for them all to reach the middle of the room, clear of any phones, alarms or other transmitters. All goes well and I think we'll get through this phase without incident. But suddenly I see rapid movement by a youngish man on my left-hand side. He gets up and is making a dash towards a red button that has been installed on the side wall of the room. I have to assume that this button is an alarm connected to the main guard force. If he gets there to push it, we will have the main armed guard here to investigate. We are no match for a highly armed and trained military force and we would kiss goodbye to our mission and probably our lives as well. I have no option. I turn and fire a short tap on the trigger of my Kalashnikov, releasing no more than three rounds. They are sufficient.

The bullets strike the young man in the right shoulder and arm, as I intend. He had tried to use that arm to reach the button. He never made it. The other seven occupants of the room seem stunned to see their colleague shot down. They meekly comply with my order and move slowly towards me as ordered. When they have reached the centre of the room and are well clear of phones and communications equipment, I tell them to stop, line up and keep their hands up.

The seven consist of five men and two women. I tell Bernd and Ed to search the men for weapons and Heidi to do the same with the two women. I notice one of the men is wearing the uniform of oberst, or full colonel, so I presume he must be Krause. But I do not address him personally yet. His turn will come. First, we must ensure we neutralise the room in terms of eliminating any chance of an alarm being given to the outside guard force.

The searches complete with no weapons found, I tell our captives to walk over to a wall that I can see is clear of phones and alarms and tell them to face the wall and keep their hands raised. We had earlier relieved Klaus of the holdall and brought it into the room with us. I tell Ed and Heidi to tie the hands of all our captives but for them to keep facing to the wall.

When this is done, then, and only then, I tell Bernd, our doctor, to tend to the young man I had shot.

Our security arrangements are not yet complete. I tell Ed he is to supervise our held captives and tell him, in a voice for all to hear, that anyone who tries to escape or reach a phone, is to be shot. No warnings are to be given.

I then tell Frederik to accompany me and we go back out to the front desk where Klaus is still covering the bovine young guard. First I talk to Klaus and tell him, "Klaus, your job here is to cover this front desk and take the young guard's place. You are to act as his "replacement". You're already wearing the right jacket so that should do. Use your radio to alert us if anyone approaches. Clear?"

"OK, sir. You can count on me"

I then turn to Frederik and tell him, "You did a great job to get us this far, there was no way we could have managed it without you. Now, we need your knowledge and expertise again, Frederik. I want you to remain outside the compound and act as our outer security cordon. Your uniform and authority allows you to move freely here. Should you become suspicious of anything or anyone, you are to contact me via the radios we got from Nikonov. Can you do that?"

"Of course I can, and you're right I'm the only one who can do this, though I must confess I would have loved to have had the chance to get at that bastard Krause myself"

"Understood, I hope you'll get the chance later."

I wish him luck and return to the outer part of the compound. I get Klaus settled behind the guard desk then I lead the young guard we've arrested back into the main office area. There, I get him to stand next to the others and task Ed to tie him up as well. I notice Ed and Heidi had used their initiative and removed our prisoners' shoes and belts. Good move!

I do a quick mental check. Outer perimeter patrolled by Frederik, entrance to the complex covered by Klaus. Both have radios to warn of any threat. Prisoners all disabled and under guard.

So far, so good. So now we can get down to the whole reason of us being in this crazy place in the midst of the Stasi Headquarters in the middle of a cold wet Berlin December night.

I turn to the man dressed in Colonel's uniform and say to him, "Colonel, what is your name?"

He answers in one word, "Krause."

I say to him. "Now I will tell you our mission. It is to talk to you colonel. That's why we are here."

Chapter Twenty-Eight

I go to Colonel Krause's desk and check there are no phones within range. I then tell Ed to untie the Colonel and bring him over to where I am. Ed does so and helps him to shuffle over in his socks. We stand face to face like that for a while.

Krause is a short and slightly overweight man in his fifties. He has puffy red cheeks and his tummy protrudes over the waist of his trousers. He wears thick lens spectacles held around his ears by a steel frame. He's not in good shape. I make him continue to stand opposite me, next to his desk. For a time we just stand there, looking at each other, saying nothing. I stare him straight in the eye. For a while he defiantly stares back. He is the first to lower his eyes.

He blurts out, "What is this intrusion about and why do you behave in such an outlandish manner? Why did you shoot one of my staff? Can't you see he needs proper medical attention? And why are you holding us here against our will? What is it you want?"

I say to him, "So many questions, Colonel. But we are the people to ask them, not you."

"How dare you come here and talk to me like that. I am a senior officer from X Division of the *Hauptverwaltung Aufklärung,* the main directorate for reconnaissance. My work is directed by Herr Werner Grossmann, the head of our division."

Ed has moved up to stand next to me. He says to Krause in a soft tone, "That must be a very important job, Colonel. Are you the head of your section here?

"Yes, I am. And I have important work to do. Your gross intrusion here is an outrage in preventing me from getting on with my work."

Ed says to me, "Could we let the Colonel sit down here at his desk. You can see he is very uncomfortable."

I hold him firmly by his shoulders, steer him to his desk. I push down so that he sits with a hard jolt. I stand behind the chair, out of his vision. Ed stands in front of him.

Krause says, "I am indeed in charge of this section and I can tell that neither one of you is German." He continues in English, "I speak and write English perfectly so we might make more progress if we speak English instead of struggling with the poor German that both of you two speak."

Ed, "Yes, Colonel, I can hear you speak excellent English. Do you know other languages?"

Krause, "Yes of course. I am equally fluent in Russian. I also speak good French."

Ed, "That's really impressive, Colonel. Yes, I know we'll make much more progress here if you will do us the favour of speaking in English. As you so rightly say, your linguistic ability is far superior to our poor German."

At first I had wondered where Ed is going with this line. But now I'm beginning to realise that Ed is a skilled interrogator. He can see that Krause is a conceited man and Ed is playing to that characteristic. I am more than content to play the "Mr Nasty" role to complement Ed's "Mr Nice".

Ed again, "What is it you do in your department here, Colonel?"

Krause, "I can't discuss that. All our work is top secret."

Ed, "Do you initiate the work or do you merely carry out the orders of Herr Grossmann?"

Krause pauses and we wait for his reply. While he's thinking, I hold his shoulders from behind. I squeeze, not too hard but enough to cause him slight pain. I then take my hands away again.

Then Krause says, "Of course I have to do it all. Grossmann has not got the intellectual ability. Nothing has been the same since our previous director retired two years ago."

Ed, "Who was that?"

Krause, "Herr Markus Wolf of course. He's a brilliant man and we bitterly regret that things have gone downhill since he left. I seem to be the only one now capable of carrying on with the same standard of work that Herr Wolf established."

Ed, "I'd heard that Grossmann is very innovative and has created new projects since he has been the director. Is that not so?"

Krause, "That's absolute rubbish! Grossmann has no idea, he's just a "yes man" to Mielke and his gang at the head of our Stasi movement."

Krause is revealing that not only is he a conceited man but he also has a big chip on his shoulder against his direct boss and the Stasi hierarchy. Ed is doing an excellent job at getting through to Krause, while I hover behind his shoulder just as a reminding menace that he'd better keep talking.

Referring to the computer on the desk, Ed says, "Colonel, that's a pretty incredible machine you have there on your desk. How does your technician operate it?"

Krause, "Of course I don't need a technician to operate it. I do that myself. My staff here merely follow my orders."

Ed, "I've not seen one like that even though I'm an American. Is it an IBM machine?"

Krause, "Certainly not. We work with "state of the art" machines. This is called a Macintosh Plus, made by the Apple company."

I'm content that we should stick to this line for a while as I can tell Ed is getting Krause to open up and show off his knowledge. This could take time and we can't afford to hang around here any longer than we have to, but we do need to get something substantive from Krause before we can leave. So Ed continues.

Ed, "When you say state of the art, what do you mean?"

Krause, "Well this is the third model in the Macintosh line. It was first introduced in 1986 following on from the 512K model and is able to run System 7 OS. It has a revolutionary 1 MB RAM which we have the software to expand to 4MB. This machine has 128KB of ROM on the motherboard, double that of previous Macs and the ROMs include the routine to support the new 800KB floppy drive disks. This has the advantage of enabling us to store all files in a single directory.

Ed, "Woo, Colonel, you're losing me! I'm only just learning to adapt to the use of computers in my office. You're way ahead of me. I suppose you must have good intellectual discussions about this with our Soviet colleagues. I hear that Mr Gorbachev is pushing for his country to embrace new technology of this type. Are you sharing data with them?"

Krause, "Bah! Never with that traitor Gorbachev. Thanks to him and all his Glasnost and Perestroika business, he has left our country vulnerable. We cannot allow that to continue. Before, when our communist movement was strong and cohesive, we knew we could always rely on our Soviet allies. Now, this man's so called new thinking is totally destabilising and is a direct threat to our principles here in the DDR."

Ed, "How do you mean – a threat?"

Krause, "We can't go on like this. Honecker is becoming more and more remote and our Stasi boss Erich Mielke seems to have lost his way ever since Herr Wolf left us two years ago. The Soviets here, with whom we used to have a close rapport and common political identity, now seem to be have changed their attitude towards us. Today, there's a sense of unease about the place and I really don't know any more if we could count on their support if there were to be a serious challenge to our SED party.

Ed, "Colonel, you told us you have very important work to do here. What is it?"

I could sense Krause tensing up. He must have realised he had already said far too much about his attitude to his bosses in the DDR. While he and Ed had been talking, Adel had come across and picked up several of the floppy disks that were at the side of Krause's desk. We noticed there was also a small pile of the new type CD-ROMs. Casually he inserts one of the disks into the Macs hard-drive. A report appears on the screen. It's written in English.

Ed, "Colonel, how impressive that is! Could you tell us what the report that we can see on your computer screen is about and who you send it to?"

Now is the time to get heavy with him. I put my hands back on his shoulders from behind, squeeze firmly and I physically turn him so that his face is pointing directly at the screen.

Ed now ceases to play the nice guy. Instead he says, "That's enough playing games, Krause, we've recorded your comments about Honecker and Mielke. Just those alone will be enough to send you off to the Hohenschönhausen. Now I'll ask you again. What can we see on your computer screen?"

Krause tries to free himself from the grip I have on his shoulders but I squeeze just a little harder and push his face closer to the screen. At that close range the words must appear to be in large bold print in front of his bespectacled eyes. I know that now we have him.

Ed resumes his quieter tone, "Tell us what your reports are about, Colonel Krause."

I keep the pressure on his shoulders and Adel begins to scroll down through the report at slow enough speed so that we can read the text. We can see it's about Soviet troop reinforcements travelling through Poland."

We can also see that Krause has had enough. He blurts out, "All right, that's an extract of a report I wrote two days ago."

Ed, "Why did you write that? Did that troop reinforcement really occur?"

Krause, "Of course not, I invented it."

Ed, "Why did you do that?"

Krause, "All right, all right, I'll tell you. We in the DDR are becoming increasing worried about the improving relations between the Soviets and the NATO countries, particularly the Americans. This détente is leaving us very vulnerable. Gorbachev's speech last week has made the situation even worse. With Mielke and Grossmann's authority, I have been producing reports suggesting a renewed built up of forces. I write these referring to Soviet moves and send them to US sources knowing they will feed them in to those agencies within the US administration that I know will be more susceptible to this type of report. I write other reports in Russian suggesting that NATO is taking advantage of the Soviet perestroika policies to strengthen its military posture. I send these to hard-line sources within the Politburo of the Kremlin."

He pauses and we wait for him to continue. He then says defiantly, "The secret is to know which agencies to send the reports to. Where they are likely to be taken seriously by the recipient who can influence changes and reactions to NATO and Soviet policy. That is my particular skill."

Ed again, "And you've been very successful, Colonel. We congratulate you. But now it has come to an end. What do you wish to do now? We will be taking all your floppies and CDs as evidence. You could come also with us to the West. If you are honest about your work with this disinformation, you will be treated fairly. But if you stay, well… we don't need to spell out the consequences."

My Soviet supplied radio starts to bleep. I operate the pressel switch to indicate "receive". It's Frederik. "Attention, Peter. Three guards are on security patrol. Heading to your compound."

That is all he says. I jump to my feet and say to all our captives. "Keep quiet everyone. Not a word, you understand! Ed, keep them covered!"

I walk briskly back towards the entrance, open the door to the corridor, pass through and close it behind me. I go to the second door which leads to the front entrance. I open this and see that Klaus is there on duty as I had instructed. I say to him, "Guards on their way, don't let them through. I've got you covered." I close the door again but leave a slight gap so that I can see through into the lobby. I have my Kalashnikov at the ready. There's no way I will let them through.

Within seconds, three uniformed guards appear and come straight into the entrance section. Their leader says to Klaus, "Night security patrol. We need to check in with Colonel Krause."

Klaus plays his role well. He says, "Not possible. The colonel is in there working on an urgent report that he has to send out tonight. He gave strict instructions he must not be disturbed. He's OK, you can take my word for it."

The patrol leader replies, "We don't do "trust". We need to be sure."

We're in a stand-off situation here. If they insist on coming on, I shall have no choice but to open fire. I'm confident that I can take the three of them out but the sound of gunfire would be bound to alert other security patrols in the area. So, I hold my fire and wait.

The patrol leader seems undecided. He stands there looking towards the door where I am hidden. I hold my breath and wait.

After what seems like an age but was probably no more than a few seconds, he makes up his mind. He says, "OK then, we'll leave it for now." He beckons to the other two guards and they move back to the compound entrance and leave.

I wait a few seconds to be sure they've genuinely left, open the door and say a "well done" to Klaus then return to the main complex office area.

"OK, relax everyone," I tell our people. But I know we can't push our luck and stay here much longer. But we still have to resolve the position of Krause. I say to him, "Colonel, you had some breathing space just now. I hope you used it well. We will be leaving here shortly. What is to be? Are you coming with us or do you prefer to stay and justify yourself to Mielke and Grossmann?"

I don't care that much what his choice is. I've already decided we will have to take him with us. Better though if he's a willing realist rather than us having to drag him all the way.

"OK, you're right," Krause says, "now you've destroyed my work, there's no future for me here. There probably never was anyway. I can see all around me that my party, the SED, which I've supported for many years, is already beginning to fall apart. I see corruption and despair with more and more of our citizens being carted off to the Hohenschönhausen just because some informer has reported something adverse about them, whether or not it's true. I hoped that my work might have set the US and Soviets against each other and reignited the old Cold War situation and therefore, restored the protection of my country by the Soviets. Now you have ruined my work, I can only imagine our citizens will become more and more emboldened to defy our communist leaders and attempt to join with the West. Maybe we can hold out as an independent country for a year or so longer, I don't know. My decision is now clear. I will come with you to the West and take my chances there."

"Right, you have made the right decision, Krause. Before we leave, show me the distribution list of your reports. I don't read Cyrillic so let's concentrate on your Western list."

Krause reaches for a file and opens it up. I decide to take this and the Russian version with us. I scan quickly through the list. Two names catch my eye. One is Suzanne Brok, Intelligence Division, NATO headquarters, Brussels. That's our ever helpful, SuziB! So, I was right to have assumed that! There's one other name I recognise too. It's John Evers, I remember that's the name of the MI6 guy who had been pushing the hard line during the meeting at the Joint Intelligence Committee in London. Well, well!! I think our analysts will have a field day with this list. I fold it neatly and put it in my pocket.

It's time to get out of here. First I go over to Bernd who had attended to the guy I had shot. Bernd tells me he will need further attention but his wounded shoulder is stabilised. He will live. I ask about the other six, who are still leaning up against the wall with their hands tied and are less their shoes and belts. They have been watching and listening throughout. I have no wish to kill them but we can't just leave them here risking they might free themselves quickly and raise the alarm. And I'm certainly not prepared to try to take them all with us: dragging along Krause will be effort enough.

Bernd says, "Look, I know I shouldn't suggest this from a medical ethics view, but I can give each an injection that will immobilise them for about an hour or so without doing any lasting harm."

That's all I need to hear. I tell him, "Do it now, Bernd!"

I call Frederik on the Soviet radio and check all is clear. He confirms it is. I tell him to return to our complex. I also check with Klaus that the front lobby area is clear. He says it is.

We ensure we have collected all the floppy disks, CDs and paper files needed as proof of Krause's reports and his means of distribution. We give Krause his shoes and belt back. Then, when Bernd confirms that all the other captives are injected and immobilised, we are ready to leave.

I get Frederik to lead us again and I follow on behind him. I get Ed to act as Krause's guardian and tell Klaus to act as our rear guard. In this formation, we retrace our steps back toward the main entrance to the Stasi complex.

We have a clear route on the way back, no incidents, no challenges. Frederik leads us back to the VIP parking area where we had left the two cars. We are sure we know exactly where the cars were parked. But the two spaces are now empty. The cars are gone.

Chapter Twenty-Nine

Frederik has the presence of mind hardly to break stride when he realises our means of transport has gone. We can only speculate what the reason may be. But speculation won't help. We have to assume the worst case that the Stasi have noted the cars were not officially authorised or logged and that they now have put the parking area under close surveillance.

We proceed on towards the main gate and I see that Ed has moved up close behind Krause to ensure he's covered should he choose to have a change of mind and try to alert the Stasi guard. At the entry/exit point to the complex, there is one wide opening for vehicles, divided into an "In and an Out" section. It's the same with the smaller pedestrian point. There are far fewer employees entering and leaving than when we had arrived. The guards seem to be doing a thorough job of checking IDs at the entry line but as far as we can see the exit point is unguarded. We keep walking towards it at a steady pace, keeping up with Frederik in his Stasi officer's uniform. We come up level with the sentry post. A guard looks our way, sees Frederik and smartly salutes him. Frederik returns the salute and keeps on walking. The rest of us follow on behind. We turn into Möllendorffstrasse in the opposite direction to where Nikonov had earlier instigated the tram crash. We can see rescue teams still working there though the earlier commotion seems to have died down. We keep on walking to be sure we are well clear of the Stasi headquarter complex.

At least we are now in the open. From my earlier planning, I know it is about eight or nine kilometres from here to the Palast der Republik near the Schlossplatz – too far for us all to walk there at this time of the evening without drawing attention, particularly as the good Colonel Krause is already wheezing with the effort. I switch my radio to the channel reserved for Nikonov and I say "DELTA!" A few seconds later I receive the reply "DELTA confirm." We had agreed this code means "We need transport". Let's hope it works.

We soon hear the sound of a truck coming up behind us, then slowing and pulling up next to us. We hope it's not a Stasi patrol. It's not. Instead it's a fearsome looking armoured personnel carrier. It has eight wheels, four each side and I notice it has a turret with both a 14.5mm heavy machine gun and a mounted 7.62mm medium machine gun. I recognise it as having the NATO designator OT-64. As far as I know, this beast of a vehicle is produced only by Poland and Czechoslovakia so how the hell Nikonov has got hold of it, and to have responded so quickly, I've no idea. He must have put together the means of supplying all the items on our code list – just in case.

Nikonov is here in person. He leaps down from the turret, runs around to the rear of the vehicle and opens up the rear door. He gives me an infectious grin, makes a little mock bow and ushers us inside. He closes the door behind us and, I imagine, resumes his position in the turret. What a star this guy is!

Inside the vehicle there is room to spare. There's a dim interior light allowing us to get our bearings and we take our places on the firm seating. I find an intercom system which I presume is connected to the command turret. I call Heidi over so that she can interpret and I soon hear she's speaking directly to Nikonov. She says something to him which I think means, "Wait a moment, I'll ask him", then she says, "He's telling me this vehicle is amphibious. Do you want us to find somewhere over the River Spree and zap through the water straight over to the Western side?"

Now, there's an idea – what a spectacular way to get us all back to West Berlin in style!! But I know it won't be that simple, as inviting as the idea seems. For a start, I have no idea where we could possibly find a point in this heavily monitored and patrolled part of Berlin where we could just drive and "swim" the vehicle through without being detected and causing a major political incident. Secondly, I have an obligation to Marshal Ogarkov to accept the support of Nikonov's team but not to the point where any action would upset the sensitivities of the present West/East balance. Charging over the River Spree could seriously fuck up everything we are trying to achieve. I'm so tempted to go for it, but I know that this option is not a goer. Fuck it, but I have to say "no".

I say to Heidi, "Tell him "Great idea but NO!" Just get us to the Palast der Republik and drop us off nearby but not right bang outside! Let's try to be discreet about it because arriving in a fucking great OT-64 is bit too crowd pulling. I'm sure he'll understand."

Heidi gets back on the intercom and gives me a thumbs-up sign indicating he's got the message. We trundle on through the snow littered streets of East Berlin in this armoured shell of a vehicle.

In the dim lighting of the interior, I look around at my fellow travellers. Adel and Bernd are sitting up close together. Both have already played their part. Bernd was quick to attend to the guy I shot and to immobilise our captives; Adel sorted out the hi-tech computer issues and uncovered all the disinformation messages. Frederik did an outstanding job in leading us in and out of the formidable Stasi complex. I can see him now, head down, resting so he will be ready for the next move. I think he knows we still have many problems yet to face. Sitting next to him is young Klaus. He's a strong guy, cool under pressure when challenged by the Stasi patrol and always ready to respond. Sitting next on the hard seats are Ed and his captive, Colonel Krause. Ed has proved his worth this evening. He and I had not even discussed how to deal with Krause but somehow, we had blended into a team when it came to interrogating him. Ed took over the lead there entirely. I've come to realise that Ed has great qualities. I think I was underestimating him in my mind and yet again I have been proved wrong. As far as Colonel Krause is concerned, I wonder what is going through his mind. I see him now sitting there, his face impassive. The events of this evening have totally changed his life. From a self-important line manager, thinking he was saving his country to… what? He tells me he's prepared to throw in his lot with us and bargain with the Western authorities, but I wonder how he will react when push comes to shove. I don't trust the guy and know we'll have to keep him under our close control until, hopefully, we can all get safely back to the West.

Heidi is now sitting close up next to me. What a day it's been since we broke free from each other's arms in the wee small hours of this morning! To Zossen and my amazing interview there with Marshal Ogarkov, to our meeting in Lichtenberg when I had to start playing the role of "the commander in charge", to our infiltration to the Stasi HQ and out again. And here we are now inside the protective shield of this monster of a vehicle! I wonder what is going to become of us. Heidi looks up and we make serious eye contact. She gives me that wonderful smile again. It's been a long time!

The OT-64 continues to trundle along and I guess we must soon be nearing the Palast area. I see the time is now 2220 hours. I try to radio through to Ruth to fix a rendezvous point but I can't get a signal. It must be due to the armoured shell of the vehicle. There's a hatch leading from the interior compartment up to the turret. It has a small aperture and I fear I might get stuck. So, I tell Heidi to go up and I see that her petite body shape has no problem slipping up through. I tell her to check with Nikonov how far we still have to go, then to contact Ruth and fix a meeting time and place. She's soon back and tells me Nikonov has chosen a spot to park the armoured vehicle in a road just adjacent to the Palast and that we will arrive there in a few minutes time. From up in the turret, she got good reception to Ruth and arranged for us to meet her at the entrance to the bowling alley that's inside the Palast building.

I tell our guys the plan and to be ready to disembark the OT-64. Frederik tells me he has actually been bowling there so I ask him to lead us once again. Ed and Klaus will stay close to Colonel Krause. We can't risk him trying to slip away.

The armoured vehicle judders to a stop and we wait while Nikonov opens the rear hatch door. We get out and find ourselves looking up at the huge brightly lit building ahead. I shake Nikonov warmly by the hand. He has responded brilliantly. I feel he's now involved with our mission and would like to accompany us further. It would certainly be an asset for him to stay with us but I know that is not politically acceptable to Marshal Ogarkov. Through Heidi, I tell him to remain on call as we have no idea what hurdles we may yet have to overcome before we can get back to the West.

Frederik resumes his position in the lead as we head straight over the road to the Palast. I have no previous knowledge of this place and am amazed by its sheer size. Ruth had explained that there is a concert on this evening given by the Leipzig symphony orchestra. It must be just concluding as we see a stream of early leavers coming down the stairs of the concert auditorium. But there are not only concert goers here. Even at this time of the evening, it is crowded and we are ourselves soon part of this crowd. This is good for our security but I'm concerned to ensure we keep a tight watch on Krause. I look over at Ed and know I don't need to be concerned. Ed and Klaus have moved either side of Krause and are poised to grip him if he were to try to escape.

Frederik leads us up a flight of stairs and past a couple of restaurants which are still open and full of customers. Ahead is a group of young East Berliners heading for a sign for a discotheque. We hear the loud bass tones of rock music as we walk past the entrance. We turn a corner and see the sign for the bowling alley up ahead. As we approach, we see Ruth.

We hardly break step but now follow on behind Ruth as she leads us up back down two long flights of stairs. At the bottom, we continue along a corridor until we reach a set of closed doors. I reckon we are now in the basement of the building. On one of the doors is a large notice, "*Privatzimmer. Kein Zutritt*" - Private, no admittance. Ruth produces a key and opens the door. We enter and she closes and locks the door behind us.

Ruth says, "We can talk here. We are now in the suite of offices and rooms that Honecker keeps exclusively for himself and his family. Normally only a few of his closest aides ever come down here. I have a key as I'm sometimes required to come in the evenings to take dictation. Other than the Honeckers themselves, only the security department also have keys. The guards sometimes do security checks so we need to be alert. The Honeckers are out of town today and are not due back for a day or two but they are expected to spend their Christmas here. We will now go on and I'll show you the entrance to the tunnel."

I can see that Ruth is more relaxed now that we have safely navigated our way through the crowds and are into this quiet area of empty rooms and offices. She acts like a tour guide, pointing out the function of each of the rooms as we pass by them. We are in another corridor and Ruth explains, "This leads to the tunnel which was built in the greatest secrecy by trusted Stasi employees. It runs under a main road to outbuildings which have direct access to the River Spree. It has not yet been used but is available at all times to Honecker as a means to escape to the West should he feel this to be necessary. Here's the key to the grille at the tunnel entrance. I'm now going – "

Ruth doesn't get to finish her sentence as we find ourselves facing a young Stasi uniformed guard. He calls out in German. "Halt, this a private property. You are intruding here."

I see he has quick reactions. As he's speaking he tries to do two things at the same time - to operate his radio and to draw his pistol. I have no choice. I free my Kalashnikov from inside my parka and fire two single shots, one at his left hand that is reaching for his radio, the second at his right arm to stop him from firing his gun. The shots find their mark and the guard slumps down in front of us. Already he is bleeding profusely. I stoop down beside him and check the radio. The guard had no time to shout an alarm but, despite that, the radio appears to be set on "send" so the sound of my shots and perhaps his challenge to us could have been received by his control room. I rip the battery out of the radio handset and hope that is enough to immobilise it. I decide we have no time to waste as guard reinforcements could be on the way.

The shooting has been too much for poor Ruth. She is shaking violently and crying. Between her sobs, she says, "I can't understand it. I came up here earlier this evening to check. No-one was here then. Now I've put you all at risk. And that poor man you shot. He was only doing his job."

I try my best to comfort her, but I know we can't hang around. I bring in Heidi to help the poor lady. I tell Ruth, "It's not your fault, you've done a great job to get us here. But you can see we now have to move on before the guards' reinforcement come to investigate."

Ruth stammers out, "I know, I know but I can't. I just can't go on. This is all my fault!"

There's no way we can calm her. But we cannot stay here. I see a door to a room next to where we are standing. I open it and see it's an empty bedroom. Heidi and I lead Ruth into the room and lay her on a bed. She doesn't resist. We'll have to leave her here. It's tough as she's been so obliging to get us to this point. But we have no choice. We must go on. We take the key she's still clutching and leave her on the bed.

As we turn the next corner, we come to the end of the corridor. In front of us is a door. It is not locked. Behind is a large metal grille. I have the key that I took from Ruth and insert it into the lock. It opens and we swing the large grille door open to expose access directly to the tunnel. It is completely dark and although we find a light switch, it doesn't work.

Klaus is still carrying the haversack we loaded up before we left for Normannenstrasse and we extract the torch that Nikonov had provided. Its beam is quite weak but at least we can see our main direction of travel. The tunnel appears to be clad in reinforced concrete and its roof must be about two metres high. None of us have to stoop. I'm amazed how well constructed it appears to be and that, according to Ruth, it's existence has been kept such a close secret.

We make our way cautiously along the tunnel. Ruth said it is only about fifty metres long so it shouldn't take us long to find our way through to the end. I keep everyone close together as we feel our way through the darkness guided by the weak beam of the torch. I regularly check that Colonel Krause is still keeping up. Having got him this far I'd hate anything to happen to him now. I can hear his rasping breath and can just make out that Ed is steering him along with a strong grip on his arm.

We've no precise information about what we can expect at the end of the tunnel. But if indeed it leads out directly onto the River Spree and a boat is moored there, as Ruth had told us, we should make it to the RV with Cheryl not long after the 2300 hours RV time. The thought of getting back to the West, and of catching up again with Cheryl, spurs me on to get to the end.

The light from our torch finally picks up a shadow up ahead of us. We move in closer. To our dismay, we find we have come up to a solid brick built wall. We shine the torch along its surface and find a stout metal door set into the brickwork of the wall. It has a handle which I turn. It's doesn't open. I still have the key which we used to open the door at the other end of the tunnel. I insert it in the lock. It doesn't work.

I hear voices coming from the entry end of the tunnel. Then shouting. It has to be the reinforcement guard. I try again to open the door with the key. It doesn't budge. I try to barge it open with my shoulder. It doesn't move. Frederik tries - no luck. He and I both try together - same result.

I tell the others to stand well back. I raise my Kalashnikov and fire a burst of rapid fire at the lock. It has the same result. The door will NOT open!

I hear the sounds of the guards making their way down the tunnel towards us. We can't open the fucking door and the guards are closing in. We know they will be fully armed. We're completely trapped!

Chapter Thirty

I've got to get a grip, and fast. We've got a fair amount of firepower between us and it might be possible to shoot our way back to the Palast. But what then? If the reinforcing guard fail to report back quickly, the Stasi will up the stakes and send in a major task force. We wouldn't stand a chance against such a force. I'm also concerned that we must do all we can to keep Colonel Krause alive. He's the crucial evidence we have come here to find.

We listen as the guards make their way towards us. They are talking quietly to each other and we can see the silhouette of their shapes in the flickering light of their torches. I can make out three shapes. There appears to be no one following up behind. Only the three guys. That makes our task easier than I had at first feared.

I call Frederik and Klaus to prepare to come forward with me. I tell them we are going to close in on them and each of us will fire off an automatic burst aiming just wide of them, enough to put the shits up them but not to hit them. After that, Frederik is to use his most authoritative Stasi voice to command them to drop their weapons. I tell Ed to stay put here with Krause and the rest of our team. We make sure our torch stays switched off.

The three of us move slowly up towards the oncoming guards. We spread out across the width of the tunnel. We can see them against the light of their torches. They cannot see us. I let the gap between us and the guards reduce down to about ten metres then I open fire with a short automatic burst with my Kalashnikov. I intentionally fire just over their heads. As I open fire both Frederik and Klaus do the same. The noise in the confines of the tunnel is deafening. As soon as we cease firing, Frederik yells out, "Drop your weapons and raise your hands. Do it now!!" There's a moment's hesitation then first one, their leader I assume, does as Frederik has ordered. The other two follow on. All three stand stock still with their hands raised in the dim light. Frederik goes forward and looms over them while Klaus goes to each of them and collects their weapons which, like ours, are also Kalashnikovs. What a nice coincidence!

Klaus remains on prisoner guard duty while I do a quick body search of each of them for additional weapons. I find none. I call out to Ed to tell him he can put the torch back on and his group should make their way back to the tunnel entrance. We need to regroup and rethink there.

We all backtrack up the tunnel and return to the Honecker suite of private rooms. Klaus continues to cover our three new captives and when we are again in full lighting, I see that they are three young men, still boys almost. They look thoroughly scared and subdued. I'll have to decide what to do with them while we revise our escape plans. More pressing is that the first guard that I had shot is still lying where he had fallen near the tunnel entrance. He is also only a slim young man. He is conscious but in pain. As soon as Bernd joins us, I ask him to attend to him as best he can.

I remember we had left Ruth lying on a bed in one of the many rooms that lead off this main corridor. I recognise the room and check inside. There is no one there, just the indentation marks of where her body was lying. I wonder where she is and hope that she has recovered and made her way safely back to the main Palast building. She was not up to this type of pressure. I wish her well.

We check on communications and find that only the patrol leader has a radio. I turn to Adel for advice and tell him that we need urgently to do what we can to keep the link between the patrol guys open and seemingly routine with their base control. With Klaus hovering over them with his Kalashnikov, Adel tells the patrol leader to send in a routine report to his base controller. The reply comes back asking why they took so long to reply to an earlier comms check. Under Adel's direction again, the leader says they were checking the tunnel and while inside there, their radio doesn't work due to the solid reinforced concrete construction. The base then asks about the first guard, the one I had shot. Again, under Adel's direction, the patrol leader says he is fine and checking out one of the Honecker rooms, adding that his own radio has a malfunction.

From the above exchange, it is reasonable to assume that the sound of our firing when we were inside the tunnel had not been heard outside. What a tribute to the tunnel builders! I tell Adel to stick with the task of directing the radio replies that the patrol leader makes to his base. If he gets any defiance from the patrol leader or the other two, Klaus will sort it out.

Bernd checks in to tell me he has taken the medical field dressings from our captives and had enough to patch up the guard I had shot earlier. He tells me his wounds are superficial and he will survive.

I feel we've bought ourselves a breathing space but this won't last for long. The main guard base will eventually suspect trouble and bring a larger force to investigate. The main problem still looming over us is how we are going to get out of here and to the West. It's not a viable option to try to get back out of the Palast and search for some other escape route. It's now after 2300 hours and the earlier crowds at the concert, bowling and restaurants will have dispersed so we would stand out if we tried to leave by the same route we used to get in. Yet we found the tunnel comes to a dead end. We don't have the key to open the metal door and it resisted our best efforts to force it open.

I can think of only one solution to get us moving on and this involves our friend Nikonov once again. I had asked him to remain on call so let's hope he still is. I find an old scrap of notepaper and a pencil in the pocket of my parka. I draw a picture and write a name in English. I ask Frederik if he is willing to return back through the Palast building and take the paper to Nikonov. He is our best choice as he is still wearing his Stasi uniform. As always, he's up for it. Before he leaves, I use my radio on the dedicated frequency to call up Nikonov. When he replies, I get Heidi to translate that I have urgent need of a particular weapon and that Frederik is en route to collect it.

Now we can only wait. Our team is still holding up well despite the frustration and disappointment we all felt when we found ourselves trapped at the dead end of the tunnel. I still hope we might somehow unearth the key to that door. Heidi is nearby and I can tell she is restless so I ask her to do a check through the rooms in General Secretary Honecker's suite to see if the key can be found. I know it's a forlorn hope, but worth a try.

Bernd has now finished administering to the wounded guard. I know he is a skilled doctor but I have another job for him if ever we get the chance. I ask him, "Bernd, what do you know about boats?"

"What don't I know about boats might be a better question, Peter! Sailing and navigation have been hobbies of mine since I was a boy. Whenever I have the free time, I go up to the coast near Rostock where I moor my own boat. Why do you ask? We're a long way from the sea here."

"Not the sea, Bernd, but the river. Do you understand about boat engines?"

"Well, I'm better at sailing, but sure, I have my own motor as a reserve when there's no wind or it's in the wrong direction! But you haven't answer my question, why do you want to know?"

"Fair point." I reply, "Look, Bernd, I still haven't given up the idea of us getting out via this tunnel. If we do, we need someone who is comfortable with boats, their engines and navigation to get us from this side of the River Spree to the other. Could you do that?"

"Of course. Just give me the chance!"

I hope I will.

Ed seems satisfied with the role he has undertaken as Colonel Krause's minder. They have taken the room where Ruth had been and found two chairs to make themselves comfortable. Ed has left the door wide open to remain in contact. I see they are in deep conversation and, knowing Ed's skills, I'm sure he has learnt a great deal more about the whole disinformation effort that the Stasi's have been engaged in. If we ever do get out of here, Ed's newfound knowledge will be invaluable to Western intelligence.

Heidi returns empty-handed from her key hunt. She tells me she searched in every unlocked room in the whole of the Honecker suite. She had no luck. No key.

The time seems to drag waiting for Frederik to return. It's already been nearly one hour. I hope he's found Nikonov and more important that the Russian is able to supply what I have asked. I just have to control my impatience and keep waiting. There's nothing else to do.

Adel comes over to me looking agitated. He tells us, "The patrol base has relayed through to our captive guards that the Stasi headquarters is in a high state of alert. They say the staff at Colonel Krause's office have raised the alarm and reported that Colonel Krause has been kidnapped. They say they had been drugged and the effects are only just wearing off."

Bernd says, "Well, the timing of the injections I gave them is not an exact science. At least they gave us time to get out of there."

"That's not all," Adel continues, "the patrol base is saying that Stasi HQ has told them they are not satisfied the Honecker suite has been comprehensively searched following earlier reports of irregularities there. A major task force is being assembled and will be sent over to the Palast shortly.

Now we are trapped here again. If we try to return back to the main Palast concourse we would surely be spotted trying to cart out Colonel Krause who the Stasi now know is kidnapped.

There's movement in the corridor and we brace ourselves. To our relief, it's Frederik. He's carrying what looks like a long pipe. It's wrapped in an outer container with a local Berlin plumber's name.

"Long story and not without complications," says Frederik. "Main thing, Peter, is I've got what you asked for. Nikonov sends it with his compliments."

We unwrap the packaging. Inside to my delight is the RPG - 7V anti-tank rocket launcher I had tasked Nikonov to provide! My heartfelt thanks go out to him and to Frederik for somehow spiriting it through to us here. I get Frederik to come with me and tell the rest to stay where they are but to be prepared to move quickly at short notice. Klaus can keep our captives under guard and bring them with us when we go.

I can see a lot of questioning faces but there's not time for explanations now that we know the Stasi will soon be visiting us again.

Frederik seems used to carrying the weight of the rocket launcher and sticks with it as we walk back down the tunnel. I'm holding the torch to keep us on track. When we are about twenty metres short of the brick wall, I tell him to stop and put the launcher of the ground. I examine it as well as is possible under the limited light thrown out by the torch. I'm familiar with the details of the weapon as we hold some for instruction in our armoury back in Ashford, but I've never actually fired one. Nikonov only supplied one rocket which was all that Frederik could reasonably carry. So I'd better get this right as there won't be a second chance.

I reckon the basic pyro dynamics are pretty similar to the UK produced 3.5 inch rocket launcher which I have fired. That gives a mighty kick if not held firmly but it's the back blast which can be lethal to anyone standing right behind the firing point. What I've read about this RPG is that it fires a HEAT, that's High Explosive Anti-Tank round capable of penetrating up to 320mm of armour. I reckon that should make mincemeat of the fucking brick wall!

I place the launcher on my right shoulder and tell Frederik to shine the torch directly ahead so I can just see the outline of the wall. While I hold the aim steady I get Frederik to ensure the rocket is firmly bedded to the firing mechanism. Now we're ready to go. I tell Frederik to kneel down on my left side. On no account must he get behind me or the backblast will take his head off.

Frederick kneels down next to me and continues to shine the torch forward to allow me to keep my aim straight. Now for it. I squeeze the trigger. There is a slight pause and for a moment I fear we have a misfire then there's a sudden jerk as the projectile leaves the tube of the launcher followed almost instantly by a thunderous roar as the HEAT round crashes through the brick wall ahead. Both Frederik and I are almost blinded by the flash of the explosion and deafened by the noise. We stand still and wait for our senses to return. We are covered in the dust that has been stirred up by the blast.

We shake ourselves down and move forward. Surprisingly the torch is still working. We reach the wall and I shine the torch at it. Right bang centre of the wall we see a gaping hole in the brickwork and a view of the night sky beyond. We move further forward to the hole. It's almost a perfect circle with a circumference big enough for a human to crawl through. I peer through the hole and can just see the outline of some steps leading down to the river's edge. At the bottom of the steps I see a small boat. I give thanks to General Secretary Honecker for his careful planning. We now have our escape route.

We hurry back to the other end of the tunnel and I tell everyone we must move without delay. I get Bernd to go first and I tell him to leg it through the hole we've blasted and to see if he can get to the boat and fix its motor ready for our river cruise across to the other side. He doesn't hesitate.

I get Ed to hurry the good Colonel Krause along. He's our special package. Then the rest of us follow on with Klaus bringing up the rear still guarding our captives.

It's quite a scrum in the tunnel but progress is good. In the flickering torchlight, I can see Bernd up ahead and his figure disappearing as he crawls though the hole at the end. I know it won't be long before the Stasi major task force reach the Honecker suite.

When we get to the wall, I tell Ed to get through the hole first, then we push Colonel Krause through with Ed on the other side to control him down the steps to the boat. Then one by one the rest of us can follow.

We hear echoing voices coming from the other end of the tunnel. It can only be the Stasi task force. Adel is through the hole and we push our captive guards though. They don't resist as Klaus is right behind them.

I can now see lights flashing and hear the sound of orders being given. The Stasi force is coming into the tunnel. I tell Heidi to go on through the hole. Frederik and I are the last two left. We change magazines on our Kalashnikovs and chamber a round ready to fire. Without me telling him, he knows we have to hold the task force soldiers up until all our people are safely away. We spread out to opposite sides of the tunnel and move slowly forward. I can now clearly see the lead soldiers moving steadily forward. They are now about thirty metres from our position.

Their flashlight enables us to pinpoint their positions exactly. I can't afford to delay any longer, hoping all our people have reached the boat. I aim directly at the lead soldier and tap a short burst. The soldier falls instantly. From across the tunnel, Frederik also fires. Another guy falls.

Our action causes the forward movement of the task force to halt but I know this will only be temporary. Then I see guys moving into position pulling an object that I can't identify. Then to my horror I see what it is. It's a flamethrower. In the confined space of the tunnel, this would be a fearsome weapon. It is however well within the range of our Kalashnikovs so I don't hesitate and I fire a rapid burst directly at the appliance and then at the two soldiers who were pulling it into position. I see the flamethrower topple on its side which I hope has made it inoperable. The escorting soldiers are lying next to it. I see the figure of another guy who was giving orders to the others. I aim at him and fire. Nothing happens. I must have used up the full thirty rounds in the magazine. I have one mag left which I fit on, ready to go. But it's my last and I need to keep some reserve for what we might encounter later. So, I take careful aim at their leader and tap a short burst. I see him fall.

There is a lack of further movement by the task force personnel. I suppose they are discussing how best to regroup and attack us again. I reckon our people should be all on board by now so I decide that Frederik and I should pull out of here. I call out to him. There's no answer. I look across and can only see a shape which is not moving. I go over to him and to my horror I see the side of his head has been shot away. In the heat of our fire exchanges he must have taken a direct hit. There is nothing I can do for him except mourn his death.

I withdraw back towards the wall. I reckon it's now my turn to go. Then I'm shocked to find that Heidi is still here, she should be on the boat by now.

"What the hell are you doing still here, Heidi," I shout at her. "Come on, we have to get out of here now."

She doesn't move but just looks at me with an expression I can't read.

I shout at her again, "Come on, Heidi, we've GOT to go."

I try to pull her towards the hole but she evades my grip. Then she says, "Peter, I'm not coming with you. I can't face what I might find in the West. I'm half East German and half Russian. This is my home. I have to stay."

I try to argue with her, to do anything I can to persuade her. But it's no use.

The task force has got itself organised again and has started firing. I watch helplessly as Heidi turns towards the entrance to the tunnel. To my horror, I see she is undoing her bullet proof vest as she starts to move back up the tunnel. She is hit by a burst of automatic fire and instantly crumbles to the ground. I fire a burst and rush forward. I pick her up but I know there's no hope. She's dead.

I cradle her in my arms and scream out uncontrollably, "You fucking bastards!! Fuck you! FUCK YOU!!!"

I look down at her sweet face and feel a flood of emotion for her. I've known her for such a short time but she filled my world while we were together. I wonder if I should carry her with me to the boat, but she insisted she wanted to stay in the East so I kiss her dead lips, gently lower her to the ground and leave her.

I fire off a final burst from my Kalashnikov to cover my withdrawal and as I struggle through the hole I realise I don't even know Heidi's surname.

Chapter Thirty-One

I'm in a complete daze as I find my way down the steps to the river. What should be a moment of euphoria that we are free has turned into a bitter sense of anguish at the loss of these two people. Frederik, the Stasi officer, belonging to an organisation that the West strongly opposes, turned out to be an absolute hero. Nothing was too difficult or too challenging for him. He made things possible when no one else could have. As one of many examples, I will never know how he managed to get the RPG rocket launcher through to us. But he did and it saved our lives.

Heidi was very, very special and, to me, a unique person. I know I will never meet anyone like her again in my lifetime. I remember the precise last words she spoke before she died. She said, "I can't face what I might find in the West." Maybe I shouldn't be so arrogant but I had told her about my wife and my children and I can't help but think she meant that she couldn't face coming into my life to upset my marriage. I shall never know.

I see the little boat on the jetty ahead of me. It's loaded up and ready to go. As I get on board I see expectant faces wondering where are Frederik and Heidi. I try to keep my voice calm as I tell them that neither of them made it – but I know I don't succeed. Bernd looks at me questioningly and I nod to him. It's time for us to go.

I can tell Bernd has done his homework. The East Germans have put up river barriers in this sector to prevent their citizens from escaping this way but there are gaps which I can't see but Bernd obviously can as he steers a positive but erratic course into the midst of the River Spree. At this mid-winter season point, the water level is high and fast flowing.

My mind is still in a bad place and I hardly notice the rest of our team as Bernd expertly navigates our little boat across the river. I know I must get a grip on myself but it doesn't happen just like that. I know for now I've got to blank out the thoughts I still have of the woman I left behind. Her character, her mesmeric face, her petite figure, the feel and warmth of her body, her amazing smile! Oh Heidi, Oh Heidi!!!!

Now we're nearing the bank on the other side of the river. As Bernd guides us through the cold dark night, I can just make out the mooring spot that he is aiming for. He throttles back on the motor and we glide silently into the point he has chosen for us to land. I wonder what lies in store for most of those on board. We are now back in West Berlin – home territory for Ed and me. But for all the rest? Bernd, Adel and Klaus are now, for them, in a new world. I hope they will adjust and find themselves a new life here. Bernd and Adel are both highly intelligent individuals. I'm sure they will be as successful here as anywhere. For Klaus, he's a young lion of a man but I think the change and pressures of his new life will take more time. I hope he will be OK. I owe so much to all of these guys, a debt I will never be able to repay.

What about Stasi Colonel Krause? I look at him now on the point of our landing. His face is impassive. I really have no idea what thoughts must be going through his mind. He started the day as the arrogant, self-important little man thinking he was saving the world with all his contrived reports. From his perspective, he could well have succeeded. Now he is reduced to having to come in front of a Western court and try to justify his activities. He's smart and I think he will find his way through.

We've also brought these four young guys with us – the Stasi guards. They used to be our enemy, our adversaries, the dreaded Stasi! I look at them now – four young lads who were only doing their duty tonight in support of a regime they probably could not begin to understand. I expect they all have mothers who will now be worrying because their sons have not returned home tonight. I vow to make sure we treat these guys well.

Bernd brings our boat to a stop and Ed helps him attach a rope to a post on the small landing jetty. It's completely dark still and cold and dank as is normal for Berlin in December. The adrenalin that had motivated everyone begins to fade as we wonder what our next move should be.

I know I have to get out of my own depressing thoughts and take some initiative. I remember Klaus had packed some flares in the rucksack we loaded up way back in Lichtenberg. It's time to use them now. Klaus is pleased to have something positive to do. He unloads the flares and sets off a pyrotechnic display. We're all cheered by the fact we can do this without a Stasi reaction. We are now in the West. But still nothing happens until at last we hear the sound of several vehicles approaching. They grind to a halt in front of our jetty. A figure emerges from the lead vehicle and strides purposefully towards us. I recognise the shape and the walk.

I say, "Good evening, Cheryl. What took you so long?"

"Whoa, looky here! Look what's the tide's washed up!" It's "bird" Colonel Cheryl Walker, United States Air Force. As always, despite it being nearly three o'clock in the morning on a cold December night, she's in her usual ebullient form. Ed and I greet her warmly. She's brought along what looks like a platoon's worth of armed US soldiers who disembark quickly from the vehicles and line up along the side of the jetty.

I segregate the Stasi soldiers and ask Cheryl for them to be taken to a detention centre for the night. They can be processed later. I stress that they should be treated well as they have all undergone a stressful night. Maybe they can be returned to their units tomorrow but that's not for me to decide. I then introduce Cheryl to Bernd, Adel and Klaus asking they be found decent billets for the night. I tell her we owe all three a great debt and I will write this in a separate report shortly. Last but far from least, there's Colonel Krause. I leave the introduction for Ed to make.

Ed says, "Now for the star turn of the night. I present to you Colonel Konrad Krause, from Department X, *Hauptverwaltung Aufklärung* of the Stasi headquarters. He is the evidence we went over to the East to find. Please protect him well. We also have a mass of supporting evidence in the form of floppy disks and CDs. Bernd and Adel have already given me the ones they took from Krause's office. It would be good to deposit these for safe keeping overnight ready for them to be documented and handed over to the appropriate authorities."

Cheryl says, "Wilco, it will all be done as you both stipulate. Now, you two boys, it's time for you to hand over your charges and let these competent guys I've brought along do their job. As far as you two gallant heroes are concerned, it's beddy byes time. It's already three o'clock in the fucking morning, for Chrissake!"

Cheryl, as always, has her way with words.

Not quite yet Cheryl, I think to myself. I don't know anything about the processing system for Eastern escapees to the West but once these guys are whisked away, it is unlikely we will meet up with them again.

Not for some time anyway. I see that Ed is having similar thoughts. Both of us go over and give a big hug and handshake to Bernd, Adel and Klaus. Three great guys who all played their parts in our adventure together. Of course, in my mind I'm also thinking about Frederik and Heidi and mourning their loss but I know I have to suppress my emotions about them for tonight.

The transport is brought forward and our guests and captives are on loaded. A special military police guard is provided for Krause. Ed and I shake his hand before he is escorted away under the charge of a competent looking US army major.

Ed, Cheryl and I are left together. Cheryl gives a wave and a smart staff car is driven up alongside. "Come on, boys," she tells us, "Time to go! Oh, and Peter, you look like shit!"

Good old Cheryl. Always the flatterer.

As we glide through the quiet streets of West Berlin, Cheryl explains that for several days, she and all her Western colleagues lost contact with both Ed and me. She continues, "We had no idea what had become of you and for a time we had to fear the worst. Then yesterday, the BRIXMIS brigadier got a call from a Soviet officer telling us you were both safe and he passed the message of our meeting point tonight. And here you are! Of course, you do realise you kept this lady waiting as I was given a 2300 hours RV time! But I'll forgive you, just this once!"

We find ourselves now back in the British zone and we pull up outside the general's residence where we had spent our first night here.

Cheryl says, "Home sweet home, boys. You've been given the same rooms as last time. So, off you both go. Breakfast will be at 0800 hours but there's a cold snack in your rooms. What's more, you'll even get a wake-up call! Sleep well!"

The room I've been allocated is warm, clean and welcoming. I strip off, and take a long hot shower. I towel myself down and can't resist devouring a couple of delicious egg and cucumber sandwiches. Then I just have time to brush my teeth before I collapse into bed. I must have fallen asleep immediately because the next thing I'm aware of is the alarm clock ringing by the side of my bed.

It's a big deal being the guest of the general. In the bathroom I find a razor, shaving soap and shampoo. I use all three and look in the mirror hoping I don't still look like shit as Cheryl had so sweetly told me last night. Next to my bed, I find that a full set of army uniform has been laid out, clean and pressed. Olive green trousers, khaki shirt, woolly pulley sweater with a full colonel's rank badges fixed to the shoulder tabs – a crown and two pips. They've even fitted two red gorgets to the lapels and provided an Intelligence Corps staple belt, Cyprus green beret with general staff badge and brown military shoes. I put these on and find they all fit perfectly. Someone must have got my measurements from the BRIXMIS quartermaster. Now I'm properly dressed, I feel refreshed and ready to go. It's with regret that I pack up all my winter kit acquired from the BRIXMIS quartermaster and leave it in the room with a "thank you" note to the brigadier.

The breakfast seating plan is the same as I remember from last time. The general is sweet talking Cheryl while Ed and I find ourselves sitting either side of Suzanne, the general's charming wife. She is fastidious in ensuring we both eat well. We don't disappoint her.

Then Suzanne says, "Peter, I hope you don't mind but I took it upon myself to call your wife Ann yesterday, as soon as we heard you were accounted for in the East. Of course, I didn't wish to alarm her in any way, just to try to reassure her. When she heard the news, I could tell she almost broke down in tears of relief as she had been so worried about you. She obviously loves you so much and has been missing you dearly while you've been away from Brussels. Perhaps you could call her before your meetings this morning."

I tell her, "Thank you for caring and for the phone call. Of course, I'll call her." Privately, I'm rather shocked about how Ann reacted. Perhaps she really does still love me. Perhaps we should try again to refresh our marriage. I only know I'll try my best when I get back home.

The general has anticipated that Ed and I would want to phone our families and had allocated two private rooms with phones for our use.

I call my home number and it's Christian who picks up. I'd forgotten the children are now on their Christmas holidays. I'm about to apologise to him for missing his rugby match but he pre-empts me, "Oh Daddy, it's you! It's just as well you weren't here for the match last week or perhaps you heard already. It was cancelled because the pitch was frozen and they said it was too dangerous to play. We were all so disappointed. But it's warmed up a bit again now. Anyway, although it's the holidays, our school teachers have arranged a special match tomorrow. We're playing on our home pitch at the BSB here at the school against our big rivals, The International School at The Hague. They're coming all the way from Holland. It starts at half past two. I'd love you to be there, Daddy. Can you?"

I say to myself. Whatever it takes, I'll make it. I tell Christian, "I'll be there. Good luck for tomorrow."

"Oh, Daddy, Mummy's right next to me. She wants to talk so I'll pass the phone over."

It's Ann. "Peter! Where are you now?"

I reassure her, "I'm in West Berlin, safe and sound."

"Thank God! The general's wife called me yesterday. Before that, I kept trying to contact you but no one could tell me anything. I've been worried sick. Thank heavens you're OK. I've missed you so much. We all have. I love you, Peter."

"Me too," I reply and hope we both really mean it. "I told Christian I'll be back to support his rugby game tomorrow."

"That's wonderful. Oh, Chloe is here and wants to say hello"

I recognise my darling daughter's voice immediately as she says, "Daddy, it's me. I love you. We all love you. Come home soon!!"

"I will," I tell her, "and I love you too."

I put the phone down and swear to myself I'll do everything I can to make it back home tomorrow - even if I have to resign my fucking commission!

I come out of the office that had been set aside and I find that Captain Berger is waiting for me. It seems an age since we flew into Berlin together after the long flight from Washington. I ask her how she's been spending her time.

She replies, "Well to be honest, Colonel, I've spent most of it worrying about you and Mr Morgan. We're all so pleased you're both back. The reason I'm here now is because Colonel Walker told me to see if there's anything I can do for you today. She told me to be at your disposal.

Wow, that's an offer I can't refuse. I say to her, "That's much appreciated, Captain. What I really need is personal, mostly for my own family. Are you sure you don't object to that?"

"Of course not, I'm only too pleased to help."

"OK, fine. First thing is I've just talked to my wife and kids and suddenly realise that it's Christmas in a couple of days. It's been impossible to sort out presents and what not. Could you help out there?"

"Sure, what can I do?"

Right. Number One. The game of rugby football. I know it's not a game many Americans play but it's my son's passion. Get on the phone or whatever and see when the English national team are next playing at Twickenham, that's in London. Should be sometime in February or March. Get me two tickets in a good place for viewing. Can you do that?"

"Noted, sir. What else?

"Have you had the chance go shopping here in Berlin?"

"Sure have, sir, there are great stores in the Kurfűrstendamm, the KaDeWe for example."

"Great, my daughter is only fourteen but she's growing up fast. I'd love to buy her a really nice winter coat. She's a little bit smaller than you are but not much. I respect your taste, Captain. Could you buy a lovely coat for her?"

"Well that's a challenge, sir, but if you trust me, I'll do my best."

"One more thing. I'm desperate to get back to Brussels tomorrow morning. That's the twenty fourth. See what the possibilities are. Any airline. I don't care."

"Will do, sir. Anything else."

"Not for now, Captain. Look, I don't yet know how to pay as all my cash was taken from me in the dreaded Hohenschönhausen prison."

"Don't worry, sir, I'm sure Uncle Sam will find a way!"

It's a busy morning. That's good because I'm eager to get on with it so that I can fuck off home as soon as I can. But now I'm smartly dressed in the Queen's uniform, I must see this project fully through.

As soon as it was known that Ed and I were safely back, a meeting has been hastily convened with all of the intelligence staffs we had met up with on our first day here in West Berlin. I make my way through the Olympic Stadium complex and meet up again with Ed on the way.

All the main sources and agencies of the intelligence business are represented and secure link communications facilities are in place connecting us up to the National Security Agency and the CIA in the US, monitored by Jo Suter, to GCHQ in UK, and there's even a link to the DGSE in Paris.

I'm pleased to see a top team of experts has been assembled. I know many of these guys and have great respect for their knowledge and experience. But I'm also introduced to other analysts who have been brought in specially to assist in what I hope will be a definitive assessment. We get down to business straightaway. The 1: 50,000 scale map is still in place from our previous meeting. I run through the "order of battle" dispositions of all the group of Soviet forces Germany and those of the East German, Czech, Hungarian and Polish forces. We spend two hours going minutely through the details of any major troop deployment changes, of any new equipment being introduced or of any sign of offensive moves. We do a complete trawl of all the agencies connected electronically.

Our conclusion is unanimous. There has been no major change to the Warsaw Pact military posture. We agree the disinformation was all the work of the East German Stasi, the author of these reports is now in our custody and being debriefed by our counterintelligence experts as we speak. I bring the meeting to a close, thank everyone for their expertise and wish them all a Happy Christmas.

We need to send a written report back to the Chairman of the UK Joint Intelligence Committee and the US Intelligence Committee in the Pentagon. Ed and I agree to keep it short and to the point. We revisit our original mission and write our report:

Mission

To determine:

One: Has there been any recent evidence of either Soviet, East German or Czech military reinforcement of combat troops in the DDR or Czechoslovakia?

Our assessment: No

Two: Who is behind the recent tensions in East Berlin – the Soviets or the East Germans?

Our assessment: The East Germans Stasi organisation. Detailed evidence attached.

Three: How should we respond to those in our (i.e. the US) nation who feel we must react now by increasing our own alert measures?

Our assessment: By exposing the reports produced by the East German Stasi – as per Two above.

We end with a short conclusion. This states:

We verify that we believe Mr Gorbachev's speech was genuine.

Ed and I jointly sign the report.

Colonel Peter Chambers, UK Army Mr Edward Morgan. Senior Agent, CIA USA

As an attachment, we give details of Colonel Krause's reports with appropriate CDs and Floppies.

We hand our report in to the British Berlin Communications unit for secure transmission to the named US, UK, French and NATO addressees.

Chapter Thirty-Two

It's about 1230 hours when Ed and I finally finish our joint report. I know there will still be more to do with wrapping up all the evidence we've got on the Stasi led DDR effort to disrupt the developing peace process. I also must find the right security channel to feed into about the Stasi informants, SuziB in our own Division of NATO and John Evers, the MI6 guy in UK. Both are well respected and established people. From the evidence we've got, I know for sure that they are both informants of the Stasi but I need to be very careful how I report them and will need to provide absolute proof.

My friend for the day, Captain Terri Berger, is there to ambush me as I walk out of the comms centre after sending our report. She's dressed in civvies and wearing a beautiful long coat.

She says, "Excuse me, Colonel, do you like my coat?"

"Very nice, but so…?"

"Well, it's not mine. I bought it for your daughter. I hope it's OK."

I take a second look at the coat. Yes, it's really beautiful and I know Chloe will love it. My only hesitation is that it's a young lady's coat, very à la mode and chic. I suppose as a father I feel defensive about my little girl growing into a young woman!

I say, "It's a great choice, Captain. Well done. I know my daughter will love it."

"Glad you like it, sir. Our head of logistics here has issued a credit card in your name. You can use it as you wish and we'll bill you later. I've already put the cost of the coat on the card. Oh, and I've got the information you asked me for about the rugby match. I've written it down and will have it sent to your room with the coat. But there's another thing, sir. The general's aide has just told me that the general wants to see you. Can you check into his office asap?"

Pheew! I think, what's this now? I reckon I've done all that has been required of me. I just want to get away from here and go and sort out my family. But to Captain Berger I say, "Sure, I'll go now and see what he wants. But please hang about, Captain. I've got more things I'd like you to do."

I check in with the general's aide who says he is available now. I knock at his office door, can see his beckoning wave, so I enter and salute as per protocol. He says:

"Ah, Peter, just the man. I understand you and Ed have now finished and despatched your report."

"Yes, General, with a copy to you of course."

"And what now?"

"Well, General, Ed and I have done all that's been required of us and I'm hoping to get a flight out of Berlin as soon as possible. Hopefully today."

"Sorry, Peter. That's not going to happen just yet. I've got some good news and some bad news for you. First I must tell you that your mission has created considerable interest among the top brass, and I mean the very top. We are to host three VIPs this evening. They are all flying in to Berlin now. There's the Supreme Allied Commander Europe or SACEUR, that's the US General who as you well know is based in Mons, Belgium. Then we're to receive the Commander, US army in Europe or Commander USAREUR as he's known. He's coming from his HQ in Wiesbaden. That's not all. Also coming is the Commander in Chief, British Forces of the Rhine or BAOR from Rheindahlen. They'll all be staying overnight with their key aides so it's going to be quite a scrum! We're having a full visitors list printed up to save any confusion as to names, appointments etc."

"So, Peter, the first bad news is that we're going to have to move you out of the room in my residence as I will be accommodating these bigwigs here overnight. 'Fraid they all outrank you! But don't worry, we've got a good room booked for you in our Officers' Mess. I'm having your things moved over there. Secondly, Peter, you and Ed are the star attractions. Our VIP generals insist they meet you both this evening and they all want to hear your stories from East Berlin. So, I'm afraid you're stuck with us for another night."

"But now for the good news. SACEUR is scheduled to fly back to Mons tomorrow morning and a seat has been set aside for you. Then we've got a car on call to drive you from there to Brussels – that's only one hour by car. Yes, I know all about your son's rugby match and we'll get you there for that. My wife Suzanne has taken a close personal interest in your welfare and she's been nagging me to make sure you'll be there for your son's big match."

I can tell the general is having a busy day so all I say is, "Thank you and your wife for your consideration, General." I salute and leave. Well, pluses and minuses I suppose!

I find that Captain Berger is waiting for me outside the general's office. She says,

"You said you may need me for some other duty, Colonel."

I look at my watch and see it's just after 1330 hours. I'm told that Ed and I have to be ready to meet the generals at 1700 hours. That gives me over three hours of free time.

"Yes, Captain, we're going shopping again. Get us a car and we'll be off. Have you seen a good jeweller's shop in your travels?"

"As a matter of fact, I have, sir. There are several around the Kurfürstendamm area. We could go there first."

I take my time with this because I'm looking for something special. I try several shops before at last I find what I want. It costs more than my colonel's salary warrants but that's too bad. I buy it anyway.

I've still got time before the meeting and I know what I want to do. I say to Captain Berger.

"Captain, I know you speak perfect German. Here's a good test for you. Drop me off at the Officers' Mess where the general says all my kit has been taken and I'll meet you at the Olympic Stadium. I don't mean the British garrison next to it. I mean the actual stadium. I'm told it is administered by the local West German authorities who are very particular about when it's open and who goes there. This is the thing. I want you to persuade, cajole, threaten, whatever it takes for me to have access. I'll be coming back here in about a half an hour and I intend to run 10,000 metres on the original 1936 Olympic Games track."

I think the captain may have blinked a bit but she takes my request in her stride. All she says is, "I'll get right on it Colonel!"

I've been running all my youth and adult life. I'm only average in many sports but running is my passion. As age began to catch up with me I found I began running longer and longer distance events. I was a pretty sharp sprinter when I was young then I moved up to eight hundred and fifteen hundred metres, we used to stick to the old half mile and mile measures in the early days. Later I moved up to five and ten thousand metres and finally to the marathon. I suppose my knees are starting to tell me to ease up but not yet. I still like to hammer round the twenty-five laps of the track which makes up the ten thousand metres. Since I was a boy, I've marvelled at the 1936 Olympics which were held right here, in this very stadium. I remember the famous black American athlete Jesse Owens winning the long jump at the games much to the consternation of the Nazis. What an atmosphere! I've always hankered after the chance to run on this track. Now, if Captain Berger can weave her magic, today is the day.

I find my new room in the Officers' Mess and get out my running kit. I haven't got a track suit but I sling on my army sweater which will keep the winter chill at bay until I've warmed up. I jog round to the stadium and find Captain Berger chatting to the custodian as if they've been old mates for years. The custodian is an older gentleman who clearly takes his responsibilities very seriously. But he also clearly takes to Captain Berger!

He says to me, "This lady has said you want to run ten thousand metres on our track. I can't allow you much time here as we have a football match to prepare for. How long will it take?"

I tell him, "Well, the world record at the moment, in 1988, stands at twenty-seven minutes and twenty-seven seconds. So, let's say about a half an hour. OK?"

He responds gruffly, "Well OK, but no longer." There's pressure!

I get onto the track – an amazing experience just to be here. I do one warm up lap then pull up near the start/finish line and take off my sweater. I line up as if in a major champion event, brace myself nervously, imagine the starting pistol is fired and off I go. I'm now in a make-believe dream world, imagining this is a major international race. Each time I complete a lap, I check my position in relation to all the other imaginary runners that I believe are competing with me. I lose myself completely in this fantasy world. I believe I'm holding my position on the track while conserving my energy until the latter stages of the race when the top runners will begin to up the pace and those with lesser ability or strength will begin to fall back.

In my mind, the event starts to turn into a real foot race as the front three runners start to break away from the rest of the field. I track these three guys and steadily close the gap between us, while still conserving my energy. I'm still feeling pretty good. We've now covered twenty-three laps of the race. Two more to go. I imagine that one guy takes off, and as we're here in Berlin, I think of him as being German. He's making a long run for home, hoping his strength and fitness will see him through. I coast past the other two and cover the move of the guy at the front. I close to within five metres as we take the bell for the final lap. He bursts again as we enter the back straight. I again cover his move but I'm now beginning to feel the pressure. He's still ahead as we round the final bend. We can now see the tape at the end of straight and I imagine the crowd in the packed stadium is on its feet thrilled by this brilliant contest. We are now striding side by side but I sense my rival has taken too much out of himself and is beginning to tire. Now is my chance to strike. I summon up my last dregs of energy and propel myself forward. Inexorably, I gain on my rival and surge forward to breast the tape in a wild euphoria of utter glory. I'm the winner!!!

I pull up having completed the twenty-five laps, slowly letting my breath and pulse rate return to normal. Then I realise, as I knew all along, that I am quite alone. There was no race, there were no competitors, no yelling crowds filling the stadium with noise and enthusiasm. It was just make believe.

I look around at the empty stands. There is one lone spectator, clapping mildly. It's Captain Berger.

"Well done, sir," she says, rather half-heartedly. "What would you like to do next?"

I've enjoyed Captain Berger's company and attention though, after my athletic high jinks, I suspect she'll be glad to see the back of this crazy Brit. I thank her for helping me today and jog back to the Officers' Mess. I take a shower and lie down on the bed. I must have nodded off for a while as when I wake up I see it's 1630 hours and time to get ready for all these VIP generals who Ed and I have to meet this evening.

I don't have a lot of clothes choice with me so I put on the neat uniform that was provided for me this morning. I meet up with Ed who has also been transferred to the Mess accommodation. He's wearing a smart suit which I suspect he bought here in Berlin today. I should have done the same – too late now! We go along to the room that has been set aside for the meeting.

I suppose I imagined some sort of conventional lay-out – chairs arranged facing a stage with lectern, etc. But not this meeting. Our host general has decided that the gathering is to be held in a more homely setting using a small reception room in his own residence building. Ed and I are bang on time but already the distinguished gentlemen (no women!) are assembled. They have clearly been here for some time as the atmosphere is informal and cordial. Cups of tea and coffee and small eats have already been served. Our host general welcomes us both and introduces us to his guests. I have not met SACEUR or the Commander USAREUR before but I have seen them on TV and at various conferences. But I do know the Commander in Chief, British Army of the Rhine as I was a student of his at the Army Staff College in Camberley, Surrey. He is a tall and rangy man whose natural good looks seem to be weathering well with age. I remember his original regiment was the Irish Hussars before he rocketed through the ranks to his present distinguished four star rank. It is good to see him again.

The generals are full of questions for Ed and me. How did we find the atmosphere in East Berlin? What about the relations between the Soviets and the ruling SED party? What did both of us do during our time in East Berlin? Who were our contacts? We both try to answer all these questions as openly as we can. Then to me personally they ask: "What were the conditions in the Hohenschönhausen prison? How did the Stasi treat you? How did you escape? Why were the Soviets so supportive?

I do my best to answer, but revisiting in my mind all these situations, brings back such strong emotions that I have about Frederik, the amazing Stasi officer and of course about Heidi. My factual replies can't come close to the emotion I am feeling about these two individuals. I think no one except Ed can begin to understand. These fine generals are treating Ed and me as some sort of heroes for bringing over Colonel Krause, the initiator of the disinformation and for exposing all these fake source reports. But both of us know the real heroes are not us at all. They are Frederik and Heidi who gave their lives and they are Adel, Bernd and Klaus who risked so much to help us succeed in our task.

The two points that seemed to intrigue the generals the most were, firstly the personal support given by Marshal Ogarkov. I'm not sure they are convinced about the report I give of my meeting with the great man in his office in Zossen-Wünsdorf. Secondly, they are astounded that Honecker should feel sufficiently insecure of his position that he built a tunnel to the West should he be forced to escape.

Ed and I conclude that, based purely on our experiences of our time in East Berlin and our conversations with East Germans there, that the regime is frightened of its own population and that the Soviets will no longer intervene to prop up the communist rulers should the population raise up against them. We feel that Gorbachev's policies in general and his UN speech in particular are the major factors in bringing about this change. We feel that a popular revolt against the SED party and its enforcers, the Stasi, could well occur within the next few months.

After our grilling that I reckon lasted about two hours, SACEUR thanks Ed and me for the successful conclusion of our mission and invites us to join the generals in a visit that has been laid on for them.

SACEUR explains, "This is to be a very special and I believe unique evening. It is being organised by your British Head of BRIXMIS at their mission house in Potsdam. Gentlemen, I am informed that our transport is waiting for us so let's go!"

Ed and I are allocated to a vehicle and the cavalcade sets off. I find it a surreal experience to be driven over the Glienicker Bridge across the narrows of the River Havel and for our party of top NATO generals to be waved through by the Soviet authorities. I remember it was only two years ago in 1986 that the most recent prisoner exchange took place. I enjoyed reading the novels of John Le Caré and Len Deighton where this famous bridge was referred to. But their stories were, I suppose, fiction. Today it's real.

Our cars pull up at the BRIXMIS mission house at 34 Seestrasse, just before 2000 hours and the brigadier is there to greet his guests. We are escorted inside into a well-furnished reception hall and join a large group of individuals who have clearly already started on the vodka. Most are in uniform, a mix of British, American and French who are acting as hosts to a number of Soviet guests. My eyes scan around and I spot Colonel Orlov, the Head of the SERB organisation who had been instrumental in my release from Hohenschönhausen prison. He sees me and immediately comes across and gives me a classic Russian bear hug greeting. I introduce him to Ed.

Orlov says: "Hi, Peter! I told you we might well meet here at the BRIXMIS Christmas drinks party. I'm so pleased you and your colleague here made it. We have much to discuss my friend."

I don't know how honest I should be talking to him. But then I reflect that if it hadn't been for him and the role he played, I would probably still be languishing in Hohenschönhausen. I look around and see our top American and British generals talking freely to their Soviet counterparts. It is truly an inspiring evening.

I start to describe our tunnel escape but Orlov interrupts me. He says, "Just hold for a moment, Peter. There's someone here who I know you would like to see again and who also wants to hear your story."

Orlov walks back to his fellow Soviet group and beckons one of them forward. It's Major Nikonov, the Special Forces guy whose inspirational assistance got us into the Palast der Republik.

I am delighted to see him again. We exchange greetings and this time we have Orlov to translate for us so we can converse freely.

I give both Soviet officers an account of what occurred to us at the Palast after Nikonov had dropped us off in his formidable OT-64 Armoured Personnel Carrier. I hope he can answer a question that has been recurring in my mind. I say to him, "My great thanks to you for providing the RPG 7 rocket launcher. You should see the mess it made of Herr Honecker's brick wall! But to me the great mystery is how Frederik got the launcher into the building without being detected."

Nikonov smiles enigmatically and tells me, "As you know, I was under orders not to compromise our Soviet position and we were only to be in support, remember? Well, let's just say Frederik did have some additional assistance to get the weapon to you. We must leave it at that!"

I know when not to press things too far. This is one of those times. I know it will remain a mystery to me forever.

It was my sad duty to tell Orlov and Nikonov about Frederik's death. It was news to them. However, I couldn't bring myself to tell them about Heidi. It still hurts too much.

Our conversation is interrupted by the sound of a gong, calling us all to attention. A new guest is just arriving. Surrounded by a group of aides, I see an officer I met just a few days ago. It's Marshal of the Soviet Union Nikolai Vasilyevich Ogarkov. Our host, the BRIXMIS brigadier makes the introductions to SACEUR and our other top NATO generals. Waiters arrive on cue with glasses of vodka and a formal toast is made for "East-West détente". We all drink to that shared aspiration.

Chapter Thirty-Three

I wake up with a sore head. That's not usual but then I realise I had a lot of vodka last night at the BRIXMIS Mission House in Potsdam. But what an occasion it had turned out to be! If ever I write my memoirs, I'll certainly include that. The highlight for me surely had to be when the marshal called me over with Major Nikonov and patted us both on the back, telling the Western generals we could relax more after what we had achieved. I insisted Ed be included.

I look at my watch and see it's nearly eight o'clock. I also realise it's Saturday 24th December. Yesterday I was told I'll be flying back on SACEUR's private plane, but I wasn't given a flight time, only that I would be informed. I ring down to the Mess reception and ask if there's any news about the flight. The receptionist tells me there's nothing from SACEUR's staff but there is a message from a Colonel Walker, US Air Force. I say I'll be down to collect it.

I take a quick shower, put on the old suit I took with me to Washington and pack all the rest of my stuff in my travel bag. I leave that together with the beautifully packaged present for Chloe and my own winter blouson so that I can grab them quickly when I get the flight call.

At reception, I pick up the message from Cheryl. It reads, "Friday, 23 Dec. I've been offered the chance to hitch a lift back to Brussels today, so I'm taking it!! Tried to get hold of you but you were doing some macho thing on the running track! Mad you! I've learnt you'll be snobbing it in SACEUR's plane tomorrow. Catch up with you later. Behave yourself. Love Cheryl. Ps. I enclose a little something for you. It's not to be opened before Christmas Eve. Promise!"

That's our Cheryl!

I leave word at reception to contact me as soon as they hear about my flight and I head into the dining hall. There's no one here who I know. I grab a self-service breakfast. I'm hungry so I go for a traditional full English fry up – couple of eggs, sausages, mushrooms and baked beans. I toast myself some bread to have with butter on the side and a large cup of steaming hot coffee. Not a good recipe for low cholesterol but there you go!

I'm restless to get moving and I'm relieved when I get the message that a car will be outside the Mess to pick me up at 1000 hours. I whip back up to my room, collect my bags and coat and wait at reception for the car.

While I'm waiting, I ask the receptionist to patch me through a call to Ed's room. It rings a long time before a sleepy voice answers. I've woken him up. I tell him, "Just to let you know I hope to be leaving shortly. It's been great knowing you and working with you. Hope we can meet up again, next time in more relaxed circumstances. Look after yourself, mate. Now, you can go back to sleep." He mumbles something like "same to you" but I disconnect and leave him in peace. I was going to ask him when he's flying out but better he continues his beauty sleep for now. Hope he gets home for Christmas.

As I put down the phone, a smart young US soldier comes up to me and says, "Colonel Chambers? I'm to drive you to meet up with SACEUR's party."

At last we're away. But it's still not that simple. I think I'm beginning to know the geography of West Berlin and I'm sure we're not heading for Tempelhof. I check with the driver.

He says, "We will be going to Tempelhof later, sir, but first we're connecting up with SACEUR's party at the Rathaus in Schöneberg. SACEUR has to make a courtesy call on the governing mayor and his leading senators. Shouldn't take long, then we'll all proceed in convoy to the airport.

I try to be patient, something I'm not good at. I rationalise that SACEUR is the most senior military officer in Western Europe and it's a big deal when he visits Berlin. So, it's only accepted protocol that he should feel obliged to call on the senior German official here. Quite right and proper. But I hope he gets a fucking move on as I need to get back to support my son's rugby match! Let's get our priorities straight!

We pull up behind a line of official cars outside the Rathaus and wait and wait and wait. I'm now getting seriously stressed about this. I try to work out timings. I reckon the flight time from Berlin to the SHAPE HQ airbase somewhere near Mons in Belgium will take about one hour forty-five minutes allowing for our required route through the Berlin corridor. Then there's a one hour drive, who knows it may be more from there to Brussels. That's cutting it fucking fine!

As I'm fretting away in the back of this car, I see SACEUR coming out of the Rathaus accompanied by a distinguished looking gentleman and other dignitaries. They shake hands while posing at the Rathaus entrance for the bevy of waiting photographers. I can see them mouthing "Happy Christmas, *Frohe Weihnachten*" to each other then, more handshakes all around.

SACEUR walks down the Rathaus steps and, to my surprise, doesn't go to the lead car but comes over to the one I'm in. He opens the door and pops his head in.

He says, "Ah, Colonel Peter Chambers. I'm glad our guys found you OK. I hope you're not in any way concerned as we know the time constraints about your son Christian's match. Relax, we'll get you there in time for the kick off or whatever it's called."

I'm stunned that he should be so conciliatory and helpful. What a stupid shit I can be sometimes. I feel terrible about fuming away in the back of the car when this top officer has gone out of his way to help me in a domestic matter. When am I fucking well going to learn?

All I can think of to say is, "I'm most grateful, sir. Thank you."

There's much opening and slamming of doors in the cars ahead and then we're away. It's not long before I see the signs for Tempelhof up ahead. There's no queuing up in line, no passport control, no customs checks. My driver gets out, goes around to open the boot of the car to get my luggage, then opens the door for me saying, "I'll look after your bags, sir, just join those gentlemen over there. Your flight is ready for you."

We've been driven right out onto the tarmac of Tempelhof and in front of us is a shiny Jet Airliner. It's compact and painted in the livery of the United States Air Force. That's good enough for me. Ahead I see SACEUR talking to a uniformed senior US Air Force officer who I reckon must be the Tempelhof station commander. He shakes his hand, they salute each other and wave as SACUR climbs the steps up to the aircraft. His staff are right behind and I follow on. A smart attendant in US Air Force uniform shows me to a seat next to an US army brigadier, final checks are carried out and we're away. Goodbye Berlin.

The brigadier next to me and I talk briefly but I can tell it's only out of politeness, by both of us. Soon after take-off, he dozes off and I hear snoring sounds as he gets deeply into it. I remember he was also enjoying the vodka at the BRIXMIS party last evening.

I'm excited at the prospect of coming home again, more so than ever before. After some of the operational combat tours, I'd come back home to find my poor frigid wife not seeming to care whether I was there or not. I'm confident this time it will be different.

I stay deep in my thoughts as I sit next to my snoring companion. I fish out of my pocket the envelope containing the note Cheryl has written and see the smaller envelop she had put inside. She tells me not to open it before Christmas evening. Well, it is now PM on the 24th so I decide to cheat a little and open it now. Inside is a ticket from the Melia hotel in London. It shows a reservation for four persons to stay for two nights, 3rd and 4th March 1989. There is also another handwritten note from Cheryl. It reads, "Captain Berger tells me she got you tickets to take your son to the Rugby in Twickenham, London on Sat 4 March. Don't be a meany, why don't you take Ann and Chloe as well and stay two nights. Your girls can always go shopping while you two do your thing! Compliments of US government!" That's all. I get quite filled up by this. Cheryl and her assistant Captain Terri Berger have played a blinder!

The steady drone of the aircraft seems to be having a soporific effect on most of the passengers, plus last night's party. But I can't sleep and I'm glad when I hear the pitch of the aircraft changing as we begin our descent. The flight attendant tells me we will shortly be landing at a Military Airbase called Chièvres, which is about twenty kilometres from Mons.

We land smoothly. SACEUR gets off first then I'm surprised to be called forward to get off the aircraft next. I walk down the steps and find that SACEUR is waiting for me. He says, "Your bags are being taken off first and loaded onto that car. Get to it, son, and make sure you root hard for your boy!" I turn and see my bags offloaded from the plane and placed into the car. I give my thanks to SACEUR, get in the car and we're away!

SACEUR is true to his word. We pull up outside my house in Woluwe, just before 1400 hours. I get out of the car to see Ann running to meet me. She's looking slim, fit and as lovely as I've ever seen her. We kiss and then she pushes me lightly back, looks up at me and says, "Welcome home, soldier! With the help of Susanne, the Berlin general's wife, we've been monitoring your progress today every bit of the way. You're right on time!"

I love to see her like this but I also realise I've got to get my skids on to get to the British School of Brussels in time for the match. I start to tell Ann but she cuts me off.

"It's OK, everything's organised. You go in, get some warm clothes on and get yourself off to the match. Christian's already gone ahead. Chloe's also not here, we'll catch up with her later. Now go!"

I can tell there's a lot of catching up to do. Suzanne, the Berlin general's wife seems to have been such a kind concerned asset. But where's Chloe? But that's for later.

I do as Ann says and change quickly into thick sweater and jeans. Then I'm back out with my blouson, wave to Ann, jump in my Golf and am away. As I driving I wonder how my car has been returned. The last time I saw it, it was parked at Zaventem airport.

I pull into the school parking and leg it over to the rugby pitch. I see the boys emerging from the changing room and warming up on the pitch. I go and join a large crowd of spectators, mostly parents of the boys and I find a place amidst them. I spot Christian wearing the scrum half number nine on the back of his shirt. He seems small compared to many of the others. But he is only ten after all. He is involved in the pre-match team talk and all the boys are in a huddle around their coach. He's Mr Collins, a teacher who I've met several times on parents' evenings. He's also Christian's geography teacher. When the team talk is over, the boys break away and limber up to keep warm. Christian hasn't seen me yet. I watch him as he looks around the crowd of spectators on the edge of the pitch. Suddenly he spots me and I can see an immediate flash of delight as we make eye contact. We wave to each other. I know he would rush over but that's not the way. We'll get to that later.

The game gets underway. The first half is rather a scrappy affair. No side gains real dominance over the other but the boys from the Dutch school are disciplined and clearly have learnt the rules of rugby very well. They have a good scrummaging technique and regularly gain the better and more cohesive push at the scrum. Christian is an energetic scrum half, making the most of the few scraps he is given by his forwards to give an accurate service to his backs or when the opposing forwards keep bearing down on him, he box kicks over them to give his backs the chance to run onto the ball as it lands in open play. The boys from The Hague School score two good tries to only one to the BSB Brussels. Half-time score: The Hague International School 12, BSB 5.

I think Mr Collins must have got a real grip on his charges during the break because the BSB team play harder and more clinically in the second half. They touch down in one corner for a try which is converted with an excellent kick from near the touch line to bring the scores level at twelve apiece. Christian continues to play well, always sniping away at his forwards feet. There's another scrum and this time the BSB boys combine well to get a good shove going which drives the other team back. Christian controls the effort to keep the ball at the feet of the number eight as the scrum moves forwards. Then it is held up and the referee shouts out to "play the ball". This is Christian's chance; he picks the ball up as the number eight heels and sets off around the scrum. He dodges a couple of players and goes to make a break through the centre where he can link up with the mid-field players. Then one the largest of the opponent's players throws himself at Christian and high tackles him around the neck. A clear and deliberate foul! Christian falls and lies still on the ground. There are boos of protest from the BEB supporters. I can hardly contain myself. I'm on the verge of rushing on and frogmarching the offending boy off the pitch. My boy has been fouled!! But I tell myself to cool it and leave it to the ref to intervene. He does and the offending boy is told to leave the field. I worry for Christian but quickly he gets back up to his feet and indicates to the ref that he's OK. I'm glad Ann isn't here to watch or she might want to ban Christian from playing rugby again.

There were no further scores and the match is declared a draw at twelve all. The boys file off back to the changing rooms but Christian takes time to turn to where I'm standing and gives a thumbs-up. As I wait for the boys to shower and dress, I feel proud of my son and so delighted I was able to keep my promise and be here to support his first representative game. Judging by the way he played today, I'm sure he will be picked for the team again.

Christian finally emerges and we make our way together to the car. Once we are alone, we then have the hug of greeting I've been so eagerly awaiting. I tell him I'm so proud of how well he played and he glows with pleasure. All the way back to Woluwe, he recaptures every moment of the game.

Back at the house, neither Ann or Chloe are here. We go inside and I see how well the house has been decorated for Christmas. I didn't even notice this when I had rushed in earlier before taking off again for Christian's match. A tree has been put up in one corner with lights that Christian switches on so I can get the full effect. Christian tells me proudly he had been put in charge of erecting the tree and fixing the lights. Chloe did the decorating. But where is Chloe? Why wasn't she here to greet me when I first got home? I ask Christian but he just looks mysterious. Something is going on. Christian says that his mother had told him that I am to get dressed respectably. I go into our bedroom and see she has laid out my only other suit which is about as shabby is the one I wore on my travels. Next to it is a clean shirt and tie. I have a quick wash and change as I've been told. When I come back to the sitting room, Christian has also smartened himself up.

"Come on, Daddy," he tells me, "we've got to go."

"Go where?" I ask "What's going on?"

"You'll soon find out. Let's go!"

We get back into the Golf and Christian directs me to a side street in Woluwe and tells me to park.

We're close to the Woluwe shopping mall but in a street opposite. I see a number of people filing into what I see is a small theatre. I've seen it there before but I've never been inside. We go in and Christian produces two tickets. I find it's beautifully furnished inside with tiered seating for stalls and balconies arranged around the sides. The rich purple curtain is lowered. Already about three quarters of the seats are filled and others are coming in behind us. Then I see Ann. She had been watching out and waves when she sees us. We excuse ourselves as we pass by others in the same row. We reach Ann and she moves over so that I am sitting between her and Christian. I glance across at Ann. She returns the glance, smiles and gently leans into my shoulder. She waits for me to speak first. I say to her, "This is very interesting, Ann. Good idea for Christmas eve. But why the mystery and where's Chloe?"

Ann replies, "You'll soon find out. I got us a copy of the programme. Take a look."

I see it's a performance of Shakespeare's "The Taming of the Shrew" being performed by a company called "The Woluwe Players." At first I think the company is part of the BSB school but I look around me and see the audience is made up of a wide international group. I look through the credits and publicity in the program then scan through the cast. Petruchio, Lucentio and so on. Then I see it. And the penny drops. The part of Katherine Minola is played by… Chloe Chambers!! So that's why my darling daughter wasn't at the house when I got home. She was rehearsing for tonight.

I look around at my wife and my son and see the smug expressions on their faces.

"You two rogues!" I tell them.

The theatre has filled, the five-minute bell has sounded and then the curtain is raised. I want to watch the complete play but naturally I'm watching out for Chloe, alias Katherine. I don't see her. Then there she is. She's dressed in her "Padua" costume and she looks like a fully grown up pretty young woman. Can this really be my little Chloe? Soon she speaks,

"I pray you, sir, is it your will
To make a stale of me amongst these mates"

She speaks clearly and with the venomous tone that her part requires. She continues:

"I'faith, sir, you shall never need to fear
I wis it is not half way to her heart."

and so on through her part. I am spellbound by her characterisation and the confidence of her delivery.

The play is well acted by all the cast. In Act V, Scene II, Katherine has her great speech when her character has changed from venomous to submissive. She starts,

"Fie, fie, unknit that threatening unkind brow
and dart not scornful glance from those eyes
to wound thy lord, thy king, thy master"

She ends this section with,

"in token of which duty if you please
My hand is ready, may it do him ease"

And Petruchio responds with,

"Why there's a wench! Come on and kiss me Kate."

That's Kate, or Katherine. In reality, it's my darling daughter, Chloe!

At the end of the play, the audience's applause is long and genuine. I feel so proud of my daughter as she takes her bows with the rest of the cast. Gone is my little shy, underweight girl. Here she is finding herself at last. This evening, she has shown poise and confidence. Perhaps all her recent negativity and weight loss was due to her inner self searching for a way to find expression. By watching her and listening to her tonight, I think she's found it. If that's where her motivation leads her, I'm sure she could one day be a great actress. It's early days of course, but it's a positive start.

I'm back with my family again. Christian proved today he's a tough little guy – fit, brave and daring as he's shown on the rugby pitch. Chloe has been living into herself until her acting ability has enabled her to move forward in her adolescence and prove to herself what she can do and become.

At last the audience has given their final applause and are beginning to collect themselves and leave the theatre. I look across at Ann. I'm sure she feels as proud of our two children as I do. They are the product of us both. I detect in her a new warmth. I remember her reaction on the phone when she knew I had returned safely from East Berlin. I remember what Susanne, the Berlin general's wife, told me after she had talked to Ann. It was, "She loves you so very much." I know we have to build on this and in some ways make a new start from the barren desert years after the Cyprus tragedy.

I look forward to tomorrow, Christmas day, when we give each other our presents. Having seen my growing up daughter this evening I'm sure she'll love the winter coat that Captain Berger chose for her. And I look forward as well to the special weekend in early March when, thanks to Cheryl, the four of us will stay in a top London hotel – England versus France for Christian and me, shopping for the girls, then all together again for the evening.

I'm also looking forward to tomorrow for another special reason, but perhaps I'll not be able to wait that long and will give it to her tonight when our children have finally gone to bed. When I was on my Berlin shopping spree, I bought something else. It is a ring, so similar to the one I bought her for our engagement all those years ago. I checked this evening and saw she is still wearing it. It's so similar in size but the ring I bought is of far superior quality. I intend to give it to my wife Ann as a symbol of renewal, of our lives together, of the love of our children, of the love we have for each other.